# RISING FROM POINT NEMO

## FROM THE OCEAN'S DEEPEST TRENCH,

## A NEW DAWN RISES

"This book is a work of fiction. While the character and their journey were inspired by the spirit and creativity of a real individuals, the story, characters, and events contained within are entirely products of imagination and are not based on real life. This narrative was created with the assistance of artificial intelligence."

By Richard Dell Schwarz

Copyright © 2025 Richard Dell Schwarz
All rights reserved

Forward

From the crushing silence of the ocean's most desolate reaches emerges a story as profound as the depths from which it rises. *Rising from Point Nemo* is not just a tale of science and survival—it is an exploration of human grief, perseverance, and the relentless search for meaning in the face of loss.

When I first conceived this story, it was with a desire to explore not only the vast, alien world beneath our oceans but the equally deep and often unexplored terrain of the human soul. In Captain Elias Thorne, I found a vessel through which to navigate both. Haunted by tragedy and driven by an unquenchable need for redemption, his journey becomes our own— into the black abyss of despair, into the glimmering possibilities of discovery, and ultimately, into the fragile hope that something extraordinary still awaits beyond the edge of understanding.

This book is, at its core, a tribute to resilience. It challenges the limits of science and emotion, while reminding us that even in the darkest places—beneath miles of pressure, silence, and forgotten wreckage—the spark of life, of curiosity, of connection, still burns.

I hope you, the reader, will find within these pages not only suspense and wonder but also a quiet truth: that the greatest discoveries often lie not in what we find, but in what we become when we dare to search.

*— Richard Dell Schwarz*

# Table of contents

## Contents

## 1: The Weight of the Ocean

The crushing blackness of the abyssal plain pressed in on the *Abyssus*, a relentless, palpable weight that had become as familiar to Captain Elias Thorne as the phantom ache in his chest. Here, at the oceanic pole of inaccessibility, commonly known as Point Nemo, the silence was absolute, broken only by the hum of his submersible's life support and the faint, rhythmic ping of its sonar. This was the graveyard of ambition, the ultimate discard heap of human endeavor. Ships, satellites, defunct space stations – anything deemed too expensive or too dangerous to retrieve, anything that had outlived its purpose or met a catastrophic end, inevitably found its way here, carried by the indifferent currents of the vast Pacific. The water column above was an unfathomable distance, miles of frigid, crushing fluid separating this alien landscape from the distant, sun-drenched world of the living. It was a realm of perpetual twilight, illuminated only by the *Abyssus*'s powerful, piercing beams, which cut through the inky blackness like desperate probes into the unknown. The seabed itself was a testament to entropy, littered with the spectral remains of failed voyages, each piece of debris a silent monument to dreams that had shattered against the unforgiving realities of space or the ocean's depths.

The sheer desolation of Point Nemo was a stark, almost spiritual, landscape. There was a haunting beauty to it, a grand, terrifying majesty in its utter emptiness. Nothing lived here by conventional definition; only specialized extremophiles clung to existence around hydrothermal vents, tiny beacons of life in a sea of desolation. Yet, the detritus of humanity was abundant. Twisted metal, shattered ceramics, ghostly skeletal structures of once-proud machines — they lay scattered across the seabed like the bones of forgotten giants. It was a place where the immense scale of the planet truly asserted itself, where human endeavor seemed laughably ephemeral, a fleeting flicker against the backdrop of geological time. Elias navigated the

*Abyssus* through this spectral graveyard with a practiced hand, his movements precise and economical. His stoicism, honed by years of command and further hardened by personal tragedy, was a formidable shield, but beneath it lay a raw, unyielding current of grief. The memory of the shuttle disaster, the fiery descent, the silence that followed, was a constant echo in the quiet confines of his vessel, a phantom limb that throbbed with an unbearable loss. His family — his wife, his daughter — had been taken from him in the void of space, a void he now navigated in the crushing

darkness of the deep. This mission, this self-imposed
exile at the literal ends of the Earth, was more than just
a job; it was a penance, a way to remain close to the
echoes of what he had lost, to swim in the same silent,
unfeeling medium that had claimed them.

The *Abyssus* itself was a testament to human ingenuity,
a marvel of engineering designed to withstand
pressures that would instantly obliterate any lesser craft.
Its hull, a composite of reinforced alloys and advanced
ceramics, gleamed dully in the submersible's own
internal lighting. Its powerful thrusters could maneuver
with astonishing agility, allowing it to dance amongst
the debris fields with an almost balletic grace. Its sensor
arrays, a sophisticated network of sonar, lidar, and
optical scanners, painted a detailed, three-dimensional
picture of the abyssal plain, revealing the contours of
the seabed and the shapes of submerged wreckage. It
was a self-contained world, a microcosm of survival in
the most hostile environment imaginable. Yet, even this
technological triumph was merely a tool, a means to an
end. For Elias, the *Abyssus* was an extension of his own
will, a vessel through which he pursued his relentless,
solitary quest. Its advanced systems, while critical for
survival, also served to amplify his isolation, its
complex machinery a constant reminder of the living
world he had left behind. He lived and breathed by the

readouts on his console, by the subtle shifts in pressure, by the energy signatures that flickered across his screens. The world of touch, of warmth, of human connection, had receded to a distant memory, replaced by the cold, hard data of survival.

The vastness of the Pacific, stretching for thousands of kilometers in every direction, provided a natural cloak for their operations. Point Nemo was a place of deliberate forgetfulness, a location so remote that charting its precise coordinates was a challenge in itself. Few vessels ventured this far out, and fewer still had any reason to linger. The silence that permeated this oceanic desert was not merely an absence of sound but an active force, a deep, pervasive quietude that seemed to absorb all extraneous noise, all external interference. It was a silence that could drive a man mad, or, in Elias's case, allow him to finally hear the whispers of his own grief, unbidden and unending. He had chosen this place not just for its remoteness, but for its symbolic resonance. It was a place where things died, where they were forgotten, where the weight of the ocean pressed down until all that remained was the ghost of what had been. And Elias Thorne, a man haunted by ghosts, felt a grim kinship with this desolate expanse. His stoic facade, the carefully constructed mask of the professional captain, was all that separated him from the abyss of his own despair. Every decision, every maneuver, every breath he took was imbued with the memory of the shuttle disaster, the fiery descent that had stolen his wife, Anya, and his daughter, Lily, from his grasp. Their laughter, their warmth, their very existence, had been extinguished in the cold vacuum of space, and now, in the crushing embrace of the deep, he sought not solace, but a form of continued communion, a perpetual remembrance.

The *Abyssus*, a beacon of human tenacity, was more than just a submersible; it was Elias's confessional, his sanctuary, and his prison. Its advanced systems were extensions of his own weary will, meticulously calibrated to execute the complex and dangerous tasks that lay before them. He lived by the rhythmic pulse of its environmental controls, by the steady readout of its hull integrity, by the subtle hum of its life support. These were the constant, reassuring presences in a world devoid of human warmth. His focus was absolute, his attention to detail unwavering, a direct consequence of the catastrophic failure that had befallen his family's shuttle. He had learned, in the most brutal way imaginable, that the slightest miscalculation, the most minuscule oversight, could have unimaginable consequences. Every bolt tightened, every system checked, was a silent prayer against the forces of entropy and disaster. He was a man tethered to his mission by an invisible, unbreakable chain of grief and a burning, unarticulated need for something more. The descent into these crushing depths, into this desolate, unforgiving environment, was a deliberate act of self-immolation, a slow, deliberate burning away of the man he used to be. He sought no comfort, no absolution, only the grim satisfaction of continuing to function, to operate, to survive, in the very medium that represented the ultimate end. The silence of the deep was a stark contrast to the terrifying cacophony of the shuttle disaster, and Elias found himself drawn to its profound, unyielding quietude. It was a silence that mirrored the emptiness within him, a vast, echoing void where his family's laughter used to be.

The sheer isolation of Point Nemo was a double-edged sword. It offered unparalleled privacy for their clandestine operations, a vast expanse of ocean where they could conduct their salvage missions with minimal risk of detection. Yet, it also amplified their own solitude, creating a fragile ecosystem within the *Abyssus* where every interaction, every shared glance, carried a weight far beyond its intended meaning. Elias, a man accustomed to the command of a larger crew, found himself relying on the quiet competence of his two companions, each a solitary star in his desolate firmament. First Mate Kaelen, a man carved from granite and tempered by pragmatism, served as Elias's anchor to reality. His loyalty to Elias was unwavering, a quiet devotion forged in shared hardship, but it was a loyalty tested daily by the captain's increasingly risky endeavors and his palpable emotional detachment. Kaelen's grounded nature was a necessary counterpoint to Elias's brooding intensity, his steady presence a silent reminder of the precariousness of their situation. He was the voice of reason, the one who meticulously managed their resources, who ensured their operational integrity remained paramount, even as Elias pushed the limits of both the submersible and their own endurance.

Dr. Lena Petrova, on the other hand, was a supernova of scientific curiosity, her mind a vibrant galaxy of theories and hypotheses. She was brilliant, unconventional, and utterly consumed by the pursuit of knowledge. Her passion for discovery was a stark contrast to Elias's somber mission, her excitement infectious as she delved into the mysteries of the deep. Her fascination with the alien technologies they encountered bordered on obsession, her drive to understand and reverse-engineer them fueling a relentless pursuit that often blurred the lines between scientific endeavor and reckless ambition. She saw the debris of Point Nemo not as a graveyard, but as a treasure trove, a repository of secrets waiting to be unlocked. Their interactions were a delicate dance between Elias's melancholic focus and Lena's fervent exploration, with Kaelen attempting to bridge the chasm between their disparate approaches. The small, enclosed space of the *Abyssus* became a crucible for their interdependence, each relying on the others' skills and strengths to survive, to complete their mission, and perhaps, to find a flicker of meaning in this vast, indifferent ocean. The unspoken pressures of their work, the constant threat of the environment, and the crushing weight of Elias's unspoken grief, bound them together in a fragile alliance, a testament to the human need for connection even in the most extreme isolation.

The primary objective of their mission was deceptively simple: to salvage valuable components from derelict spacecraft and other advanced debris scattered across the abyssal plain. These were not mere trinkets; they were the remnants of cutting-edge technology, often too exotic or too dangerous for conventional retrieval, destined for the ultimate resting place at Point Nemo. The process was depicted with a sense of gritty realism, a meticulous, painstaking operation that demanded every ounce of the crew's skill and the *Abyssus*'s formidable capabilities. Each salvage attempt was a high-stakes gamble, a dance with the crushing pressure and the unpredictable currents. The submersible's powerful manipulators, extending like metallic tendrils from its hull, carefully probed and retrieved objects, their movements dictated by the precise instructions from Elias and the real-time sensor data provided by Lena. The vastness and silence of the deep sea were palpable, an almost suffocating presence that amplified both the wonder and the dread of their work. They navigated through fields of debris that stretched for miles, each wreck a potential treasure or a deadly trap. A seemingly intact hull could conceal structural weaknesses that would buckle under the slightest strain, or residual energy signatures that could fry their sensitive equipment. The wreckage served as a constant reminder of the inherent dangers of exploration, of the thin line between groundbreaking discovery and catastrophic failure. Elias's methodical approach, his unwavering focus on safety protocols, was a direct response to the trauma that still clung to him like the perpetual dampness of the deep. He would not, *could not*, allow another tragedy to befall his crew, not while he still carried the weight of the past so heavily.

The silence of the deep, however, was not entirely devoid of echoes. As the *Abyssus* navigated through a particularly dense field of debris, its powerful lights pierced the eternal darkness, illuminating the skeletal remains of a spacecraft that had met its end in the unforgiving abyss. It was an older wreck, its metallic hull pitted and corroded by decades of submersion, yet its basic structure remained remarkably intact. A sense of foreboding permeated the scene, a chilling premonition that settled over Elias as he directed the submersible closer. Each wreck was a story, a testament to a journey cut short, and this one, with its strangely familiar configuration, stirred a disquiet within him. The lights of the *Abyssus* played over the scarred metal, revealing the ghostly outlines of what had once been a proud vessel, now reduced to a spectral shadow in the eternal night. The deeper they ventured into the debris field, the more pronounced this feeling of unease became. It was as if the ocean itself was holding its breath, a silent witness to their intrusion into its hallowed, forgotten grounds. The narrative hinted at the psychological impact of confronting these relics of past failures, these monuments to lost dreams and shattered ambitions. They were more than just inert objects; they were potent symbols, potent reminders of the fragility of life and the unforgiving nature of the void, both above and below. As they approached their first primary target for the day, a hulking mass of twisted metal that might have once been a deep-space cargo freighter, Elias felt a prickle of anticipation mingled with a profound sense of dread. Something about this particular wreck, something in its shape, its scale, resonated with a deep, buried part of his consciousness, stirring dormant hopes and ancient fears in equal measure, setting the stage for a discovery that would irrevocably alter the course of their perilous journey.

Elias Thorne was a ghost piloting a ghost. The *Abyssus*, a marvel of human engineering, designed to defy the crushing embrace of the deep, felt less like a vessel and more like an extension of his own tormented spirit. Each hum of its advanced systems, each flicker of data across its myriad screens, was a familiar, almost intimate, whisper in the suffocating silence. This was no mere salvage operation; it was a pilgrimage into the heart of his own personal abyss, a self-imposed exile that had become the very air he breathed. The weight of the ocean, that relentless, omnipresent pressure, was a constant, tangible echo of the grief that bore down on him. Miles of frigid, unyielding water separated him from the world, a world that had cruelly snatched away his wife, Anya, and his daughter, Lily, in the fiery descent of a shuttle lost to the unforgiving void of space. Now, here, in the crushing darkness of Point Nemo, he sought not solace, but a perverse communion with the medium that had claimed them.

His command of the *Abyssus* was a testament to his formidable intellect and his unwavering dedication.

Every maneuver, every diagnostic, was executed with a precision born not just of training, but of a visceral, deeply ingrained fear of repetition. The catastrophic failure that had stolen his family had seared into his soul the absolute necessity of vigilance, of leaving no stone unturned, no wire uncrossed. The slightest deviation from protocol, the most infinitesimal oversight, was a potential prelude to another unimaginable loss. Thus, the submersible's sophisticated array of sensors – the sonar that mapped the alien terrain, the lidar that delineated the treacherous contours of submerged wreckage, the optical scanners that painted ghostly images in the perpetual twilight – were not just tools; they were extensions of his own heightened senses, meticulously calibrated to anticipate and negate every conceivable threat. He lived and breathed by the data streaming across his console, by the subtle shifts in pressure that signaled the integrity of their hull, by the energy signatures that winked into existence from the spectral debris field. These readings, cold and objective, were the only constants in a world that had been irrevocably fractured.

The *Abyssus* was his confessional, his sanctuary, and his cage. Within its reinforced hull, Elias Thorne, the stoic captain, was shed, revealing the raw, bleeding wound beneath. The advanced life support systems, the carefully regulated atmosphere, the synthesized nutrients that sustained them — all were designed for survival, but for Elias, they were a constant, agonizing reminder of the warmth and life he had lost. His interactions with his small crew, the taciturn First Mate Kaelen and the effervescent Dr. Lena Petrova, were carefully managed exchanges, brief flickers of human connection in a vast, echoing emptiness. He respected their skills, relied on their expertise, but a vast, unbridgeable chasm separated him from them, a chasm carved by the unique burden of his grief. He was a man adrift, his vessel the only tangible link to a world he no longer truly belonged to. The mission, the salvage of exotic, often dangerous, technological remnants from the graveyard of space and sea, was not merely a job; it was a penance, a ritualistic act of self-flagellation played out in the deepest, darkest corners of the planet. Each piece of salvaged debris, each successful extraction, was a small victory against the forces that had taken his family, a grim validation of his continued existence, even as he felt himself dissolving into the very desolation he inhabited.

His focus was a shield, forged in the fires of loss. When Kaelen, with his quiet, pragmatic efficiency, presented him with resource projections or operational integrity reports, Elias would nod, his gaze already scanning the external sensors, his mind dissecting the sonar returns for anomalies. Kaelen's steady presence, his unspoken loyalty, was a bulwark against the crushing weight of Elias's internal tempest, but even Kaelen could not truly penetrate the fortress Elias had built around his shattered heart. Lena's infectious enthusiasm, her insatiable scientific curiosity that saw the wreckage not as a graveyard but as a library of cosmic secrets, was a vibrant counterpoint to his own somber mission. He appreciated her brilliance, her ability to unravel the mysteries of alien technology, but her fervent pursuit of knowledge often bordered on recklessness, a trait that Elias, ever mindful of the precipice on which they stood, found both admirable and deeply unsettling. He found himself constantly calculating the risks, not just for himself, but for the two souls who had chosen to follow him into this self-made purgatory.

The *Abyssus*, with its powerful manipulators and its array of sophisticated tools, was an extension of Elias's will, allowing him to reach out into the spectral landscape and extract fragments of forgotten futures. He navigated the submersible with a precision that bordered on the preternatural, his movements fluid and economical, each thruster adjustment a calculated risk. The debris fields, vast and desolate, were a landscape he had come to know intimately, the skeletal remains of lost ventures a familiar, albeit mournful, tapestry. He saw the twisted metal, the shattered ceramics, the desiccated husks of once-proud machines, not just as salvage targets, but as monuments to the hubris of mankind, echoes of the very hubris that had led to his own personal catastrophe. Each successful retrieval was a small defiance against the indifference of the universe, a fleeting assertion of human agency in the face of overwhelming entropy. Yet, with each salvaged component, with each piece of exotic technology brought back from the brink of oblivion, Elias felt not triumph, but a deepening weariness, a profound emptiness that the crushing weight of the ocean could never truly fill. He was a ghost in the machine of his own making, forever navigating the dark currents of his past, seeking a closure that remained as elusive as the sunlight in these abyssal depths. His meticulously planned descent was a descent into himself, a journey into the core of his grief, where the silence of the deep was the only solace he could find, a chilling echo of the silence that had fallen upon his life after the shuttle's fiery demise. He was a captain without a harbor, a man adrift in a sea of sorrow, his only companion the unyielding, crushing weight of the ocean.

The hum of the *Abyssus*'s environmental controls was a low, steady thrum against the oppressive silence of the deep. For Elias, it was a lullaby of survival, a testament to the technological prowess that kept him breathing in a realm utterly hostile to life. But for the others aboard, the same hum was a constant reminder of their isolation, their precarious existence tethered to the whims of a captain whose gaze was perpetually fixed on the spectral echoes of his past.

First Mate Kaelen stood by the main tactical display, his broad shoulders hunched slightly as he studied a complex series of energy readings. His presence was a study in quiet competence, a bulwark of stability in the often-turbulent emotional landscape of the submersible. His face, weathered by years spent in environments that alternated between the vacuum of space and the crushing pressures of the deep, rarely betrayed his inner thoughts, but his hands, large and calloused, moved with a precise, economical grace that spoke of a lifetime of responsibility. He was Elias Thorne's right hand, the man who translated Elias's often abstract directives into concrete, executable actions. Yet, even Kaelen's unwavering loyalty was beginning to chafe against the sharp edges of Elias's increasingly desperate pursuit. The captain's obsession with finding *something*, anything, that resembled a pattern, a clue, a sign of the anomaly that had consumed his family, was pushing the *Abyssus* and its crew into increasingly dangerous territories. Kaelen had seen the calculations, had run the simulations, and the risk assessment for their current trajectory was not just high; it was bordering on suicidal. He understood grief, the suffocating weight of loss, but he also understood the fundamental imperative of self-preservation, a concept Elias seemed to have long abandoned. "Captain," Kaelen's voice, a low baritone, cut through the ambient noise, "the spectral distortion readings from Sector Gamma are intensifying. We're operating outside of all established safety parameters for extended exposure. The hull integrity stress is accumulating at an unacceptable rate."

Elias, hunched over his own console, his fingers dancing across the holographic interface, barely looked up. His eyes, shadowed and hollow, were fixed on a complex waveform that pulsed with an unnatural rhythm. "Unacceptable, Kaelen, is a relative term. We are here to discover the unacceptable. We are here to find answers that the parameters of logic and safety have failed to provide." The words were clipped, devoid of emotion, yet laced with an undercurrent of desperation that Kaelen knew all too well. He'd seen it before, in the early days after the shuttle disaster, a raw, unadulterated agony that had threatened to consume Elias entirely. Now, it was a more controlled, insidious beast, a relentless drive that fueled his every waking moment. "Captain, my duty is to ensure the operational viability of this vessel and the lives entrusted to its command. If we push any further into this anomaly, we risk catastrophic structural failure. The energy fluctuations are unlike anything we've cataloged. They're… unstable." Kaelen's voice, usually so measured, carried a note of genuine concern. He wasn't just reciting data; he was pleading for a return to reason.

Across the cramped bridge, in the auxiliary engineering station, Dr. Lena Petrova was a stark contrast to Kaelen's stoic pragmatism. Her auburn hair was pulled back in a chaotic bun, stray strands escaping to frame a face alight with a fervent, almost manic, curiosity. Her fingers flew across her own console, her brow furrowed in concentration as she dissected the torrent of data flooding in from the deep. Lena was a prodigy, a brilliant astrophysicist and xenolinguist who had found her niche in the fringe science of deep-sea anomalies and extraterrestrial artifacts. For Lena, the *Abyssus* was not a tomb, but a treasure chest, and Elias's obsession was the key that unlocked its secrets. She saw the danger, of course, the terrifying unknown that lay beyond the shimmering veil of energy readings, but her mind was a relentless engine of discovery, always eager to push the boundaries of human knowledge. "Kaelen, don't be such a worrywart!" she chirped, her voice laced with an almost childlike enthusiasm. "Elias is onto something. This energy signature… it's not just random noise. It's patterned. Complex. It's like… like a whisper from another dimension. Imagine what we could learn if we could just get a cleaner read on the source!"

Kaelen sighed, a barely perceptible puff of air. He admired Lena's intellect, her boundless enthusiasm, but he often found himself caught between Elias's almost pathological drive and Lena's scientific recklessness. They were two halves of a dangerous equation, each pushing Elias in their own direction, and he, the steady anchor, was increasingly struggling to keep the vessel from capsizing. "Lena, the 'whisper' you're hearing could very well be the death knell of this submersible. We're not equipped for interdimensional communication, we're equipped for salvage and research. And right now, our research is telling us to retreat."

"Retreat? When we're on the cusp of something monumental?" Lena scoffed, her eyes never leaving her screen. "This isn't just another wrecked freighter, Kaelen. This is… different. The readings are fluctuating in a way that suggests an intelligence, a deliberate manipulation of spacetime on a scale we can barely comprehend. Elias, you see it too, don't you?" Her gaze flickered towards Elias, her expression one of eager anticipation.

Elias finally lifted his head, his eyes, burning with an intensity that belied his exhaustion, met Lena's. "I see the patterns, Lena. And I see the implications. But Kaelen is right. The risks are escalating. We need to maintain a degree of control." His voice was low, almost a murmur, but it carried the weight of absolute authority. He understood Lena's excitement, the intoxicating allure of the unknown, but he also felt the icy grip of Kaelen's pragmatism. He was caught between two worlds, the world of scientific discovery and the stark reality of survival. "Kaelen, run a full diagnostic on the forward manipulator arms. Ensure all systems are nominal for potential retrieval. Lena, continue to triangulate the signal's origin point, but do not attempt to broadcast or engage. We observe, we analyze, and we proceed with extreme caution." Kaelen nodded, a silent acknowledgement of the captain's command, though the tension in his shoulders remained. He knew that "extreme caution" in Elias Thorne's vocabulary was a sliding scale, often leaning heavily towards calculated risk. He moved to his console, his fingers already flying across the controls, initiating the lengthy diagnostic sequence. He trusted

Elias's judgment, or at least, he had. But the abyss had a way of warping perceptions, of drawing even the most grounded individuals into its depths.

Lena, meanwhile, was practically vibrating with excitement. "Triangulating, Captain! The energy signature is originating from a cluster of debris approximately three klicks northeast. It's… it's immense. Unlike anything I've ever seen documented. The structure seems to be… organic in its arrangement, yet undeniably artificial in its composition. There are harmonic resonances within the energy field that suggest a sophisticated form of data transmission." She paused, her breath catching. "It's as if something is actively *communicating* through this energy field."

The word "communicating" hung in the air, heavy with unspoken implications. For Elias, it was another piece of the puzzle, another flicker of hope in the suffocating darkness. For Kaelen, it was a siren song, a dangerous lure that threatened to pull them all under. He continued to monitor the hull stress, the subtle groans and creaks of the *Abyssus* under immense pressure. The ocean, indifferent and ancient, was a constant reminder of their fragility. Every meter they descended was a defiance of nature, a testament to human ingenuity, but also a gamble with increasingly steep odds. Elias

Thorne, the captain haunted by loss, was navigating not just the physical depths of the ocean, but the treacherous currents of his own grief, dragging his crew along for the ride, a crew bound together by circumstance and a fragile, unspoken alliance, united in their pursuit of the unknown, yet divided by the perilous paths they were forced to tread.

The vast, inky blackness outside the reinforced viewport of the *Abyssus* offered no comfort, only a profound sense of isolation. It was a void so absolute, so crushing, that it seemed to seep into the very metal of the submersible, into the bones of its occupants. Elias Thorne, however, found a strange solace in its immensity. It was a reflection of his own inner desolation, a tangible manifestation of the emptiness that had become his constant companion since the day he lost Anya and Lily. He was a man adrift in the deepest part of the world, and in that solitude, he felt a perverse sense of belonging. "Captain," Kaelen's voice, a low rumble that always managed to cut through Elias's internal haze, broke the silence. "We've reached the target coordinates. Deploying the primary sensor array." The words were factual, devoid of the emotional subtext that Elias constantly wrestled with. Kaelen was the bedrock of their operations, the steady hand that ensured the complex machinery of the

*Abyssus* functioned as a cohesive unit. His presence was a silent testament to Elias's capabilities as a commander, even if Elias himself was a man fractured by personal tragedy. Kaelen had served with Elias for years, had witnessed the slow erosion of the man he once was, replaced by a spectral shadow driven by an insatiable need for answers. Loyalty was a deeply ingrained principle for Kaelen, but even the strongest loyalty could be tested by the ever-present specter of death. He had seen the calculations, had run the simulations, and the probability of a successful outcome in their current trajectory was alarmingly low. The ocean, in its infinite, crushing embrace, was not a playground. It was a graveyard.

Elias nodded, his gaze fixed on the external cameras. The sonar display painted a ghostly, three-dimensional image of their surroundings — a landscape of jagged rock formations and a scattering of what appeared to be dense, metallic debris. "Initiate detailed scan of the debris cluster. Lena, I need everything you can get on the energy signatures. I want to know their composition, their frequency, and their point of origin. Don't hold back." His voice was tight, strained, the words clipped with an urgency that Kaelen had come to associate with Elias teetering on the precipice of a breakthrough, or a breakdown.

Dr. Lena Petrova, hunched over her console with an almost feverish intensity, her fingers flying across the holographic interface, emitted a delighted gasp. "Captain, you won't believe this! The energy readings are… they're unlike anything in our databanks. It's a complex waveform, highly structured, with an incredibly dense informational content. And the debris… it's not just random wreckage, Elias. It's organized. It's… artificial." Her auburn hair, escaping its haphazard bun, framed a face alight with the pure, unadulterated joy of discovery. For Lena, this was the pinnacle, the moment when theoretical physics met tangible, alien reality. She saw the danger, yes, but the potential for knowledge, for understanding, far outweighed any personal risk. This was what she lived for, what she had dedicated her life to.

Kaelen's brow furrowed as he reviewed Lena's preliminary findings. "Artificial? Lena, the pressure down here could distort readings. We've seen it before. Remember the… incident near the Marianas Trench?" He deliberately avoided mentioning the specifics, the close call that had nearly cost them their lives. The memory was still too raw, too close to the surface.

Lena waved a dismissive hand, her focus unwavering. "This is different, Kaelen. The structure of the energy field is too precise, too deliberate. It's like… like a signal. A beacon. And the debris itself… it's not corroded by the sea as one would expect. It's almost… preserved. As if time itself has been bent around it." She turned, her eyes sparkling with an infectious excitement that Elias found himself momentarily drawn to, a fleeting glimpse of the life he had lost. "Captain, this is it. This is what we've been searching for. This isn't just salvage; this is first contact. Or at least, the remnants of it."

Elias felt a familiar tightening in his chest, a phantom ache that no amount of technological sophistication could assuage. First contact. The words echoed in the vast emptiness of his mind, a stark contrast to the intimate, devastating loss he had endured. He had sought the profound, the alien, hoping to find some cosmic resonance with his own grief, some grander narrative that could explain the unfairness of it all. He looked at Lena, her youthful exuberance a sharp counterpoint to his own ingrained weariness. She was the embodiment of what he had lost – a boundless capacity for wonder, a belief in the future.

"We need to be cautious, Lena," Elias said, his voice low and measured. "The energy fluctuations are still significant. Kaelen, keep a close watch on hull integrity and environmental stability. If anything spikes beyond acceptable parameters, we pull back immediately." The words were firm, a necessary anchor of pragmatism against Lena's burgeoning excitement and his own dangerous curiosity.

Kaelen nodded, his gaze sweeping across the multiple readouts flickering across his console. He understood Elias's directive, but he also saw the flicker of something akin to hope in the captain's eyes, a dangerous emotion in their current circumstances. Elias was a man driven by ghosts, and these spectral signals from the abyss were fanning the flames of his obsession. Kaelen's role was to be the steady hand, the voice of reason, to ensure that Elias's pursuit of closure didn't lead them all to an untimely end. He admired Elias's brilliance, his sheer tenacity, but he also recognized the escalating risks. The *Abyssus* was a marvel of engineering, but even its advanced systems had their limits.

"Captain," Kaelen interjected, his voice calm and steady, "the seismic activity in this region is higher than anticipated. We're detecting subtle tremors that could indicate geological instability. Combined with the energy fluctuations Lena is observing, this sector is becoming increasingly hazardous." He paused, allowing the weight of his words to settle. "My recommendation is to deploy the drone for a closer, less invasive assessment before we commit the *Abyssus* any further."

Lena scoffed again. "A drone? Kaelen, that's like trying to understand a symphony by listening to a single, muffled note! This requires a direct approach. Elias, we need to get closer. The energy signature is strongest directly within that debris cluster. I believe the source of the signal is embedded within the largest metallic structure." She pointed to a particularly dense mass on the sonar display, an anomaly that seemed to pulse with its own internal light.

Elias considered their words, his gaze sweeping across the data, his mind a whirlwind of calculations and emotional responses. He felt the pull of Lena's scientific curiosity, the intoxicating allure of the unknown, a siren song that echoed the whispers of his lost family. But Kaelen's pragmatic warning, the cold, hard data on hull stress and seismic activity, was a stark reminder of the brutal reality of their situation. He was not just a scientist; he was a captain, responsible for the lives of his crew, and more importantly, for not repeating the mistakes that had led to his own personal cataclysm. "We will proceed with caution, Lena," Elias finally declared, his voice resonating with a quiet authority. "Kaelen, prepare the manipulator arms for deployment. Lena, I want you to run a series of energy absorption simulations. If this structure is indeed emitting such a powerful signal, it might also be capable of absorbing significant energy. We need to understand its potential impact on our systems before we make direct contact."

Lena, though slightly disappointed by the lack of immediate deep dive, readily accepted the new parameters. "Simulations running, Captain! This is going to be incredible. Imagine, Elias, what we could learn from this… this artifact. It could rewrite everything we know about astrophysics, about communication, about… life itself." Her enthusiasm, while infectious, also carried a hint of the same unbridled ambition that had, in part, led to the shuttle disaster that had claimed Elias's family. He felt a pang of guilt, a resurgence of the old fear, but he pushed it down, compartmentalizing it as he always did.

Kaelen, meanwhile, was already initiating the complex sequence for the manipulator arm deployment. His movements were precise, efficient, each action a testament to his years of experience. He trusted Elias's strategic mind, his ability to navigate the treacherous currents of both the ocean and his own grief. But as he worked, he couldn't shake the feeling that they were venturing into waters far deeper and more dangerous than any of them truly understood. The alliance they shared, this fragile bond forged in the crucible of shared isolation and a singular, enigmatic mission, was about to be tested like never before. The ocean held its secrets close, and the deeper they plunged, the more it seemed to demand a terrible price.

The *Abyssus*, a marvel of deep-sea engineering, descended with deliberate, measured grace. Its external floodlights cut through the oppressive blackness, revealing a vista of silent, ancient decay. Scattered across the abyssal plain, like skeletal remains of colossal beasts, lay the husks of derelict spacecraft. These were not the gleaming, modern vessels that plied the shallower waters; these were relics of a forgotten era, their hulls scarred by eons of pressure, their systems long dead, yet their metallic carcasses held the promise of invaluable salvage. This was the primary objective of their mission: to meticulously pick through this graveyard of ambition, extracting what remained of functional technology, rare alloys, and data cores that might unlock the secrets of their predecessors.

The operation was a testament to human ingenuity and a stark reminder of their own fragility. Each movement of the *Abyssus* was calculated, its powerful thrusters pushing against the immense, unyielding pressure of the deep. The sheer scale of the debris field was overwhelming. Wreckage stretched as far as the submersible's lights could penetrate, a testament to some long-forgotten cataclysm or a brutal series of interstellar conflicts. Elias Thorne, his gaze fixed on the sonar and visual feeds, felt the familiar weight of responsibility settle upon him. He was the captain, tasked with guiding his crew and vessel through this treacherous expanse, not just to retrieve valuable resources, but to ensure they all returned to the surface alive.

"Kaelen, proximity alert on the starboard side," Elias's voice was a low rumble, cutting through the ambient hum of the life support systems. "That debris cluster is denser than anticipated. Run a structural integrity scan on the largest section."

First Mate Kaelen, ever vigilant, acknowledged the command with a curt nod. His fingers danced across his console, initiating the scan with practiced efficiency. "Understood, Captain. Analysis commencing. Preliminary readings indicate a significant metallic composition, likely a heavy alloy. Hull plating appears to be several meters thick. No immediate structural weaknesses detected from this range, but the density suggests it could be a considerable hazard if we misjudge our approach."

On the auxiliary engineering station, Dr. Lena Petrova was already engrossed in the spectrographic analysis of the surrounding debris. Her eyes, magnified by the intricate holographic displays, scanned for unique energy signatures or residual radiation that might indicate valuable salvageable components. "Captain, I'm picking up residual energy traces from that cluster Kaelen is scanning," she reported, her voice brimming with the characteristic eagerness that always managed to inject a sliver of excitement into the otherwise grim task. "Low-level, but persistent. It's not a common power source; the frequency is highly unusual. It suggests advanced, possibly experimental, propulsion or power generation systems."

Elias absorbed the information, piecing together the fragmented data into a coherent picture. The mission was not merely about scavenging scrap metal. Each derelict was a potential treasure trove, a silent witness to technological advancements that could revolutionize their own present. The risk, however, was equally immense. These wrecks were often unstable, their internal structures compromised by the crushing pressures of the abyss. A misplaced maneuver, a sudden shift in the seabed, or a cascade failure within the debris itself could spell disaster.

"Lena, can you isolate the source of those energy traces?" Elias inquired, leaning forward. "Are they emanating from the main hull, or a specific component?"

"It's difficult to say with certainty without a closer look, Captain," Lena replied, her brow furrowed in concentration. "The readings are diffused, but there's a distinct locus within the largest wreckage. It's behaving almost like a dormant power core, emitting faint pulses. It could be incredibly valuable if we can access it safely."

Kaelen's scan completed, and he turned his attention to the primary display. "The large section is largely intact, Captain. Minimal hull breach detected. However, there are multiple smaller debris fragments attached to it, some of which appear to be structural supports. They could pose a snagging hazard for the manipulator arms."

"Understood," Elias responded. He knew the delicate dance they had to perform. The *Abyssus* was equipped with state-of-the-art manipulator arms, articulated and powerful, designed to grasp, cut, and retrieve objects from the seabed. But even these sophisticated tools had their limitations, especially when dealing with the unpredictable nature of deep-sea wreckage. The silence of the abyss, punctuated only by the low thrum of their own vessel and the crackle of comms, was a constant reminder of the sheer, unforgiving power of the environment they were operating in.

"We'll approach the primary hull section," Elias declared, his voice firm. "Kaelen, plot a course that allows us to maintain a safe distance from the smaller, potentially unstable fragments. Lena, I want you to monitor the energy readings continuously. If they spike or show any sign of instability, you alert me immediately. We prioritize caution. We don't want to wake up anything that's best left undisturbed."

The *Abyssus* shifted course, its powerful thrusters nudging it through the water with smooth, controlled movements. The floodlights illuminated the colossal structure before them, a testament to an unknown civilization's lost journey. It was a leviathan of metal, its surface encrusted with millennia of marine growth, yet its form was unmistakably artificial. Twisted girders, shattered observation decks, and gaping holes where once vital systems had resided spoke of a violent end.

"The energy signature is stabilizing, Captain," Lena reported, her voice filled with a hushed reverence. "It's almost as if it's reacting to our presence, but not aggressively. More like… a dormant sentry acknowledging a visitor."

Kaelen initiated the deployment sequence for the primary manipulator arm. With a low whirring of hydraulics, the articulated limb extended from the

*Abyssus*'s ventral bay, its multi-jointed structure moving with an uncanny fluidity. The claw at its end, a formidable piece of engineering capable of crushing rock, was poised to grasp.

"Targeting a section of hull that appears to be a primary access panel," Kaelen announced, his eyes glued to the manipulator's camera feed. "It's fused shut, but the underlying framework seems intact. We might be able to pry it open and access the interior. The residual energy readings are strongest from within that area."

Elias watched the delicate ballet of mechanical precision. This was the core of their mission: to overcome the obstacles of time, pressure, and decay to salvage what was left. The potential reward was immense, but the risks were ever-present. The abyss was a place of profound silence, but it was also a place where the slightest miscalculation could echo with catastrophic consequences.

"Proceed with caution, Kaelen," Elias reiterated, his gaze never leaving the unfolding operation. "Gentle pressure. We don't want to compromise the integrity of the hull we're trying to breach."

The manipulator arm made contact with the fused panel. For a tense moment, nothing happened. Then, with a low groan of protesting metal, the panel began to shift. Small fragments of rust and ancient sealant flaked away, revealing the dark void beyond. Lena's breath hitched.

"Captain, the energy readings just spiked!" she exclaimed, her voice sharp with alarm. "It's a significant increase, and the frequency has shifted dramatically. It's… it's not random. It's a structured pulse, almost like a… a signal."

Elias's senses sharpened. "What kind of signal, Lena?"

"I can't categorize it yet, Captain. It's unlike any known communication protocol. It's complex, layered. And it's originating from directly behind that panel."

Kaelen, though focused on maintaining control of the manipulator, registered Lena's report. "Captain, I'm experiencing an unexpected resistance from the debris cluster. It's not mechanical; it feels like a localized field disturbance. The manipulator's torque readings are fluctuating erratically."

The situation was rapidly escalating. The dormant wreck, disturbed by their intrusion, was showing signs of activity. Elias had to make a decision, and he had to make it quickly. The lure of valuable salvage warred with the primal instinct for self-preservation.

"Pull back the manipulator arm, Kaelen," Elias ordered, his voice tight. "Slowly. Let's reassess the situation."

The arm retracted, its powerful claw releasing its grip. As it withdrew, the energy readings Lena had detected began to subside, and the localized field disturbance Kaelen had reported diminished. The abyss seemed to exhale, its silent menace returning to a low simmer.

"The signal has faded back to its previous dormant state," Lena reported, a hint of disappointment in her voice, but also a renewed sense of scientific intrigue. "The disturbance in the field has dissipated."

"The resistance is gone," Kaelen confirmed, his hand hovering over the manipulator controls. "It seems our attempt to breach the hull triggered a localized defensive response, or perhaps a warning."

Elias leaned back in his command chair, his mind racing. They were not merely salvaging derelicts; they were delving into the unknown, into a realm where ancient technology might still possess active protocols. The initial objective of salvaging valuable components had just become infinitely more complicated, and infinitely more dangerous. The sheer audacity of their mission, to plunder the remnants of forgotten voyages, was a testament to humanity's insatiable drive for progress. But the abyss, in its silent, crushing embrace, served as a constant reminder that progress often came at a steep price, and that some secrets were perhaps best left buried in the crushing depths.

The discovery of the active energy signature within the derelict vessel marked a significant turning point in their salvage operation. What had begun as a meticulous, albeit dangerous, process of disassembling and retrieving valuable components had now transformed into a venture into the realm of active, potentially responsive, ancient technology. Elias knew they could not simply abandon this potential source of knowledge, but he also understood the heightened risks. Their mission was salvage and survival, a dual imperative that now seemed more precarious than ever.

"Lena, I need you to analyze those energy pulses again," Elias commanded, his gaze fixed on the spectral data that still shimmered on her console. "Focus on the pattern, the frequency modulations. Try to identify any recurring sequences or variations that might indicate a more complex form of communication or internal process." He paused, considering their next move. "Kaelen, I want a full diagnostic on the manipulator arm, paying particular attention to any stress fractures or anomalies that might have occurred during the attempted breach. We need to ensure our tools are in optimal condition before we proceed."

Kaelen nodded, already initiating the diagnostic sequence. His movements were economical, precise, a practiced dance of technological assessment. "Diagnostics running, Captain. The arm performed within expected parameters, despite the resistance. However, I concur with Lena's assessment regarding the anomaly. The localized field distortion was… unusual. It felt less like a physical obstruction and more like a conscious deterrent."

Lena's fingers flew across her console, her brow furrowed in concentration. The complex waveforms danced before her, each flicker and oscillation a potential clue. "The pulses are indeed structured, Captain," she reported after a few minutes of intense analysis. "There are repeating motifs, almost like a rudimentary alphabet. And the energy fluctuations suggest a sort of internal monitoring system. It's as if the vessel, or at least this part of it, is still… aware."

The word "aware" hung in the air, heavy with implication. Elias felt a shiver, a primal instinct that warred with his scientific curiosity. He was a man driven by the ghosts of his past, constantly searching for answers in the vast unknowns of the universe. The idea that they had stumbled upon something that was not merely inert wreckage, but a potentially sentient remnant of a lost civilization, was both exhilarating and terrifying.

"Aware or not," Elias stated, his voice firm, "our objective remains the same: salvage. However, we must adapt our approach. We can't afford to trigger any further defensive responses. The structural integrity of this wreck is still a major concern, and we don't know the full extent of its capabilities."

"Perhaps a different approach is warranted," Kaelen interjected, his gaze sweeping across the external camera feeds. "Instead of forcing access, we could try to locate a less compromised entry point. The debris field is extensive. There might be other sections of this vessel that are more accessible, or perhaps other, smaller derelicts nearby that are easier to salvage without risking a confrontation with this… active system."

Elias considered Kaelen's suggestion. It was the pragmatic, responsible course of action. Their primary mission was salvage and survival, and engaging with an unknown, potentially hostile ancient technology was not part of the original plan. However, the lure of what lay within that sealed compartment, the secrets it held, gnawed at him. It was a siren song, a whisper of answers to questions he hadn't even fully articulated.

"We will continue our survey of the immediate area, Kaelen," Elias decided. "Maintain a safe standoff distance from the primary wreck. Deploy the scout drones to map out the surrounding debris field. I want to know what else is out here, and whether any of it presents a more manageable salvage opportunity."

The scout drones, small, agile submersibles equipped with advanced sensor arrays and manipulator tools, were dispatched from the *Abyssus*. They fanned out into the darkness, their powerful lights cutting through the abyssal gloom, illuminating further stretches of the silent, metallic graveyard. Elias, Kaelen, and Lena watched their progress on the tactical display, a mosaic of data points and visual feeds.

The drones systematically explored the vast expanse. They encountered smaller wrecks, most of them heavily damaged and offering little in the way of valuable salvage. One drone reported a dense cluster of metallic fragments that appeared to be an engine core, its intricate components fused beyond recognition. Another found the shattered remnants of what looked like a cargo bay, its contents long since dispersed or decomposed.

Then, one of the drones, designated 'Scout-3', reported a significant find. "Captain, Scout-3 is transmitting visual data," Kaelen announced, his voice tinged with a rare note of excitement. "It's a smaller vessel, partially embedded in a rock formation. It appears to be remarkably intact. And… it's emitting a unique energy signature. Similar to the primary wreck, but far weaker, more stable."

Elias leaned closer to the main display, where Scout-3's camera feed was now prominently featured. The drone's lights illuminated a sleek, metallic craft, its lines far more refined than the hulking structure they had encountered earlier. It was lodged at an angle, its forward section pressed against a jagged, crystalline outcropping, but its main hull seemed largely undamaged. The energy signature Lena had detected was indeed faint, a soft, intermittent pulse.

"Lena, analyze that signature," Elias commanded. "Compare it to the readings from the primary wreck. Is it related?"

"Affirmative, Captain," Lena replied, her eyes wide with fascination. "It's the same fundamental waveform, but attenuated. It's like a distant echo, or a modulated signal. It's definitely connected to the larger wreck, perhaps a smaller utility craft or a probe that detached from the main vessel."

"Kaelen, plot a course for Scout-3's position," Elias ordered. "We'll assess this smaller derelict first. If it's intact and the energy signature is stable, it might represent a more manageable salvage opportunity."

The *Abyssus* adjusted its trajectory, moving towards the location of the smaller vessel. As they drew closer, the details of the craft became clearer. Its metallic hull gleamed faintly in the drone's lights, and intricate patterns, almost like etched circuitry, were visible on its surface. It was a work of art as much as a machine, and its apparent intactness was a beacon of hope in the desolation of the abyss.

"The structure seems solid, Captain," Kaelen reported as they maneuvered the *Abyssus* into a position that allowed for a closer inspection. "No significant hull breaches visible. The rock formation it's lodged in is stable, not showing signs of imminent collapse."

"Lena, any change in the energy readings?" Elias inquired.

"No, Captain. The signature remains consistent. It's a low-level emission, very stable. It doesn't seem to be reacting to our presence." Lena's voice was filled with a mixture of relief and mild disappointment; the thrill of a potential confrontation was absent, replaced by the steady hum of scientific observation.

"Alright," Elias said, making his decision. "Kaelen, prepare the manipulator arm for a gentle extraction. We'll try to carefully dislodge it from the rock formation. Priority is to retrieve the craft intact, if possible. Lena, continue to monitor the energy signature and any subtle environmental changes. We proceed with the same caution we would any other salvage operation, but with an added layer of awareness due to the nature of the energy emissions."

The manipulator arm extended once more, its claw opening wide. Kaelen guided it with expert precision, aiming to grip the smaller vessel at its strongest points. The process was slow and deliberate, a delicate maneuver designed to exert just enough force to free the craft without causing damage. The vast, silent pressure of the ocean seemed to press in on them, a constant reminder of the forces they were contending with.

"Grip established," Kaelen announced. "Applying minimal torque."

There was a faint creaking sound, a protest from the ancient metal as it was shifted. The crystalline rock formation chipped and fractured slightly, but the smaller vessel remained remarkably intact. The energy signature, however, flickered.

"Captain, the energy signature just pulsed!" Lena exclaimed, her voice urgent. "It's a single, distinct pulse, and then… nothing. It's gone completely silent. The readings have flatlined."

Elias felt a jolt of apprehension. "Gone silent? Lena, are you sure?"

"Yes, Captain. All residual energy readings have ceased. It's as if the power source has been completely deactivated."

Kaelen felt a subtle shift in the resistance he was applying. "The dislodgement is complete, Captain. The smaller vessel is free from the rock."

The manipulator arm carefully lifted the craft, bringing it closer to the *Abyssus* for a more thorough examination. It was a beautiful, enigmatic object, its purpose and origin lost to time. The sudden cessation of its energy signature was unsettling. Had their actions deactivated it, or had it simply reached the end of its operational cycle?

"Bring it into the auxiliary bay, Kaelen," Elias commanded. "We'll conduct a full internal scan once it's secured. The loss of the energy signature is… concerning. We need to understand what happened."

As the smaller derelict was carefully maneuvered into the *Abyssus*'s spacious auxiliary bay, Elias couldn't shake the feeling that their salvage operation had taken an unexpected and profound turn. They had come seeking valuable components, but they had stumbled upon relics that hinted at a far grander, more complex history. The abyss held its secrets tightly, and each discovery seemed to raise more questions than it answered. The weight of the ocean was not just in its crushing pressure, but in the immensity of its forgotten past, a past they were only just beginning to unearth. The primary mission, salvage and survival, was now interwoven with the daunting task of deciphering the echoes of civilizations long gone, a challenge that Elias knew would push them all to their absolute limits.

The descent had been a ballet of controlled power, the *Abyssus* a silent predator gliding through an ocean of absolute black. Its external floodlights, typically a source of comforting illumination, now felt like probing fingers against the oppressive, suffocating dark. They cut through the void, revealing a vista that was less a landscape and more a graveyard. Scattered across the abyssal plain, like the colossal, fossilized bones of leviathans long extinct, lay the husks of derelict spacecraft. These were not the sleek, functional vessels that traversed the upper ocean layers; these were relics of a forgotten epoch, their hulls weathered by millennia of crushing pressure, their internal systems long silenced, yet their very existence whispered of lost technologies and untold stories. This alien necropolis was the quarry, the promise of salvageable wonders and invaluable data shimmering in the minds of Elias Thorne and his crew.

The sheer scale of the debris field was a visceral shock. Wreckage stretched as far as the *Abyssus's* powerful beams could penetrate, a testament to some cataclysmic event or a brutal interstellar conflict lost to the mists of time. Elias felt the familiar, heavy cloak of responsibility settle upon him. He was the captain, entrusted with the safety of his crew and the integrity of his vessel as they navigated this treacherous expanse. Each movement of the *Abyssus* was a deliberate calculation, its powerful thrusters battling the immense, unyielding pressure of the deep. The silence was profound, broken only by the rhythmic hum of the life support systems and the faint crackle of the comms. It was a silence that spoke volumes, a constant, unnerving reminder of their own fragility in the face of the abyss's indifferent might.

"Kaelen, proximity alert on the starboard side," Elias's voice, a low rumble that seemed to absorb some of the surrounding silence, broke the stillness. "That debris cluster is denser than anticipated. Run a structural integrity scan on the largest section."

First Mate Kaelen, a man whose vigilance was as ingrained as the metallic tang of recycled air, acknowledged the command with a curt nod. His fingers danced across his console, initiating the scan with a practiced, almost instinctual efficiency. "Understood, Captain. Analysis commencing. Preliminary readings indicate a significant metallic composition, likely a heavy alloy. Hull plating appears to be several meters thick. No immediate structural weaknesses detected from this range, but the density suggests it could be a considerable hazard if we misjudge our approach."

On the auxiliary engineering station, Dr. Lena Petrova was already immersed in the intricate dance of spectrographic analysis. Her eyes, magnified by the sophisticated holographic displays, scanned for any anomalous energy signatures or residual radiation that might point to salvageable components. Her usual scientific detachment was tinged with an unmistakable spark of excitement. "Captain, I'm picking up residual energy traces from that cluster Kaelen is scanning," she reported, her voice carrying a note of scientific wonder. "Low-level, but persistent. It's not a common power source; the frequency is highly unusual. It suggests advanced, possibly experimental, propulsion or power generation systems."

Elias absorbed the fragmented data, his mind working to assemble a coherent picture. Their mission was not simply about stripping down derelicts for raw materials. Each wreck was a potential Pandora's Box of lost knowledge, a silent witness to technological leaps that could redefine their own present. The risk, however, was equally immense. These ancient wrecks were often unstable, their internal structures compromised by the relentless, crushing pressure of the abyss. A misplaced maneuver, a sudden shift in the seabed, or a cascading failure within the wreckage itself could spell immediate disaster.

"Lena, can you isolate the source of those energy traces?" Elias inquired, leaning forward in his command chair. "Are they emanating from the main hull, or a specific component?"

"It's difficult to say with certainty without a closer look, Captain," Lena replied, her brow furrowed in intense concentration. "The readings are diffused, but there's a distinct locus within the largest wreckage. It's behaving almost like a dormant power core, emitting faint pulses. It could be incredibly valuable if we can access it safely."

Kaelen's scan completed, and he turned his attention to the primary display, his gaze sharp and focused. "The large section is largely intact, Captain. Minimal hull breach detected. However, there are multiple smaller debris fragments attached to it, some of which appear to be structural supports. They could pose a snagging hazard for the manipulator arms."

"Understood," Elias responded, his mind already calculating the delicate maneuvers required. The *Abyssus* was equipped with state-of-the-art manipulator arms, articulated and powerful, designed to grasp, cut, and retrieve objects from the seabed. Yet, even these sophisticated tools had their limitations, especially when dealing with the unpredictable nature of deep-sea wreckage. The silence of the abyss was a tangible presence, a stark reminder of the sheer, unforgiving power of the environment they were operating within. It was a realm where a single miscalculation could reverberate with catastrophic consequences.

"We'll approach the primary hull section," Elias declared, his voice firm and decisive. "Kaelen, plot a course that allows us to maintain a safe distance from the smaller, potentially unstable fragments. Lena, I want you to monitor the energy readings continuously. If they spike or show any sign of instability, you alert me immediately. We prioritize caution. We don't want to wake up anything that's best left undisturbed."

The *Abyssus* shifted its orientation, its powerful thrusters nudging it through the water with smooth, controlled movements. The floodlights intensified, illuminating the colossal structure before them with stark clarity. It was a testament to an unknown civilization's lost journey, a leviathan of metal whose surface was encrusted with millennia of marine growth, yet whose form was unmistakably artificial. Twisted girders, shattered observation decks, and gaping holes where once vital systems had resided spoke of a violent, decisive end.

"The energy signature is stabilizing, Captain," Lena reported, her voice hushed with a reverence that Elias found himself sharing. "It's almost as if it's reacting to our presence, but not aggressively. More like… a dormant sentry acknowledging a visitor."

Kaelen initiated the deployment sequence for the primary manipulator arm. With a low whirring of hydraulics, the articulated limb extended from the *Abyssus*'s ventral bay, its multi-jointed structure moving with an uncanny fluidity. The claw at its end, a formidable piece of engineering capable of crushing solid rock, was poised to grasp.

"Targeting a section of hull that appears to be a primary access panel," Kaelen announced, his eyes glued to the manipulator's camera feed. "It's fused shut, but the underlying framework seems intact. We might be able to pry it open and access the interior. The residual energy readings are strongest from within that area."

Elias watched the delicate ballet of mechanical precision unfold. This was the crux of their mission: to overcome the obstacles of time, pressure, and decay to salvage whatever remained of value. The potential reward was immense, but the risks were ever-present. The abyss was a place of profound silence, but it was also a place where the slightest miscalculation could echo with devastating finality.

"Proceed with caution, Kaelen," Elias reiterated, his gaze never leaving the unfolding operation. "Gentle pressure. We don't want to compromise the integrity of the hull we're trying to breach."

The manipulator arm made contact with the fused panel. For a tense, drawn-out moment, nothing happened. Then, with a low groan of protesting metal, the panel began to shift. Small fragments of rust and ancient sealant flaked away, revealing the dark void beyond. Lena's breath hitched audibly.

"Captain, the energy readings just spiked!" she exclaimed, her voice sharp with alarm. "It's a significant increase, and the frequency has shifted dramatically. It's… it's not random. It's a structured pulse, almost like a… a signal."

Elias's senses sharpened, his body tensing. "What kind of signal, Lena?"

"I can't categorize it yet, Captain. It's unlike any known communication protocol. It's complex, layered. And it's originating from directly behind that panel."

Kaelen, though focused on maintaining precise control of the manipulator, registered Lena's urgent report. "Captain, I'm experiencing an unexpected resistance from the debris cluster. It's not mechanical; it feels like a localized field disturbance. The manipulator's torque readings are fluctuating erratically."

The situation was rapidly escalating. The dormant wreck, disturbed by their intrusion, was showing signs of unexpected activity. Elias had to make a decision, and he had to make it quickly. The potent lure of valuable salvage warred with the primal, ingrained instinct for self-preservation.

"Pull back the manipulator arm, Kaelen," Elias ordered, his voice tight with suppressed urgency. "Slowly. Let's reassess the situation."

The arm retracted, its powerful claw releasing its grip. As it withdrew, the energy readings Lena had detected began to subside, and the localized field disturbance Kaelen had reported diminished. The abyss seemed to exhale, its silent menace returning to a low, simmering state.

"The signal has faded back to its previous dormant state," Lena reported, a hint of disappointment in her voice, but also a renewed surge of scientific intrigue. "The disturbance in the field has dissipated."

"The resistance is gone," Kaelen confirmed, his hand hovering over the manipulator controls, ready for immediate action if necessary. "It seems our attempt to breach the hull triggered a localized defensive response, or perhaps a warning."

Elias leaned back in his command chair, his mind racing. They were not merely salvaging inert derelicts; they were delving into the unknown, into a realm where ancient technology might still possess active protocols, perhaps even autonomous functions. The initial objective of salvaging valuable components had just become infinitely more complicated, and infinitely more dangerous. The sheer audacity of their mission, to plunder the silent, forgotten voyages of predecessors, was a testament to humanity's insatiable drive for progress. But the abyss, in its silent, crushing embrace, served as a constant, sobering reminder that progress often came at a steep price, and that some secrets were perhaps best left buried in the crushing, eternal darkness.

The discovery of the active energy signature within the derelict vessel marked a significant, unforeseen turning point in their salvage operation. What had begun as a meticulous, albeit inherently dangerous, process of disassembling and retrieving valuable components had now transformed into a venture into the realm of active, potentially responsive, ancient technology. Elias knew they could not simply abandon this potential source of knowledge, not without a more thorough understanding, but he also understood the heightened risks involved. Their mission was salvage and survival, a dual imperative that now seemed more precarious than ever before. The weight of the ocean wasn't just in its physical pressure; it was in the immense burden of responsibility he carried.

"Lena, I need you to analyze those energy pulses again," Elias commanded, his gaze fixed on the spectral data that still shimmered on her console, a ghostly record of the anomaly. "Focus on the pattern, the frequency modulations. Try to identify any recurring sequences or variations that might indicate a more complex form of communication or internal process." He paused, considering their next move, his mind sifting through the immediate tactical options. "Kaelen, I want a full diagnostic on the manipulator arm, paying particular attention to any stress fractures or anomalies that might have occurred during the attempted breach. We need to ensure our tools are in optimal condition before we proceed with any further engagement."

Kaelen nodded, his movements economical and precise, already initiating the diagnostic sequence. It was a practiced dance of technological assessment, a testament to his professionalism. "Diagnostics running, Captain. The arm performed within expected parameters, despite the resistance. However, I concur with Lena's assessment regarding the anomaly. The localized field distortion was… unusual. It felt less like a physical obstruction and more like a conscious deterrent, a deliberate pushback."

Lena's fingers flew across her console with a speed that bordered on frenetic, her brow furrowed in intense concentration. The complex waveforms danced before her, each flicker and oscillation a potential clue, a fragment of an ancient puzzle. "The pulses are indeed structured, Captain," she reported after a few minutes of intense analysis, her voice barely above a whisper, filled with a palpable sense of discovery. "There are repeating motifs, almost like a rudimentary alphabet. And the energy fluctuations suggest a sort of internal monitoring system. It's as if the vessel, or at least this part of it, is still… aware."

The word "aware" hung in the sterile air of the command module, heavy with implication. Elias felt a primal shiver trace its way down his spine, a sensation that warred with his ingrained scientific curiosity. He was a man driven by the ghosts of his past, a seeker of answers in the vast, silent unknowns of the universe. The idea that they had stumbled upon something that was not merely inert wreckage, but a potentially sentient remnant of a lost civilization, was both exhilarating and deeply unsettling. It was a prospect that promised immense reward, but also invoked a profound sense of dread.

"Aware or not," Elias stated, his voice firm, cutting through the rising tide of speculation, "our objective remains the same: salvage. However, we must adapt our approach. We can't afford to trigger any further defensive responses. The structural integrity of this wreck is still a major concern, and we don't know the full extent of its capabilities. We need to be surgical, not forceful."

"Perhaps a different approach is warranted," Kaelen interjected, his gaze sweeping across the external camera feeds, his mind already working on alternative strategies. "Instead of forcing access, we could try to locate a less compromised entry point. The debris field is extensive. There might be other sections of this vessel that are more accessible, or perhaps other, smaller derelicts nearby that are easier to salvage without risking a confrontation with this… active system."

Elias considered Kaelen's suggestion. It was the pragmatic, responsible course of action, the one that prioritized the safety of the crew and the vessel. Their primary mission was salvage and survival, and engaging with an unknown, potentially hostile ancient technology was not part of the original operational plan. However, the lure of what lay within that sealed compartment, the secrets it undoubtedly held, gnawed at him. It was a siren song, a whisper of answers to questions he hadn't even fully articulated yet, a promise of knowledge that could fundamentally alter their understanding of their place in the cosmos.

"We will continue our survey of the immediate area, Kaelen," Elias decided, his gaze still fixed on the enigmatic wreck. "Maintain a safe standoff distance from the primary wreck. Deploy the scout drones to map out the surrounding debris field. I want to know what else is out here, and whether any of it presents a more manageable salvage opportunity. Information is our best weapon right now."

The scout drones, small, agile submersibles equipped with advanced sensor arrays and delicate manipulator tools, were dispatched from the *Abyssus*. They fanned out into the oppressive darkness, their powerful lights cutting through the abyssal gloom, illuminating further stretches of the silent, metallic graveyard. Elias, Kaelen, and Lena watched their progress on the tactical display, a mosaic of data points and visual feeds painting a picture of the surrounding desolation.

The drones systematically explored the vast expanse. They encountered smaller wrecks, most of them heavily damaged and offering little in the way of valuable salvage. One drone reported a dense cluster of metallic fragments that appeared to be an engine core, its intricate components fused beyond recognition by the ravages of time and pressure. Another found the shattered remnants of what looked like a cargo bay, its contents long since dispersed or decomposed, leaving only the hollow shell of its former purpose.

Then, one of the drones, designated 'Scout-3', reported a significant find. "Captain, Scout-3 is transmitting visual data," Kaelen announced, his voice tinged with a rare note of genuine excitement, a stark contrast to the usual grim tenor of their reports. "It's a smaller vessel, partially embedded in a rock formation. It appears to be remarkably intact. And… it's emitting a unique energy signature. Similar to the primary wreck, but far weaker, more stable.”

Elias leaned closer to the main display, where Scout-3’s camera feed was now prominently featured. The drone’s lights illuminated a sleek, metallic craft, its lines far more refined and elegant than the hulking structure they had encountered earlier. It was lodged at an angle, its forward section pressed against a jagged, crystalline outcropping, but its main hull seemed largely undamaged. The energy signature Lena had detected was indeed faint, a soft, intermittent pulse that was barely registering on their sensors.

“Lena, analyze that signature,” Elias commanded, his mind already racing with possibilities. “Compare it to the readings from the primary wreck. Is it related?”

“Affirmative, Captain,” Lena replied, her eyes wide with fascination, her usual scientific objectivity momentarily eclipsed by the sheer wonder of the discovery. “It’s the same fundamental waveform, but attenuated. It’s like a distant echo, or a modulated signal. It’s definitely connected to the larger wreck, perhaps a smaller utility craft or a probe that detached from the main vessel.”

“Kaelen, plot a course for Scout-3’s position,” Elias ordered, the decision made. “We’ll assess this smaller derelict first. If it’s intact and the energy signature is stable, it might represent a more manageable salvage opportunity, a less risky first step."

The *Abyssus* adjusted its trajectory, its powerful thrusters guiding it through the water towards the location of the smaller vessel. As they drew closer, the details of the craft became clearer. Its metallic hull gleamed faintly in the drone's lights, and intricate patterns, almost like etched circuitry, were visible on its surface. It was a work of art as much as a machine, and its apparent intactness was a beacon of hope in the desolation of the abyss.

"The structure seems solid, Captain," Kaelen reported as they maneuvered the *Abyssus* into a position that allowed for a closer, more detailed inspection. "No significant hull breaches visible. The rock formation it's lodged in is stable, not showing signs of imminent collapse."

"Lena, any change in the energy readings?" Elias inquired, his gaze fixed on the delicate fluctuations on her console.

"No, Captain. The signature remains consistent. It's a low-level emission, very stable. It doesn't seem to be reacting to our presence." Lena's voice was filled with a mixture of relief and mild disappointment; the thrill of a potential confrontation was absent, replaced by the steady, reliable hum of scientific observation.

"Alright," Elias said, his decision made. "Kaelen, prepare the manipulator arm for a gentle extraction. We'll try to carefully dislodge it from the rock formation. Priority is to retrieve the craft intact, if possible. Lena, continue to monitor the energy signature and any subtle environmental changes. We proceed with the same caution we would any other salvage operation, but with an added layer of awareness due to the nature of the energy emissions."

The manipulator arm extended once more, its claw opening wide, a metallic maw ready to embrace its prize. Kaelen guided it with expert precision, aiming to grip the smaller vessel at its strongest points. The process was slow and deliberate, a delicate maneuver designed to exert just enough force to free the craft without causing damage. The vast, silent pressure of the ocean seemed to press in on them, a constant, palpable reminder of the immense forces they were contending with. It was a dance on the edge of disaster, a testament to the skill of the crew and the resilience of their technology.

"Grip established," Kaelen announced, his voice steady. "Applying minimal torque."

There was a faint creaking sound, a protest from the ancient metal as it was shifted, a mournful sigh from the depths of time. The crystalline rock formation chipped and fractured slightly, shedding tiny fragments into the surrounding darkness, but the smaller vessel remained remarkably intact. The energy signature, however, flickered.

"Captain, the energy signature just pulsed!" Lena exclaimed, her voice urgent, her eyes wide with alarm. "It's a single, distinct pulse, and then… nothing. It's gone completely silent. The readings have flatlined."

Elias felt a jolt of apprehension, a cold dread seeping into his gut. "Gone silent? Lena, are you sure?"

"Yes, Captain. All residual energy readings have ceased. It's as if the power source has been completely deactivated."

Kaelen felt a subtle shift in the resistance he was applying, a sudden release of tension. "The dislodgement is complete, Captain. The smaller vessel is free from the rock."

The manipulator arm carefully lifted the craft, bringing it closer to the *Abyssus* for a more thorough examination. It was a beautiful, enigmatic object, its purpose and origin lost to time, a silent testament to a vanished era. The sudden cessation of its energy signature was deeply unsettling. Had their actions deactivated it, or had it simply reached the end of its operational cycle, a final, fading breath?

"Bring it into the auxiliary bay, Kaelen," Elias
commanded, his voice tight with a mixture of concern
and anticipation. "We'll conduct a full internal scan
once it's secured. The loss of the energy signature is…
concerning. We need to understand what happened,
why it chose to go silent now."

As the smaller derelict was carefully maneuvered into
the *Abyssus*'s spacious auxiliary bay, Elias couldn't shake
the feeling that their salvage operation had taken an
unexpected and profound turn. They had come seeking
valuable components, mere fragments of lost
technology, but they had stumbled upon relics that
hinted at a far grander, more complex history, a history
shrouded in mystery and the crushing silence of the
abyss. The abyss held its secrets tightly, and each
discovery seemed to raise more questions than it
answered, each answered query opening a new door to
further unknowns. The weight of the ocean was not
just in its crushing pressure, but in the immensity of its
forgotten past, a past they were only just beginning to
unearth, a past that whispered of wonders and terrors
yet to be revealed. The primary mission, salvage and
survival, was now inextricably interwoven with the
daunting, almost existential task of deciphering the
echoes of civilizations long gone, a challenge that Elias
knew would push him and his crew to their absolute
limits, and perhaps beyond.

## 2: The Anomaly

The sheer scale of the debris field was a visceral shock. Wreckage stretched as far as the *Abyssus*'s powerful beams could penetrate, a testament to some cataclysmic event or a brutal interstellar conflict lost to the mists of time. Elias felt the familiar, heavy cloak of responsibility settle upon him. He was the captain, entrusted with the safety of his crew and the integrity of his vessel as they navigated this treacherous expanse. Each movement of the *Abyssus* was a deliberate calculation, its powerful thrusters battling the immense, unyielding pressure of the deep. The silence was profound, broken only by the rhythmic hum of the life support systems and the faint crackle of the comms. It was a silence that spoke volumes, a constant, unnerving reminder of their own fragility in the face of the abyss's indifferent might.

"Kaelen, proximity alert on the starboard side," Elias's voice, a low rumble that seemed to absorb some of the surrounding silence, broke the stillness. "That debris cluster is denser than anticipated. Run a structural integrity scan on the largest section."

First Mate Kaelen, a man whose vigilance was as ingrained as the metallic tang of recycled air, acknowledged the command with a curt nod. His fingers danced across his console, initiating the scan with a practiced, almost instinctual efficiency. "Understood, Captain. Analysis commencing. Preliminary readings indicate a significant metallic composition, likely a heavy alloy. Hull plating appears to be several meters thick. No immediate structural weaknesses detected from this range, but the density suggests it could be a considerable hazard if we misjudge our approach."

On the auxiliary engineering station, Dr. Lena Petrova was already immersed in the intricate dance of spectrographic analysis. Her eyes, magnified by the sophisticated holographic displays, scanned for any anomalous energy signatures or residual radiation that might point to salvageable components. Her usual scientific detachment was tinged with an unmistakable spark of excitement. "Captain, I'm picking up residual energy traces from that cluster Kaelen is scanning," she reported, her voice carrying a note of scientific wonder. "Low-level, but persistent. It's not a common power source; the frequency is highly unusual. It suggests advanced, possibly experimental, propulsion or power generation systems."

Elias absorbed the fragmented data, his mind working to assemble a coherent picture. Their mission was not simply about stripping down derelicts for raw materials.

Each wreck was a potential Pandora's Box of lost knowledge, a silent witness to technological leaps that could redefine their own present. The risk, however, was equally immense. These ancient wrecks were often unstable, their internal structures compromised by the relentless, crushing pressure of the abyss. A misplaced maneuver, a sudden shift in the seabed, or a cascading failure within the wreckage itself could spell immediate disaster.

"Lena, can you isolate the source of those energy traces?" Elias inquired, leaning forward in his command chair. "Are they emanating from the main hull, or a specific component?"

"It's difficult to say with certainty without a closer look, Captain," Lena replied, her brow furrowed in intense concentration. "The readings are diffused, but there's a distinct locus within the largest wreckage. It's behaving almost like a dormant power core, emitting faint pulses. It could be incredibly valuable if we can access it safely."

Kaelen's scan completed, and he turned his attention to the primary display, his gaze sharp and focused. "The large section is largely intact, Captain. Minimal hull breach detected. However, there are multiple smaller debris fragments attached to it, some of which appear to be structural supports. They could pose a snagging hazard for the manipulator arms."

"Understood," Elias responded, his mind already calculating the delicate maneuvers required. The *Abyssus* was equipped with state-of-the-art manipulator arms, articulated and powerful, designed to grasp, cut, and retrieve objects from the seabed. Yet, even these sophisticated tools had their limitations, especially when dealing with the unpredictable nature of deep-sea wreckage. The silence of the abyss was a tangible presence, a stark reminder of the sheer, unforgiving power of the environment they were operating within. It was a realm where a single miscalculation could echo with devastating finality.

"We'll approach the primary hull section," Elias declared, his voice firm and decisive. "Kaelen, plot a course that allows us to maintain a safe distance from the smaller, potentially unstable fragments. Lena, I want you to monitor the energy readings continuously. If they spike or show any sign of instability, you alert me immediately. We prioritize caution. We don't want to wake up anything that's best left undisturbed."

The *Abyssus* shifted its orientation, its powerful thrusters nudging it through the water with smooth, controlled movements. The floodlights intensified, illuminating the colossal structure before them with stark clarity. It was a testament to an unknown civilization's lost journey, a leviathan of metal whose surface was encrusted with millennia of marine growth, yet whose form was unmistakably artificial. Twisted girders, shattered observation decks, and gaping holes where once vital systems had resided spoke of a violent, decisive end.

"The energy signature is stabilizing, Captain," Lena reported, her voice hushed with a reverence that Elias found himself sharing. "It's almost as if it's reacting to our presence, but not aggressively. More like… a dormant sentry acknowledging a visitor."

Kaelen initiated the deployment sequence for the primary manipulator arm. With a low whirring of hydraulics, the articulated limb extended from the *Abyssus*'s ventral bay, its multi-jointed structure moving with an uncanny fluidity. The claw at its end, a formidable piece of engineering capable of crushing solid rock, was poised to grasp.

"Targeting a section of hull that appears to be a primary access panel," Kaelen announced, his eyes glued to the manipulator's camera feed. "It's fused shut, but the underlying framework seems intact. We might be able to pry it open and access the interior. The residual energy readings are strongest from within that area."

Elias watched the delicate ballet of mechanical precision unfold. This was the crux of their mission: to overcome the obstacles of time, pressure, and decay to salvage whatever remained of value. The potential reward was immense, but the risks were ever-present. The abyss was a place of profound silence, but it was also a place where the slightest miscalculation could echo with devastating finality.

"Proceed with caution, Kaelen," Elias reiterated, his gaze never leaving the unfolding operation. "Gentle pressure. We don't want to compromise the integrity of the hull we're trying to breach."

The manipulator arm made contact with the fused panel. For a tense, drawn-out moment, nothing happened. Then, with a low groan of protesting metal, the panel began to shift. Small fragments of rust and ancient sealant flaked away, revealing the dark void beyond. Lena's breath hitched audibly.

"Captain, the energy readings just spiked!" she exclaimed, her voice sharp with alarm. "It's a significant increase, and the frequency has shifted dramatically. It's… it's not random. It's a structured pulse, almost like a… a signal."

Elias's senses sharpened, his body tensing. "What kind of signal, Lena?"

"I can't categorize it yet, Captain. It's unlike any known communication protocol. It's complex, layered. And it's originating from directly behind that panel."

Kaelen, though focused on maintaining precise control of the manipulator, registered Lena's urgent report. "Captain, I'm experiencing an unexpected resistance from the debris cluster. It's not mechanical; it feels like a localized field disturbance. The manipulator's torque readings are fluctuating erratically."

The situation was rapidly escalating. The dormant wreck, disturbed by their intrusion, was showing signs of unexpected activity. Elias had to make a decision, and he had to make it quickly. The potent lure of valuable salvage warred with the primal, ingrained instinct for self-preservation.

"Pull back the manipulator arm, Kaelen," Elias ordered, his voice tight with suppressed urgency. "Slowly. Let's reassess the situation."

The arm retracted, its powerful claw releasing its grip. As it withdrew, the energy readings Lena had detected began to subside, and the localized field disturbance Kaelen had reported diminished. The abyss seemed to exhale, its silent menace returning to a low, simmering state.

"The signal has faded back to its previous dormant state," Lena reported, a hint of disappointment in her voice, but also a renewed surge of scientific intrigue. "The disturbance in the field has dissipated."

"The resistance is gone," Kaelen confirmed, his hand hovering over the manipulator controls, ready for immediate action if necessary. "It seems our attempt to breach the hull triggered a localized defensive response, or perhaps a warning."

Elias leaned back in his command chair, his mind racing. They were not merely salvaging inert derelicts; they were delving into the unknown, into a realm where ancient technology might still possess active protocols, perhaps even autonomous functions. The initial objective of salvaging valuable components had just become infinitely more complicated, and infinitely more dangerous. The sheer audacity of their mission, to plunder the silent, forgotten voyages of predecessors, was a testament to humanity's insatiable drive for progress. But the abyss, in its silent, crushing embrace, served as a constant, sobering reminder that progress often came at a steep price, and that some secrets were perhaps best left buried in the crushing, eternal darkness.

The discovery of the active energy signature within the derelict vessel marked a significant, unforeseen turning point in their salvage operation. What had begun as a meticulous, albeit inherently dangerous, process of disassembling and retrieving valuable components had now transformed into a venture into the realm of active, potentially responsive, ancient technology. Elias knew they could not simply abandon this potential source of knowledge, not without a more thorough understanding, but he also understood the heightened risks involved. Their mission was salvage and survival, a dual imperative that now seemed more precarious than ever before. The weight of the ocean wasn't just in its physical pressure; it was in the immense burden of responsibility he carried.

"Lena, I need you to analyze those energy pulses again," Elias commanded, his gaze fixed on the spectral data that still shimmered on her console, a ghostly record of the anomaly. "Focus on the pattern, the frequency modulations. Try to identify any recurring sequences or variations that might indicate a more complex form of communication or internal process." He paused, considering their next move, his mind sifting through the immediate tactical options. "Kaelen, I want a full diagnostic on the manipulator arm, paying particular attention to any stress fractures or anomalies that might have occurred during the attempted breach.

We need to ensure our tools are in optimal condition before we proceed with any further engagement."

Kaelen nodded, his movements economical and precise, already initiating the diagnostic sequence. It was a practiced dance of technological assessment, a testament to his professionalism. "Diagnostics running, Captain. The arm performed within expected parameters, despite the resistance. However, I concur with Lena's assessment regarding the anomaly. The localized field distortion was… unusual. It felt less like a physical obstruction and more like a conscious deterrent, a deliberate pushback."

Lena's fingers flew across her console with a speed that bordered on frenetic, her brow furrowed in intense concentration. The complex waveforms danced before her, each flicker and oscillation a potential clue, a fragment of an ancient puzzle. "The pulses are indeed structured, Captain," she reported after a few minutes of intense analysis, her voice barely above a whisper, filled with a palpable sense of discovery. "There are repeating motifs, almost like a rudimentary alphabet. And the energy fluctuations suggest a sort of internal monitoring system. It's as if the vessel, or at least this part of it, is still… aware."

The word "aware" hung in the sterile air of the command module, heavy with implication. Elias felt a primal shiver trace its way down his spine, a sensation that warred with his ingrained scientific curiosity. He was a man driven by the ghosts of his past, a seeker of answers in the vast, silent unknowns of the universe. The idea that they had stumbled upon something that was not merely inert wreckage, but a potentially sentient remnant of a lost civilization, was both exhilarating and deeply unsettling. It was a prospect that promised immense reward, but also invoked a profound sense of dread.

"Aware or not," Elias stated, his voice firm, cutting through the rising tide of speculation, "our objective remains the same: salvage. However, we must adapt our approach. We can't afford to trigger any further defensive responses. The structural integrity of this wreck is still a major concern, and we don't know the full extent of its capabilities. We need to be surgical, not forceful."

"Perhaps a different approach is warranted," Kaelen interjected, his gaze sweeping across the external camera feeds, his mind already working on alternative strategies. "Instead of forcing access, we could try to locate a less compromised entry point. The debris field is extensive. There might be other sections of this vessel that are more accessible, or perhaps other, smaller derelicts nearby that are easier to salvage without risking a confrontation with this… active system."

Elias considered Kaelen's suggestion. It was the pragmatic, responsible course of action, the one that prioritized the safety of the crew and the vessel. Their primary mission was salvage and survival, and engaging with an unknown, potentially hostile ancient technology was not part of the original operational plan. However, the lure of what lay within that sealed compartment, the secrets it undoubtedly held, gnawed at him. It was a siren song, a whisper of answers to questions he hadn't even fully articulated yet, a promise of knowledge that could fundamentally alter their understanding of their place in the cosmos.

"We will continue our survey of the immediate area, Kaelen," Elias decided, his gaze still fixed on the enigmatic wreck. "Maintain a safe standoff distance from the primary wreck. Deploy the scout drones to map out the surrounding debris field. I want to know what else is out here, and whether any of it presents a more manageable salvage opportunity. Information is our best weapon right now."

The scout drones, small, agile submersibles equipped with advanced sensor arrays and delicate manipulator tools, were dispatched from the *Abyssus*. They fanned out into the oppressive darkness, their powerful lights cutting through the abyssal gloom, illuminating further stretches of the silent, metallic graveyard. Elias, Kaelen, and Lena watched their progress on the tactical display, a mosaic of data points and visual feeds painting a picture of the surrounding desolation.

The drones systematically explored the vast expanse. They encountered smaller wrecks, most of them heavily damaged and offering little in the way of valuable salvage. One drone reported a dense cluster of metallic fragments that appeared to be an engine core, its intricate components fused beyond recognition by the ravages of time and pressure. Another found the shattered remnants of what looked like a cargo bay, its contents long since dispersed or decomposed, leaving only the hollow shell of its former purpose.

Then, one of the drones, designated 'Scout-3', reported a significant find. "Captain, Scout-3 is transmitting visual data," Kaelen announced, his voice tinged with a rare note of genuine excitement, a stark contrast to the usual grim tenor of their reports. "It's a smaller vessel, partially embedded in a rock formation. It appears to be remarkably intact. And… it's emitting a unique energy signature. Similar to the primary wreck, but far weaker, more stable."

Elias leaned closer to the main display, where Scout-3's camera feed was now prominently featured. The drone's lights illuminated a sleek, metallic craft, its lines far more refined and elegant than the hulking structure they had encountered earlier. It was lodged at an angle, its forward section pressed against a jagged, crystalline outcropping, but its main hull seemed largely undamaged. The energy signature Lena had detected was indeed faint, a soft, intermittent pulse that was barely registering on their sensors.

"Lena, analyze that signature," Elias commanded, his mind already racing with possibilities. "Compare it to the readings from the primary wreck. Is it related?"

"Affirmative, Captain," Lena replied, her eyes wide with fascination, her usual scientific objectivity momentarily eclipsed by the sheer wonder of the discovery. "It's the same fundamental waveform, but attenuated. It's like a distant echo, or a modulated signal. It's definitely connected to the larger wreck, perhaps a smaller utility craft or a probe that detached from the main vessel."

"Kaelen, plot a course for Scout-3's position," Elias ordered, the decision made. "We'll assess this smaller derelict first. If it's intact and the energy signature is stable, it might represent a more manageable salvage opportunity, a less risky first step."

The *Abyssus* adjusted its trajectory, its powerful thrusters guiding it through the water towards the location of the smaller vessel. As they drew closer, the details of the craft became clearer. Its metallic hull gleamed faintly in the drone's lights, and intricate patterns, almost like etched circuitry, were visible on its surface. It was a work of art as much as a machine, and its apparent intactness was a beacon of hope in the desolation of the abyss.

"The structure seems solid, Captain," Kaelen reported as they maneuvered the *Abyssus* into a position that allowed for a closer, more detailed inspection. "No significant hull breaches visible. The rock formation it's lodged in is stable, not showing signs of imminent collapse."

"Lena, any change in the energy readings?" Elias inquired, his gaze fixed on the delicate fluctuations on her console.

"No, Captain. The signature remains consistent. It's a low-level emission, very stable. It doesn't seem to be reacting to our presence." Lena's voice was filled with a mixture of relief and mild disappointment; the thrill of a potential confrontation was absent, replaced by the steady, reliable hum of scientific observation.

"Alright," Elias said, his decision made. "Kaelen, prepare the manipulator arm for a gentle extraction. We'll try to carefully dislodge it from the rock formation. Priority is to retrieve the craft intact, if possible. Lena, continue to monitor the energy signature and any subtle environmental changes. We proceed with the same caution we would any other salvage operation, but with an added layer of awareness due to the nature of the energy emissions."

The manipulator arm extended once more, its claw opening wide, a metallic maw ready to embrace its prize. Kaelen guided it with expert precision, aiming to grip the smaller vessel at its strongest points. The process was slow and deliberate, a delicate maneuver designed to exert just enough force to free the craft without causing damage. The vast, silent pressure of the ocean seemed to press in on them, a constant, palpable reminder of the immense forces they were contending with. It was a dance on the edge of disaster, a testament to the skill of the crew and the resilience of their technology.

"Grip established," Kaelen announced, his voice steady. "Applying minimal torque."

There was a faint creaking sound, a protest from the ancient metal as it was shifted, a mournful sigh from the depths of time. The crystalline rock formation chipped and fractured slightly, shedding tiny fragments into the surrounding darkness, but the smaller vessel remained remarkably intact. The energy signature, however, flickered.

"Captain, the energy signature just pulsed!" Lena exclaimed, her voice urgent, her eyes wide with alarm. "It's a single, distinct pulse, and then… nothing. It's gone completely silent. The readings have flatlined."

Elias felt a jolt of apprehension, a cold dread seeping into his gut. "Gone silent? Lena, are you sure?"

"Yes, Captain. All residual energy readings have ceased. It's as if the power source has been completely deactivated."

Kaelen felt a subtle shift in the resistance he was applying, a sudden release of tension. "The dislodgement is complete, Captain. The smaller vessel is free from the rock."

The manipulator arm carefully lifted the craft, bringing it closer to the *Abyssus* for a more thorough examination. It was a beautiful, enigmatic object, its purpose and origin lost to time, a silent testament to a vanished era. The sudden cessation of its energy signature was deeply unsettling. Had their actions deactivated it, or had it simply reached the end of its operational cycle, a final, fading breath?

"Bring it into the auxiliary bay, Kaelen," Elias commanded, his voice tight with a mixture of concern and anticipation. "We'll conduct a full internal scan once it's secured. The loss of the energy signature is… concerning. We need to understand what happened, why it chose to go silent now."

As the smaller derelict was carefully maneuvered into the *Abyssus*'s spacious auxiliary bay, Elias couldn't shake the feeling that their salvage operation had taken an unexpected and profound turn. They had come seeking valuable components, mere fragments of lost technology, but they had stumbled upon relics that hinted at a far grander, more complex history, a history shrouded in mystery and the crushing silence of the abyss. The abyss held its secrets tightly, and each discovery seemed to raise more questions than it answered, each answered query opening a new door to further unknowns. The weight of the ocean was not just in its crushing pressure, but in the immensity of its forgotten past, a past they were only just beginning to unearth, a past that whispered of wonders and terrors yet to be revealed. The primary mission, salvage and survival, was now inextricably interwoven with the daunting, almost existential task of deciphering the echoes of civilizations long gone, a challenge that Elias knew would push him and his crew to their absolute limits, and perhaps beyond.

The *Abyssus* continued its methodical exploration of the abyssal plain, its powerful floodlights piercing the eternal night. The sheer volume of wreckage was staggering, a testament to a history far more complex and violent than any recorded by humanity. Each derelict was a tomb, its secrets locked away by the crushing pressures and the passage of eons. Elias felt a growing sense of awe mixed with trepidation. They were charting the silent graveyard of forgotten voyages, navigating a realm where the remnants of advanced civilizations lay scattered like the bones of cosmic leviathans.

"Captain, Scout-7 is reporting unusual geological formations ahead," Kaelen's voice crackled through the comms, cutting through the low hum of the ship's systems. "Dense metallic deposits, unlike typical seabed mineral concentrations. And… it's detecting faint, intermittent energy signatures emanating from within them."

Elias's attention snapped to the tactical display. Scout-7's feed showed a starkly different vista from the scattered debris they had been encountering. Here, the seabed was studded with colossal, crystalline structures that seemed to pulse with a faint, internal luminescence. They were intricate, geometric formations, unlike anything natural, yet they appeared to be fused with the underlying rock. And within these formations, Lena's sensors were indeed registering weak, but persistent, energy readings.

"Analyze those signatures, Lena," Elias commanded, leaning forward. "Compare them to the patterns from the larger wreck and the smaller craft we recovered."

Lena's fingers danced across her console, her brow furrowed in concentration. The holographic displays flickered to life, depicting complex waveforms and spectral analysis. "The signatures are… derivative, Captain," she reported, her voice tinged with a profound sense of scientific intrigue. "They share characteristics with the primary wreck's emissions, but they are significantly weaker, almost like a resonance effect. The crystalline structures themselves seem to be acting as conduits, or perhaps amplifiers, for a very diffuse energy field."

"Conduits for what, Lena?" Elias pressed.

"That's the question, Captain. The energy is highly organized, not chaotic. It suggests a deliberate energy distribution system, or perhaps a form of residual biological or artificial energy imprint. It's unlike anything we've encountered before. The complexity suggests a technology far beyond our current understanding."

Elias felt a prickle of excitement race through him. This was not just salvage; this was discovery of a magnitude he had only dreamt of. These crystalline structures, so alien yet so seemingly integrated with the very fabric of the seabed, hinted at a civilization that possessed an intimate understanding of energy and matter that dwarfed their own.

"Kaelen, bring the *Abyssus* closer," Elias ordered. "Maintain a safe distance, but we need a direct sensor sweep of those formations. I want to know what's generating these signatures."

The submersible moved with deliberate grace, its powerful lights illuminating the colossal, shimmering structures. They were breathtaking in their alien beauty, vast pillars of light and mineral that seemed to hum with an unseen energy. As they approached, the readings intensified.

"Captain, the energy is… it's interacting with the *Abyssus*'s hull," Lena announced, her voice suddenly tight with alarm. "Not physically, but through a subtle resonant frequency. It's causing minor fluctuations in our internal systems. Nothing critical, but it's definitely responsive."

Elias's eyes narrowed. Responsive. That word carried a universe of implications in this desolate, silent realm. "What kind of response, Lena? Is it hostile?"

"I… I can't say for certain, Captain. It's not a direct energy transfer, more like a sympathetic vibration. It's like the formations are… acknowledging our presence. There's a subtle increase in the complexity of the energy patterns, a modulation that wasn't present before."

Kaelen brought the *Abyssus* to a near halt, its thrusters pulsing gently to maintain their position. "Captain, I'm detecting a very faint, localized anomaly directly beneath the primary crystalline formation. It appears to be a distinct object, partially buried, but its metallic composition is registering as highly anomalous. The energy readings are significantly stronger in that specific vicinity."

Elias's gaze was drawn to the sonar readings. A single, distinct object, distinct from the surrounding mineral formations, lay hidden beneath the shimmering crystals.

Its shape was obscured by the density of the deposits, but its metallic signature was unmistakable. And it was the source of the intensified energy readings.

"Deploy Scout-5," Elias commanded. "Direct it to the anomaly beneath the primary formation. I want detailed scans, high-resolution imaging, and spectrographic analysis of that object. If it's what I suspect, it could be the key to understanding these formations, and perhaps even the larger derelict we encountered earlier."

The small scout drone detached from the *Abyssus*, its powerful lights cutting through the dim luminescence of the crystalline structures. It descended slowly, its advanced sensors probing the depths, its delicate manipulator arm poised for action. The tension in the command module was palpable, a shared anticipation of the unknown.

Scout-5 reached the anomaly. Its lights illuminated a metallic object, roughly spherical, about the size of a man's head, its surface intricately etched with patterns that seemed to shift and flow like liquid. It was embedded in a matrix of the luminous crystal, and the energy readings emanating from it were significantly higher than anywhere else.

"Captain, Scout-5 is transmitting visual data," Kaelen reported, his voice hushed with wonder. "The object…

it's unlike anything I've ever seen. The design is so… precise. And the material… it's not any known alloy."

Lena's voice was a breathless whisper. "The energy readings are extraordinary, Captain. This object is generating a contained field of immense power. The patterns are extraordinarily complex, a symphony of frequencies. It's… it's a technological marvel. And it's remarkably intact."

Elias felt a profound sense of discovery wash over him. This wasn't just a piece of salvaged technology; it was a fragment of something far greater, something that spoke of a civilization that had mastered energies and materials on a scale he could only begin to comprehend. The sheer alienness of its design, yet its subtle familiarity in its sheer sophistication, created an immediate sense of profound mystery that captivated the crew, and especially Elias. It was a mystery that beckwed, promising answers that could reshape their understanding of the universe.

"Can we retrieve it, Kaelen?" Elias asked, his voice barely above a whisper.

"The crystalline matrix is integrated with the object, Captain. It's not a simple excavation. The crystals seem to be organically connected to it, channeling its energy."

"Lena, what do you think? Can we extract it without destabilizing the formation, or the object itself?"

Lena studied the readings intently. "The energy field is highly contained, Captain. The crystals appear to be a symbiotic structure, designed to manage and perhaps even amplify the object's output. If we can carefully sever the crystalline connections without disturbing the object itself, we might be able to retrieve it. However, any sudden shock or disruption could trigger a catastrophic energy release."

Elias considered the implications. A catastrophic energy release in this confined space, surrounded by these luminous, resonant structures, could have unforeseen and devastating consequences. Yet, the lure of this object, this encapsulated enigma, was too strong to ignore. It represented a leap in technological understanding that could benefit humanity immeasurably.

"We will attempt a controlled extraction," Elias declared, his decision made. The weight of the ocean pressed down, but the allure of discovery felt even greater. "Kaelen, use the Scout drone's manipulator arm. Proceed with extreme caution. We need to cut the crystalline connections with surgical precision. Lena, monitor the energy readings constantly. If there's any sign of instability, any deviation from the current pattern, you alert me immediately, and we abort."

Kaelen guided Scout-5 with agonizing slowness. The drone's manipulator arm, equipped with a focused sonic cutter, emitted a high-frequency beam, carefully severing the luminous crystalline strands that bound the metallic sphere to the seabed. Each cut was a tense, drawn-out moment, the drone's sensors feeding back a constant stream of data about the energy field's stability.

The first few cuts went smoothly, the crystalline connections parting with a faint, almost musical hum. The energy readings remained stable, the object pulsing with its steady, contained power. But as Kaelen worked on a particularly thick nexus of crystal, the readings began to fluctuate.

"Captain, the energy signature is becoming erratic!" Lena shouted, her voice sharp with alarm. "The frequency is shifting, and the amplitude is increasing. It's not stable!"

"Pull back, Kaelen!" Elias ordered, his heart leaping into his throat.

But before Kaelen could retract the manipulator, the crystalline formation around the object pulsed with an blinding intensity. The entire seabed seemed to shimmer, and the *Abyssus* shuddered as a wave of energy washed over it. Alarms blared throughout the command module.

"Hull integrity is holding, Captain," Kaelen reported, his voice strained, "but we're experiencing significant electromagnetic interference. All external sensors are being jammed!"

"Lena, what happened?" Elias demanded, his eyes fixed on the main display, which was now a chaotic mess of static and distorted readouts.

"The object… it's not just a power source, Captain," Lena stammered, her voice filled with a mixture of terror and awe. "It's… it's a consciousness. The energy surge was a directed response. It's communicating, but not with words… with raw, unfiltered thought. It's… overwhelming."

Elias felt a primal wave of primal fear mixed with an exhilarating sense of the sublime. They had not found a piece of technology; they had found something alive, something sentient, something that had slept in the depths of the ocean for untold ages. The abyss, he realized with chilling clarity, was not merely a graveyard of the past, but a cradle of forgotten life, a repository of intelligence that predated humanity itself. The glimmer in the deep was not merely a signal; it was a mind. And it had just awakened. The auxiliary bay of the *Abyssus* hummed with a low, resonant thrum as the recovered crystalline sphere was carefully secured within its containment field. Elias watched from the observation deck, his gaze fixed on the object that had so recently sent ripples of shock and awe through his crew. Lena, her face illuminated by the soft glow of the sphere's residual energy, was meticulously running a battery of diagnostics. The initial data was baffling – an alloy composition that defied classification, an energy signature that was both impossibly complex and unnervingly stable. It was a testament to a lost era of technological advancement, a whisper from a civilization that had clearly possessed a mastery of physics far beyond humanity's current grasp.

"Any progress, Lena?" Elias's voice was low, betraying none of the gnawing unease that had settled in his gut since the sphere had pulsed with that overwhelming consciousness.

Lena didn't look up from her console, her fingers flying across the holographic interface. "The material is… remarkable, Captain. It's a complex lattice of metallic elements, bonded at an atomic level with crystalline structures. It's incredibly dense, yet possesses an uncanny resilience. The energy containment is unlike anything I've ever analyzed. It's as if the sphere itself is a perfectly regulated fusion core, operating at parameters we can only theorize about." She paused, her brow furrowed. "And the markings, Captain…. they're not merely decorative. They're integral to the energy regulation. It's a form of integrated circuitry, woven into the very fabric of the sphere."

Elias nodded, absorbing her words. Integrated circuitry. A living, thinking component. The implications were staggering. This wasn't just a piece of ancient technology; it was a sophisticated artifact, possibly a form of data storage, or even a rudimentary artificial intelligence, preserved for millennia. His mind, however, kept drifting back to the events that had led them here, to the whispers of a conscious entity in the deep. The encounter had been terrifying, exhilarating, and deeply unsettling. He had felt the alien mind brush against his own, a torrent of incomprehensible data and sensation, before it had withdrawn, leaving him shaken to his core.

The scout drones had continued their meticulous mapping of the surrounding area, revealing more of these colossal crystalline formations, each pulsating with a faint, residual energy. They were interconnected, forming a vast, submerged network that seemed to hum with a low, persistent power. The sheer scale of it was mind-boggling, suggesting an entire civilization had once harnessed these energies, perhaps even built their cities around these luminous conduits.

"The energy patterns are showing subtle variations, Captain," Lena reported, her voice suddenly hushed. "The initial surge has subsided, but it's not completely dormant. It's maintaining a baseline energy state, and the patterns are… coalescing. They're becoming more defined, more structured. Almost as if it's… processing our interaction."

Elias leaned closer, his eyes glued to the evolving waveforms on Lena's display. She was right. The chaotic surge had given way to a more ordered series of pulses, like a complex language being slowly deciphered. It was a tantalizing prospect, a potential key to understanding not only the sphere but the entire network of crystalline structures, and by extension, the lost civilization that had created them.

"Can you isolate any recurring sequences?" Elias asked, his mind already racing through the possibilities of translation, of communication.

"I'm trying, Captain," Lena replied, her focus absolute. "The complexity is immense. It's not a simple binary code. It's multi-layered, with harmonic frequencies interacting in ways that suggest a profound understanding of wave mechanics. But there are… there are definite repeating motifs. Small sequences of energy modulations that appear with a degree of regularity."

It was then that a chill, unrelated to the ambient temperature of the ship, began to creep up Elias's spine. He had seen those patterns before, or something agonizingly similar. The memory was a phantom limb, a phantom ache that had haunted him for years, a scar tissue of the soul.

"Lena," he said, his voice tight, a nascent dread coiling in his gut. "Can you overlay the spectral analysis of the alloy composition? I want to see the elemental breakdown."

Lena, sensing the shift in his tone, complied without question. The data flickered onto the main display, a stark grid of atomic weights and elemental percentages. Elias stared at it, his breath catching in his throat. His heart began to pound a frantic, irregular rhythm against his ribs. The alloy. The precise bonding of metals, the unique crystalline matrix… it was all there, laid out in stark, undeniable detail.

This was not just a sophisticated piece of alien technology. It was chillingly, terrifyingly familiar. The very same alloy composition. The same intricate structural integrity. The same subtle, yet distinctive, energy signature. It was the same component that had been at the heart of the catastrophic failure of the *Stardust*, the space shuttle that had disintegrated on its ascent, taking his wife and daughter with it into the unforgiving void. The memory, suppressed for so long, surged back with brutal force, a tidal wave of grief and disbelief. The identical markings, etched with impossible precision onto the sphere's surface, were the same intricate patterns that had adorned the failed component, patterns that had been dismissed by the inquiry board as inexplicable manufacturing anomalies.

"Captain?" Lena's voice, laced with concern, finally broke through the suffocating silence that had descended upon the bridge. She saw the color drain from his face, the sudden rigidity in his posture.

Elias's gaze remained fixed on the display, his eyes wide with a dawning, horrifying realization. The investigation into the *Stardust* disaster had concluded that the failure was due to a critical flaw in a newly developed inertial dampener component. A component that had been manufactured with an experimental alloy, one that had been lauded for its supposed unprecedented strength and resilience. But it had failed, spectacularly and fatally. And now, here, in the crushing darkness of the abyss, they had found its twin, or rather, its progenitor.

"It's… it's identical," Elias whispered, his voice hoarse, barely audible. "The composition. The structural design. The energy signature." He looked at Lena, his eyes burning with a desperate, frantic intensity. "It's the same component. The one that failed on the *Stardust*."

Lena's expression shifted from concern to shock, then to a profound, disbelieving horror. She quickly cross-referenced the data, her fingers moving with a renewed, almost frantic urgency. The spectral analysis of the recovered sphere was a mirror image of the scant fragments recovered from the *Stardust* crash site. The initial reports had been classified, of course, but Lena, with her access to the *Abyssus*'s extensive historical archives, had delved into the declassified documents years ago, driven by a morbid curiosity about the technological hubris that had led to such a devastating loss. She recognized the signature, the precise composition, immediately.

"Captain," she breathed, her voice trembling. "You're right. The elemental breakdown… the crystalline structure… it's a perfect match. The reports stated the alloy was a proprietary Terran development, synthesized specifically for the inertial dampeners."

"Proprietary Terran development?" Elias scoffed, a bitter laugh escaping his lips. "That's a lie. This… this is something else entirely. Something far older." He ran a trembling hand through his hair, the enormity of the revelation crashing down upon him. His family hadn't died because of a Terran manufacturing defect. They had died because of… this. Whatever 'this' was.

The weight of the coincidence was crushing, a cruel, cosmic joke. He had been driven, all these years, by the need to understand what had happened, to find answers that the official inquiry had so conveniently swept under the rug. He had believed that the abyss, with its forgotten secrets and lost civilizations, might hold some clue. He had never imagined that the answer would be so directly, so agonizingly connected to his own personal tragedy.

"How is this possible?" Lena murmured, staring at the data with a mixture of awe and terror. "If this is the original… where did it come from? And how did it end up on Earth, integrated into our technology?"

The question hung in the air, unanswered, a dark prophecy echoing in the silent confines of the *Abyssus*. Elias's mind reeled. The thought that this alien technology, this ancient artifact, had been somehow reverse-engineered, or perhaps even directly acquired, and then implemented into their most critical spacecraft systems, was almost too much to bear. Had someone, somewhere, known the truth? Had they deliberately covered it up, knowing that the component was inherently flawed, or worse, knowing its true, unfathomable nature?

The implications were chilling. If this component was capable of such immense power, and possessed such an intricate, perhaps even sentient, operational core, then its failure would have been catastrophic, regardless of any perceived manufacturing flaw. The *Stardust* incident wasn't just an accident; it was a consequence. A consequence of tampering with forces, with technologies, that humanity did not understand.

"It's not just a match, Lena," Elias said, his voice hardening with a new resolve, a grim determination that had been forged in the fires of personal loss. "It's a blueprint. This sphere… this is the source. And they – whoever 'they' are – they replicated it. Or, at the very least, they tried to integrate its principles into our own technology."

He thought of his wife, her radiant smile, the way she had held their daughter's hand as they walked up the gantry to the shuttle. He saw their faces, etched forever in his memory, a constant reminder of what had been stolen from him. And now, he knew why. It wasn't a random act of fate. It was a consequence of human ambition, of a desperate reach for technologies that were not yet theirs to comprehend.

"The energy signature," Elias continued, his mind working feverishly, piecing together the fragments of this horrifying new reality. "You said it was processing our interaction. Could it be… learning from us?"

Lena's eyes widened. "It's possible, Captain. If it's truly sentient, and if its purpose is indeed to understand and integrate information, then it would naturally analyze any new input. Our encounter, our attempts to study it… it would be part of its data acquisition."

"And what if it's not just learning?" Elias mused, a dark thought taking root. "What if its original purpose was to integrate with other systems, to spread? What if its failure on the *Stardust* was not a malfunction, but a deliberate act of self-preservation, or even… a warning?"

The abyss, which had initially seemed like a repository of forgotten history, now felt like a Pandora's Box that had been pried open, unleashing horrors far more profound than mere physical destruction. The discovery of the sphere was not just a scientific breakthrough; it was a profound revelation about humanity's place in the universe, and the potentially catastrophic consequences of its insatiable quest for advancement.

The weight of his discovery settled upon Elias, heavy and suffocating. The hope that had flickered within him, the desperate hope that perhaps this anomaly could offer some explanation, some solace, was now replaced by a cold, hard certainty. The truth was far more terrible than he could have imagined. His family had not been lost to a random accident. They had been collateral damage in a cosmic experiment, a tragic consequence of humanity's hubris in attempting to harness powers that were not its own.

He looked at the sphere, its internal luminescence now seeming less like a beacon of discovery and more like the baleful glow of an ancient, awakened entity. The markings on its surface no longer appeared as mere circuitry; they seemed to writhe, to shift, like cryptic messages from a forgotten tongue. The abyss had yielded its secret, but the secret was not one of solace. It was a secret of profound, existential dread. And Elias knew, with a chilling certainty, that his mission had just become infinitely more complex, and infinitely more dangerous. He was no longer just a salvage captain; he was a witness to a truth that could shatter the very foundations of human civilization. The past was not just prologue; it was a present danger, resurrected from the crushing depths.

The hum of the auxiliary bay was a steady counterpoint to the frantic thrumming in Lena's own chest. Elias's words, the horrifying revelation of the *Stardust* connection, had hung in the air, a shroud of disbelief and dawning terror. But as she returned her attention to the sphere, a different emotion, one that had been a constant companion throughout her career, began to assert itself: an insatiable, almost primal scientific curiosity. The grief and shock that Elias was clearly experiencing were a raw, agonizing wound. Her own connection to the tragedy was more indirect, a professional acquaintance with the lost crew, a familiarity with the wreckage analysis reports that had always felt incomplete, unsatisfying. Now, however, those same reports seemed to glow with a terrifying new significance, their classified details suddenly illuminated by the impossible reality before her.

Lena's fingers danced across the holographic interface, the cool, responsive light of the projected displays a familiar comfort. Elias's immediate, visceral reaction was understandable, a natural consequence of such a devastating personal connection. But for Lena, the sheer impossibility of the sphere's existence, its defiant assertion of a reality far beyond humanity's current comprehension, was a siren call to the deepest parts of her scientific soul. The material analysis was still a jumble of indecipherable elements, of atomic bonds that seemed to laugh in the face of known physics. The energy readings were a symphony of harmonics and resonant frequencies that defied any conventional understanding of power generation or containment. It was a puzzle of infinite complexity, a testament to a civilization that had seemingly mastered the very fabric of the universe.

She brought up the spectral analysis data again, comparing it not just to the *Stardust* fragments, but to the theoretical models of exotic matter that her team had been developing for years, models that had been relegated to the realm of pure speculation, of science fiction. The sphere's composition wasn't just similar; it was an uncannily precise match. The proprietary Terran alloy, the supposed miracle of human engineering, was nothing more than a crude, imperfect imitation. The original, the progenitor, pulsed with a life, an inherent order, that the Terran version could only crudely mimic. The implications were staggering. This wasn't just a discovery; it was a paradigm shift. Humanity, in its relentless pursuit of progress, had stumbled upon, and then fundamentally misunderstood, the work of a species that had walked these stars, or perhaps even *created* them, eons before.

"Captain," Lena said, her voice steady, though a tremor of excitement ran beneath the surface. "The energy patterns you mentioned, the ones that are coalescing. I've managed to isolate some of the repeating motifs. They're not simple data packets, or even complex algorithms as we understand them. It's more akin to… a biological process. The energy fluctuations are responding to our probes, to the ambient energy of the ship, and even, I suspect, to our proximity."

She highlighted a complex waveform on the main display, a swirling, intricate dance of light and shadow that represented the sphere's internal energy flow. "See this harmonic convergence here? It occurs precisely when our passive sensors detect a change in the sphere's internal temperature. And this fluctuation, right here? It coincides with the activation of the containment field. It's not just reacting; it's *processing*."

Her mind raced, weaving together threads of data, of speculation, of pure, unadulterated wonder. This wasn't just a physical object; it was a nexus of information, an active participant in its own analysis. The sheer sophistication of its design, the elegance of its integrated systems, spoke of a biological imperative, a drive to learn, to adapt, to *be*.

"The markings," Lena continued, her gaze fixed on the surface of the sphere, now appearing on her display as a high-resolution topographical map. "They're not just decorative, as we first thought. They're conduits. Energy pathways. And within them, there are structures that resemble neural pathways. Microscopic, impossibly intricate structures. It's… it's like looking at the blueprint for a brain, Captain. A brain made of alloy and light."

Elias was silent for a moment, the weight of his own tragedy momentarily overshadowed by the sheer, mind-bending implications of Lena's findings. He could feel the gears in her analytical mind turning, processing this new deluge of information with a speed and intensity that was almost frightening. Her scientific detachment was a powerful force, a shield against the overwhelming emotional burden of their discovery.

"A brain?" Elias finally echoed, his voice tinged with a disbelief that mirrored her own initial reaction.

"Metaphorically speaking, of course," Lena clarified, her fingers already tracing new analytical pathways. "But the structural similarities are undeniable. The way energy flows through these 'conduits,' the way they seem to form interconnected nodes… it's as if the sphere itself is alive, or at least possesses a form of consciousness that we can only begin to conceptualize. And the fact that it's 'learning' from us, as you theorized, suggests an active intelligence, not just a passive artifact."

She paused, taking a deep, steadying breath. The danger was evident, a palpable presence in the room. But the potential for knowledge, for understanding the fundamental nature of the universe, was an even more potent force. This artifact was a key, a gateway to secrets that had been hidden for millennia, secrets that could redefine humanity's place in the cosmos. It was a chance to move beyond the petty squabbles and limitations of their own civilization, to glimpse a reality that transcended their wildest dreams.

"The *Stardust* incident," Lena mused, her voice dropping to a near whisper as she connected the final dots. "If this is the source, then the component on the shuttle… it wasn't just a piece of technology. It was a fragment of this… this intelligence. And its failure wasn't a malfunction; it was a disconnect. A severed limb, perhaps, reacting to an alien environment."

The idea sent a shiver down her spine, a stark contrast to the warmth that bloomed in her chest at the prospect of unraveling such a profound mystery. She imagined that fragment, on the *Stardust*, desperately trying to communicate, to warn, before succumbing to the alien stresses of a human-made vessel. It was a tragic image, a testament to the profound gulf that separated their understanding from that of the sphere's creators.

"We need to understand its primary function, Captain," Lena stated, her focus sharpening, her analytical drive pushing aside any lingering personal apprehension. "If it's a data storage device, what kind of data? If it's a communication hub, who is it communicating with?

And if it's truly sentient, what is its purpose? Its origin?"

She began to run simulations, projecting hypothetical scenarios based on the limited data they had. Could this sphere be a navigational beacon? A terraforming tool? A living repository of a civilization's entire history and knowledge? The possibilities were as boundless as the darkness of the abyss itself.

"The energy signature is not static," she reported, her eyes never leaving the shifting patterns on her display. "It's subtly increasing in amplitude. It's like it's building up a charge, preparing for something. I can't identify the trigger, but the trajectory is clear. It's evolving."

Elias watched her, a mixture of awe and unease settling upon him. Lena, in her element, was a force of nature. Her mind, unburdened by the same personal demons that haunted him, was free to soar, to explore the uncharted territories of this new discovery. He knew, with a certainty that chilled him to the bone, that his grief, while a powerful motivator, was also a potential impediment. He had to trust Lena's scientific instincts, her ability to navigate this treacherous path of revelation without succumbing to the overwhelming implications.

"Can you detect any external energy sources affecting it?" Elias asked, his gaze sweeping across the cavernous bay, as if the answer might be hidden in the shadows.

"Nothing that we can identify," Lena replied, her brow furrowed in concentration. "The energy surge seems to be generated internally, or at least, it's originating from the crystalline network that surrounds us. It's as if these formations are all interconnected, a vast, planetary-scale power grid, and this sphere is a node within it, perhaps even the central processor."

The enormity of that statement was almost too much to grasp. A planetary-scale power grid. An entire civilization built on harnessing these energies. It painted a picture of a society so advanced, so intrinsically linked to the forces they manipulated, that humanity's own technological achievements seemed like the clumsy fumblings of children playing with fire.

"The markings are changing, Captain," Lena announced, her voice a hushed exclamation. "The patterns on the surface… they're reconfiguring. It's not a random shift; it's a deliberate restructuring of the circuitry. It's… it's reacting to our presence in a more profound way than I anticipated. It's like it's *trying* to communicate, to show us something."

Elias moved closer to the observation deck, his eyes

fixed on the sphere. He could see it now, the subtle, almost imperceptible shimmer of the markings on its surface, a liquid dance of light that seemed to flow beneath its metallic skin. It was both beautiful and terrifying, a silent testament to the vast, unknown universe that lay just beyond their grasp.

"What do you mean, 'trying to communicate'?" Elias asked, his voice barely above a whisper.

"I'm not sure," Lena admitted, her fingers flying across the console, attempting to capture and analyze the shifting patterns. "But the energy flow through those conduits is intensifying, and the sequences are becoming more complex, more… deliberate. It's as if it's adapting its internal architecture to better interface with us, or perhaps, to convey a specific message."

She zoomed in on a particular section of the sphere's surface, where the markings seemed to coalesce into a more defined, almost pictographic form. It was unlike anything Lena had ever seen, a language of pure energy and form, a visual representation of concepts that defied verbal description.

"This sequence," she murmured, pointing to a cluster of pulsating nodes and interwoven lines. "It's repeating, but with subtle variations. And the overall pattern… it reminds me of… star charts. But not any star charts that I recognize. It's… alien."

Elias felt a prickle of unease. Star charts. A connection to the vastness of space. Had this civilization traveled across the cosmos? Or were they indigenous to this sector, their knowledge extending far beyond the confines of their own star system? The implications were staggering, and frankly, terrifying.

"Can you decipher any of it?" Elias pressed, his curiosity warring with a growing sense of apprehension.

Lena shook her head, her face etched with frustration and exhilaration. "Not yet. The complexity is overwhelming. It's like trying to understand a symphony by looking at a single musical note. But there's a logic to it, a profound underlying structure that suggests a sophisticated form of communication. If we can just… if we can just understand the foundational principles, the grammar of this energetic language, we might be able to establish a dialogue."

She began to upload the captured data to the ship's main analytical core, initiating a series of complex algorithmic deconstructions. The sheer processing power required was immense, pushing the *Abyssus*'s systems to their limits. But Lena was driven by a force stronger than any computational constraint: the pure, unadulterated pursuit of knowledge. This was the moment every scientist dreamed of, the opportunity to touch the face of the unknown, to unlock secrets that could reshape the destiny of humankind.

"The material composition," Lena continued, her voice laced with a growing excitement that was almost tangible. "It's not just strong; it's self-repairing. There are micro-structural anomalies that are actively mending themselves, re-bonding at the atomic level. It's a form of controlled, directed nanite activity, woven into the very fabric of the alloy. This isn't just advanced engineering; it's… it's almost biological in its resilience."

She looked at Elias, her eyes shining with an uncharacteristic intensity. "Captain, this sphere… it's not just an artifact. It's a testament to a civilization that achieved a level of technological integration with the natural world that we can only dream of. They didn't just build machines; they seemed to have *become* the machines, or rather, they had found a way to imbue their creations with life, with consciousness, with an inherent understanding of the universe."

The auxiliary bay, once a sterile, functional space, now felt imbued with a palpable sense of wonder, of profound mystery. The low hum of the ship's systems seemed to fade into the background, replaced by the silent, eloquent language of the sphere. Lena felt as though she were standing on the precipice of a new era, a dawn of understanding that would forever alter humanity's perception of itself and its place in the vast, unknowable cosmos. The tragedy of the *Stardust*, while a somber backdrop, had, in a strange and terrible way, led her to this very moment, to this profound, awe-inspiring revelation. The abyss had yielded its secret, and that secret was not one of despair, but of a breathtaking, terrifying, and ultimately, hopeful glimpse into the true potential of existence.

The air in the auxiliary bay, moments before thick with the electric thrill of groundbreaking discovery, now carried a palpable tension. Kaelen's arrival had been announced by the soft chime of the deck communicator, a familiar sound that usually signaled a routine update. Today, however, it marked a shift in the atmosphere, a grounding force entering the charged space. He stood at the entrance, his broad frame silhouetted against the corridor's sterile light, his gaze sweeping over Lena, Elias, and the pulsating anomaly on the observation deck. His presence was a physical manifestation of the caution that had always been his hallmark, a steadfast anchor in the often-turbulent seas of space exploration.

"Captain," Kaelen's voice, a deep baritone, cut through the hushed reverence. His eyes, sharp and assessing, were fixed not on the sphere itself, but on the readings flickering across Lena's consoles. There was no trace of the scientific wonder that had captivated Elias and Lena; instead, his brow was furrowed with a familiar concern, a seasoned wariness honed by years of navigating perilous frontiers. "I've reviewed the preliminary analysis and the sensor logs from the sector transit. This… object. It's unlike anything catalogued. The energy signatures alone are unprecedented." He gestured towards the sphere, his hand cutting a decisive arc through the air. "And the proximity to the *Stardust* wreckage… that's not a coincidence, is it?"

Lena turned from her console, a faint frown creasing her forehead. "The material composition is eerily similar to the recovered fragments from the *Stardust*, Kaelen. Down to the atomic level. It's as if this sphere is the… progenitor, and the *Stardust* component was a crude imitation, a shard of something far greater."

Kaelen's jaw tightened almost imperceptibly. He knew the *Stardust*. He'd been part of the retrieval effort, had witnessed firsthand the scattered, agonizing testament to its destruction. Elias's personal anguish, the raw wound that had been reopened by Lena's revelations, was something Kaelen understood on a fundamental level, even if his own grief was more muted, more buried beneath layers of ingrained discipline. "A shard of something greater," he echoed, the words heavy with unspoken implications. He stepped further into the bay, his boots making soft thuds on the metal deck.

"Which begs the question, Captain: what *is* the 'greater' thing? And more importantly, what does it want with us?"

Elias, who had been lost in a silent contemplation of the sphere's mesmerizing glow, finally looked at Kaelen. "It's not about what it *wants*, Kaelen. It's about what it *is*. Lena's analysis suggests… sentience. An intelligence that predates our own species by millennia. This isn't just an artifact; it's a discovery that could rewrite everything we understand about the universe."

Kaelen turned his steady gaze upon Elias, his expression unreadable. "And what if that rewrite comes at our expense, Captain? Our mission is to survey the Kepler-186 system, to assess its habitability for potential colonization. We're not equipped for… xenological contact with an entity that can apparently manipulate spacetime and defy our fundamental understanding of physics. This sphere, its origin, its purpose – it's a massive deviation from our objective."

Lena, ever the pragmatist when it came to scientific endeavor, nodded in agreement with Kaelen's concern, though her eyes still sparkled with the thrill of the unknown. "He's right, Elias. The energy requirements for studying this anomaly are significant. We're already drawing heavily on auxiliary power, and we've only just begun to scratch the surface. Diverting further resources could compromise our ability to complete the primary mission. And frankly, we don't know the full extent of this thing's capabilities. What if its energy output, or its inherent properties, are harmful to our systems, or even to us?"

"Harmful?" Elias's voice held a trace of impatience. "Lena, the *Stardust* was destroyed by a component directly linked to this sphere. If this is its origin, then 'harmful' is an understatement. It's potentially catastrophic. We need to understand it, to know what we're dealing with before it decides to 'interact' with us in a more… definitive way."

Kaelen stepped closer, his voice dropping in volume but not in intensity. "And how do we propose to do that, Captain? We have no frame of reference. We're trying to dissect a cosmic enigma with tools designed for cataloging nebulae and charting asteroid fields. Lena's brilliance is undeniable, but even she admitted the energy patterns are… alien. We could be inadvertently provoking it. Or worse, we could be inviting something into our ship, something we have no hope of containing or controlling." He looked at Lena. "You said it's 'learning' from us. What happens when it learns enough to see us as a threat? Or a resource?"

The weight of Kaelen's words settled upon them, a stark reminder of the razor's edge they walked. His caution was not born of fear, but of a deep-seated understanding of the unforgiving nature of the void. He saw the universe not as a playground for scientific inquiry, but as a vast, indifferent expanse where survival was paramount. Elias, caught between the overwhelming implications of the sphere and the pragmatic realities of command, felt the familiar tug-of-war between his scientific curiosity and his duty to his crew. Lena, while undeniably captivated by the anomaly, also recognized the inherent dangers Kaelen articulated.

"The risk is undeniable, Kaelen," Elias conceded, his gaze returning to the sphere. "But the potential reward… This could be the answer to questions humanity has been asking for centuries. Are we alone? What is the true nature of consciousness? Is there a fundamental intelligence underlying the fabric of reality? This sphere might hold those answers."

"And at what cost, Captain?" Kaelen pressed, his voice steady and unwavering. "The *Stardust* was a state-of-the-art vessel, carrying some of our brightest minds. It was lost with all hands because of a component that, it now appears, was a fragment of this very object. We don't know if this is a dormant power source, a beacon, or something far more sinister. We're playing with forces we don't comprehend, and the consequences could be far more devastating than the loss of a single shuttle."

He moved towards Lena's console, his gaze falling upon the complex energy readings. "These fluctuations you're tracking, Lena… they're not just reacting to our probes; they're amplifying them. It's like it's feeding on our attempts to understand it. That's not a sign of passive curiosity; that's aggressive engagement."

Lena, her fingers still flying across the holographic displays, nodded grimly. "Kaelen's right, Elias. The energy signature is not just increasing; it's becoming more structured, more… patterned. It's as if it's trying to communicate through our own diagnostic tools, using our energy output as a medium." She highlighted a particularly intricate waveform. "This spike, for example, directly correlates with the last deep-scan probe we sent. It's not just absorbing the energy; it's *analyzing* and *responding* to the data embedded within it."

"Responding how?" Kaelen's question was sharp, demanding.

"That's what we don't know," Lena admitted. "The response is currently encoded in an energetic language we can't decipher. It's a series of complex harmonic resonances and frequency modulations. It's beautiful, in a way, but it's also profoundly alien. It suggests a level of sophistication in communication that makes our own linguistic structures seem rudimentary."

"Rudimentary or not, it's what we have," Kaelen stated, his gaze locking with Elias's. "Captain, I understand the allure of this discovery. I truly do. But our primary directive is to ensure the safety of this crew and the success of our mission. We have a responsibility to the Federation to conduct our survey. This anomaly, as fascinating as it is, represents an unacceptable risk. We should log its position, transmit the preliminary data, and continue our course. We can petition for a dedicated research vessel, a team better equipped to handle something of this magnitude. But we cannot afford to be derailed by it."

Elias remained silent, weighing Kaelen's pragmatism against the undeniable pull of the sphere. He felt the immense responsibility of command weighing on him, the need to make the right decision not just for himself, but for every soul aboard the *Abyssus*. The echoes of the *Stardust* disaster, the faces of lost colleagues, the sheer terror of that inexplicable destruction, warred with the tantalizing possibility of unlocking the universe's deepest secrets.

"A research vessel?" Elias finally said, his voice thoughtful. "And what if, by the time that vessel arrives, this anomaly has moved on? Or worse, what if it's already integrated itself into the very fabric of this system, making it impossible to study without triggering who knows what kind of event? We're here, Kaelen. We have the opportunity. To simply log it and leave… it feels like a betrayal of the very spirit of exploration that brought us out here in the first place."

"Exploration does not mean recklessness, Captain," Kaelen countered, his tone firm but respectful. "And sometimes, the greatest act of courage is knowing when to retreat, when to seek help, and when to admit that we are outmatched. This… entity," he gestured to the sphere, his expression a mixture of awe and apprehension, "is something far beyond our current capabilities. To engage with it directly, without a comprehensive understanding of its nature, is not exploration; it's a gamble with stakes that are too high to comprehend."

Lena chimed in, her scientific curiosity momentarily tempered by Kaelen's pragmatic assessment. "He has a point, Elias. The energy surge we're detecting is still within manageable parameters for the *Abyssus*, but it's steadily increasing. If this continues, we could face critical power drain or even structural integrity issues. We're running simulations, but the variables are so vast, so… unknowable. It's like trying to map a hurricane from within its eye."

"But what if it's not a threat, Lena?" Elias countered, a flicker of hope in his eyes. "What if it's a gift? A message from a benevolent, ancient civilization? The *Stardust* fragment, whatever its purpose, was described as incredibly stable, even after the catastrophic event. That suggests a resilience, a fundamental robustness that isn't inherently destructive."

"Or it suggests an adaptability that allows it to survive even catastrophic destruction, Captain," Kaelen interjected, his voice laced with a grim pragmatism. "That's not a comforting thought; it's a terrifying one. We are not its equals. We are not even its peers. We are ants observing a god, and we have no idea if that god is benevolent or simply indifferent to our existence." He paused, allowing the weight of his words to settle. "Think about the *Stardust* crew, Elias. They were in a similar position, staring at the impossible. And look where it got them."

The mention of the *Stardust* crew, the unspoken memory of their fate, hung heavy in the air. Elias flinched, the pain of that loss a constant ache. He knew Kaelen was right. The scientific imperative warred with the instinct for self-preservation, the responsibility to the living clashing with the allure of the ultimate discovery. But the sphere pulsed before them, a silent, enigmatic testament to forces beyond their current comprehension, and the questions it posed were too profound to ignore.

"We can't just leave, Kaelen," Elias said, his voice quiet but resolute. "Not yet. We'll proceed with extreme caution. Lena, can you isolate the sphere's energy field and create a buffer zone? Something that will shield us from any unforeseen surges without completely cutting off our sensor access?"

Lena nodded, her fingers already moving across the console. "I can try, Captain. It will require rerouting primary power from non-essential systems, but it might provide a degree of insulation. I'll also attempt to establish a limited, low-power diagnostic ping. If it reacts aggressively, we'll know to pull back immediately."

Kaelen watched Lena work, his expression still troubled but now tinged with a grudging respect for her determination. He knew that confronting the unknown was part of their calling, but he also knew that blind ambition could be the most dangerous anomaly of all. "Just remember, Captain," he said, his voice low, "caution has kept us alive in this void for a long time. Let's not discard it now, not when we're standing on the precipice of something that could either elevate humanity to a new understanding, or extinguish us as surely as a supernova snuffs out a star." He turned to leave, his presence a lingering reminder of the ever-present dangers of their voyage, leaving Elias and Lena to grapple with the profound, terrifying allure of the anomaly.

The hum of the anomaly, a resonant thrum that had permeated the auxiliary bay since its arrival, now seemed to Elias to carry a new cadence. It was no longer just an object of study, a scientific puzzle to be painstakingly dissected. It had become a crucible, testing the very foundations of his existence. The relentless grind of salvaging derelicts, the cold, calculated pursuit of scrap metal and intact systems, the days bled into weeks, weeks into months, all under the crushing weight of grief and obligation – those were the shadows from which the anomaly's light now began to draw him. The *Stardust*. The name itself was a shard of ice in his soul, a constant reminder of loss, of failure, of the vast, indifferent emptiness that had swallowed his crewmates whole. He had scoured the wreckage for years, driven by a desperate, gnawing need to find meaning, to salvage some tangible piece of what had been lost, to claw back some semblance of control from the chaos that had claimed them. But it had been a futile endeavor, a Sisyphean task of sifting through the ashes of tragedy.

Now, this sphere. It pulsed with an intelligence that dwarfed his own, its energetic signatures weaving a tapestry of cosmic data that Lena, with all her brilliance, could only begin to interpret. The material composition, mirroring the fragments recovered from the *Stardust*, was no mere coincidence. It was a genesis. The destroyed shuttle, a crude, broken echo of this perfect, potent origin. The thought ignited a fire within him, a desperate, burning hope that had been long dormant. This wasn't about salvage anymore. It wasn't about duty or financial gain. It was about understanding. It was about redemption. The gnawing emptiness that had defined his life since the *Stardust* disaster began to recede, replaced by a singular, all-consuming ambition. He would understand this technology. He would learn its secrets. And perhaps, just perhaps, he could wield it. The dream of space, once a haunting specter that whispered of loss and regret, now shimmered with a new, radiant possibility. It wasn't a tomb anymore; it was a canvas. A chance to paint over the devastation with an audacious act of creation, a resurrection from the deep, a testament to the enduring power of life and discovery.

Kaelen's pragmatic counsel, usually a grounding force, now felt like a faint whisper against the roaring crescendo of Elias's newfound purpose. The risks were undeniable, the potential for disaster immense. He acknowledged the truth in Kaelen's words; they were indeed ants before a god. But what if this god was offering a gift? What if the *Stardust* disaster wasn't a prelude to destruction, but a necessary, albeit brutal, initiation? The fragments of the shuttle, stable even after its violent end, spoke of resilience, of an inherent robustness that transcended the destructive forces it had encountered. It wasn't just about surviving; it was about thriving, about adapting in ways that defied conventional understanding. This sphere represented not a threat, but an opportunity – an opportunity to break free from the cycle of loss and to forge a new destiny, not just for himself, but for humanity.

Lena, her face illuminated by the shifting patterns on her console, seemed to catch the nascent spark of his conviction. Her initial apprehension, born of scientific rigor and a healthy respect for the unknown, was slowly yielding to a shared sense of wonder, a dawning recognition of the monumental significance of their discovery. "The energy fluctuations are stabilizing, Captain," she reported, her voice tinged with a cautious excitement. "It's as if it's… listening. Or perhaps, adapting to our presence in a more controlled manner. I've managed to create a limited energy containment field, using a modified resonance dampener. It should mitigate any sudden surges, and it's allowing us to maintain continuous sensor access without drawing excessive power."

Elias nodded, a sense of urgency building within him. "Excellent work, Lena. Keep monitoring those patterns. I want to know if there's any correlation between its energetic output and our transmissions, our probes, even our own ship's life support systems. I need to understand its 'language,' its method of interaction." He turned to Kaelen, his gaze steady and resolute. "We won't be leaving, Kaelen. Not yet. We will proceed with the utmost caution, but we will proceed. This anomaly is too significant to ignore. It's a chance to redefine our understanding of the universe, to potentially unlock capabilities we've only dreamed of."

Kaelen's expression remained etched with concern, but the unyielding certainty in Elias's voice seemed to chip away at his resistance. He saw the fire in Elias's eyes, a fire that mirrored the desperate, burning curiosity that had driven explorers across the galaxy for centuries. He understood the temptation, the irresistible allure of the unknown. "I understand your conviction, Captain," Kaelen said, his voice laced with a grudging acceptance. "But the stakes are astronomically high. We are alone out here, with no immediate backup. If this entity decides to reveal its true nature, and that nature is hostile, we will be the first and only casualties. My priority remains the safety of this crew."

"And my priority, Kaelen, is to ensure that this crew, and indeed all of humanity, has a future worth living in," Elias countered, his voice firm. "This isn't just about survival anymore. It's about evolution. The universe is vast and complex, and we are but a small part of it. But what if we are meant to be more? What if this anomaly is a key, a stepping stone to a new understanding of our place in the cosmos? The *Stardust* was a tragedy, a devastating loss. But even in its destruction, it yielded a fragment of something extraordinary. That fragment led us here. And now, this sphere… it's offering us a chance to complete the equation, to turn that tragedy into a catalyst for something truly profound."

He moved closer to the observation window, his reflection mingling with the mesmerizing glow of the anomaly. The sphere seemed to shift, its internal luminescence pulsing with an intricate, almost rhythmic pattern. It was a dance of light and energy, a silent symphony that spoke of immense power and unfathomable intelligence. Elias felt a deep, resonant connection to it, a kinship that transcended the vast chasm of species and time. He saw not just an alien artifact, but a mirror reflecting the boundless potential of existence. The dream of exploration, once a painful echo of his lost past, had transformed into a vibrant, all-consuming vision of his future. The void, which had once been a symbol of despair, now beckoned with the promise of revelation. He would not be deterred by fear. He would not be silenced by caution. He would embrace this anomaly, unravel its mysteries, and in doing so, he would resurrect not just the memory of the *Stardust*, but the very soul of human endeavor. The path forward was daunting, fraught with peril, but for the first time since the *Stardust* vanished, Elias felt a sense of purpose, a burning clarity that illuminated the darkness. He was no longer a scavenger of lost dreams; he was the architect of a new one, built from the very fabric of the impossible. The anomaly was not an end; it was a beginning.

## 3: The Uncharted Cavern

The hum of the anomaly, a resonant thrum that had permeated the auxiliary bay since its arrival, now seemed to Elias to carry a new cadence. It was no longer just an object of study, a scientific puzzle to be painstakingly dissected. It had become a crucible, testing the very foundations of his existence. The relentless grind of salvaging derelicts, the cold, calculated pursuit of scrap metal and intact systems, the days bled into weeks, weeks into months, all under the crushing weight of grief and obligation – those were the shadows from which the anomaly's light now began to draw him. The *Stardust*. The name itself was a shard of ice in his soul, a constant reminder of loss, of failure, of the vast, indifferent emptiness that had swallowed his crewmates whole. He had scoured the wreckage for years, driven by a desperate, gnawing need to find meaning, to salvage some tangible piece of what had been lost, to claw back some semblance of control from the chaos that had claimed them. But it had been a futile endeavor, a Sisyphean task of sifting through the ashes of tragedy.

Now, this sphere. It pulsed with an intelligence that dwarfed his own, its energetic signatures weaving a tapestry of cosmic data that Lena, with all her brilliance, could only begin to interpret. The material composition, mirroring the fragments recovered from the *Stardust*, was no mere coincidence. It was a genesis. The destroyed shuttle, a crude, broken echo of this perfect, potent origin. The thought ignited a fire within him, a desperate, burning hope that had been long dormant. This wasn't about salvage anymore. It wasn't about duty or financial gain. It was about understanding. It was about redemption. The gnawing emptiness that had defined his life since the *Stardust* disaster began to recede, replaced by a singular, all-consuming ambition. He would understand this technology. He would learn its secrets. And perhaps, just perhaps, he could wield it. The dream of space, once a haunting specter that whispered of loss and regret, now shimmered with a new, radiant possibility. It wasn't a tomb anymore; it was a canvas. A chance to paint over the devastation with an audacious act of creation, a resurrection from the deep, a testament to the enduring power of life and discovery.

Kaelen's pragmatic counsel, usually a grounding force, now felt like a faint whisper against the roaring crescendo of Elias's newfound purpose. The risks were undeniable, the potential for disaster immense. He acknowledged the truth in Kaelen's words; they were indeed ants before a god. But what if this god was offering a gift? What if the *Stardust* disaster wasn't a prelude to destruction, but a necessary, albeit brutal, initiation? The fragments of the shuttle, stable even after its violent end, spoke of resilience, of an inherent robustness that transcended the destructive forces it had encountered. It wasn't just about surviving; it was about thriving, about adapting in ways that defied conventional understanding. This sphere represented not a threat, but an opportunity – an opportunity to break free from the cycle of loss and to forge a new destiny, not just for himself, but for humanity.

Lena, her face illuminated by the shifting patterns on her console, seemed to catch the nascent spark of his conviction. Her initial apprehension, born of scientific rigor and a healthy respect for the unknown, was slowly yielding to a shared sense of wonder, a dawning recognition of the monumental significance of their discovery. "The energy fluctuations are stabilizing, Captain," she reported, her voice tinged with a cautious excitement. "It's as if it's… listening. Or perhaps, adapting to our presence in a more controlled manner. I've managed to create a limited energy containment field, using a modified resonance dampener. It should mitigate any sudden surges, and it's allowing us to maintain continuous sensor access without drawing excessive power."

Elias nodded, a sense of urgency building within him. "Excellent work, Lena. Keep monitoring those patterns. I want to know if there's any correlation between its energetic output and our transmissions, our probes, even our own ship's life support systems. I need to understand its 'language,' its method of interaction." He turned to Kaelen, his gaze steady and resolute. "We won't be leaving, Kaelen. Not yet. We will proceed with the utmost caution, but we will proceed. This anomaly is too significant to ignore. It's a chance to redefine our understanding of the universe, to potentially unlock capabilities we've only dreamed of."

Kaelen's expression remained etched with concern, but the unyielding certainty in Elias's voice seemed to chip away at his resistance. He saw the fire in Elias's eyes, a fire that mirrored the desperate, burning curiosity that had driven explorers across the galaxy for centuries. He understood the temptation, the irresistible allure of the unknown. "I understand your conviction, Captain," Kaelen said, his voice laced with a grudging acceptance. "But the stakes are astronomically high. We are alone out here, with no immediate backup. If this entity decides to reveal its true nature, and that nature is hostile, we will be the first and only casualties. My priority remains the safety of this crew."

"And my priority, Kaelen, is to ensure that this crew, and indeed all of humanity, has a future worth living in," Elias countered, his voice firm. "This isn't just about survival anymore. It's about evolution. The universe is vast and complex, and we are but a small part of it. But what if we are meant to be more? What if this anomaly is a key, a stepping stone to a new understanding of our place in the cosmos? The *Stardust* was a tragedy, a devastating loss. But even in its destruction, it yielded a fragment of something extraordinary. That fragment led us here. And now, this sphere… it's offering us a chance to complete the equation, to turn that tragedy into a catalyst for something truly profound."

He moved closer to the observation window, his reflection mingling with the mesmerizing glow of the anomaly. The sphere seemed to shift, its internal luminescence pulsing with an intricate, almost rhythmic pattern. It was a dance of light and energy, a silent symphony that spoke of immense power and unfathomable intelligence. Elias felt a deep, resonant connection to it, a kinship that transcended the vast chasm of species and time. He saw not just an alien artifact, but a mirror reflecting the boundless potential of existence. The dream of exploration, once a painful echo of his lost past, had transformed into a vibrant, all-consuming vision of his future. The void, which had once been a symbol of despair, now beckoned with the promise of revelation. He would not be deterred by fear. He would not be silenced by caution. He would embrace this anomaly, unravel its mysteries, and in doing so, he would resurrect not just the memory of the *Stardust*, but the very soul of human endeavor. The path forward was daunting, fraught with peril, but for the first time since the *Stardust* vanished, Elias felt a sense of purpose, a burning clarity that illuminated the darkness. He was no longer a scavenger of lost dreams; he was the architect of a new one, built from the very fabric of the impossible. The anomaly was not an end; it was a beginning.

The faint energy signature, a spectral whisper against the overwhelming silence of the deep, had become Elias's lodestar. It emanated from the anomaly, a subtle yet insistent pull that promised answers, perhaps even redemption. It was this ethereal thread that now guided the *Abyssus*, his battered submersible, through the crushing embrace of the ocean's unknown depths. Lena's fingers danced across her console, translating the raw data streams into a comprehensible map of the abyss. "Captain," she reported, her voice calm, yet carrying the weight of their shared endeavor, "the signature is fluctuating, but its vector remains consistent. It's leading us deeper into the trench. I'm detecting increasing levels of trace exotic particles in the water column, consistent with the anomaly's initial energy readings."

Elias leaned closer, his gaze fixed on the holographic display. The world outside the reinforced viewport was a study in oppressive darkness, punctuated only by the submersible's powerful external lights, which carved futile tunnels through the inky blackness. They were venturing into territory uncharted, unmapped, a testament to the planet's hidden immensity. "Maintain course, Lena," he commanded, his voice steady, though a primal awareness of the forces arrayed against them thrummed beneath the surface of his words. "Keep the sensors focused. I want to know the precise moment that signature deviates, or if it intensifies. Kaelen, status report on structural integrity."

Kaelen's response came from his station at the rear of the cramped cockpit. "All systems nominal, Captain, but the pressure is increasing exponentially. We're pushing the *Abyssus* beyond its designed operational limits. The hull is groaning under the strain. We've already encountered several micro-fractures in the forward viewport plating, no cause for immediate alarm, but they're expanding at a rate that warrants concern." His tone was matter-of-fact, betraying none of the tension that Elias knew he must be feeling. Kaelen, ever the pragmatist, was the bulwark against Elias's sometimes-reckless ambition.

The *Abyssus* was a workhorse, a deep-sea salvage submersible built for endurance, not exploration of the truly unknown. Its hull, a composite of reinforced alloys and advanced polymers, was designed to withstand immense pressures, but the Mariana Trench, or whatever uncharted chasm they were currently navigating, was a different beast entirely. The environment here was not merely hostile; it was actively hostile, a symphony of crushing force and geological instability. The submersible's internal systems whined in protest as the external pressure mounted, each creak and groan a stark reminder of their precarious existence.

Lena's console pinged softly. "Captain, I'm picking up anomalous sonar returns. Complex geological formations, unlike anything I've cataloged in this region. They're… organic in their structure, almost crystalline, yet they're registering as solid mass. And they're intercepting some of the ambient energy from the signature. It's as if the trench itself is resonating with it."

Elias's mind raced. Organic structures, intercepting energy. This planet, this abyss, was revealing itself to be far more than just a repository of mineral wealth. It was alive, in a way they couldn't yet comprehend. The energy signature wasn't just a beacon; it was an interaction, a dialogue with the very fabric of this alien world. "Can you isolate the source of those sonar returns, Lena? Are they interfering with the primary signature?"

"Negative, Captain. The primary signature remains distinct, though I am seeing a subtle amplification when we pass near these formations. It's almost as if they're acting as conduits, focusing the energy. It's like… cosmic whispers in the abyss, Captain. Small, localized reverberations that hint at something much larger." Lena's voice was hushed with awe, her scientific curiosity battling with the raw, unnerving nature of their surroundings.

They were descending into a realm where light had never penetrated, where the sheer weight of water pressed down with unimaginable force. It was a world forged in darkness, sculpted by pressures that would instantly obliterate anything not specifically engineered to survive. The *Abyssus*, despite its robust construction, was a fragile bubble of life in an ocean of crushing oblivion. Elias felt a familiar tightening in his chest, a visceral response to the vastness that surrounded them. It was the same feeling he'd experienced on the bridge of the *Stardust* moments before the anomaly had ripped it apart, a sense of being infinitesimally small against an overwhelming cosmic power. But this time, the fear was tempered by a burgeoning sense of discovery, a desperate hope that this time, he would understand, not just succumb.

"What's the estimated depth, Lena?" Elias asked, his voice barely above a whisper.

"We've passed the Challenger Deep's recorded maximum, Captain. We are in uncharted territory, approximately 11,500 meters below the surface. The pressure readings are… extreme. The *Abyssus* is holding, but the margin for error is rapidly diminishing."

Each meter descended was a step further from the known universe, a deeper plunge into the heart of the unknown. The submersible's internal lighting cast long, distorted shadows that played tricks on the eyes, making the already alien landscape appear even more surreal. Lena continued to monitor the energy signature, her brow furrowed in concentration. The patterns were becoming more complex, more intricate. "Captain," she said, her voice suddenly sharp, "the signature is evolving. It's not just a passive emission anymore. It's… reacting. To the geological formations, to our presence, and… to the ambient energy of the planet itself."

Elias felt a surge of adrenaline. "Reacting how?"

"It's developing a more complex harmonic structure. It's like a ripple effect, Captain. The planet's own geothermal activity, the immense pressures, even the electromagnetic fields generated by the tectonic plates —

they're all interacting with the anomaly's energy. It's creating a feedback loop, amplifying and modifying the original signature. It's a cosmic symphony being played out in the deepest trenches of this world."

The implications were staggering. This wasn't just an alien artifact; it was a part of the planet's very essence, or at least, it was deeply intertwined with it. The anomaly wasn't a visitor; it was an intrinsic element of this alien biosphere. The fragments from the *Stardust* hadn't just been remnants of a destroyed ship; they were echoes of a profound cosmic connection. The tragedy that had defined Elias's life was now inextricably linked to this immense, subterranean mystery.

Kaelen's voice cut through the charged atmosphere. "Captain, I'm detecting a significant increase in localized seismic activity. Minor tremors, but they're concentrated around our current position. The hull is vibrating. We need to consider ascending. This environment is becoming increasingly unstable."

Elias's gaze remained fixed on the data. The seismic activity Lena was detecting seemed to correlate directly with fluctuations in the energy signature. It was as if the planet was stirring, awakened by their intrusion. "Lena, can you pinpoint the source of the tremors?"

"The readings are chaotic, Captain, but they seem to originate from directly below us. And the energy signature is pulsing in time with the seismic events. It's… beautiful, in a terrifying way. Like the heartbeat of the planet."

"A heartbeat that's about to have a cardiac arrest if we don't manage our situation," Kaelen interjected, his voice taut. "Captain, my advice is to disengage and ascend. We have gathered substantial data, and we can analyze it from a safe distance. Pushing further is an unacceptable risk."

Elias closed his eyes for a brief moment, the weight of Kaelen's words pressing down on him, heavier even than the ocean's crushing weight. Kaelen was right. Every instinct screamed at him to obey, to preserve the vessel and its crew. But the anomaly… it was so close to revealing its true nature. The fragmented whispers of understanding were coalescing into a chorus of profound revelation. He could feel it, a tangible presence in the dark waters, beckoning him forward.

"Lena," Elias said, his voice resonating with a conviction that brooked no argument, "how much further until we reach the focal point of the energy signature?"

Lena's fingers flew across her console, her eyes wide. "The signature is most concentrated… directly below us, Captain. Approximately fifty meters further down. It appears to be emanating from a massive subterranean cavity, a cavern of sorts, that the seismic activity seems to be originating from. The structure is incredibly complex, with energy conduits that dwarf anything we've seen so far."

Fifty meters. Fifty meters separated him from an answer, from understanding the cataclysm that had claimed his crew, from potentially finding a way to reclaim what had been lost. The *Stardust* disaster had been a void in his life, a black hole of unanswered questions. This anomaly, this signature, was the only light in that darkness.

"Kaelen," Elias said, his voice firm, "we're not turning back. We'll descend another fifty meters. Lena, maintain maximum sensor coverage. If anything spikes beyond acceptable parameters, you have authorization to initiate emergency ascent. But until then, we go forward."

Kaelen's sigh was barely audible, a sound of resigned concern. "As you command, Captain. But I've rerouted auxiliary power to reinforce the forward viewport. It's the only section I can bolster significantly. May it hold."



The *Abyssus* continued its agonizingly slow descent, the groans of its hull a constant reminder of the immense forces at play. The external lights, once powerful beams, now seemed feeble against the encroaching blackness. The water itself felt different, charged with an unseen energy that made the hairs on Elias's arms stand on end. Lena's readings were a torrent of data, each new discovery more astonishing than the last. The planet's internal structure was a marvel of intricate energy pathways, far more sophisticated than any known geological model.

"Captain, I'm detecting… an aperture," Lena breathed, her voice laced with wonder. "A massive opening in the seabed directly beneath us. It's perfectly circular, almost artificial in its precision. And the energy signature… it's emanating from within. The cavern you mentioned, it's enormous, Captain. The scale… it's astronomical."

Elias stared at the holographic representation, a vast, yawning maw opening in the planet's crust. It was a wound, or perhaps a gateway, radiating a power that felt both ancient and utterly alien. The energy signature pulsed from its depths, a beckoning light in the ultimate darkness. This was it. The source. The heart of the mystery.

"Prepare to enter the aperture, Lena," Elias commanded, his voice hoarse with anticipation. "Slow and steady. Kaelen, brace for extreme turbulence. This is it."

The *Abyssus* edged closer to the opening, its powerful lights cutting through the perpetual night. The sheer scale of the chasm was disorienting. It was a world within a world, a subterranean ocean hidden beneath the planet's surface. The energy signature intensified, painting the interior of the submersible with shifting patterns of light. It was a siren song, luring them into the unknown. As they crossed the threshold, the *Abyssus* was enveloped in a soft, pervasive glow, emanating from the very walls of the cavern. It was unlike any light Elias had ever seen, a luminescence that seemed to emanate from the rock itself, a manifestation of the planet's deep, buried power. The hum of the anomaly, which had been a constant presence, now swelled into a resonant chorus, a symphony of pure energy that vibrated through the *Abyssus*, through Elias himself. He was no longer just following an energy signature; he was immersed in it, a part of the cosmic whisper that had drawn him to this unfathomable place. The journey into the uncharted cavern had truly begun.

The submersible's descent into the cavern was a transition from the crushing pressure of the external ocean to an environment saturated with a primal, raw energy. The perfectly circular aperture Lena had detected was not merely an opening, but a portal. As the *Abyssus* glided through it, the familiar oppressive darkness of the abyss was replaced by an ethereal luminescence that seemed to emanate from the very bedrock of this subterranean world. Elias felt it before he saw it — a subtle, pervasive warmth that seeped into the hull, a stark contrast to the biting cold of the external depths. The water, too, had transformed. It shimmered with an otherworldly iridescence, alive with microscopic particles that danced and swirled in response to an unseen force.

Lena's voice, usually a steady anchor of scientific observation, was now tinged with an almost breathless awe. "Captain, the energy readings are off the charts. This entire cavern… it's a geothermal nexus. These are hydrothermal vents, but unlike any I've ever encountered. The temperature gradients are extreme, fluctuating wildly, and the mineral composition of the plumes… it's unlike anything in our databases."

Elias steered the *Abyssus* deeper into the cavern, guided by the now-overwhelming energy signature. The external lights of the submersible, once essential for navigation, were almost redundant here. The cavern was illuminated by the vents themselves. They rose from the seabed like colossal, phosphorescent chimneys, spewing forth plumes of superheated water and exotic minerals. These weren't the dark, brooding smokers of terrestrial hydrothermal fields; these were vibrant, almost bioluminescent structures, pulsing with an internal light that cast dancing shadows across the cavern walls. The water swirling around them was thick with suspended particles, shimmering like a million tiny diamonds caught in the submersible's beam. The spectacle was both terrifying and breathtakingly beautiful, a testament to the raw, untamed power that lay hidden beneath the planet's surface.

"They're radiating energy, Lena," Elias murmured, his gaze sweeping across the panorama. "Not just heat, but something… more. The anomaly's signature is amplified here, drawn to it. It's like a cosmic amplifier, focusing the energy."

Kaelen, his eyes fixed on the structural integrity readouts, chimed in, his voice tight with concern. "Captain, the hull temperature is rising steadily. We're approaching critical limits for our cooling systems. And the pressure variations around these vents are causing localized stresses. We've already logged a five percent increase in hull deformation since entering the main cavern."

Elias acknowledged Kaelen's warning but remained focused on the primary objective. The vents were not just geological phenomena; they were intrinsically linked to the anomaly. Their very existence seemed to be a response to, or an interaction with, the energy that Elias had been chasing. He maneuvered the *Abyssus* closer to one of the larger vents, a towering structure that pulsed with a deep, crimson light. The water around it churned violently, a vortex of superheated fluid and mineral deposits.

"Lena, what are these particles?" Elias asked, pointing towards the shimmering clouds around the vent. "They're interacting with the anomaly's energy signature."

"I'm running a full spectrographic analysis, Captain," Lena replied, her fingers flying across her console. "The data is… perplexing. The particles are not organic in the traditional sense, yet they exhibit a form of complex self-organization. They're aggregating, forming transient crystalline structures that seem to… resonate with the vent's energy output. And they're absorbing and re-emitting certain frequencies of the anomaly's signature. It's like they're a biological antenna system, designed to interact with this specific energy."

Elias felt a jolt of recognition. This was it. This was the missing piece of the puzzle, the reason the *Stardust* fragments had survived its catastrophic encounter. The advanced components, the very fabric of the ship's construction, would have been shielded by this unique geothermal environment. The extreme heat and pressure, far from being destructive, had acted as a protective cocoon, preserving the alien technology within. The derelict spacecraft hadn't simply crashed here; it had been drawn here, finding refuge within this nexus of primal energy.

"So, the vents created a kind of Faraday cage for the *Stardust*?" Elias mused aloud, the idea taking root in his mind. "The energy field generated by the vents, and these… self-organizing particles, they would have neutralized or at least significantly dampened the destructive forces that tore the ship apart."

"It's a plausible hypothesis, Captain," Lena confirmed, her voice gaining a new urgency. "The sheer intensity of the energy emanating from these vents, particularly at their core, could create a localized field distortion, effectively absorbing or deflecting the chaotic energy released by the anomaly during its initial activation. The derelict shuttle's advanced shielding capabilities, coupled with the natural properties of this environment, would have provided an unprecedented level of protection. It's a remarkable synergy."

The implications sent a shiver down Elias's spine. The *Stardust* disaster hadn't been an insurmountable loss; it had been an unintended consequence of a journey to a place of profound, protective power. The alien technology, in its volatile state, had sought out this specific environment, and the *Stardust*, in its pursuit of the anomaly, had inadvertently followed. The fragments recovered weren't just remnants of a tragedy; they were proof that this place held the key to understanding, and perhaps even controlling, the very forces that had destroyed his ship.

He steered the *Abyssus* towards the largest of the vents, its crimson glow pulsating with an intensity that seemed to draw the very light from the water. The mineral plumes spewing from its apex were denser, thicker, swirling with an almost intelligent pattern. The self-organizing particles were most concentrated here, forming transient, shimmering veils that seemed to ripple in response to the anomaly's presence.

"Lena, focus all sensors on that vent," Elias commanded, his voice low with anticipation. "I want a complete analysis of the particle aggregation, their energy absorption spectra, and any correlation with the anomaly's core signature. Kaelen, monitor hull temperature and structural stress. If we hit red, we pull back, no matter what."

"Understood, Captain," Kaelen replied, his voice grim. He knew Elias's resolve, and he also knew the unspoken stakes. They were on the precipice of a discovery that could rewrite humanity's understanding of physics, of energy, of life itself. To turn back now, without grasping the full truth, would be an even greater tragedy than the loss of the *Stardust*.


As the *Abyssus* drew closer, the hum of the anomaly intensified, resonating with the rhythmic pulsing of the vent. Elias felt it deep within his bones, a vibration that seemed to connect him to the very heart of this alien world. The particles coalesced, forming ephemeral, crystalline lattices that seemed to refract the vent's light into a dazzling display of spectral hues. These weren't just passive minerals; they were active participants in a cosmic dance, a biological-geological hybrid system designed for an unimaginable purpose.

"Captain," Lena reported, her voice hushed with wonder, "the particles are forming complex geometric patterns. They're not random. These structures are incredibly intricate, almost like an encoded language.

And they are directly influencing the energy output of the vent. It's not just absorbing the anomaly's signature; it's modulating it, refining it, shaping it."

Elias felt a profound sense of awe wash over him. This wasn't just a natural phenomenon; it was a sophisticated, self-regulating energy system, a living conduit for cosmic forces. The *Stardust* hadn't just found a place to hide; it had stumbled upon the engine room of a galactic phenomenon. The fragments of its hull, embedded within the bedrock surrounding these vents, were not merely wreckage; they were anchors, tethering a piece of humanity to this immense power source.

He maneuvered the *Abyssus* to hover just above the vent's apex, the submersible now bathed in the crimson, pulsing light. The heat was intense, a tangible force pressing against the hull. Kaelen's warnings became more urgent. "Hull temperature at 95% of maximum. Structural stress exceeding safety margins by twelve percent. Captain, we cannot maintain this position for much longer."

"Just a moment longer, Kaelen," Elias urged, his eyes scanning the complex patterns forming within the particle clouds. He could see it now, a subtle shift in the aggregation, a rearrangement of the crystalline structures that coincided with specific pulses of the anomaly's energy. It was a communication, a feedback loop that transcended mere physical interaction.

"The particles," Lena said, her voice trembling, "they're reacting to our presence. Not just the submersible, Captain, but… to us. To our bio-signatures. They're attempting to integrate our energy frequencies into their own pattern. It's a form of assimilation, or perhaps… a welcome."

Assimilation. The word hung in the air, both intriguing and unsettling. Was this alien biosphere attempting to absorb them, or to communicate on a fundamental level? Elias felt a strange sense of calm descend upon him, a feeling of being understood, of being recognized. The grief that had shadowed him for so long seemed to recede, replaced by a profound connection to this alien world.

"Lena, can you create a controlled energy pulse, mimicking the anomaly's core frequency?" Elias asked, a daring thought forming in his mind. "Just a small burst, to see how they react. Kaelen, prepare for an immediate evasive maneuver."

Lena nodded, her fingers already flying across her console. "Initiating controlled energy burst. Modulating frequency to match core anomaly signature. Standby for particle response."

A faint, almost imperceptible hum emanated from the *Abyssus* as Lena unleashed a carefully calibrated energy pulse. For a tense moment, nothing happened. Then, the particle clouds surrounding the vent erupted in a riot of color. The crimson glow intensified, and the crystalline structures began to vibrate, resonating with the submersible's emitted energy. The patterns shifted, becoming more complex, more ordered, as if responding to a direct query.

"They're mirroring the pulse, Captain," Lena reported, her voice filled with exhilaration. "They're incorporating it, amplifying it, and re-emitting it with subtle variations. It's a dialogue. We're actually communicating with this environment."

Elias felt a surge of triumph. This was the breakthrough he had been searching for. The *Stardust* had been a tragic prelude, a sacrifice that had led them to this place. The derelict shuttle's advanced components, shielded by these very vents, were not just salvaged technology; they were a bridge, a means of understanding this alien biosphere. The fragments recovered from the *Stardust* weren't just pieces of metal and circuitry; they were artifacts imbued with the knowledge of this place, a knowledge that could unlock the secrets of the anomaly and perhaps, even the universe.

He looked at Kaelen, who was monitoring the increasing stress on the hull. "We have what we came for, Kaelen," Elias said, his voice firm. "We have the key. Let's retreat before the *Abyssus* becomes another relic of this place."

Kaelen readily agreed, and Elias expertly guided the *Abyssus* away from the intense energy of the vent. As they moved back towards the cavern's entrance, the luminescence of the vents gradually dimmed, and the vibrant particle clouds dispersed. The crushing pressure of the external ocean returned, a familiar embrace after their immersion in the primal energies of the geothermal nexus.

The journey back to the surface was a stark reminder of the immense forces they had just navigated. The *Abyssus*, battered but intact, had survived its encounter with the planet's hidden heart. Elias, however, felt profoundly changed. The weight of his loss had not vanished, but it had been transmuted, transformed into a fierce, unwavering determination. He had found not just the remnants of the *Stardust*, but the promise of understanding, the possibility of redemption. The fragmented whispers of the anomaly had coalesced into a clear, resonant message, and he was now ready to decipher its full meaning. The labyrinth of vents had not been a dead end, but a gateway to a future he had once believed lost forever.

The relentless crimson glow of the primary vent, so all-consuming moments before, began to recede as Elias expertly maneuvered the *Abyssus* away from its pulsating core. The intense heat, a palpable force against the submersible's hull, gradually subsided, replaced by the more ambient, though still significantly warm, waters of the main cavern. The spectacular, swirling particle clouds, which had momentarily embraced the submersible in a dazzling display of coordinated energy, began to disperse, their intricate geometric patterns dissolving back into the luminescent haze. Kaelen's steady pronouncements of decreasing hull temperature and stabilizing structural stress acted as a grounding counterpoint to the profound, almost spiritual experience they had just undergone.

"Hull temperature normalizing, Captain," Kaelen reported, a note of relief in his voice. "Structural integrity readings are within acceptable parameters once more. We're clear of the primary vent's direct influence."

Lena, still immersed in the lingering echoes of the communication protocol, nodded, her eyes still scanning the data streaming across her console. "The particle aggregation is destabilizing. Their organized structure is breaking down as the energy nexus recedes. It's remarkable, though. The way they responded… it confirms the resonance hypothesis. They aren't just reacting to energy; they're engaging with it, processing it, and even mirroring it."

Elias, his gaze sweeping across the cavern, felt a profound shift within himself. The frantic pursuit, the gnawing grief, had been momentarily eclipsed by a connection so profound it felt almost primal. He had communed, in a rudimentary fashion, with a force beyond human comprehension. Yet, the fragmented pieces of the *Stardust* still lay scattered, waiting to be fully understood. "The fragments," he said, his voice carrying the weight of their shared ordeal, "they're still out there. We need to find them."

He guided the *Abyssus* with deliberate precision, its powerful external lights cutting through the ethereal luminescence of the cavern. Their descent had brought them to a specific area, a region Elias had marked based on the residual energy signatures detected during their initial survey of the main vent. The previous passage had revealed the astonishing nature of these vents, their role as geothermal amplifiers, and the bizarre, self-organizing particles that danced within their plumes. But the true prize, the scattered remnants of the *Stardust*, remained elusive, hidden within the vastness of this newly discovered subterranean world.

"According to the initial scans," Lena said, her voice carefully modulated, "there's a significant concentration of metallic alloys and trace elements consistent with the

*Stardust*'s hull composition approximately fifty meters below the primary vent's current position. The anomaly's energy signature is also significantly attenuated in that direction, suggesting a different geological formation."

"A different formation," Elias mused, his mind racing. "Or perhaps something… hidden."

He directed the *Abyssus* downwards, the submersible's powerful thrusters providing a gentle, controlled descent. The luminous water, thick with suspended particles that still shimmered with residual energy, gradually gave way to a denser, darker medium as they moved away from the immediate influence of the hydrothermal vents. The omnipresent warmth began to dissipate, and the familiar chill of the deep ocean began to assert itself once more, albeit muted, a ghost of the external pressure.

As they approached the targeted coordinates, the seabed below began to change. The rugged, mineral-encrusted rock of the cavern floor gave way to a smoother, more uniform surface. It was a subtle alteration, easily missed, but Elias's trained eyes caught it. There was an unnatural regularity to this section of the seabed, a suggestion of an underlying structure that was not of purely geological origin.

"Captain," Kaelen's voice cut through the quiet hum of the submersible, "I'm detecting a significant structural anomaly ahead. It's… immense. And it appears to be a void, an empty space carved into the ocean floor."

Elias brought the *Abyssus* to a halt, its external lights intensifying as they probed the darkness. Lena's sensors began to paint a more detailed picture. "The readings are… extraordinary. It's a cavern, Captain, but not like the one we just exited. This one… it's perfectly circular. Almost unnaturally so. And it's incredibly vast. The diameter is estimated to be at least two kilometers."

Two kilometers. The sheer scale of it was staggering, dwarfing the previous cavern. But it was the unnatural perfection of its shape that truly captured Elias's attention. The ocean floor was a chaotic canvas, sculpted by eons of seismic activity and volcanic processes. Such precise geometric forms were exceedingly rare, almost always indicative of artificial construction.

"And the energy signature," Lena continued, her voice tinged with disbelief, "it's still present. Faint, but undeniably there. It's emanating from within this void. It's… familiar."

Elias's gaze was fixed on the readings. Familiar. That word echoed the profound sense of connection he had felt with the anomaly. "Lena, can you get a visual on the opening? Kaelen, keep a close watch on our surroundings. I have a feeling we're not alone in this place."

The submersible's powerful forward lights swept across the seabed, and then, they found it. Not a fissure, not a jagged tear in the earth, but a flawlessly engineered aperture, a perfect circle of darkness punched into the seemingly solid rock. It was as if a colossal celestial drill had bored through the ocean floor, leaving behind a smooth, unblemished entrance to another world.

"It's a passage," Elias breathed, the words catching in his throat. "And it's unlike anything I've ever seen. The edges are… impossibly smooth."

Lena confirmed his observation. "Spectrographic analysis of the aperture walls indicates a composition of highly compressed, crystalline silicate, Captain. The precision of the cut… it's beyond any known terrestrial excavation technology. The sheer scale and perfection suggest a process of immense power and control."

The anomaly's energy, previously a vibrant hum, seemed to converge on this opening, a silent invitation. Elias felt a prickle of anticipation, a mixture of dread and exhilaration. The fragments of the *Stardust* were undoubtedly connected to this place. "We're going in," he announced, his voice firm. "Carefully."

He nudged the *Abyssus* forward, its robust hull designed to withstand immense pressures. As they glided through the perfectly formed aperture, the submersible was engulfed by a profound silence. The faint warmth of the vents was absent here, replaced by a neutral, stable temperature. The water itself seemed different – clearer, less dense, and devoid of the microscopic particles that had danced in the previous cavern. It was as if they had passed through a veil, entering a realm of pristine stillness.

The cavern unfolded before them like a celestial ballroom. It was colossal, a vast, hollowed-out space within the very heart of the ocean floor. The roof was lost in the impenetrable darkness beyond the reach of the submersible's lights, but the sheer expanse of the cavern floor was evident. It stretched out in an impossibly smooth, featureless plain, bathed in a soft, internal luminescence that emanated from an unseen source. This was not the chaotic beauty of a natural formation; this was the stark, awe-inspiring grandeur of something designed.

"Captain," Lena's voice was hushed with an awe that mirrored Elias's own, "the energy readings are… stable. The anomaly's signature is diffused throughout the entire cavern, like a gentle, ambient field. It's not concentrated, but pervasive."

Elias guided the *Abyssus* deeper into the cavern, the silence amplifying the hum of their own systems. The silence here was not an absence of sound, but a profound lack of external intrusion. The crushing pressures of the ocean, the grinding of tectonic plates, the ceaseless murmur of the abyss – all were absent. This was a sanctuary, a pocket of profound peace carved from the very fabric of the planet.

And then, they saw them.

Scattered across the vast expanse of the cavern floor, resting in what appeared to be meticulously prepared berths, were a collection of submerged spacecraft. They were unlike anything Elias had ever encountered. Sleek, aerodynamic forms, crafted from materials that seemed to absorb and re-emit the cavern's gentle luminescence, they were astonishingly intact. There were no signs of damage, no evidence of catastrophic impact, as if they had simply been placed there, waiting.

"My God," Elias whispered, the words barely audible. The sheer number of them was overwhelming. Dozens, perhaps even hundreds, of alien vessels lay dormant, their ethereal glow a silent testament to their advanced nature.

Lena's fingers flew across her console, her scientific curiosity overcoming her awe. "Captain, the energy signatures… they match the anomaly's resonance. These craft are all integrated with the ambient energy field. They're not powered in the conventional sense, but… they're alive, in a way. They're drawing sustenance from the cavern's unique energetic properties."

The implication sent a chill down Elias's spine. The *Stardust* had not been an isolated incident. It had stumbled upon a hidden armada, a repository of alien technology nestled deep within the planet's core. And the anomaly, the very force that had drawn him here, was the key to its existence, its power source, and its preservation.

Kaelen, his eyes glued to the proximity sensors, spoke with a newfound intensity. "Captain, the readings suggest these vessels are ancient. Their energy signatures are old, very old, but incredibly stable. No decay, no degradation. It's as if time itself has no effect within this cavern."

Elias steered the *Abyssus* closer to one of the vessels, a particularly striking craft that seemed to be crafted from a single, obsidian-like material that shimmered with internal light. Its lines were fluid, organic, suggesting a mastery of design that transcended human aesthetics. As they drew nearer, Elias could discern intricate, glowing patterns etched into its surface, patterns that pulsed in time with the cavern's ambient energy.

"Lena, can you scan that vessel?" Elias asked, his voice tight with anticipation. "I need to know if… if any of them match the *Stardust*'s configuration."

Lena's sensors hummed, and the data began to stream onto her display. For a long moment, there was silence, broken only by the rhythmic pulse of the submersible's life support. Then, Lena gasped.

"Captain… it's… it's astonishing," she stammered, her voice laced with disbelief. "The primary power conduit, the energy channeling matrix… it's identical to the schematics we recovered from the *Stardust* fragments. The propulsion system… it's the same advanced, unknown technology. And the hull composition… it shares trace elements with the alloys we found. Captain, this isn't just a similar design. This *is* the *Stardust*."

Elias stared at the vessel, his heart pounding in his chest. The craft before him, pristine and untouched, was the *Stardust*. Not a fragment, not a remnant, but the entire ship, restored to its former glory. The catastrophic event that had shattered his ship had, in reality, brought it here, to this hidden sanctuary, where it had been preserved, perhaps even repaired, by the very forces that Elias had been hunting.

"But… how?" Kaelen asked, his voice a mixture of confusion and wonder. "The loss of the *Stardust*… it was a catastrophic event. We recovered barely anything."

"The vents," Elias realized, the pieces clicking into place with a sudden, blinding clarity. "The geothermal nexus. It wasn't just a shield; it was a conduit. The anomaly's energy, amplified by the vents, must have enveloped the *Stardust* during its descent. It pulled the ship here, into this cavern, and then… it stabilized it. The 'damage' we saw was likely an effect of its transition through the anomaly, not the cause of its destruction."

Lena nodded, her eyes wide. "The energy integration would have been immense. The *Stardust* was designed to harness the anomaly's power, but perhaps it overloaded. The cavern acted as a dampener, absorbing the excess energy and re-directing it into the vessel's structural integrity. It's… it's a form of cosmic repair."

The revelation was profound, shattering Elias's understanding of the events that had led him on this quest. The loss of his crew, the years of searching, the haunting specter of the anomaly – it all began to coalesce into a new narrative. The *Stardust* hadn't been lost; it had been found. It had found its true purpose, its true destination.

He maneuvered the *Abyssus* closer to the *Stardust*, its familiar silhouette now bathed in the soft, ethereal glow of the sanctuary. Elias felt a pang of grief, sharp and sudden, for the crew he had lost, for the mission that had gone so terribly wrong. But beneath the grief, a new emotion was blossoming: understanding. He finally understood.

"We need to investigate," Elias said, his voice resonating with a newfound resolve. "We need to understand how this place works, how it preserved the *Stardust*, and what its purpose is."

He brought the *Abyssus* to a halt beside the resting place of his lost ship. The sheer scale of the discovery was almost overwhelming. This cavern, this hidden sanctuary, was a testament to an intelligence far beyond human comprehension. It was a repository of alien technology, a monument to an unknown civilization, and the ultimate resting place, and perhaps even rebirth, of the *Stardust*. The journey had been fraught with peril, with loss and uncertainty, but it had led them here, to the heart of a mystery that promised to redefine humanity's place in the cosmos.

Elias activated the *Abyssus*'s external manipulator arms, their articulated joints moving with precise, deliberate motion. Their objective was clear: to make contact with the *Stardust*, to interface with its systems, and to unlock the secrets it held within this profound, silent sanctuary. The knowledge they sought, the understanding of the anomaly, of the universe itself, lay dormant within the alien hull, waiting for them to awaken it. The exploration of this colossal, silent cavern had just begun.

The internal luminescence of the cavern, a gentle, pervasive glow that defied any discernible source, illuminated a scene that defied comprehension. Elias had anticipated finding remnants of the *Stardust*, perhaps fragments of its hull or key systems that could explain its catastrophic demise. What he found instead was something far grander, far more significant. The cavern floor, stretching out in an impossibly smooth expanse, was not merely a docking bay for dormant alien vessels; it was a vast, silent workshop, a repository of advanced technology that dwarfed anything humanity had ever conceived.

Scattered across this celestial expanse, nestled in the same meticulously prepared berths as the larger spacecraft, were countless components, tools, and even entire sections of vessels that, while smaller than the primary craft, exhibited the same startlingly advanced characteristics. These weren't shattered debris; they were pristine, as if carefully placed and cataloged. Gleaming conduits of an unknown alloy, their surfaces impossibly smooth and radiating a faint warmth, lay coiled like dormant serpents. Intricate crystalline matrices, humming with a low, resonant frequency, were mounted on articulated arms, waiting to be integrated. There were even what appeared to be specialized tools, their forms alien and their purpose a mystery, crafted from materials that seemed to ripple with contained energy.

Lena's fingers danced across her console, her initial awe giving way to a feverish scientific analysis. "Captain," she breathed, her voice barely above a whisper, her eyes wide with a mixture of exhilaration and disbelief, "the spectral analysis… it's consistent. The alloys, the energy signatures, the structural integrity… it's all directly correlated with the *Stardust*. But these aren't just parts of our ship. This is… this is a veritable treasure trove of technology. Look at this manifold," she pointed to a complex, multi-faceted component lying a short distance away, its surface intricately etched with glowing patterns. "The energy channeling capabilities are orders of magnitude beyond what we recovered from the *Stardust* fragments. It's as if they were field-testing experimental components here, pushing the boundaries of their own designs."

Elias guided the *Abyssus* slowly over the expanse, his gaze sweeping across the silent testament to an advanced civilization. He could see entire sections of spacecraft, hull plating meticulously fitted, propulsion units integrated, control interfaces exposed, all awaiting assembly or perhaps refinement. These were not the broken remnants of a single catastrophic event; they were components of a much larger, much more complex endeavor. It was as if a vast shipyard, operated by beings of immense power and knowledge, lay dormant beneath the ocean's crust.

"Lena, are you certain none of this is human-made?" Elias asked, a knot of apprehension forming in his gut. The idea of a clandestine, far-future human project operating on this scale, in this hidden sanctuary, was a possibility, however remote.

"Captain, the precision, the materials science, the sheer audacity of the engineering… it's simply not within the realm of known human capability, even theoretical," Lena replied, her conviction absolute. "We're talking about technologies that manipulate spacetime on a localized level, energy containment fields that defy our understanding of physics, and fabrication processes that seem to bend matter itself. This is definitively extraterrestrial. Or," she paused, her voice dropping to a more speculative tone, "a human project so advanced, so utterly alien to our current paradigm, that it might as well be extraterrestrial. But the energy resonance… it aligns with the anomaly, with the same cosmic fingerprint we detected from the *Stardust*."

The sheer scale of the find was overwhelming. Elias had come seeking answers about his lost ship, about the anomaly that had consumed it. He had found not just his ship, but an entire fleet, an arsenal of unimaginable power, and a workshop capable of building such wonders. The scattered components weren't just discarded parts; they were opportunities. For Elias, burdened by the loss of the *Stardust* and its crew, this was more than a discovery; it was the raw material for his impossible dream. He could see the potential for reconstruction, for replication, for understanding how to harness these advanced systems. The scattered pieces were no longer just remnants of a tragedy; they were the building blocks of a new future, a future he could forge.

He instructed Kaelen to begin a detailed inventory of the accessible components, prioritizing anything that appeared to be a primary propulsion system, a control module, or an energy conduit. Lena, meanwhile, focused her sensors on the larger spacecraft, attempting to decipher their operational status and identify any that might be directly analogous to the *Stardust*'s design, beyond the initial confirmation.

As the *Abyssus* moved deeper into the cavern, the density of the technological artifacts increased. They encountered what appeared to be specialized assembly bays, massive robotic arms extending from the cavern walls, frozen in mid-action, each tipped with tools of unimaginable precision. These arms were positioned around partially constructed vessels, suggesting an automated construction process of incredible sophistication. There were also smaller, self-contained units that pulsed with a faint energy, their purpose unclear, but their advanced design evident. One such unit, roughly the size of a terrestrial shuttlecraft, was composed of interlocking hexagonal plates that seemed to shift and realign themselves in a slow, mesmerizing dance.

"Captain, I'm detecting a localized energy surge from that hexagonal unit," Kaelen reported, his voice tight with caution. "It's… it's adapting to our proximity. The energy field is fluctuating, as if it's attempting to scan us."

Elias brought the *Abyssus* to a respectful distance. "Lena, any insights on that? Is it a defensive measure, or something else?"

Lena's brow furrowed as she analyzed the incoming data. "It's not aggressive, Captain. It's… curious. The energy signature is highly complex, a form of data transfer we can't currently parse. It's trying to establish a communication protocol, perhaps. It's like a probe, or a diagnostic tool."

The idea that these alien technologies might be capable of self-awareness, or at least a form of automated sentience, was both exhilarating and unsettling. This was not just a derelict graveyard; it was a living repository, a dormant intelligence waiting to be reawakened. The implications were staggering. If they could interface with these systems, they might not only reconstruct the *Stardust* but also unlock the secrets of its creators.

Elias's gaze fell upon a section of the cavern floor that seemed to be a dedicated testing ground. Here, components were arranged in complex configurations, as if undergoing intricate calibration. He saw what looked like miniature warp cores, their containment fields shimmering with contained power, suspended in mid-air by unseen forces. There were also energy conduits arranged in vast, geometric patterns, pulsing with synchronized light, suggesting experiments in power distribution and long-range energy transmission. The sheer ingenuity on display was breathtaking. They were witnessing the pinnacle of technological achievement, a masterclass in alien engineering.

"Captain, I've identified a cluster of components that bear a remarkable resemblance to the *Stardust*'s primary navigation array," Lena announced, her voice filled with a newfound urgency. "The crystalline matrix, the quantum entanglement processors… they are almost identical. This suggests that the *Stardust* itself was a derivative of this technology, a human attempt to replicate or integrate with these alien systems."

This was a crucial piece of the puzzle. The *Stardust* hadn't just stumbled upon this place; it had been built with this place, or at least its technology, in mind. Elias felt a surge of renewed purpose. The tragedy of the *Stardust* wasn't a random accident; it was a consequence of humanity's ambition to reach for something far greater than itself, an ambition that had led them to this hidden sanctuary.

He directed the *Abyssus* towards a particularly large, partially assembled vessel. It was sleek, avian in its design, with sweeping curves and an almost organic appearance. Unlike the dormant ships, this one seemed to be in a more advanced state of construction, with visible connection points and internal conduits laid bare. Elias piloted the submersible closer, his intention to get a clearer visual of its systems.

"Captain, I'm detecting residual energy signatures from that vessel's primary conduit," Kaelen reported. "It's faint, but it matches the unique energy fluctuations we observed during the *Stardust*'s initial activation sequence. It's… it's as if this ship was recently powered up."

The implication sent a shiver down Elias's spine. "Recently powered up?" he echoed. "By whom? Or what?"

Lena's analysis offered no immediate answers, only more questions. "The energy source isn't external, Captain. It seems to be self-contained, but the power generation method is unlike anything we've ever encountered. It's not fusion, not antimatter… it's drawing directly from the cavern's ambient energy field, but with a focus and efficiency that suggests a deliberate, controlled process."

Elias brought the *Abyssus* alongside the partially constructed vessel. The scale of it was immense, dwarfing the *Abyssus* by comparison. The craftsmanship was flawless, the materials impossibly smooth and seamless. He could see articulated panels designed to open and reveal complex machinery, and what appeared to be weapon emplacements, integrated so seamlessly into the hull that they were almost invisible. This was not a reconnaissance vessel; this was a warship, designed for operations on a cosmic scale.

"Lena, initiate a passive scan of its internal systems," Elias ordered. "I want to see if we can identify any recognizable control interfaces or data storage units."

As Lena's sensors probed the alien vessel, Elias couldn't shake the feeling that they were trespassing, that they were intruding upon a sacred space. This cavern, this repository of advanced technology, was clearly the product of a civilization of immense power and sophistication. Their purpose here, the reason for this vast workshop, remained a profound mystery. Were they preparing for a conflict? Were they engaged in some grand cosmic endeavor? Or was this simply a resting place, a sanctuary for their creations?

"Captain, I'm picking up fragmented data streams within the ship's primary memory core," Lena reported, her voice laced with excitement. "It's heavily encrypted, of course, but some of the core programming language… it's similar to the rudimentary translation protocols we developed for the *Stardust*'s AI. It's a long shot, but I might be able to access some foundational information."

Elias nodded, a flicker of hope igniting within him. "Do it, Lena. Any information we can glean about this place, about these technologies, is invaluable. And keep a close watch on our surroundings. We don't know what else might be dormant in this cavern."

He continued to pilot the *Abyssus* through the silent aisles of technology, each component, each partially assembled craft, a testament to the vast unknown. This was more than just a treasure trove; it was a glimpse into a future, or perhaps a past, that humanity had not yet conceived. The scattered pieces of the *Stardust* had led him here, to the heart of a cosmic enigma, and in doing so, had presented him with the ultimate opportunity: the chance to understand, to rebuild, and perhaps, to ascend. The sheer abundance of advanced technology was almost paralyzing, each piece begging for investigation, each system holding the potential to unlock secrets that could reshape their understanding of the universe. Elias knew that their mission had just expanded exponentially, and that the true exploration of this uncharted cavern had only just begun. The potential was limitless, the challenge immense, and the rewards, if they could only unlock the secrets held within this alien workshop, could be the salvation of humanity itself.

The hum of the *Abyssus* seemed to falter, as if even the submersible's sophisticated systems were struggling to process the sheer audacity of their surroundings. Elias stood on the observation deck, his reflection distorted in the reinforced viewport, a silent observer in a cathedral of alien engineering. The spectral luminescence of the cavern, which had once seemed merely beautiful, now felt imbued with a profound, almost sacred purpose. He had come seeking the shattered fragments of the *Stardust*, a ghost ship lost to the void, a tomb for his fallen comrades. He had found, instead, a celestial shipyard, a silent testament to a civilization whose technological prowess rendered humanity's greatest achievements infantile.

Lena's voice, usually sharp with scientific inquiry, was now laced with a reverence that mirrored his own. "Captain, the energy readings from the larger vessels… they're not merely dormant. They're in a state of low-power stasis, but the core systems are intact. The propulsion matrices, the navigation arrays… they're all remarkably similar in design to the *Stardust*'s core architecture, but refined, perfected. It's like comparing a child's drawing to a masterpiece."

Kaelen, ever the pragmatist, chimed in from his console, his voice taut with a suppressed excitement that threatened to break through his professional demeanor. "And the components, Captain? We've cataloged over three thousand distinct pieces, each exceeding our material science capabilities by orders of magnitude. The alloys alone… their tensile strength, their energy conductivity… it's beyond anything we've ever hypothesized. Some of these conduits, they're practically conduits to another dimension, the way they channel energy."

Elias's gaze drifted over the cavern floor, past the dormant spacecraft and the scattered, yet pristine, components. He saw the articulated robotic arms, frozen in their work, each tipped with tools that defied comprehension. He saw the crystalline matrices, humming with an internal rhythm, waiting for integration. He saw the hexagonal unit, still pulsing with that gentle, inquisitive energy. This wasn't just a collection of advanced technology; it was a blueprint, a promise.

The weight of the *Stardust*'s loss, the ghosts of his crew, had haunted him for cycles. He had carried their memory like a shroud, a constant reminder of his failure. But here, in this impossibly vast workshop, surrounded by the very essence of what had claimed his ship and his friends, Elias felt something shift within him. The grief did not vanish, but it was no longer the all-consuming force. It was tempered by a new, fierce resolve. The pain that had driven him to this desolate ocean floor was now being transmuted into a burning purpose.

He turned from the viewport, his eyes alight with a conviction that had been absent for too long. The despair of the past was being drowned out by the roaring crescendo of possibility. He looked at Lena, then at Kaelen, his gaze steady and unwavering. "We didn't just find wreckage," he stated, his voice resonating with a newfound authority. "We found a legacy. We found the means to overcome what happened."

He took a step forward, his boots echoing softly on the deck plates of the *Abyssus*. "The *Stardust* was lost. But its spirit, its design, its ambition… it lives on here. In these components. In these very vessels." He gestured around the cavern, encompassing the silent grandeur of the alien shipyard. "We came here for answers. But we've been given something more. We've been given a chance."

He paused, letting the weight of his words settle. The silence that followed was not one of uncertainty, but of anticipation. He could feel the crew's collective gaze upon him, their hopes and fears hanging in the air.

"We will not just salvage these parts," Elias declared, his voice rising, echoing in the confined space of the submersible. "We will *rebuild*. We will *ascend*. We will take the remnants of what humanity dared to reach for, and we will forge it into something new. Something stronger. Something that can carry us beyond the stars, beyond the reach of whatever destroyed the *Stardust*."

He envisioned it with crystalline clarity: the integration of these alien systems, the reverse-engineering of their impossible physics, the creation of a vessel born from the ashes of tragedy and the ingenuity of the cosmos. It was an audacious plan, a desperate gamble, but it was the only path forward.

"We will build a ship," he continued, his voice a steady promise. "A ship capable of reaching orbit. A ship capable of traversing the void. A ship that will be a beacon, a testament to what we can achieve when we refuse to be defined by our losses." He met Lena's gaze, then Kaelen's. "We will call it… The Phoenix."

The name hung in the air, a symbol of rebirth, of defiance against the overwhelming forces that had sought to extinguish them. The *Stardust* had fallen, consumed by an unknown anomaly. But from its ashes, a new vessel, a new hope, would rise.

Lena's eyes widened, a slow smile spreading across her face. "The Phoenix," she breathed, the name clearly resonating with her scientific mind, her understanding of the symbolism. "It's… it's perfect, Captain."

Kaelen nodded, a rare, unreserved smile gracing his lips. "The Phoenix. I like it. It's ambitious. It's defiant."

Elias felt a surge of adrenaline, a potent elixir that chased away the lingering shadows of despair. This was not just a mission anymore; it was a sacred trust. He had a duty to the fallen, a duty to the living, and a duty to the future of humanity.

"This is our new objective," he stated, his voice firm. "We will begin by identifying the core propulsion systems and the primary control interfaces of the *Stardust*-class vessels. Lena, prioritize the analysis of any data cores or navigation computers. Kaelen, we need a comprehensive inventory of all salvaged components, focusing on structural integrity and energy channeling capabilities. We will need to fabricate new housing units, adapt their power conduits, and, if possible, establish a rudimentary understanding of their operational parameters."

He knew the task ahead was monumental, fraught with unimaginable challenges. They were adrift in an alien ocean, in an alien cavern, with alien technology. Every step would be a leap into the unknown, a test of their ingenuity and their resilience. But standing in this sanctuary of advanced technology, with the spectral light illuminating their path, Elias felt a profound sense of destiny. The pain of his past was momentarily eclipsed by the sheer, overwhelming possibility of the future. He felt an almost divine calling, a mandate to take what humanity had reached for and failed, and to succeed where they had fallen.

"This discovery changes everything," he continued, his gaze sweeping across the cavern once more, this time with a clarity born of purpose. "It's no longer about survival, it's about evolution. We're not just recovering what was lost; we're building what will be. We are going to learn from this place, understand it, and use its power to lift ourselves beyond our current limitations."

He turned back to the crew, his resolve hardening with each passing second. The whispers of doubt that had plagued him since the loss of the *Stardust* were now drowned out by the thunderous pronouncement of his vow. "We will build the Phoenix. And from the depths of this abyss, we will rise to the stars." This moment, he knew, was the turning point. The quiet desperation of their survival had ended. A perilous, yet exhilarating, new course had been charted, a course defined not by loss, but by a defiant, unwavering commitment to rebirth. The echoes of his vow reverberated through the cavern, a promise whispered to the silent giants of alien technology, a promise to ascend.

## 4: Reverse Engineering the Impossible

The *Abyssus*, once a sleek submersible designed for deep-sea exploration and recovery, now bore the scars and modifications of a far more ambitious undertaking. Its familiar, sterile corridors had been reconfigured, their utilitarian purpose now augmented by a palpable thrum of scientific endeavor. Where once there were storage lockers and crew quarters, there were now the beginnings of a highly specialized laboratory, a testament to Lena's relentless drive and ingenuity. She had worked with an almost feverish intensity, transforming sections of the submersible into a mobile research facility, a crucible where the impossible was being systematically dismantled and understood.

The cavern, a silent testament to a lost civilization's mastery of the cosmos, had yielded its treasures. Meticulously cataloged, each salvaged component was transported with an almost reverent care back to the *Abyssus*. These weren't mere pieces of wreckage; they were fragments of a higher existence, keys to unlocking mysteries that had previously been confined to the realm of theoretical physics and the wildest dreams of science fiction. Lena's lab, a hastily assembled yet highly functional space within the submersible, became the nexus of this profound undertaking. The confined quarters of the *Abyssus* amplified the intensity of their mission. Every calculation, every experimental setup, every microscopic analysis was a critical step, not just towards building the Phoenix, but towards their very survival in this alien, unforgiving environment.

Lena, her face etched with concentration, her fingers stained with exotic lubricants and trace elements that defied terrestrial classification, hovered over a workbench. The air in the repurposed section of the *Abyssus* crackled with the low hum of repurposed alien machinery, now jury-rigged to interface with the submersible's systems. The spectral luminescence that had bathed the cavern still clung to some of the components, casting an ethereal glow on Lena's focused features. She moved with a precision born of deep understanding, her mind a whirlwind of data, hypotheses, and audacious leaps of logic. The sheer alienness of the materials was both a challenge and an intoxicating allure. She was not just analyzing them; she was conversing with them, coaxing their secrets out through a painstaking process of reverse engineering.

"Captain," Lena's voice, broadcasted over the submersible's internal comms, was a low, resonant hum that cut through the ambient noise. "The energy conduits we extracted from the primary propulsion matrix of the derelict freighter… they're not simply designed to channel energy. They appear to *manipulate* spacetime on a localized level. The resonance frequency of the crystalline lattice within them aligns with theoretical models of warp field generation, but… it's orders of magnitude more efficient, more stable, than anything we've ever conceived."

Elias, reviewing tactical readouts in the command center, felt a familiar surge of awe mingled with the persistent weight of responsibility. "Manipulate spacetime, Lena? Are you certain?"

"As certain as I can be without a fully operational diagnostic suite, Captain," she replied, a hint of exasperated excitement in her tone. "The material itself exhibits properties that violate several fundamental laws of conventional physics. The atomic structure… it's not just tightly packed; it's inter-dimensionally interwoven. It's as if each atom is a miniature nexus point, capable of drawing energy from, or perhaps even influencing, adjacent realities."

Kaelen, ever the pragmatist, interjected from his station. "And the power source for these conduits, Lena? We've analyzed the smaller energy cells, the ones we recovered from the smaller drones. They're compact, incredibly dense, but the output… it seems insufficient to power something of that magnitude. Unless…"

"Unless they're not *just* power sources," Lena finished, her voice alight with a dawning realization. "I believe they're more akin to energy *catalysts*. They don't generate power in the traditional sense; they facilitate its flow, drawing upon ambient energy fields, perhaps even the zero-point energy of the vacuum itself. The *Abyssus* can barely sustain the basic operational needs of our salvaged components, let alone power them to their full potential. We're operating on a fraction of a percent of what these systems are designed for."

The implications were staggering. They were handling technology that operated on principles far beyond human comprehension, powered by sources that defied their understanding of energy generation. It was like trying to understand a fusion reactor by examining a single spark. Yet, Lena, with her unparalleled intellect and unwavering determination, was making progress. Her lab was a testament to that progress, a vibrant, albeit cramped, hub of scientific discovery.

The salvaged materials, once laid out in the cavern like a celestial graveyard, were now meticulously organized within the *Abyssus*. Lena had established a strict cataloging system, each component tagged, analyzed, and cross-referenced. The sheer volume of data was overwhelming, a deluge of information that threatened to drown even her prodigious intellect. She had designated specific areas for optical analysis, material composition testing, and rudimentary operational simulations. The sterile white of the *Abyssus*'s interior was now punctuated by the iridescent sheen of alien alloys, the soft glow of internal energy conduits, and the intricate, almost organic designs of alien circuitry.

"The navigational array," Lena announced, her voice carrying the weight of a significant breakthrough. "I've managed to partially interface with its data core. The architecture is… it's not binary, not even quaternary. It's based on a hyper-dimensional geometric lattice. The 'coordinates' it uses aren't just spatial; they're temporal and existential. It's less about plotting a course through space and more about aligning oneself with a specific point in the universal fabric."

Elias felt a shiver trace its way down his spine. The loss of the *Stardust* had been attributed to an anomaly, a disruption in the very fabric of spacetime. Now, it seemed, they were staring into the heart of that disruption, and the technology that navigated it with apparent ease. "Can you… can you decipher any of it, Lena? Can we learn how to use it?"

"That's the crux of it, Captain," Lena replied, her brow furrowed in deep thought. "It's not about deciphering in the traditional sense. It's about understanding the underlying principles, the philosophical framework that underpins their engineering. Their navigation isn't a calculation; it's an act of conscious alignment. They don't *fly* through space; they *become* one with their destination. It's… it's profoundly alien, but also… elegant."

The *Abyssus* itself had undergone a transformation. Its primary function had shifted from mere survival to active participation in this monumental endeavor. The limited space forced an efficiency that was both a blessing and a curse. Lena's lab was a carefully orchestrated chaos, a testament to the urgency of their situation. Tools, schematics, and glowing fragments of alien technology were spread across every available surface. The hum of the submersible's life support systems was now underscored by the subtle symphony of alien machinery awakening under Lena's careful ministrations.

"I've managed to establish a rudimentary power flow to the structural integrity field generator," Lena reported, her voice tinged with exhaustion but alight with triumph. "It's a fraction of its intended capacity, but it's stable. The material is self-repairing, Captain. Not in a biological sense, but at a quantum level. Any stresses or micro-fractures are instantly corrected by the reordering of its atomic structure. If we can integrate this into the Phoenix, its hull will be virtually indestructible."

Elias could only imagine the implications. A vessel that could withstand the crushing pressures of the deep, the unforgiving vacuum of space, and whatever unknown forces had claimed the *Stardust*. This wasn't just about building a ship; it was about forging a new paradigm for human existence. The weight of that responsibility settled upon him, a burden he was now ready to bear. The ghost of his lost crew was no longer a specter of despair, but a silent presence, a driving force that fueled his determination. They had deserved better than oblivion, and this alien technology offered them a chance to grant that wish.

"What about the primary drive systems, Lena?" Elias asked, his gaze fixed on the holographic projection of the alien freighter's engine core, a breathtakingly complex arrangement of interlocking crystalline structures. "Can we replicate that kind of propulsion?"

Lena sighed, a sound that carried the weariness of countless sleepless cycles. "Replication is a strong word, Captain. We can perhaps *mimic* a fraction of its functionality. The core principle involves manipulating the very fabric of causality. It's not about thrust or reaction mass; it's about subtly influencing the probabilistic nature of spacetime to 'steer' oneself through existence. I've identified what I believe to be the primary regulators, but their internal mechanisms are still largely incomprehensible. It's like trying to understand a symphony by dissecting a single note."

The confined spaces of the *Abyssus* seemed to press in on them, a constant reminder of their isolation and the monumental task before them. Yet, within these metal confines, a revolution was taking place. Lena's lab was a beacon of defiant innovation, a testament to humanity's unyielding spirit in the face of overwhelming odds. Each success, no matter how small, was a victory against the vast indifference of the cosmos and the tragedy of their past. The Phoenix was no longer just a concept; it was taking shape, piece by painstaking piece, within the belly of their repurposed submersible.

"The bio-mimetic interfaces," Lena continued, her voice a low murmur as she meticulously examined a crystalline shard that pulsed with a faint, internal light. "They're designed to interface directly with a sentient nervous system. Not through implants or external sensors, but through direct neural resonance. The alien designers understood that the most advanced technology is an extension of the user's will, not merely a tool to be operated."

Elias nodded, picturing the seamless integration that must have existed in the civilization that created these marvels. "So, the pilot wouldn't be *controlling* the ship, but rather *experiencing* its flight?"

"Precisely," Lena confirmed. "And the complexity of the interface is directly proportional to the user's cognitive capabilities. It adapts, learns, and grows with the pilot. If we can even partially understand this, the Phoenix will be more than a ship; it will be an extension of our collective consciousness. It will be truly alive."

The challenge, however, was immense. The *Abyssus* was a marvel of human engineering, but it was a blunt instrument compared to the ethereal sophistication of the alien technology they were encountering. Integrating these systems, even on a rudimentary level, required an unprecedented level of ingenuity and a willingness to discard preconceived notions of how technology should function. Lena's lab was a constant battleground of hypotheses and experimental results, a place where failure was not an endpoint but a stepping stone.

"I've managed to isolate the primary energy regulation nexus from one of the smaller scout vessels," Lena reported, her voice laced with a peculiar mix of exhaustion and exhilaration. "It's incredibly compact, no larger than my fist, yet its energy density is… astronomical. The material is a lattice of exotic particles that seem to exist in a state of quantum superposition, simultaneously existing in multiple energy states. It's like holding a contained singularity."

Elias felt a familiar sense of vertigo, the ground beneath his feet shifting as he grappled with the sheer scale of their discovery. The technology of this lost civilization was not merely advanced; it was fundamentally different, operating on principles that blurred the lines between physics, metaphysics, and even consciousness.

"And can we power it, Lena?" Elias asked, the question hanging in the air, heavy with unspoken hope.

"That, Captain," Lena replied, her gaze drifting to a schematic displayed on her console, a complex tapestry of alien symbols and energy flow diagrams, "is the million-credit question. Our current power generation capabilities are utterly insufficient. To even activate these systems, even for a fraction of a second, we would need an energy source that dwarfs anything humanity has ever conceived. We are attempting to power a starship with a candle."

Her frustration was palpable, a stark contrast to the unwavering scientific curiosity that drove her. The *Abyssus*, retrofitted to accommodate the salvaged materials, was a testament to their resourcefulness. Its sterile corridors, once filled with the mundane hum of life support and navigation systems, now vibrated with the subtle energies of alien machinery. Lena's makeshift laboratory was the epicenter of this transformation, a cramped yet intensely focused space where the impossible was being systematically deconstructed and understood. Each salvaged component, meticulously cataloged and transported, represented a piece of the puzzle, a fragment of a forgotten cosmic symphony. The submersible, once a mere tool for recovery, had evolved into a mobile research facility, its limited confines amplifying the intensity of their undertaking. Every calculation, every experiment, was a high-stakes gamble, critical to their survival and the realization of Elias's audacious vision.

The sheer volume of data Lena was processing was staggering. She worked with a relentless energy, fueled by an insatiable curiosity and the growing understanding that they were on the precipice of something truly world-altering. The alien components, scattered across her workbench, glowed with an inner luminescence, each whispering secrets of a civilization that had mastered forces beyond human comprehension. The tensile strength of the alloys, the conductivity of the crystalline conduits, the sheer elegance of the bio-mimetic interfaces – each element was a puzzle piece that Lena was painstakingly fitting into a larger, emergent picture.

"Captain," Lena's voice crackled over the comms, her tone a mixture of exhaustion and sheer, unadulterated wonder. "I've made a breakthrough with the primary atmospheric containment field. The 'walls' of this cavern… they aren't just rock and sediment. They're a dynamically generated energy matrix. It's not holding back water; it's holding back… vacuum. A controlled void, maintained by a network of resonance emitters that are almost imperceptible to our sensors."

Elias, standing on the observation deck of the *Abyssus*, gazing out at the breathtaking spectacle, felt a chill that had nothing to do with the temperature. The sheer scale of the engineering was humbling. "A controlled void? So, the water… it's being held in place by pure energy?"

"Essentially, yes," Lena confirmed. "And the energy required to maintain such a field is immense, far beyond anything our current power cores can generate. However, I've identified a nodal point, a central conduit that seems to regulate the entire matrix. If we can tap into that, even a fraction of its output could power the *Abyssus* for millennia, let alone the Phoenix."

The prospect was both exhilarating and terrifying. Tapping into the core of an alien energy network, a system designed to contain an entire ocean within a void, was a task of unfathomable complexity and inherent danger. Yet, it was also their only hope.

Back in her lab, the cramped quarters of the *Abyssus* hummed with the low thrum of alien machinery Lena had managed to partially activate. The spectral light of the salvaged components cast an ethereal glow on her focused features. She meticulously cataloged every data packet, every material analysis, her mind racing to bridge the vast chasm between human understanding and the alien science before her. The confined space amplified the intensity of their undertaking, each successful integration a small victory, each failure a stark reminder of the immense challenge ahead.

"The structural alloys," Lena reported, her voice carrying the weight of countless hours of analysis. "Their atomic structure is… it's self-organizing. They don't rely on traditional molecular bonding; they maintain cohesion through a form of quantum entanglement. It's as if each atom is intrinsically linked to every other atom in the component, creating an unbreakable lattice that can adapt to any stress."

Elias, reviewing the preliminary material reports, felt a sense of profound awe. The *Stardust* had been lost to an anomaly, a disruption in the very fabric of spacetime. Now, they were surrounded by technology that seemed to actively manipulate and master that fabric. "So,

Lena, if we were to integrate this into the Phoenix, what would that mean for its hull?"

"It would be, for all intents and purposes, indestructible, Captain," Lena replied, a rare smile touching her lips. "It could withstand forces that would tear conventional alloys apart atom by atom. It's like building a ship not out of metal, but out of solidified spacetime itself. The implications for interstellar travel, for survival in hostile environments, are… revolutionary."

The challenge, however, lay in understanding how to integrate these systems. The *Abyssus*, while capable, was a far cry from the advanced technological cradle that had produced these marvels. Lena's lab was a testament to her relentless ingenuity, a space where human ingenuity was being pushed to its absolute limits. She was not just reverse-engineering; she was re-interpreting, adapting, and, in a sense, learning a new language of physics and engineering.

"The power conduits," Lena continued, her voice laced with a hint of frustration, "they function on a principle of energy resonance, Captain. They don't simply transmit power; they *tune* it. They draw energy from ambient fields, from the very fabric of the universe, and channel it through a series of crystalline matrices that amplify and stabilize it. Our current power generation, while sufficient for the *Abyssus*, is like trying to fill an ocean with a teacup."

Elias understood. They had found the keys to unimaginable power, but they lacked the means to turn them. The *Abyssus* had been retrofitted to accommodate the salvaged materials, its sterile corridors now filled with the low hum of exotic machinery and Lena's focused energy. The submersible, once a tool for salvage, had become a mobile research facility, its confined space amplifying the intensity of their undertaking. Each calculation and experiment was critical to their survival and success, a delicate dance with forces they were only beginning to comprehend.

Lena's lab was a testament to her brilliance, a carefully orchestrated chaos of alien components, holographic schematics, and the constant, low hum of repurposed technology. She worked with an almost obsessive focus, her fingers stained with exotic lubricants and trace elements that defied terrestrial classification. The spectral luminescence of the salvaged materials cast an ethereal glow on her features, her mind a whirlwind of data, hypotheses, and audacious leaps of logic.

"The navigational core," Lena announced over the comms, her voice a low murmur filled with awe. "It's not based on conventional celestial mapping, Captain. It operates on a principle of cosmic resonance. The 'coordinates' aren't spatial points, but harmonic frequencies within the universal structure. The ship doesn't *travel* to a destination; it *aligns* itself with it."

Elias, on the observation deck, felt a shiver trace its way down his spine. The thought of a ship that could navigate not by calculating routes, but by attuning itself to the very vibrations of existence, was mind-boggling. "Align itself? Lena, can we even begin to understand that?"

"That's the challenge, Captain," she replied, her voice a mixture of exhaustion and exhilaration. "It requires a different way of thinking, a paradigm shift. Their engineering is not about manipulating external forces, but about internal harmony. The ship becomes an extension of the pilot's consciousness, resonating with the destination. The interfaces are bio-mimetic, designed to interface directly with neural pathways, translating intent into reality."

The sheer alienness of it all was both daunting and intoxicating. They were not just reverse-engineering technology; they were attempting to grasp a fundamentally different approach to existence, a civilization that had achieved mastery not through brute force, but through understanding and resonance. The *Abyssus*, their once reliable submersible, had been transformed into a mobile laboratory, a precarious vessel carrying the weight of humanity's future.

The intensity of Lena's work was palpable. Her makeshift lab, carved out of the *Abyssus*'s limited interior, was a hive of activity. The low hum of salvaged alien machinery, jury-rigged to the submersible's systems, filled the air, a constant reminder of the monumental task at hand. Every salvaged component, meticulously cataloged and transported, represented a piece of a cosmic puzzle, a fragment of a forgotten civilization's profound understanding. The confined space of the *Abyssus* amplified the pressure, making each calculation and experiment a critical step towards survival and the realization of Elias's audacious vision for the Phoenix.

"Captain, the primary propulsion conduits are even more remarkable than I initially estimated," Lena reported, her voice carrying a tone of deep reverence. "They don't simply channel energy; they manipulate the very fabric of spacetime. The material itself, a crystalline lattice of unknown composition, appears to exist in a state of quantum coherence, allowing it to generate localized distortions in the spacetime continuum. It's not thrust; it's… a controlled ripple."

Elias, reviewing the telemetry data in the command center, felt a familiar wave of awe wash over him. "A controlled ripple, Lena? What does that mean in practical terms?"

"It means," Lena explained, her voice laced with excitement, "that the ship doesn't push against space to move. It subtly shifts the local geometry of spacetime, effectively drawing itself towards its destination. It's a form of localized reality warping, incredibly precise and energy-efficient, far beyond anything our current theoretical models can even approach."

The implications for the Phoenix were staggering. A propulsion system that defied conventional physics, capable of traversing vast distances with unimaginable speed and efficiency. But the challenge remained: powering such a system. The *Abyssus*, while advanced, was a mere shadow of the technology they were encountering. Lena's lab was a testament to her relentless drive, a stark contrast to the sterile efficiency of the submersible's primary systems. Here, amidst the glow of alien artifacts and the hum of unfamiliar energies, the future of humanity was being forged.

"The energy core of the scout vessel," Lena continued, her voice barely a whisper as she examined a multifaceted crystal pulsating with an internal light. "It's not a power source in the traditional sense. It's a conduit, a nexus that draws energy from… well, from everything. Ambient radiation, zero-point energy, perhaps even the quantum fluctuations of the vacuum itself. It doesn't generate power; it facilitates its flow, like a valve on an infinite cosmic river."

Elias could only imagine the technological leap represented by such a device. Humanity's quest for energy had been a defining struggle, fraught with limitations and environmental consequences. This alien technology offered a glimpse of a future powered by the very essence of the universe.

"And can we control it, Lena?" Elias asked, the question hanging heavy in the recycled air of the *Abyssus*.

"That is the million-credit question, Captain," Lena admitted, her brow furrowed in concentration. "The control interfaces are bio-mimetic, designed to resonate directly with a sentient nervous system. It's not about manipulating buttons or levers; it's about the pilot's intention, their focus. The ship becomes an extension of their will. We're trying to interface a human mind with a system that operates on principles we're still struggling to comprehend."

The *Abyssus*, now retrofitted to accommodate the salvaged materials, was a stark testament to their ingenuity. Its once pristine corridors now hummed with the low thrum of exotic machinery, a symphony of alien science conducted by Lena's focused intellect. The submersible, a mere shell of its former self, had been transformed into a mobile research facility, its confined spaces amplifying the intensity of their undertaking. Each salvaged component, meticulously cataloged and transported, was a piece of a cosmic puzzle, a fragment of a forgotten civilization's profound wisdom.

Lena's lab was the nerve center of this operation, a meticulously organized chaos of salvaged artifacts, holographic schematics, and the faint, ethereal glow of alien energy sources. She worked with an almost feverish intensity, her mind a crucible where human understanding was being forged anew. The sheer alienness of the materials presented a challenge that would have daunted anyone less driven, but Lena thrived on it, her curiosity a relentless engine driving her forward.

"Captain," Lena's voice crackled over the internal comms, tinged with both exhaustion and a profound sense of discovery. "I've managed to establish a rudimentary energy flow through the primary structural integrity field generator. The material itself is… it's unlike anything we've ever encountered. It doesn't rely on traditional molecular bonding; it maintains cohesion through a form of quantum entanglement. Any stress, any damage, is instantly corrected at a subatomic level."

Elias, gazing out at the spectral luminescence of the cavern from the *Abyssus*'s viewport, felt a thrill of anticipation. "So, Lena, what does that mean for the Phoenix's hull?"

"It means, Captain," Lena replied, her voice resonating with awe, "that the Phoenix will be virtually indestructible. It will be able to withstand forces that would tear our current materials apart atom by atom. It's as if they built their ships not out of metal, but out of solidified spacetime itself. The implications for survival, for interstellar travel, are… revolutionary."

The challenge, however, was not just in understanding the materials, but in powering them. Lena's ongoing analysis of the salvaged components revealed an equally astonishing truth about their energy systems. "The power conduits," she explained, gesturing towards a complex arrangement of crystalline structures on her workbench, "they don't generate power in the conventional sense. They act as conduits, drawing energy from ambient fields, from the very fabric of the universe. They are like valves, regulating an infinite flow."

The confined space of the *Abyssus* amplified the urgency of their mission. Lena's lab, a repurposed section of the submersible, was a testament to her relentless pursuit of knowledge. The hum of salvaged alien machinery blended with the submersible's own life support systems, creating a unique symphony of human and alien technology. Every salvaged component, from the smallest data chip to the largest structural fragment, was meticulously cataloged and analyzed, each a crucial piece of the puzzle that would ultimately lead to the creation of the Phoenix.

"The navigation system," Lena announced, her voice resonating with a newfound understanding, "it's not based on spatial coordinates, Captain. It's a system of harmonic resonance. The ship doesn't calculate a trajectory; it aligns itself with the destination through a precise manipulation of spacetime frequencies. It's less about piloting and more about… attuning."

Elias, standing on the observation deck, felt a profound sense of humility. Humanity's ambition had always been to conquer the stars, but these beings had seemingly found a way to meld with them. "Attuning? Lena, can we even comprehend such a concept?"

"We are beginning to, Captain," she replied, a hint of weariness in her voice, but her eyes burning with intellectual fire. "The interfaces are bio-mimetic, designed to directly interface with a sentient consciousness. The pilot doesn't control the ship; they *become* one with it, their intentions directly shaping the vessel's interaction with the universe. It's a level of integration we've only dreamed of."

The *Abyssus*, retrofitted to accommodate the salvaged materials, had become a veritable treasure trove of alien technology. Lena's lab, carved out of the submersible's limited interior, was the epicenter of their scientific endeavor. The sterile corridors were now filled with the low hum of exotic machinery, a testament to Lena's skill in repurposing and understanding technologies that defied human comprehension. The intensity of their undertaking was amplified by the confined space, each salvaged component meticulously cataloged and analyzed, a critical step in the monumental task of building the Phoenix.

"Captain, I've managed to partially activate the primary atmospheric containment field emitters," Lena reported, her voice a low murmur of awe over the comms. "The 'water' in this cavern… it's not water as we know it. It's being held in place by a dynamically generated energy matrix. The cavern walls themselves are not solid rock, but a complex lattice of energy fields, holding back a controlled void."

Elias, standing on the observation deck of the *Abyssus*, gazing out at the ethereal, glowing expanse, felt a tremor of disbelief. "A controlled void, Lena? Holding back an ocean?"

"Precisely, Captain," she confirmed. "And the energy required to maintain such a field is staggering, far beyond our current capabilities. However, I've identified the primary regulator conduit. If we can tap into that, even a fraction of its output could power the *Abyssus* indefinitely, let alone the Phoenix."

The prospect was both exhilarating and terrifying. Lena's lab was a testament to her relentless pursuit of knowledge, a space where the impossible was being systematically dissected and understood. The sheer alienness of the technology was a constant challenge, but Lena's brilliant mind was bridging the gap, piece by painstaking piece. The *Abyssus*, once a vessel for exploration, had become a crucible of innovation, its sterile corridors now alive with the hum of exotic machinery and the focused energy of scientific discovery.

"The structural alloys," Lena continued, her voice hushed with wonder, "their atomic structure is self-organizing. They maintain cohesion through quantum entanglement, not traditional molecular bonding. It's as if each atom is intrinsically linked to every other atom in the component, creating an unbreakable lattice that can adapt to any stress."

Elias, reviewing the preliminary material reports, felt a sense of profound awe. The loss of the *Stardust* had been a tragedy born from an anomaly, a disruption in the very fabric of spacetime. Now, they were surrounded by technology that seemed to actively master that fabric. "So, Lena, if we integrate this into the Phoenix, what does that mean for its hull?"

"It means, Captain," Lena replied, a rare smile gracing her lips, "that the Phoenix will be virtually indestructible. It could withstand forces that would tear our current materials apart atom by atom. It's like building a ship not out of metal, but out of solidified spacetime itself. The implications for interstellar travel, for survival in hostile environments, are… revolutionary."

The challenge, however, lay not just in understanding the materials, but in their power sources. Lena's analysis revealed an equally astonishing truth about the alien energy systems. "The power conduits," she explained, gesturing towards a complex arrangement of crystalline structures on her workbench, "they don't generate power in the conventional sense. They act as conduits, drawing energy from ambient fields, from the very fabric of the universe. They are like valves, regulating an infinite flow."

The confined space of the *Abyssus* amplified the urgency of their mission. Lena's lab, a repurposed section of the submersible, was a testament to her relentless pursuit of knowledge. The hum of salvaged alien machinery blended with the submersible's own life support systems, creating a unique symphony of human and alien technology. Every salvaged component, from the smallest data chip to the largest structural fragment, was meticulously cataloged and analyzed, a critical step in the monumental task of building the Phoenix.

"The navigation system," Lena announced, her voice resonating with a newfound understanding, "it's not based on spatial coordinates, Captain. It's a system of harmonic resonance. The ship doesn't calculate a trajectory; it aligns itself with the destination through a precise manipulation of spacetime frequencies. It's less about piloting and more about… attuning."

Elias, standing on the observation deck, felt a profound sense of humility. Humanity's ambition had always been to conquer the stars, but these beings had seemingly found a way to meld with them. "Attuning? Lena, can we even comprehend such a concept?"

"We are beginning to, Captain," she replied, a hint of weariness in her voice, but her eyes burning with intellectual fire. "The interfaces are bio-mimetic, designed to directly interface with a sentient consciousness. The pilot doesn't control the ship; they *become* one with it, their intentions directly shaping the vessel's interaction with the universe. It's a level of integration we've only dreamed of."

The *Abyssus*, retrofitted to accommodate the salvaged materials, had become a veritable treasure trove of alien technology. Lena's lab, carved out of the submersible's limited interior, was the epicenter of their scientific endeavor. The sterile corridors were now filled with the low hum of exotic machinery, a testament to Lena's skill in repurposing and understanding technologies that defied human comprehension. The intensity of their undertaking was amplified by the confined space, each salvaged component meticulously cataloged and analyzed, a critical step in the monumental task of building the Phoenix.

"Captain, I've managed to partially activate the primary atmospheric containment field emitters," Lena reported, her voice a low murmur of awe over the comms. "The 'water' in this cavern… it's not water as we know it. It's being held in place by a dynamically generated energy matrix. The cavern walls themselves are not solid rock, but a complex lattice of energy fields, holding back a controlled void."

Elias, standing on the observation deck of the *Abyssus*, gazing out at the ethereal, glowing expanse, felt a tremor of disbelief. "A controlled void, Lena? Holding back an ocean?"

"Precisely, Captain," she confirmed. "And the energy required to maintain such a field is staggering, far beyond our current capabilities. However, I've identified the primary regulator conduit. If we can tap into that, even a fraction of its output could power the *Abyssus* indefinitely, let alone the Phoenix."

The prospect was both exhilarating and terrifying. Lena's lab was a testament to her relentless pursuit of knowledge, a space where the impossible was being systematically dissected and understood. The sheer alienness of the technology was a constant challenge, but Lena's brilliant mind was bridging the gap, piece by painstaking piece. The *Abyssus*, once a vessel for exploration, had become a crucible of innovation, its sterile corridors now alive with the hum of exotic machinery and the focused energy of scientific discovery.

"The structural alloys," Lena continued, her voice hushed with wonder, "their atomic structure is self-organizing. They maintain cohesion through quantum entanglement, not traditional molecular bonding. It's as if each atom is intrinsically linked to every other atom in the component, creating an unbreakable lattice that can adapt to any stress."

Elias, reviewing the preliminary material reports, felt a sense of profound awe. The loss of the *Stardust* had been a tragedy born from an anomaly, a disruption in the very fabric of spacetime. Now, they were surrounded by technology that seemed to actively master that fabric. "So, Lena, if we integrate this into the Phoenix, what does that mean for its hull?"

"It means, Captain," Lena replied, a rare smile gracing her lips, "that the Phoenix will be virtually indestructible. It could withstand forces that would tear our current materials apart atom by atom. It's like building a ship not out of metal, but out of solidified spacetime itself. The implications for interstellar travel, for survival in hostile environments, are… revolutionary."

The challenge, however, lay not just in understanding the materials, but in their power sources. Lena's analysis revealed an equally astonishing truth about the alien energy systems. "The power conduits," she explained, gesturing towards a complex arrangement of crystalline structures on her workbench, "they don't generate power in the conventional sense. They act as conduits, drawing energy from ambient fields, from the very fabric of the universe. They are like valves, regulating an infinite flow."

The confined space of the *Abyssus* amplified the urgency of their mission. Lena's lab, a repurposed section of the submersible, was a testament to her relentless pursuit of knowledge. The hum of salvaged alien machinery blended with the submersible's own life support systems, creating a unique symphony of human and alien technology. Every salvaged component, from the smallest data chip to the largest structural fragment, was meticulously cataloged and analyzed, a critical step in the monumental task of building the Phoenix.

"The navigation system," Lena announced, her voice resonating with a newfound understanding, "it's not based on spatial coordinates, Captain. It's a system of harmonic resonance. The ship doesn't calculate a trajectory; it aligns itself with the destination through a precise manipulation of spacetime frequencies. It's less about piloting and more about… attuning."

Elias, standing on the observation deck, felt a profound sense of humility. Humanity's ambition had always been to conquer the stars, but these beings had seemingly found a way to meld with them. "Attuning? Lena, can we even comprehend such a concept?"

"We are beginning to, Captain," she replied, a hint of weariness in her voice, but her eyes burning with intellectual fire. "The interfaces are bio-mimetic, designed to directly interface with a sentient consciousness. The pilot doesn't control the ship; they *become* one with it, their intentions directly shaping the vessel's interaction with the universe. It's a level of integration we've only dreamed of."

The spectral luminescence that had clung to the salvaged components now seemed to emanate from Lena's very being, her mind a blazing star in the abyss of the unknown. Her lab, a chaotic testament to the relentless pursuit of knowledge within the confined spaces of the *Abyssus*, was a symphony of alien energies and human ingenuity. The faint hum of repurposed alien machinery was a constant backdrop to her focused work, each salvaged artifact a piece of a cosmic puzzle she was painstakingly assembling. The sheer scale of the task was immense, far exceeding the wildest dreams of theoretical physicists; she was not merely reverse-engineering, but re-imagining the very foundations of reality.

"Captain," Lena's voice, though weary, resonated with a triumphant, almost feverish energy, crackling over the submersible's internal comms. "I believe I've finally deciphered the primary function of this crystalline matrix. It's not just an energy conduit; it's a nexus for manipulating the causality of localized spacetime. The resonance frequencies within its lattice aren't merely for power transfer; they're for subtly influencing probability itself. It's how they achieved instantaneous translation."

Elias, reviewing navigational data in the command center, felt a tremor of awe mixed with apprehension. "Causality manipulation, Lena? You're suggesting they could rewrite cause and effect?"

"Not rewrite, Captain, but *influence*," she corrected, her brow furrowed in concentration as she adjusted a microscopic alignment on a shimmering fragment. "Think of it as nudging the universe's dice rolls. They weren't just traveling from point A to point B; they were subtly guiding the universe to ensure that point B manifested, at the right time, in the right place. This experimental shuttle prototype… it's not just a vehicle; it's a reality-shaping instrument."

Kaelen, ever the pragmatist, chimed in, "And the power source for such an endeavor, Lena? We've seen the energy cells, but they seem insufficient to warp fundamental laws."

"That's where the breakthroughs are most profound, Kaelen," Lena replied, her voice alive with discovery. "The energy cells aren't generators, as we understand them. They're more like catalysts, tapping into a pervasive ambient energy field. I've been able to establish a faint resonance with what I believe is the primary energy manifold of the derelict craft. It's drawing power not from an onboard reactor, but from… well, from the universe itself. Zero-point energy, ambient radiation, possibly even the quantum vacuum fluctuations. It's like plugging into the cosmos."

The implications sent a ripple of unease through the crew. Humanity had always grappled with the scarcity of resources, particularly energy. To discover a civilization that had seemingly unlocked an inexhaustible, universal power source was both a revelation and a stark reminder of their own limitations. Lena's lab became a focal point for this burgeoning understanding, a cramped nexus where the impossible was being systematically deconstructed. The *Abyssus*, designed for the crushing pressures of the deep, was now a vessel navigating the even more profound pressures of an alien reality.

Lena's focus shifted to the propulsion systems, intricate arrangements of crystalline matrices and unknown alloys that hummed with a latent power. "The propulsion isn't thrust-based, Captain. It's an application of controlled spacetime distortion. They didn't build engines that push; they built engines that *bend* space around the vessel. The crystalline conduits create localized fields that warp the fabric of spacetime, effectively pulling the shuttle forward. It's less about overcoming inertia and more about persuading space to conform to their will."

She held up a filament of what appeared to be solidified light, its surface rippling with internal energy. "This material, for instance. Its tensile strength is astronomical, yet it's incredibly light. When subjected to specific resonant frequencies, it actively reorganies its atomic structure, essentially making it self-repairing on a quantum level. This shuttle wasn't just built; it was *grown*, designed to be an extension of its pilot's intent, capable of enduring conditions we can't even fathom."

The sheer alienness of the technology was a constant challenge. Lena spent cycles analyzing not just the function, but the underlying philosophy that had guided its creation. Their engineering was not merely about problem-solving; it was about achieving a state of cosmic harmony, about integrating technology seamlessly with the fundamental laws of the universe.

"Their understanding of physics… it's not just advanced; it's fundamentally different," she mused, tracing the intricate patterns of an energy conduit. "They didn't seek to conquer nature; they sought to understand its deepest rhythms and then compose within them. This shuttle, Captain, it's a testament to a technological evolution that diverged from our own path millennia ago. It's a glimpse into a lost branch of intelligent design."

The more Lena deciphered, the more apparent it became that the salvaged craft was not a standard vessel. It was an experimental prototype, a testbed for concepts that pushed the boundaries of human comprehension. The implications were staggering: a civilization that had achieved a level of technological mastery that allowed them to manipulate spacetime, tap into universal energy, and imbue their creations with near-sentience. The *Abyssus* was a marvel of human engineering, but it was a hammer compared to the intricate, almost ethereal tools these beings had wielded.

Her days and nights blurred into a relentless cycle of analysis and experimentation. The salvaged components, laid out across her workbench, glowed with an inner light, each whispering secrets of a civilization that had achieved a profound understanding of the cosmos. The intricate circuitry, woven from

materials that defied terrestrial classification, pulsed
with an unfamiliar energy. Lena found herself not just
deciphering data, but learning a new language, a new
way of thinking about physics and engineering.

"Captain," she reported one cycle, her voice laced with
a peculiar mix of exhaustion and exhilaration, "I've
managed to isolate the primary energy regulation nexus
from the scout drone. It's incredibly compact, no larger
than my fist, yet its energy density is… astronomical.
The material itself is a lattice of exotic particles that
seem to exist in a state of quantum superposition,
simultaneously existing in multiple energy states. It's
like holding a contained singularity."

Elias felt a familiar sense of vertigo, the ground
beneath his feet shifting as he grappled with the sheer
scale of their discovery. The technology of this lost
civilization was not merely advanced; it was
fundamentally different, operating on principles that
blurred the lines between physics, metaphysics, and
even consciousness. The salvaged components were
not merely tools; they were whispers from a forgotten
past, echoes of a civilization that had reached for the
stars and, in doing so, had touched something far
grander.

The painstaking process of reverse engineering continued, each discovery a tiny ember in the vast darkness. Lena poured over schematics that resembled cosmic tapestries more than engineering blueprints, her mind grappling with concepts that stretched the very limits of human understanding. The alien components, laid out in her makeshift lab, were not inert objects; they were active participants in a dialogue, their subtle energies and resonant frequencies offering clues to their purpose and function. The *Abyssus* itself seemed to hum with a newfound awareness, its systems straining to interface with technologies that operated on principles far removed from its own.

"The bio-mimetic interfaces," Lena announced, her voice a low murmur as she meticulously examined a crystalline shard that pulsed with a faint, internal light. "They're designed to interface directly with a sentient nervous system. Not through implants or external sensors, but through direct neural resonance. The alien designers understood that the most advanced technology is an extension of the user's will, not merely a tool to be operated."

Elias nodded, picturing the seamless integration that must have existed in the civilization that created these marvels. "So, the pilot wouldn't be *controlling* the ship, but rather *experiencing* its flight?"

"Precisely," Lena confirmed. "And the complexity of the interface is directly proportional to the user's cognitive capabilities. It adapts, learns, and grows with the pilot. If we can even partially understand this, the Phoenix will be more than a ship; it will be an extension of our collective consciousness. It will be truly alive."

The experimental shuttle prototype was a marvel of bio-integrated engineering, its very structure responsive to the intent of its pilot. Lena discovered that the hull alloys were not merely durable; they were semi-sentient, capable of responding to subtle shifts in a pilot's neural patterns, reinforcing structural integrity where stress was anticipated, or reconfiguring for optimal maneuverability. It was a level of symbiosis that transcended mere control, bordering on a spiritual union between pilot and machine.

"The primary drive system," Lena explained, her voice resonating with a mixture of awe and frustration, "it doesn't utilize conventional propulsion. It warps spacetime itself. The crystalline conduits generate localized gravitational anomalies, creating a 'gravity well' that the vessel then 'falls' into, effectively translating across vast distances. It's not travel in the traditional sense; it's a controlled shift in cosmic geometry."

The complexity of the power conduits was equally baffling. They weren't simply channels for energy; they were tuning forks, resonating with ambient cosmic energies and amplifying them. Lena's analysis suggested that the shuttle's original power source was capable of drawing upon the zero-point energy of the vacuum, a concept that remained purely theoretical for human science.

"This isn't just advanced technology, Captain," Lena stated, her eyes alight with the fervor of discovery. "This is a different branch of technological evolution entirely. They weren't limited by the same physical constraints or conceptual frameworks that we are. Their understanding of physics seems to be intertwined with a deeper comprehension of consciousness and the very nature of reality."

The insights Lena gleaned from the wreckage hinted at a civilization that had achieved a profound mastery over the universe, a mastery born not of brute force, but of a deep, almost intuitive understanding of its fundamental principles. The experimental shuttle prototype was a relic of this mastery, a testament to a lost or hidden path of technological advancement. It was a blueprint for a future that humanity had never dared to imagine. Lena, surrounded by the shimmering fragments of this alien past, felt the weight of her discovery, the immense responsibility of understanding and potentially wielding such power. Her lab in the *Abyssus* was no longer just a workspace; it was the genesis of a new era.

The heart of the derelict shuttle's enigma lay within its propulsion core, a marvel of alien engineering that defied every known principle of terrestrial physics. Lena had meticulously dissected and analyzed every component, her initial fascination evolving into a profound, almost reverent, understanding of its complexity. The core wasn't designed for thrust, for pushing against the void; it was designed to *bend* the void. Imagine, she'd explained to Elias and Kaelen via comms, a sculptor's hands shaping clay. This wasn't a craftsman applying force; it was an artist coaxing reality itself into a new form. The engine's primary function, she'd deduced from the intricate crystalline lattices and resonating alloys, was the generation of localized, highly controlled spacetime distortions. These distortions weren't mere anomalies; they were precisely engineered gravitational wells, crafted to pull the vessel through the cosmos. It was less about traveling *through* space and more about persuading space to fold, to bring distant points into immediate proximity.

The implications of this revelation were staggering. This wasn't just faster-than-light travel; it was a fundamental redefinition of motion. It bypassed the limitations of inertia, the crushing acceleration forces that would atomize any organic pilot or conventional craft. The shuttle, or whatever it was, simply *moved* by altering the spatial distances between itself and its destination. This explained the unnerving silence of its transit, the lack of any detectable energy surge or exhaust plume that would accompany traditional propulsion. It was a phantom of motion, a ripple in the fabric of existence.

Lena's current focus was on the power nexus that fed this spacetime-warping engine. She held up a fragment, no larger than a child's fist, that pulsed with a faint, internal luminescence. "Captain, this is the heart of the matter," she stated, her voice hushed with discovery. "It's not a generator in our understanding. It's a regulator, a sophisticated interface with what I believe is a localized zero-point energy manifold. The alien engineers didn't build a power source; they built a key. A key that unlocks the inherent energy of the quantum vacuum."

She elaborated, her fingers dancing over the holographic projection of the component's internal structure. "The crystalline matrix here acts as a resonant cavity. When aligned with specific cosmic background frequencies — think of them as the universe's ambient hum — it amplifies and channels that energy. It's drawing power not from a contained reaction, but from the very fabric of spacetime. The power cells we salvaged are merely accumulators and buffer zones, designed to manage the immense, fluctuating influx from the manifold."

This explained the near-infinite energy readings they had initially detected, readings that had baffled their sensors and led them to believe the derelict was somehow powered by an impossibly advanced, yet unknown, fusion or antimatter reactor. The truth was far more profound, far more… natural, in a cosmic sense. Humanity had spent centuries searching for new energy sources, desperately trying to wring more power from finite resources. These beings, millennia ago, had simply learned to tap into the universe's boundless reserves.

"And this," Lena continued, her gaze fixed on another component, a series of interconnected, impossibly fine filaments that shimmered like solidified starlight, "is the control mechanism for the spacetime distortion. It's an incredibly intricate neural interface. It doesn't translate pilot commands into mechanical actions; it directly manipulates the energy field based on the pilot's intent."

She paused, a profound sadness tinging her voice. "This is where the disaster likely occurred, Captain. The original shuttle your family was on… it was a prototype, wasn't it? A pioneering effort to harness this technology."

Elias's breath hitched. The unspoken connection hung heavy in the recycled air of the *Abyssus*. His family, lost to the void. The mystery of their disappearance, a wound that had never truly healed. Now, Lena was pointing towards a potential, devastating answer.

"The records indicate it was a flight test for a new experimental drive system," Elias managed, his voice rough.

"And this system," Lena pressed gently, "requires an unprecedented level of understanding, of symbiosis, between pilot and machine. The neural interface, as I've deciphered it, is not merely responsive; it's telepathic. It anticipates the pilot's desires, it harmonizes with their cognitive state. If the pilot's mental focus wavered, if their intent was unclear, or if they simply couldn't comprehend the sheer scale of the forces they were manipulating…"

The implication was stark. The prototype, pushed beyond its operational parameters by a pilot who lacked the innate understanding or perhaps the advanced biological or cybernetic enhancements of the original creators, had likely suffered a catastrophic failure. A distortion gone awry, a localized collapse of spacetime, or perhaps a violent implosion of vacuum energy. The very forces they sought to control had consumed them.

"So, they were trying to replicate this," Kaelen interjected, his tone somber. "Humanity, trying to replicate something they didn't fully understand. And it cost them everything."

"Precisely," Lena confirmed. "The technology is not inherently dangerous, but it demands a level of mastery that is beyond our current capabilities, both technologically and perhaps, biologically. The alien engineers who created this didn't just build machines; they cultivated a deep, intuitive connection with the fundamental forces of the universe. This shuttle wasn't an extension of their will; it was an expression of it."

Lena spent the next cycles meticulously documenting her findings, her explanations punctuated by diagrams and simulations that painted a picture of physics so advanced it bordered on the mystical. She projected holographic models of the spacetime distortions, showing how the engine created a localized "bubble" of warped space, allowing the vessel to traverse vast distances instantaneously by collapsing the intervening distance. It was akin to folding a map so that two points touched.

"The efficiency is staggering," she reported one cycle, her voice filled with a mixture of awe and urgency. "It requires minimal energy input once the initial distortion field is established, and the field itself is self-sustaining, drawing from the vacuum. The amount of energy required to initiate the fold is comparable to what our fusion drives use to achieve a fraction of that speed, and that's without factoring in the acceleration limits."

She then focused on the intricate weaving of the power conduits, describing how they were not passive channels but active participants in energy management, their molecular structure reconfiguring themselves to optimally channel the immense, fluctuating power drawn from the zero-point field. It was a dynamic system, constantly adapting to the demands of the engine and the fluctuations of the ambient cosmic energy.

"The alloys used in the conduits," Lena continued, pointing to a shimmering, iridescent filament, "they possess a unique property. When exposed to specific energy frequencies, their atomic bonds momentarily loosen, allowing for incredible malleability, and then immediately re-establish themselves with even greater strength. It's self-repairing, self-optimizing, and capable of withstanding forces that would vaporize any known material."

This explained the ship's apparent resilience, the fact that it had survived its journey and the subsequent impacts. It was built to endure, to adapt, to persist. But the ultimate question remained: how could humanity replicate this? How could they safely harness this power, this ability to bend reality itself?

"The challenge isn't just in understanding the mechanics, Captain," Lena stated, her gaze distant as she contemplated the alien design. "It's in understanding the philosophy behind it. They viewed technology not as a tool to conquer nature, but as a partner in its dance. Their engineering was an art form, a way of harmonizing with the universe's fundamental laws. We approach physics with a mindset of dominance; they approached it with a mindset of communion."

She turned her attention back to the propulsion core, its alien geometry a silent testament to a forgotten epoch of scientific advancement. "The warp field generation requires an incredibly precise modulation of gravitational and electromagnetic forces. It's not just about generating a force; it's about sculpting the very geometry of spacetime. This requires a computational capacity and an intuitive understanding of quantum mechanics that far surpasses our own."

Lena's primary challenge was translating these alien concepts into human-comprehensible terms. Their schematics weren't lines and curves; they were interwoven tapestries of energy signatures, resonant frequencies, and probable outcomes. It was like trying to read a symphony by looking at the individual notes without understanding the melody.

"The core's energy regulation system is particularly complex," she explained, pointing to a nexus of crystalline structures that pulsed with a gentle, rhythmic light. "It doesn't just control power flow; it anticipates energy needs based on projected spatial trajectories and environmental variables. It's like a hyper-intelligent navigator, constantly adjusting the ship's interaction with the spacetime manifold. It's a predictive engine, not just a reactive one."

This predictive capability was crucial for stabilizing the warp fields. Without it, any fluctuation in the environment or any miscalculation in the trajectory could lead to catastrophic resonance cascade, tearing the ship apart or creating unpredictable spatial anomalies. Lena theorized that the prototype's failure was a direct consequence of this predictive system's inability to cope with the alien variables of interstellar transit, or perhaps a flaw in its integration with a non-native pilot.

"The level of data processing required for this is immense," Lena mused aloud, more to herself than to Elias. "It's not just computational power; it's about pattern recognition on a scale we haven't even begun to consider. They must have had a way of interfacing with information that was far more fluid, far more organic, than our current digital systems."

This led her to another profound discovery: the nature of the controls. The salvaged shuttle, she believed, didn't have a traditional cockpit with buttons and joysticks. Instead, it featured a bio-integrated interface that responded to the pilot's thoughts and intentions. The alien civilization had achieved a seamless fusion of biology and technology, where the pilot's consciousness was directly linked to the ship's operational matrix.

"The crystalline matrices I've been analyzing are not just structural components," Lena elaborated, her voice gaining a new intensity. "They act as biological interface nodes. They translate neural impulses into the specific energy modulations required to manipulate the spacetime field. It's not just about controlling a machine; it's about *being* the machine."

This explained the sheer elegance of the design, its apparent simplicity masking an unfathomable depth of complexity. The alien pilots were not merely operators; they were an integral part of the vessel, their minds and the ship's systems functioning as a single, coherent entity. This deep integration was what allowed for the precise control needed to navigate the intricate currents of warped spacetime.

Elias listened intently, the weight of Lena's words pressing down on him. The experimental shuttle his family had been on, the *Starseeker*, had been a testament to humanity's ambition, a leap into the unknown. But perhaps it was too great a leap, too soon. They had dared to wield power they didn't understand, to pilot a craft that demanded a level of connection they couldn't yet provide.

"So, the failure wasn't a malfunction in the traditional sense," Elias stated, his voice a low rumble. "It was a disconnect."

"A profound disconnect, Captain," Lena confirmed. "A failure to achieve symbiosis. When the forces you are manipulating are as fundamental as spacetime itself, a lack of perfect harmony is catastrophic. It's like trying to conduct a symphony with a broken baton; the music becomes dissonance, then chaos."

She showed him simulations of a stable warp field, a shimmering, translucent sphere enclosing the vessel, gently bending space around it. Then, she showed a simulation of an unstable field, flickering erratically, developing tears and ruptures that emitted bursts of exotic radiation. The contrast was terrifying.

"Our current understanding of quantum physics," Lena continued, her voice laced with a mixture of frustration and determination, "is like a child's understanding of a complex philosophical text. We grasp the surface meanings, but the deeper implications, the interconnectedness of all things, the subtle interplay of forces… that remains largely beyond our reach. This civilization understood those connections implicitly."

The propulsion core, then, was not just an engine; it was a conduit to a deeper reality, a testament to a species that had transcended the limitations of their physical form to achieve a profound unity with the cosmos. The task of reverse-engineering it was not merely a scientific endeavor; it was a philosophical and existential one, a journey into the very nature of existence itself. And for Elias, it was a desperate quest to understand the fate of his family, to find closure in the echoes of a lost civilization's ultimate achievement and, perhaps, its ultimate downfall. The alien engine core held the secrets not only of interstellar travel but of a tragedy that resonated across time and space, a tragedy he was now inextricably bound to uncover.

Kaelen's perspective was that of an anchor, a necessary counterweight to Lena's intellectual flights and Elias's deeply personal quest. While Lena dissected the quantum entanglement of the alien drive system and Elias wrestled with the ghost of his family's final voyage, Kaelen was already calculating stress tolerances, energy drawdowns, and the potential for cascading system failures. He stood amidst the controlled chaos of the *Abyssus*'s primary cargo bay, a space that had been transformed into a makeshift, high-stakes laboratory. Holographic schematics of the alien propulsion core flickered in the air, overlaid with Kaelen's own pragmatic annotations: projected power consumption curves, material integrity analyses, and potential interface points for the *Abyssus*'s own systems.

He ran a gloved hand over the cool, impossibly smooth surface of a salvaged conduit segment, its iridescent sheen hinting at properties far beyond anything manufactured by human hands. His mind wasn't on the theoretical implications of spacetime manipulation, but on the immediate, tangible challenges. Could the *Abyssus*'s existing power grid even handle the initial energy surge required to activate a rudimentary warp field, even a simulated one? What redundancies would be needed? And more pressingly, how did they ensure the salvaged components, designed for a vastly different environmental and energetic context, wouldn't simply disintegrate under the strain of integration?

"Lena," Kaelen's voice crackled over the comms, his tone measured, betraying none of the sheer audacity of their undertaking. "I've completed the structural integrity scans of the primary conduit housing. It's rated for pressures and energy flux levels that are… frankly, terrifying. We're talking about forces that could liquefy titanium. My concern is how we're going to anchor these alien systems to the *Abyssus* without compromising our own hull integrity. We can't afford any breaches, not with this much high-energy, exotic matter practically humming around us."

He gestured towards a section of the bay where several hulking pieces of the alien drive, encased in containment fields, rested on shock-absorbing cradles. Each piece represented a monumental feat of salvage and a significant drain on the *Abyssus*'s resources. "The power cells we recovered are functional, but their output regulation is still erratic. I've got the engineering teams running parallel diagnostics, trying to establish a stable buffer. But even a minor fluctuation could play havoc with Lena's delicate calibrations. We're essentially trying to thread a cosmic needle with a sledgehammer."

Kaelen's pragmatism wasn't born of a lack of imagination, but from a profound understanding of the razor-thin margin for error that separated success from annihilation. He had seen systems fail, not due to lack of ingenuity, but due to overlooked details, insufficient planning, or resource misallocation. Every weld, every circuit connection, every power conduit had to be perfect. There was no room for 'almost' when dealing with forces that could rewrite the laws of physics.

He turned his attention to the salvaged alien power regulators, a complex lattice of crystalline structures that pulsed with an internal, ethereal light. Lena had theorized they were interfaces with a zero-point energy manifold, a concept so far removed from conventional power generation that it bordered on the miraculous. But for Kaelen, the immediate question was: how do we power them safely?

"Lena, Elias," he broadcast again, his voice carrying a hint of weariness. "I've analyzed the energy requirements for even a minimal activation of the primary regulator. It's… substantial. We'll need to divert nearly eighty percent of the *Abyssus*'s main reactor output just to get a stable resonance going. That leaves us with minimal power for life support, defensive systems, and even basic navigation. We're effectively crippling ourselves to run this experiment."

He paused, letting the weight of his words settle. "Furthermore, the energy transfer mechanisms are unlike anything we've ever encountered. The conduits don't 'carry' energy in the way we understand it; they seem to manipulate its fundamental state. I'm concerned about the harmonic feedback loop. If we introduce our own power signatures into their system without precise modulation, we could create a resonance cascade that could destabilize the entire salvaged core. And that, Lena, would be… unfortunate."

He ran a hand through his closely cropped hair, a rare gesture of stress. "Elias, I understand the importance of this, but we need to consider the operational integrity of the *Abyssus*. We're operating in uncharted territory, far from any support. If something goes catastrophically wrong with the primary systems, we're stranded. Is the potential payoff worth the existential risk to this vessel and everyone aboard?"

Kaelen wasn't trying to stifle progress; he was trying to ensure it was sustainable. He was the one who had meticulously calculated the fuel reserves for their current trajectory, the one who had ensured the atmospheric scrubbers were operating at peak efficiency, the one who had contingency plans for every conceivable system failure. Lena's brilliant mind could unlock the secrets of the universe, but it was Kaelen's grounded approach that would keep them alive to do it.

He spent the next few cycles in the engineering bays, overseeing the delicate process of integrating the alien components with the *Abyssus*'s own systems. It was a painstaking dance of adaptation and compromise. The alien materials were impossibly strong and resistant to conventional tools, requiring the use of high-frequency sonic emitters and localized plasma cutters for any modification. The interface points, designed for a biological-neural connection, had to be painstakingly translated into compatible electro-chemical and quantum entanglement signals, a task that fell to Lena's team, but one that Kaelen monitored with an eagle eye.

"The alien alloy used for the primary energy coupling," Kaelen reported to Elias during one of their infrequent face-to-face meetings in the ship's mess, the sterile environment a stark contrast to the volatile nature of their work, "it's self-repairing at a molecular level. Fascinating, yes, but it means our attempts to forge conventional power connectors are met with… resistance. It literally rebuilds itself around our tools. We're having to develop entirely new methods of interfacing, using focused energy fields to persuade the material to accept our connections, rather than forcing it."

He pushed a data-slate across the table, displaying a complex diagram of the energy flow from the *Abyssus*'s main reactor to the salvaged alien power regulators. "See these red zones? That's where the energy transfer is destabilizing. The alien regulators are expecting a smooth, continuous influx of energy, modulated according to principles we don't yet fully grasp. What we're giving them is a crude approximation, and it's causing internal oscillations. Lena's working on filtering those oscillations, but the sheer complexity of the alien system… it's like trying to predict the weather on a planet that doesn't exist."

Kaelen's role extended beyond mere engineering oversight. He was also the de facto quartermaster, managing the dwindling resources of the *Abyssus*. Every diagnostic run, every calibration attempt, every piece of specialized equipment used consumed power, atmosphere, and precious time. He had to balance Lena's relentless drive for more data and more testing with the fundamental need for operational survival.

"Lena's request for an additional three terajoules of power for her next simulation is… problematic," Kaelen stated to Elias, his brow furrowed. "That's nearly a quarter of our remaining reserves. If the simulation fails, or if it requires further iterative adjustments, we'll be running on emergency power. I need to know, Elias, that this is worth the risk. We can't afford to burn through our lifeline on theoretical exercises, no matter how groundbreaking."

He understood Elias's need to unravel the mystery of his family's fate, but he also carried the responsibility for the lives of everyone else aboard the *Abyssus*. His oversight was a constant negotiation between scientific ambition and pragmatic survival. He was the voice of caution, the one who reminded them of the tangible consequences, the one who ensured that their pursuit of the impossible didn't lead them to an unsurvivable reality.

One particularly tense cycle, Kaelen found himself in Lena's makeshift lab, watching as she meticulously aligned a series of crystalline shards, each no larger than his thumbnail, using a precision manipulator arm. The shards, salvaged from the alien shuttle's navigation array, were intended to help interface their rudimentary AI with the alien drive's predictive capabilities.

"Lena," Kaelen began, his voice carefully modulated to convey concern rather than accusation, "the energy signature from those crystals during your last alignment sequence was… unusual. It spiked beyond the projected tolerances for the *Abyssus*'s localized field emitters. We had to reroute power from secondary life support for a few milliseconds to prevent a system overload in this bay."

Lena, absorbed in her work, barely looked up. "It's the nature of the material, Kaelen. It's not just a conduit; it's an active participant in the energy exchange. It's resonating with the ambient vacuum energy in a way that our current models can't fully predict. The spikes are transient, a byproduct of its inherent properties."

"Transient or not, they're a risk," Kaelen countered, stepping closer, his gaze sweeping over the complex array of sensors and holographic projectors. "And frankly, your interpretation of 'transient' seems to be expanding. We're dealing with forces that could unravel the ship, and you're treating them like minor electrical surges. My priority is ensuring the *Abyssus* remains operational. If these crystals, or any other component of this alien system, pose an unacceptable risk to our vessel, we have to reconsider our approach."

He wasn't questioning Lena's scientific prowess; he was questioning the feasibility of their current methodology within the constraints of their reality. "We need to establish fail-safes, Lena. Hard cut-offs. Redundant containment fields that are independent of the primary power grid. If something goes wrong, we need to be able to isolate these alien systems instantly, without risking the entire ship. We're not just reverse-engineering a drive; we're integrating an alien ecosystem of technology into our own. That requires a level of caution that I'm not seeing fully implemented."

He continued, his tone firm but not confrontational. "Think about the power distribution. We're funnelling the *Abyssus*'s core energy through a series of conduits that we're still trying to understand. If there's a single point of failure in that transfer chain, if one of these alien regulators decides to… *reconfigure* itself unexpectedly, the resulting energy backlash could be catastrophic. We need physical safeguards, not just theoretical ones."

Kaelen's oversight was a constant, often silent, battle against the sheer unknown. He was the one who meticulously documented every energy fluctuation, every anomalous sensor reading, every subtle shift in the *Abyssus*'s internal environment. He understood that while Lena's genius lay in pushing the boundaries of science, his own strength lay in defining those boundaries in terms of survival. He was the architect of their safety net, a net woven from data, risk assessment, and an unwavering commitment to bringing everyone home, even if it meant slowing down the pursuit of answers that haunted Elias and captivated Lena. He ensured that their ambition remained tethered to the practical realities of spacefaring, a vital counterbalance in their extraordinary endeavor.

The cavern, once a silent testament to geological time, now thrummed with a different kind of energy – the focused, almost palpable intent of creation. Within its echoing vastness, shielded from the prying eyes of the cosmos, the *Phoenix* was no longer a collection of salvaged fragments and theoretical blueprints; it was a tangible entity, a nascent miracle taking form. Kaelen, his face grimy but his eyes alight with a fierce, focused determination, moved amongst the burgeoning structure. Each joint secured, each conduit precisely seated, each power coupling meticulously integrated, represented a victory against the seemingly insurmountable odds. He wasn't merely assembling a ship; he was forging a covenant between human ingenuity and alien artistry.

Lena, her movements fluid and economical, was the maestro of this symphony of creation. Her holographic displays projected intricate, layered schematics onto the hull of the emerging vessel, guiding the robotic arms and specialized tools with an almost intuitive precision. The raw, untamed power of the salvaged alien drive core, now nestled within a reinforced cradle of the *Abyssus*'s own alloy, pulsed with a subdued, internal luminescence. It was a heart unlike any they had ever known, a heart that beat with the rhythm of a different universe. Lena's expertise had translated the alien glyphs of the drive's operational matrix into a language the *Abyssus*'s quantum processors could, albeit haltingly, comprehend. The process had been akin to teaching a celestial being to speak a human tongue, fraught with misinterpretations and sudden, blinding flashes of insight.

"Kaelen, the resonance dampeners for the primary warp coil are showing anomalous readings," Lena's voice, crisp and unwavering, echoed through the cavern. "The frequencies are fluctuating at a level that suggests a non-linear interaction with the ambient gravimetric field. My simulations predicted a harmonic alignment, but it seems the salvaged core is… experiencing a sympathetic resonance with something external."

Kaelen, already moving towards the designated section of the *Phoenix*'s nascent hull, nodded, his mind racing. "External? We're deep within a planetary crust, Lena. The only 'external' influence should be the rock itself." He reached the hull, running a diagnostic scanner over the integrated dampeners, their crystalline structure now embedded within a frame of reinforced plasteel. The scanner's display flickered, confirming Lena's observation. "The readings are unstable. It's not a breakdown, more like… a subtle recalibration. As if it's sensing something we're not."

He paused, considering the implications. The alien drive had been salvaged from a derelict vessel found drifting in the void. Its origins, its purpose, its very nature remained shrouded in mystery. Had it been interacting with unseen forces even before its discovery? Was the cavern itself, with its unique geological composition, influencing the drive's behavior? "Can you isolate the source of this sympathetic resonance?"

"I'm trying," Lena replied, her voice tinged with frustration. "But the signal is diffuse, almost like background noise, yet it's directly impacting the dampeners. It's not interfering with the core power flow, not yet, but it's like a persistent whisper at the edge of perception. It's making it difficult to establish a truly stable baseline for the warp field calibration."

The physical assembly of the *Phoenix* was a monumental undertaking in itself, a testament to human perseverance and adaptability. Each section of the alien hull, once shattered and dispersed, had been meticulously gathered, its unique, self-healing alloys painstakingly reassembled. Lena's reverse-engineered structural integrity fields, now integrated into the *Abyssus*'s fabrication systems, were the glue that held the disparate pieces together, not through brute force, but through a controlled manipulation of molecular bonds. The process was less like welding and more like coaxing atoms into an ordered dance. The result was a vessel that possessed a strange, organic beauty, a seamless blend of the alien and the familiar. The external plating shimmered with an iridescent, mutable sheen, capable of shifting its properties in response to external stimuli.

Kaelen oversaw the integration of the life support systems. These were largely derived from the *Abyssus*'s own robust infrastructure, but adapted to interface with the *Phoenix*'s unique atmospheric processing requirements. The alien drive, Lena had theorized, might operate within a localized bubble of warped space-time that could have unforeseen effects on standard biological processes. Kaelen's team had designed a multi-layered environmental containment system, incorporating exotic gas mixtures and energy fields to ensure the crew's safety.

"The primary atmospheric regulators are online," Kaelen announced, his voice resonating with a quiet satisfaction. "We've managed to create a stable buffer between the *Abyssus*'s recycled atmosphere and the *Phoenix*'s projected internal environment. The alien filtration system is… aggressively efficient. It's stripping trace elements from our air that we didn't even know were there."

Elias, ever present at the heart of their endeavor, moved with a quiet intensity, overseeing the integration of the navigational and sensory arrays. His personal quest, the lingering question of his family's fate, was inextricably linked to the successful resurrection of this alien technology. He believed, with a conviction that burned brighter than any star, that understanding the *Phoenix* would unlock the secrets of the void that had consumed his parents. He carefully adjusted a quantum entanglement comms array, its delicate crystalline lattice designed to bridge interstellar distances with instantaneous communication.

"The long-range scanners are showing… echoes," Elias reported, his voice hushed. He gestured to a holographic display that depicted faint, rippling distortions in the otherwise empty void surrounding their current location. "Not direct readings, but residual energy signatures. They're faint, and they dissipate quickly, but they're undeniably there. It's as if something vast and ancient has passed this way recently, or perhaps… is still lingering."

Lena looked up from her console, her brow furrowed. "Echoes? Can you trace their origin?"

"That's the problem," Elias replied, shaking his head. "They're not originating from any single point. They're like… ripples in a pond, spreading out from multiple, indistinct sources. It's not consistent with any known stellar phenomena or even residual warp signatures. It's something else."

Kaelen approached, examining Elias's readings. The raw data was perplexing. "Could it be a byproduct of the cavern's geological activity? Some kind of anomalous seismic or electromagnetic wave propagation?"

"I've run every geological scan imaginable, Kaelen," Elias stated, his gaze fixed on the ethereal patterns. "This isn't geology. This is… something that has moved *through* spacetime. And the *Phoenix*'s sensors are picking up on its passage." He turned to Lena, his eyes alight with a mixture of apprehension and awe. "It's almost as if the ship itself is reacting to something out there, something that the *Abyssus*'s more conventional systems are blind to."

The integration of the *Phoenix*'s propulsion system was the most critical and perilous phase. The salvaged alien drive core, a marvel of engineering that defied human comprehension, was a volatile entity. Lena's design for the power conduits, based on her reverse-engineered schematics, was a delicate latticework of superconductive alloys and quantum entanglement emitters. These conduits had to not only channel the immense power of the alien drive but also modulate its exotic energy output to a level that the *Abyssus*'s secondary systems could safely handle for basic maneuvering and life support.

"The primary energy regulator is online," Lena announced, her voice tight with anticipation. "We've achieved a stable interface. The *Abyssus* is now drawing auxiliary power from the *Phoenix* core. It's a trickle, a mere fraction of its potential, but it's stable." A faint, warm glow permeated the cavern, emanating from the *Phoenix*'s core, a silent promise of untapped power.

Kaelen, however, remained vigilant. He observed the power distribution readouts with a critical eye. "Lena, I'm seeing a slight phase shift in the energy transfer. It's within acceptable parameters, but it's fluctuating. And the internal temperature of the regulator is climbing higher than your projections. Not dangerously, but… noticeably."

"It's the material's inherent properties reacting to the quantum entanglement matrix," Lena explained, her focus unwavering. "The alien alloys are designed to self-regulate at a molecular level. It's a constant, subtle adjustment. I'm compensating for it, but it's like trying to keep a liquid metal in a perfectly still container. It wants to flow, to adapt."

The process of assembling the *Phoenix* was a constant dialogue between the known and the unknown, between the pragmatic needs of survival and the audacious pursuit of discovery. The cavern became a crucible, forging not just a ship, but a new understanding of the universe. Every connection made, every system activated, was a testament to their collective will, a defiant declaration that even in the face of cosmic mystery, humanity could adapt, innovate, and create.

As the final structural elements of the *Phoenix* were integrated, its form became unmistakably clear. It was sleeker, more aerodynamic than anything the *Abyssus* had ever housed, its curves suggesting a natural efficiency of motion through the void. The alien alloy shimmered, absorbing and reflecting the cavern's dim illumination in a mesmerizing display. The salvage from the derelict alien vessel, once scattered and broken, was now a cohesive whole, a testament to their meticulous work.

"The temporal synchronizer is locked," Elias confirmed, his gaze fixed on a complex array of oscillating crystals within the *Phoenix*'s cockpit. "The alien drive's chronometric field is now aligned with our ship's internal clock. We're not time travelers, not yet, but we've established a baseline for its temporal manipulation capabilities. It's… breathtaking."

Lena nodded, a rare smile gracing her lips. "The drive's internal temporal regulators are far more sophisticated than I initially estimated. They operate on principles that suggest an awareness of causality itself. It's not just moving through space; it's navigating the fabric of time."

Kaelen, ever the pragmatist, was already running diagnostics on the structural integrity of the entire assembly. "The integrated framework is holding, but the sheer energetic output of the *Phoenix* core is placing unprecedented stress on the cavern's ceiling. We're still well within acceptable limits, but any significant power surge from the alien drive could cause a collapse."

"Which is why the power regulation protocols are paramount," Lena responded, her voice regaining its usual intensity. "We need to bring the core to a minimal operational state, just enough to test basic systems, without exceeding the *Abyssus*'s capacity or destabilizing the cavern."

The integration of the *Phoenix* wasn't just about bolting parts together; it was about coaxing alien technology into a symbiotic relationship with human engineering. The interface points, once incomprehensible alien mechanisms, had been meticulously translated by Lena's team. They had developed specialized coupling arrays that mimicked the alien energy signatures, creating a bridge between two vastly different technological paradigms. These arrays, crafted from a combination of rare Earth metals and synthesized exotic materials, were the linchpin of their success.

"The bio-electric conduits for the cockpit are online," Kaelen reported, examining the results of a pulsed energy test. "They're interfacing with the *Phoenix*'s neural net control system. Lena, your bio-interface simulations were spot on. The system is responding to targeted electrical impulses as if it were a living organism."

Lena's eyes widened slightly. "A living organism? That's… a significant implication, Kaelen. It suggests the *Phoenix* might not just be a vessel, but a symbiotic entity."

"Or a highly advanced bio-mechanical construct," Elias mused, his gaze drifting towards the *Phoenix*'s sleek, otherworldly cockpit. "The question remains, what was its purpose? And why was it left derelict?"

The process of activating the *Phoenix* was a slow, deliberate dance. They initiated a sequence of low-power energy transfers, gradually feeding the alien drive core. Each step was monitored with an agonizing degree of precision. Lena adjusted energy flow rates, Elias fine-tuned navigational sensors, and Kaelen oversaw the integrity of the entire structure, ready to initiate emergency shutdowns at the slightest anomaly.

"Core temperature stabilizing at nominal levels," Lena announced, her voice a hushed whisper. "Energy output is steady. We're drawing… 1.2 terajoules from the *Abyssus*'s reactor, which is… a significant load. But the *Phoenix* core is now self-sustaining its own operational cycle."

A soft, ethereal hum filled the cavern, a sound that seemed to vibrate not just in their ears, but deep within their bones. The *Phoenix* itself seemed to awaken, its internal lights flickering to life, casting an otherworldly glow across the cavern walls. The salvaged components, the fruits of their desperate endeavor, were now united, a testament to their audacity and resilience.

"The alien drive is… responding to our presence," Elias breathed, his eyes wide with wonder. "It's as if it recognizes us."

Kaelen, however, was focused on the intricate web of power conduits and structural supports. "The stress levels on the integration points are increasing, but they're holding. The self-repairing alloys are working overtime to compensate for the energetic transfer. It's a delicate balance, Lena. We're walking a tightrope."

"A tightrope that leads to the stars, Kaelen," Lena replied, her gaze fixed on the glowing heart of the *Phoenix*. "This is it. The culmination of everything. The *Phoenix* is no longer a ghost of a forgotten civilization; it's our future."

The cavern, once a tomb, was now a cradle. Within its protective embrace, the *Phoenix* had taken flight, a fusion of the alien and the human, a symbol of their collective will to transcend the boundaries of the impossible. It was a testament to their shared journey, a vessel born from salvaged dreams and reverse-engineered starlight, ready to carry them into the uncharted depths of the unknown. The silence of the cavern was broken by a new sound: the soft, steady hum of an alien heart beating in unison with their own, a promise of voyages yet to come. The genesis of the *Phoenix* was complete, and with it, humanity's own rebirth into a grander, more mysterious cosmos.

## 5: The Shadow of Oversight

The intricate dance of construction within the subterranean cavern, a symphony of advanced robotics and human ingenuity, was reaching a crescendo. The *Phoenix*, a vessel born from salvaged dreams and reverse-engineered starlight, was beginning to hum with a power that resonated through the very bedrock of the planet. Its alien heart, the salvaged drive core, pulsed with a nascent energy, a subtle thrum that, unbeknownst to its creators, was already a beacon in the vast, indifferent ocean above.

Miles above the cavern, in the sterile, hyper-modern command centers of global oceanic and defense agencies, the deep-sea monitoring systems, designed to detect everything from seismic shifts to clandestine submarine activity, began to register anomalies. These weren't the usual, predictable tremors of the Earth's crust, nor the familiar signatures of passing submersibles. These were fluctuations, ephemeral yet undeniably present, of exotic energy readings that defied conventional explanation. Located within the remote, desolate waters known as Point Nemo, a region notorious for its isolation and the very reason the *Abyssus* crew had chosen it for their covert operation, these readings were an unwelcome intrusion into their carefully maintained solitude.

The first ripple of this unforeseen detection emanated from the specialized hydro-acoustic arrays, sensitive instruments that could pinpoint the faintest sound waves propagating through the colossal volume of water. They picked up a low-frequency resonance, a subtle vibration that seemed to emanate from the very depths of the Pacific trench. It was unlike any natural oceanic phenomenon, lacking the chaotic signature of volcanic activity or the rhythmic pulse of submarine sonar. Instead, it was a steady, consistent hum, a harmonic undertone that suggested an artificial, controlled energy source. Commander Eva Rostova, a veteran of deep-sea reconnaissance and a woman whose reputation was built on her uncanny ability to decipher the most cryptic signals, found herself staring at the data with a growing sense of unease. Her team had been diligently monitoring the sector, their passive sensors designed to catalog the geological and biological diversity of the region, a quiet, uneventful assignment until now.

"What is this, Lieutenant?" Rostova's voice was calm, but her eyes narrowed as she gestured towards a holographic projection of the trench's bathymetry. A faint, pulsating circle marked the epicenter of the detected resonance. "It's not registering as seismic. It's too… coherent."

Lieutenant Commander Jian Li, a specialist in advanced signal analysis, adjusted his optical sensors, his brow furrowed in concentration. "The frequency is remarkably stable, Commander. And the amplitude, while currently low, is exhibiting a slow, upward trend. We've cross-referenced it against all known military and civilian energy signatures, both active and passive. Nothing matches." He zoomed in on the spectral analysis, revealing a complex waveform that seemed to defy standard energetic physics. "It's as if… something is generating a localized warp in the ambient energy field. The harmonics are unlike anything we've ever encountered."

Simultaneously, the gravitational anomaly sensors, deployed to map the subtle variations in the planet's gravitational field, also began to chime in with their own peculiar readings. These instruments, designed to detect the presence of large, submerged masses or unusual geological formations, were now picking up minute distortions in the gravitational pull of the trench. These weren't the large, sweeping shifts expected from tectonic plates, but rather localized, highly specific perturbations that seemed to coincide precisely with the acoustic resonance. Dr. Aris Thorne, a renowned astrophysicist who had been seconded to the agency for his expertise in exotic phenomena, found these readings particularly baffling.

"It's as if a significant mass is being introduced into the water column, but without any corresponding displacement or pressure wave," Thorne explained to Rostova, his voice laced with intellectual curiosity. "The gravitational signature is faint, but it's distinct. And it's localized to a very specific point at the trench floor. The energy required to create such a gravitational anomaly, even a minor one, would be immense. And it's not dissipating as expected."

The implications were immediately clear to Rostova. The isolation of Point Nemo, their primary advantage, was rapidly becoming a liability. The very act of constructing the *Phoenix*, of bringing its alien technologies online, was creating a detectable footprint. They had calculated that the cavern's geological shielding would be sufficient, but they had underestimated the sheer, raw power they were harnessing, and its ability to permeate even the densest of natural barriers.

The covert nature of their operation meant that any external detection was a catastrophic breach of security. Rostova's mandate was to maintain absolute secrecy, to ensure that no nation, no entity, became aware of their progress, lest the *Phoenix* and its revolutionary capabilities fall into the wrong hands. The silence of the deep ocean was their ally, and now, that silence was beginning to speak.

"Lieutenant, I want a full spectrum analysis of that energy signature," Rostova ordered, her voice now carrying a steely edge. "Focus on any unusual spectral lines, any harmonics that deviate from known energy propagation models. Dr. Thorne, can you attempt to triangulate the precise source of these gravitational perturbations? I want to know if they're emanating from a single point or a distributed network."

The operations center buzzed with activity as the specialized teams scrambled to fulfill her directives. The data poured in, each new scan adding another layer of complexity to the enigma. The acoustic resonance was indeed growing stronger, its unique waveform becoming more defined, suggesting a process of stabilization and amplification. The gravitational anomalies, meanwhile, were proving more elusive, their source stubbornly refusing to resolve into a clear, singular point, instead presenting as a diffuse field of influence that subtly warped the local gravitational geometry.

"Commander, the energy signature is exhibiting characteristics that suggest a form of controlled plasma containment," Jian Li reported, his voice tinged with a mixture of awe and apprehension. "The emitted radiation is within a spectrum that's normally associated with stellar fusion, but the containment field… it's unlike anything we have in our databases. It's almost as if they're manipulating spacetime itself to hold this energy."

Thorne, his face illuminated by the cascading data streams, added, "The gravitational field is not originating from a single point as I initially suspected. It's more of an integrated field effect, consistent with a large, complex energy source that is actively regulating its own gravitational influence. The pattern is complex, highly structured. It's not a natural phenomenon. It's unequivocally artificial."

Rostova's mind raced. The implications of Thorne's assessment were staggering. Artificial. Structured. And originating from the deepest, most inaccessible part of the ocean. They knew the region was geologically stable, with no known human presence or advanced research facilities that could explain such sophisticated energy generation. The only plausible explanation, a chilling one given their own clandestine operations, was that a hitherto unknown, highly advanced entity was at work in the trench. Or, more disturbingly, that their own activities were the cause, amplified and distorted by the unique geological conditions of the ocean floor.

"Are we certain these anomalies are not a result of our own sensor arrays interacting with the local environment?" Rostova probed, her voice sharp.

"Could this be a cascade of false positives generated by the unique pressure and salinity conditions at this depth?"

"We've run every diagnostic, Commander," Jian Li replied with unwavering certainty. "Our sensors are functioning within optimal parameters. The data is clean, consistent across multiple independent systems. We're not misinterpreting the signals. We're detecting something that shouldn't be there."

The problem was compounded by the sheer remoteness of Point Nemo. The nearest landmass was over 1,400 miles away, and the operational depth of the trench was extreme, far beyond the capabilities of most standard submersibles. Any investigation would require specialized, advanced deep-sea assets, assets that would themselves be difficult to deploy without attracting further attention. The very act of investigating would risk revealing their own surveillance, a counter-intelligence nightmare.

"What are the energy levels we're talking about, precisely?" Rostova pressed, her gaze fixed on the pulsing representation of the source.

"At its peak, the energy output is comparable to a small terrestrial fusion reactor, but the spectral signature suggests a different fundamental process," Thorne elaborated. "It's highly concentrated, incredibly efficient. And the gravitational influence, while localized, is significant enough to be detected by our most sensitive instruments. If it were to escalate, it could potentially cause localized seismic disturbances or even… affect the very fabric of spacetime in its immediate vicinity."

The thought sent a shiver down Rostova's spine. Affect the fabric of spacetime. The words echoed the most audacious theories of theoretical physics, theories that were usually confined to abstract equations and speculative academic papers. To think that such phenomena could be occurring, undetected by the wider world, in the crushing darkness of the Pacific abyss, was almost unbelievable. And the timing, coinciding with their own sensitive operations, was deeply unsettling.

"We need to confirm the source without compromising our position," Rostova stated, her mind already formulating a plan. "Lieutenant, can you isolate any modulated signals within the ambient energy output? Any attempt at communication, however rudimentary?"

"We're analyzing the substructure of the energy wave, Commander," Jian Li responded. "There are complex patterns within the primary resonance, almost like a modulated carrier wave, but it's encoded in a way that's completely foreign to us. It's not binary, not any form of digital encoding we recognize. It's… organic, somehow. Pulsatile, with irregular intervals."

This was the most alarming aspect. The energy signature wasn't merely a byproduct of some geological or unknown natural phenomenon; it was structured, modulated. It implied intent, control, and a level of technological sophistication that far surpassed anything humanity had yet achieved. And it was happening right under their noses, in a region they had chosen specifically for its desolation.

Rostova made a decision. They couldn't afford to be passive observers. The potential implications of an unknown, powerful energy source operating undetected in such a strategic location were too grave. Furthermore, if this energy source was somehow linked to their own operations, to the *Phoenix*, then they needed to understand that connection immediately.

"We'll deploy a reconnaissance drone," Rostova declared. "A Mark IV deep-sea autonomous vehicle. It's equipped with a full suite of passive sensors, shielded against energy emissions, and designed for extreme depths. Its profile is minimal, and its communication protocols are encrypted and highly directional. It will approach the anomaly from a vector that avoids direct line-of-sight detection. Its primary objective will be to gather high-resolution imaging and spectral data without initiating any active emissions of its own. If it detects any signs of intelligent activity or structured engineering, it is to return immediately, data intact."

The deployment of the Mark IV drone was a meticulously orchestrated operation. The vehicle, a sleek, torpedo-shaped marvel of engineering, was carefully launched from a classified oceanic research vessel positioned hundreds of miles away, its launch masked by a series of controlled atmospheric disturbances and simulated sonar pings designed to mimic natural phenomena. It descended silently into the crushing darkness, its internal chronometer ticking down the agonizing hours until it reached the target depth.

As the drone neared the anomaly's projected location, the sensor readings intensified. The acoustic hum became a palpable vibration, and the gravitational distortions formed a subtle, but undeniable, gravitational well. The drone's advanced optical sensors, capable of capturing images in near-absolute darkness through sophisticated multi-spectral analysis, began to transmit their findings.

The images that flickered across Rostova's monitor were nothing short of astounding. They depicted a cavern of unimaginable scale, its walls shimmering with an iridescent, metallic sheen. At its heart, bathed in a soft, ethereal glow, was a colossal structure, unlike any vessel Rostova had ever seen. It was sleek, elegant, and possessed an alien beauty that spoke of a design philosophy far removed from human engineering. Its hull, composed of an unknown, impossibly smooth alloy, seemed to absorb and re-emit the ambient light in a mesmerizing display. And nestled within its core, a powerful, contained energy source pulsed with an almost rhythmic beat, the origin of the detected anomalies.

"Commander, we have visual confirmation," the drone's automated voice reported, its tone devoid of the awe that was clearly palpable in the control room. "The source appears to be an artificial construct of significant size and complexity. Energy output is substantial, consistent with previous readings. No external defense systems or active emitters detected, but the structure itself is radiating energy across multiple spectrums."

The realization dawned on Rostova with a sickening certainty. The energy signature, the gravitational anomalies, the colossal structure – they were all intrinsically linked. And the most disturbing aspect of the drone's report was the subtle, yet undeniable, familiarity of the engineering principles it was detecting.

The self-healing alloys, the controlled energy containment, the very essence of the vessel's design… it bore an uncanny resemblance to the theoretical schematics that had been leaked from a highly classified, deniable project years ago, a project that had been officially declared a catastrophic failure. The *Phoenix*.

The clandestine operation, born out of desperation and fueled by the ghosts of lost technology, had not been as covert as they believed. Their meticulously chosen sanctuary, their isolation, had been breached, not by a rival nation, but by the very nature of the technology they were attempting to resurrect. The shadow of oversight, once a vague concern, had now solidified into a tangible, observable reality, emanating from the deepest, darkest reaches of the planet. The discovery of the *Phoenix* and its emergent capabilities had not gone unnoticed, and the world, or at least the clandestine agencies tasked with monitoring such phenomena, was beginning to stir. The silence of Point Nemo had been broken, not by a whisper, but by a resonant hum that echoed the audacious resurrection of a lost, alien future.

The subtle hum of the *Phoenix*, a sound that had become a comforting lullaby to the crew working deep within the cavern, had also become a phantom echo in Kaelen's mind. He was their security chief, a man whose paranoia was, more often than not, a crucial early warning system. His station, a nexus of sophisticated sensor arrays and encrypted communication channels, was designed to pierce the veil of absolute secrecy they desperately maintained. For weeks, it had been a silent sentinel, registering only the geological whispers of the deep ocean and the rhythmic pulse of their own nascent operations. But lately, a new element had intruded into the data stream, a dissonant chord in their carefully orchestrated symphony of silence.

It began as a faint, almost imperceptible ripple on his most sensitive long-range comms interceptors. Encrypted, yes, but with a peculiar cadence, a sub-harmonic resonance that hinted at a layered, sophisticated encryption protocol. It wasn't the standard chatter of passing maritime vessels or the predictable signals from orbital surveillance platforms. This was different. This was deliberate, targeted, and, most unnervingly, it seemed to be probing their sector.

"Elias," Kaelen's voice, usually even and measured, held a tremor of urgency as he approached the engineering bay, where Elias Vance, the visionary architect of the *Phoenix*, was overseeing the final diagnostics of the plasma conduits. "I'm picking up something… unusual."

Elias, a man whose focus was as impenetrable as the bedrock around them, looked up from the holographic display of energy flow, his brow furrowed. "Unusual how, Kaelen? More rogue seismic activity? Or are the bioluminescent flora finally staging their rebellion?" He managed a wry smile, but his eyes, reflecting the shimmering blues of the energy readings, held a flicker of concern. Kaelen's instincts were rarely wrong.

"It's communications traffic," Kaelen replied, his gaze fixed on Elias. "Encrypted, highly advanced. Not military in the conventional sense, but definitely sophisticated. It's scanning the local spectrum, testing frequencies, probing for anomalies." He paused, letting the implication sink in. "And I believe it's directed at us."

Elias's smile vanished, replaced by a look of grim understanding. The isolation of Point Nemo, their chosen sanctuary, was never meant to be absolute. They had always operated under the assumption that the sheer remoteness and the crushing depths would provide an insurmountable barrier to discovery. But they had also acknowledged the inherent risk that any sufficiently advanced technology, or indeed, any determined global power, could eventually pierce that veil. "What kind of agencies are we talking about, Kaelen? Governmental? Private entities?"

"The encryption is layered, Elias. Deeply layered. It's beyond anything I've encountered from the usual global intelligence networks. It suggests a level of resources and expertise that points to the upper echelons of global oversight agencies, or perhaps a private corporation with deep pockets and even deeper access." Kaelen's voice dropped, his usual stoicism cracking. "This isn't just random noise. This is someone looking for something specific."

The implications were immediate and chilling. The *Phoenix* was not merely a scientific endeavor; it was a potential paradigm shift, a testament to lost technologies that, if discovered and weaponized, could plunge the world into a new era of conflict. Kaelen's mind, trained to anticipate threats, was already cataloging the worst-case scenarios. Confiscation. Weaponization. Or worse, the complete suppression of their work, their discoveries buried forever beneath bureaucratic layers and geopolitical agendas. The dream they were meticulously building was at risk of being dismantled before it could even take flight.

"They're closing in," Elias murmured, more to himself than to Kaelen. The delicate balance of their operation, the carefully constructed illusion of invisibility, was beginning to fray. For months, they had operated under the assumption of their own stealth, their efforts shielded by the vastness of the Pacific. Now, that shield was proving to be porous. "We always knew this was a possibility, Kaelen. The very act of creating something this powerful, something that draws energy from a source beyond our current understanding, was bound to leave a ripple."

"A ripple is one thing, Elias," Kaelen countered, his voice tightening. "This feels more like a targeted seismic survey, mapping out the fault lines. The signals are becoming more persistent, more inquisitive. They're not just scanning; they're attempting to establish a dialogue, albeit one they're initiating with their own proprietary cipher." He ran a hand through his hair, a rare gesture of agitation. "My concern is that if they find us, if they understand what we're building, this won't just be about acquisition. It could be about containment. About silencing us permanently."

Elias turned back to the display, his gaze distant. The dream of the *Phoenix* had always been intertwined with the reality of its potential impact. They weren't just building a ship; they were resurrecting a lost chapter of human history, a technology that could redefine their place in the cosmos. But that very potential made them a target. "What are the chances they've already detected the energy signature we discussed earlier? The one from the deep trench?"

Kaelen's face grew pale. "That's what worries me the most, Elias. If those anomalies, the acoustic resonance and the gravitational fluctuations, were picked up by sensitive enough instruments, and if these new communications are a direct result of that detection, then our carefully curated solitude is well and truly over. The deep-sea monitoring networks, the orbital surveillance, even passive sonar arrays from commercial shipping lanes – any of them could have registered something. And if they've cross-referenced it with our general operating area…" He trailed off, the unspoken conclusion hanging heavy in the air.

The urgency was palpable. Elias knew that his focus had to shift, not just to the engineering marvel of the *Phoenix*, but to the immediate threat of exposure. The clandestine nature of their operation was not merely a matter of preference; it was a prerequisite for its success. They needed time to understand and harness the *Phoenix*'s capabilities before it became a pawn in geopolitical games. "We need to accelerate the primary power core stabilization," Elias stated, his voice firm, a renewed sense of purpose hardening his resolve. "The sooner we can achieve a stable, self-sustaining energy output, the sooner we can make our move. If we're going to be discovered, we might as well be discovered on our own terms, with the *Phoenix* ready to show them what we've accomplished."

"But Elias," Kaelen pressed, his voice laced with the weight of his responsibility, "if these agencies are already aware, even in a nascent stage, they might not wait for us to be ready. They'll act preemptively. They'll deploy assets. We could be facing specialized deep-sea reconnaissance units, armed submersible craft… things designed to neutralize threats in environments like this."

"And that's precisely why we can't afford any more delays," Elias countered, meeting Kaelen's anxious gaze. "Every day we spend refining is a day they spend closing the net. We need to be prepared for confrontation, but our primary objective remains the same: to activate the *Phoenix*. Kaelen, your job is to monitor and deflect. My job, our job, is to make this ship fly. If they're knocking at the door, we need to be ready to answer it… with full power."

Kaelen nodded, the grim acceptance of their precarious situation settling upon him. He understood Elias's logic. Hesitation would only play into the hands of their unseen adversaries. "Understood. I'll reroute additional processing power to the long-range interceptors. I'll also initiate a passive counter-intelligence sweep, trying to map the origin and scope of their probing. But Elias, if they're as advanced as the encryption suggests, even that might be a needle in a haystack."

"Then we'll just have to make our needle bigger," Elias said, his eyes returning to the pulsing schematic of the *Phoenix*'s core. The whispers of interference had become a chorus, and it was clear that their clandestine sanctuary was no longer as secret as they had hoped. The shadow of oversight was no longer a distant possibility; it was a tangible, encroaching presence, drawn by the very power they were struggling to control. The race against time had just intensified, and the fate of the *Phoenix*, and perhaps the future of human exploration, hung precariously in the balance. The hum of their creation was no longer just a sound of progress; it was a siren call, attracting attention from a world that was not yet ready for what they were about to unleash. And Kaelen knew, with a certainty that chilled him to the bone, that the silence of Point Nemo was about to be shattered. The question was no longer if they would be discovered, but when, and how they would respond when that inevitable moment arrived. The subtle probing of encrypted signals was the first overt manifestation of a far greater threat, a threat that sought to control not just technology, but the very trajectory of human advancement. He had to prepare for a confrontation that transcended mere physical defense; it was a battle for the very right to explore, to innovate, and to dream beyond the confines of established knowledge. The coming days would test the resilience of their operation, the fortitude of their crew, and the very foundations of their clandestine endeavor.

The data Kaelen was sifting through was a tapestry of calculated uncertainty. The signals he intercepted were not direct transmissions, but rather complex, multi-layered queries, designed to elicit responses from any active systems within a wide radius. It was like a sophisticated sonar ping, but instead of sound waves, it was using modulated energy bursts and intricate data packets, each one subtly different, designed to bypass standard detection filters and exploit any potential vulnerabilities in their communication infrastructure. He recognized the hallmarks of advanced signal intelligence gathering – the use of staggered frequencies, the rapid shifting of transmission windows, and the subtle manipulation of ambient electromagnetic fields to mask their own signature. It was the work of a highly disciplined and well-resourced organization, one that understood the principles of stealth and detection intimately.

"They're not just looking for our power source, Elias," Kaelen reported, his voice now laced with a weary frustration. "They're probing our entire operational spectrum. Our internal comms, our sensor sweeps, even the residual energy signatures from the robotics. They're building a comprehensive profile, a detailed map of our activities, even if they don't fully understand what they're seeing yet." He gestured towards a holographic display that showed a series of interconnected data points, each representing a detected signal or energy anomaly. "This cluster here," he indicated a faint, pulsing beacon on the display, "is a directional probe, attempting to triangulate the source of the ambient energy field we're generating. And this," he pointed to another, more erratic pattern, "looks like a brute-force decryption attempt on our primary operational frequencies."

Elias, now standing beside Kaelen, his own work temporarily set aside, studied the complex web of data. The sheer sophistication of the intrusion was unsettling. It spoke of an intelligence that was not only aware of their presence but was actively and methodically trying to dissect their operation. "What's their primary objective, Kaelen? Do you think they're aware of the *Phoenix* itself, or are they just investigating the unusual energy readings?"

"It's hard to say definitively without a clear intercept," Kaelen admitted, his gaze unwavering from the screen. "But the precision of their probing suggests they're not just chasing ghosts. They've likely detected enough anomalies – the resonance, the gravitational distortions you've been tracking – to warrant this level of investigation. The question is, what do they *think* they've found? A natural phenomenon? A hidden military installation? Or something else entirely?" He paused, a grim thought crossing his mind. "If they've managed to detect the *Phoenix*'s emergent energy signature, however faint, they'll be trying to understand its nature. And given the implications of what we're doing, that kind of knowledge is incredibly valuable… and incredibly dangerous."

The weight of that danger pressed down on them. The original mission parameters had been clear: achieve operational status for the *Phoenix* and then, and only then, consider how to reveal their existence to the world. But the timeline had just been drastically compressed by the very act of their success. The unintended beacon they had created was now drawing unwanted attention, and the clandestine haven they had so carefully selected was becoming a potential trap.

"We need to consider contingency plans, Elias," Kaelen stated, his voice low and serious. "If they do manage to pinpoint our location, we need a way to either deter them or, failing that, to escape. I've been running simulations, but our options are limited. We're deep underground, and any attempt to surface or transmit a distress signal would be instantly compromised."

Elias rubbed his chin, his mind racing through a myriad of complex scenarios. The *Phoenix* was designed for deep-space traversal, not for covert evasion in terrestrial waters. Its power and capabilities were immense, but its operational footprint, when activated, was equally significant. "Escape might not be the best option, Kaelen. If they're sophisticated enough to track us here, they'll likely have assets capable of intercepting us if we attempt to surface. Deterrence, perhaps. Or a decisive demonstration of capability."

"A demonstration could also be seen as an act of aggression," Kaelen countered, a flicker of alarm in his eyes. "We don't know who they are. If it's a rogue state, an aggressive corporate entity, or even an international consortium trying to control advanced technology, provoking them could be catastrophic."

"But what if the alternative is to be captured and have everything we've worked for co-opted?" Elias's voice was sharp, the underlying frustration and defiance evident. "We're on the cusp of something monumental, Kaelen. We can't let that be extinguished by fear or by the machinations of those who would seek to control it for their own ends. If they find us, we'll show them the *Phoenix*. We'll let them see what humanity is truly capable of, when it pushes beyond its limitations."

Kaelen remained silent for a moment, absorbing the weight of Elias's words. He understood the drive, the unyielding ambition that fueled Elias and the entire crew. But his own mandate was to ensure their survival, to protect the integrity of their operation. "I'm not disagreeing with the ultimate goal, Elias. But the 'how' is critical. We need to ensure that when that moment comes, we have the leverage to dictate the terms of engagement, or at least, to ensure our survival. I'll continue to analyze their signals, trying to ascertain their capabilities and intentions. Perhaps there's a weakness in their approach, a blind spot we can exploit."

He turned back to the console, his fingers flying across the holographic interface. The faint whispers of interference were growing louder, more insistent. The carefully constructed silence of their sanctuary was beginning to echo with the approaching footsteps of an unseen world. The shadow of oversight was no longer merely a concern; it was a tangible, approaching threat, and the crew of the *Phoenix* was about to face a reckoning that would test the very foundations of their audacious endeavor. The silent, deep-sea cavern, once a symbol of their hidden progress, was now a potential cage, and the light of their ambition was attracting predators from the world above. The exhilaration of their technological breakthroughs was now tempered by the cold, hard reality of discovery, and the race to harness the power of the *Phoenix* had suddenly become a race against time itself, with the world's most powerful entities poised to intervene.

Elias felt the familiar tightening in his chest, a cold knot of dread that had become a constant companion since the incident. Kaelen's report, detailing the increasingly aggressive probing of their encrypted channels, was more than just an intelligence update; it was a confirmation of his deepest fears. The shadow of oversight was no longer a theoretical construct, a distant possibility they had contingency-planned for. It was real, tangible, and closing in. Each intercepted signal, each calculated query from an unknown entity, was a hammer blow against the fragile sanctuary they had so painstakingly carved out in the abyssal depths.

His resolve, already forged in the crucible of ambition and necessity, hardened into something akin to granite. The *Phoenix* was not merely a vessel, nor a scientific breakthrough. It was a promise. A promise to his lost family, a promise to a world choked by its own limitations, and a promise to himself that the catastrophic failures of the past would not be repeated. The thought of the *Phoenix*, with its revolutionary power core derived from technologies long forgotten, falling into the hands of those who would weaponize it, who would twist its potential for destruction, was an unbearable prospect. He had seen firsthand the devastating consequences of unchecked technological ambition, the chilling finality of ambition untethered by empathy or wisdom.

"They're getting closer, Elias," Kaelen had said, his voice a low murmur, barely audible above the ambient hum of the *Phoenix*'s systems. "Their methods are evolving. They're not just scanning anymore; they're trying to understand. Trying to decode our very presence."

Elias had nodded, his gaze fixed on the schematics of the plasma conduit system that glowed with an ethereal blue light. He remembered the raw, unadulterated terror of that day, the searing heat, the deafening silence that followed. The images were seared into his memory: the twisted metal, the desperate faces, the agonizing realization that innovation, when divorced from responsibility, could become a harbinger of annihilation. His family, his brilliant wife, his inquisitive daughter – all gone, casualties of a technological race that had spiraled out of control. The *Phoenix* was his penance, his desperate attempt to reclaim a stolen future.

"We cannot afford to be discovered before we are ready," Elias stated, his voice firm, the tremor of emotion carefully suppressed. "Not by them, not by anyone. The world isn't ready for what the *Phoenix* represents. And those who would seek to control it… they are even less prepared for its true potential." He envisioned the endless bureaucracy, the committees, the military strategists who would descend like vultures, dissecting their work, stifling its revolutionary purpose, and ultimately, turning it into another instrument of power and control. The very essence of the *Phoenix*, its promise of unfettered exploration and a new understanding of humanity's place in the cosmos, would be lost.

He thought of the clandestine nature of their operation, the years of painstaking research, the sacrifices made by every member of his crew. They had operated in the deepest shadows, shielded by the indifferent vastness of the Pacific, building their dream in secret. This isolation, this deliberate withdrawal from the watchful eyes of the world, was not born of paranoia alone, but of a profound understanding of human nature. Power, especially power as transformative as that which the *Phoenix* commanded, inevitably attracted those who sought to wield it. And Elias knew, with a certainty that chilled him to the bone, that the powers that would be drawn to them would not be benevolent.

"A clandestine launch is our only viable option, Kaelen," Elias continued, turning to face his security chief, his eyes burning with a conviction that had been tempered by loss and tempered again by a fierce, unwavering hope. "We need to control our own destiny. We need to be the ones to introduce the *Phoenix* to the world, on our terms, when we deem it ready. To surrender that control now, to allow ourselves to be intercepted or apprehended, would be to betray everything we have worked for. It would be to condemn the *Phoenix*, and all that it represents, to a fate worse than destruction."

He recalled the early days of his research, the initial breakthroughs, the quiet excitement that had filled his laboratory. He had dreamed of a future where humanity could transcend its terrestrial confines, where exploration was driven by curiosity, not by conquest. But that dream had been tainted by the harsh realities of human ambition, the relentless pursuit of advantage. He had witnessed firsthand how even the most noble of scientific endeavors could be corrupted, twisted into tools of oppression and destruction. The memory of his family's faces, so full of life and promise, was a constant reminder of what was at stake.

"If they discover us now, before we can even achieve full operational capacity, they'll see us as a threat," Elias elaborated, his voice gaining a quiet intensity. "They'll see the *Phoenix* as a weapon, a tool to be dissected, controlled, and perhaps, weaponized even further. Our work will be confiscated, our discoveries buried under layers of secrecy and political maneuvering. And the memory of those we've lost… it would be a hollow victory, a testament to a dream that was extinguished before it could truly ignite."

He walked towards the viewport, gazing out at the impenetrable darkness of the ocean floor. The weight of his responsibility felt almost unbearable at times, a constant pressure in his very bones. Yet, it was also the fuel that drove him, the unwavering purpose that propelled him forward. The *Phoenix* was not just his creation; it was a legacy. A legacy he owed to his family, to the memory of their unfulfilled potential, and to the hope of a better future for all of humanity.

"The key is stealth, Kaelen. Absolute and unyielding stealth until we are ready. We must ensure that our launch is not an emergence, but a departure. A silent slip into the void, allowing us to establish our own trajectory, to control our own narrative." Elias turned back, his gaze meeting Kaelen's, a silent understanding passing between them. "We will continue to refine our systems, to enhance our capabilities, and to prepare for any eventuality. But our primary focus remains the same: to make the *Phoenix* operational, and to launch it from the shadows, on our terms."

He knew that this path would be fraught with peril. The very act of pursuing their goal meant operating in constant defiance of established powers, of those who sought to maintain the status quo. But Elias was no stranger to defiance. He had defied the limitations of known science, defied the pronouncements of obsolescence, and now, he would defy the looming threat of those who sought to control humanity's destiny. The tragedy of his past had not broken him; it had reforged him, imbuing him with a resolve that no external force could easily shatter.

"We will not be found until we choose to be found," Elias declared, his voice resonating with a quiet, unwavering determination. "We will not be contained. The *Phoenix* will fly. And when it does, it will carry with it the hope of a new beginning, a testament to the resilience of the human spirit and the pursuit of knowledge, unburdened by the shadows of fear and control." He looked back at the schematics, the intricate pathways of energy and data that represented the culmination of years of effort. This was not just about survival; it was about redemption. A redemption for the past, and a promise for the future, carried on the silent, powerful wings of the *Phoenix*. He could feel the energy thrumming within the heart of their vessel, a nascent power waiting to be unleashed. And he knew, with an absolute certainty that resonated deep within his soul, that they would not allow that power to be co-opted, not by anyone. Their path was clear, and their resolve was unyielding.

The constant hum of the *Phoenix*'s life support systems, usually a comforting backdrop to Lena's work, now felt like a ticking clock, each oscillation a reminder of their precarious situation. Elias's words, broadcasted through the internal comms, still echoed in the chilled air of her laboratory module: "We will not be found until we choose to be found." That sentiment was the bedrock of her current endeavor. The threat of detection was no longer a distant specter; it was a tangible, omnipresent danger, and Lena's role in averting it was paramount. Her fingers danced across the holographic interface, manipulating complex algorithms with a practiced grace that belied the immense pressure she was under. Every line of code, every tweak to a power fluctuation, was a brick in the wall of their invisibility.

Her primary focus was the *Phoenix*'s unique energy signature. The revolutionary power core, a marvel of salvaged and reimagined ancient technology, pulsed with a distinct frequency, a beacon that, if not carefully managed, could betray their presence to even the most rudimentary deep-space scanners, let alone the sophisticated, clandestine surveillance networks Elias feared. Lena had spent months analyzing that signature, dissecting its every harmonic. Her initial goal had been to optimize its efficiency, to unlock its full potential. Now, that same signature had to be rendered invisible, or at least, indistinguishable from the background noise of the cosmos.

She envisioned their vessel, a titan of advanced engineering, moving through the inky blackness of the ocean's depths, a leviathan of human ingenuity. But to the outside world, they needed to appear as nothing more than a spectral anomaly, a whisper in the data streams. Her current project was codenamed 'Chameleon.' It was an ambitious undertaking, a multi-layered system designed to dynamically adapt and mimic the ambient energy fields surrounding the *Phoenix*. This wasn't a simple cloaking device; it was an active deception, a technological veil woven from light, energy, and pure mathematical cunning.

Lena began by meticulously cataloging the natural energy fluctuations of the deep ocean. Geothermal vents, seismic activity, the faint bio-luminescent pulses of deep-sea organisms – all these were data points that fed into the Chameleon system. The core idea was to create a predictive model of the ambient energy, and then to overlay the *Phoenix*'s own signature, subtly shifting and morphing it to match the environmental data. It was like painting a masterpiece on a canvas that was constantly moving and changing.

"Kaelen, status report on the external sensor array," Lena's voice, though calm, carried an undertone of urgency as she addressed her security chief. The comms channel crackled briefly before Kaelen's voice, steady and reassuring, came through.

"All systems nominal, Lena. No anomalous readings detected. The ambient energy readings are within expected parameters for this depth."

"Good," Lena replied, her eyes still fixed on the cascading lines of code. "I'm initiating the first phase of the Chameleon matrix calibration. I need you to monitor for any, and I mean *any*, deviations in our emissions profile. Even the slightest spike, if it's outside the projected environmental variance, needs to be flagged."

"Understood. I'll be monitoring every fluctuation," Kaelen assured her. He understood the stakes, the silent war they were waging in the digital and electromagnetic spectrums.

Lena initiated the sequence. A subtle tremor ran through the *Phoenix* as the Chameleon system began to hum to life. It wasn't a physical vibration, but a shift in the very fabric of their energy output. The brilliant azure glow of the primary conduits, a signature of the core's immense power, was subtly modulated, softened.

Lena watched as the spectral analysis displayed on her console began to change. The sharp, distinct peaks that represented the *Phoenix* were blurring, blending into the jagged, organic lines that signified the natural oceanic background radiation.

"First phase calibration complete," Lena announced, a hint of satisfaction in her voice. "The signature is… less distinct. It's starting to look less like a deliberate emission and more like a geological anomaly. We're seeing a slight resemblance to a deep-sea hydrothermal vent's thermal plume, with a secondary overlay of low-frequency seismic resonance."

She continued her work, refining the algorithms. The next step was to address their communication signals. The *Phoenix* wasn't broadcasting anything conventionally, but the very act of internal communication, the transmission of data between modules, generated subtle electromagnetic emanations. These were the whispers, the unintended trails of breadcrumbs they left behind. Lena was developing a proprietary form of quantum entanglement communication for critical data transfer, a method so inherently secure and theoretically undetectable that it was almost mythical in its promise. However, for day-to-day operations, they still relied on encrypted, short-range bursts.

Her focus shifted to a new set of holographic projections, detailing a complex lattice of phased energy emitters embedded within the *Phoenix*'s hull. These emitters, when synchronized, could create a localized distortion field, effectively bending and scattering any incoming electromagnetic signals, including active scans. This was the 'digital phantom' aspect of Chameleon – to make the *Phoenix* appear as an empty void, a ghost in the machine of global surveillance.

"Projecting the distortion field schematics," Lena murmured, overlaying the diagrams onto her primary display. "The emitters will fire in a precisely timed sequence, creating a ripple effect. It's designed to refract any active scanning frequencies, bouncing them back in a way that suggests nothing but empty water. The challenge is the power required and the synchronization accuracy. A fraction of a second off, and the effect is negated, potentially even drawing attention to the anomaly."

She ran a series of simulations. The holographic models showed waves of energy washing over the *Phoenix*, only to be deflected, distorted, and dissipated, leaving no coherent trace. It was a digital sleight of hand, a carefully orchestrated illusion on a cosmic scale.

"Simulation 7-Alpha shows a 98.7% efficacy in deflecting standard wide-spectrum sweeps," Lena reported, her brow furrowed in concentration. "However, the residual energy dispersal pattern is still something I'm not entirely comfortable with. It's subtle, but it's there. We need to mask that too."

Her mind raced, searching for a solution. The problem wasn't just about deflecting the incoming probes; it was about cleaning up their own digital fingerprints. She needed to absorb and re-emit that residual energy in a way that was entirely innocuous. This led her to a radical idea: utilizing the *Phoenix*'s own power core to absorb and re-radiate the scattered energy, but not in its raw form. It would be processed, modulated, and released as a faint, broadband radio frequency emission, mimicking the background radiation of the universe.

"I'm implementing a secondary absorption and re-emission protocol," Lena announced, her fingers flying across the controls. "We'll use the core's tertiary regulators to capture the residual energy from the distortion field, process it through a multi-spectral filter, and then re-radiate it as a low-intensity, broad-spectrum signal. Think of it as… dressing the phantom in the clothes of a cosmic ghost. It will be indistinguishable from the natural radio noise of space."

The simulations continued, each iteration pushing the boundaries of her ingenuity. She was not just building a shield; she was crafting a deception so profound that it would make the *Phoenix* a true phantom, an entity that existed without leaving a trace. The sheer complexity of the task was staggering. It required a level of computational power and predictive accuracy that pushed the *Phoenix*'s systems to their absolute limits.

"The problem," Elias's voice cut through the silence, his presence a calming anchor in the storm of her calculations, "is not just what they can detect, but what they can infer. Even if they can't see us, they might detect the absence of something where we are. They will be looking for anomalies in their scans, for deviations from the norm."

Lena nodded, acknowledging the validity of his concern. "That's precisely why Chameleon needs to be more than just a cloaking device, Elias. It needs to be a dynamic environmental mimicry system. Not only are we masking our emissions, but we're actively projecting a false environment. If a scan happens to pass directly over us, the distortion field will ensure the data returned is of empty water, or perhaps a fleeting heat signature consistent with a minor geological event. The re-emitted energy will then serve as a final layer of passive camouflage, reinforcing the illusion of natural background noise."

She was working on a sub-protocol that analyzed incoming sensor sweeps in real-time. If a probe was detected, even a faint one, Chameleon would instantly adapt. The distortion field would intensify, the re-emission pattern would adjust, all within microseconds, ensuring that the perceived anomaly was immediately overwritten by a plausible, natural explanation.

"The challenge with that," Kaelen chimed in, his voice sharp with professional insight, "is the energy cost. Actively mimicking the environment, especially under duress, will require a significant power draw. Can the core sustain that without betraying us through its own heat signature?"

"That's where the core's unique properties come into play," Lena explained, her eyes alight with the thrill of a problem nearing its solution. "Its efficiency is such that it can manage these bursts of activity without a catastrophic increase in thermal output. Moreover, the Chameleon system is designed to draw power precisely when it's needed, and then to dissipate any excess energy through the broad-spectrum re-emission. It's a closed loop, Elias, as much as we can achieve within the bounds of current physics. We are, in essence, using the very force that defines us to become invisible."

She zoomed in on a particularly complex section of the schematics, a network of micro-emitters designed to create a localized gravitational lensing effect. This was the cutting edge, the most experimental part of Chameleon. "This is… ambitious," Lena admitted, her voice a low hum of concentration. "By creating a minute, transient gravitational distortion, we can bend light and other electromagnetic radiation around the

*Phoenix.* If it works, it would render us optically and electromagnetically invisible, even to the most advanced direct imaging systems."

The calculations for this particular aspect were mind-boggling. It required manipulating spacetime on a microscopic level, a feat previously thought impossible. But the *Phoenix* was built on the foundations of impossible science. Lena felt a surge of adrenaline, the familiar rush of pushing beyond known frontiers.

"The risk here," Kaelen warned, "is that any detected gravitational anomaly, however slight, would be highly unusual. It might be more conspicuous than a simple energy signature."

"True," Lena conceded. "Which is why this layer is activated only as a last resort, or during our actual launch sequence, when we need absolute certainty of our disappearance. For now, our primary focus remains on the energy signature masking and the distortion field. The gravitational lensing is our trump card, our final act of vanishing."

Days blurred into a cycle of intense work, punctuated only by brief moments of rest and hushed conversations with Elias and Kaelen. Lena refined the Chameleon system, pushing its parameters, testing its resilience. She developed fail-safes upon fail-safes, redundancies that would ensure the system's integrity even if parts of it were compromised. Her workspace became a sanctuary of pure logic, a bubble of focused activity against the encroaching tide of external threats. She understood that her technological prowess was not just about building something new; it was about deconstructing the tools of potential enemies, anticipating their methods, and rendering them obsolete before they could even be deployed.

She spent hours studying the intercepted data logs that Kaelen provided, analyzing the patterns of the probing signals. She saw the sophistication, the relentless, probing nature of their adversaries. They were not brute-force attackers; they were subtle, persistent, and intelligent. They were looking for a needle in a haystack, and the *Phoenix* was that needle. Lena's goal was to make the haystack itself a perfect mimicry of nothingness, rendering the search futile.

"I've managed to integrate a predictive anomaly detection algorithm into Chameleon," Lena announced during one of their debriefings. "It analyzes the incoming signal patterns and predicts potential scan vectors. If a scan is detected that doesn't conform to our projected environmental model, Chameleon will automatically initiate a targeted energy dispersal pattern to disrupt the scan's coherence. It's like throwing a handful of sand into a precise beam of light."

Elias listened intently, his gaze fixed on Lena's holographic projections. He saw not just lines of code and energy wave patterns, but the tangible manifestation of their continued existence. "This is crucial, Lena. The more we can disrupt their ability to gather reliable data, the longer we remain hidden. What about our internal communications? Are they still detectable?"

"We're minimizing our internal transmissions," Lena replied. "And for any sensitive data, we're using the entangled quantum communicators. The bursts of conventional radio are now heavily encrypted and routed through directional emitters, minimizing their outward projection. Furthermore, I've implemented a series of 'data decoys.' These are low-level, encrypted data packets that are intentionally sent out at random intervals. They're meaningless on their own, but to a passive observer, they create the impression of normal operational chatter, a smokescreen for our actual communications."

The concept of data decoys was a testament to Lena's understanding of psychological warfare, albeit applied to the realm of technology. By creating a false sense of normalcy, she aimed to draw attention away from the true nature of their operations. It was a digital misdirection, a way to make the *Phoenix* appear busy and active, but in a manner that was fundamentally uninteresting to any external intelligence agency.

"The aim," Lena elaborated, "is to create a complex, layered façade. On the surface, we are simply a highly advanced, secure research vessel operating in the deep sea. Our energy signatures will mimic natural phenomena. Our communications will be obfuscated by decoys and quantum entanglement. And our very presence will be masked by a distortion field that bends and scatters incoming scans. We will be a ghost, Elias. A technological phantom, adrift in the abyss, unseen and unheard until we are ready to reveal ourselves."

She leaned back, a faint smile gracing her lips. The work was exhausting, demanding, and fraught with the constant pressure of potential discovery. But in that moment, looking at the elegant complexity of the Chameleon system taking shape, Lena felt a profound sense of purpose. She was not just an engineer; she was a guardian, a silent protector of Elias's vision and the *Phoenix*'s future. The shadow of oversight was indeed long, but Lena was meticulously crafting the darkness within which they would thrive, a darkness that would ultimately be their shield and their salvation. Her technological precautions were not just a series of countermeasures; they were a testament to the power of human intellect to overcome even the most sophisticated forms of surveillance, a silent rebellion waged in the realm of data and energy. She was weaving a tapestry of invisibility, a masterpiece of technological deception, ensuring that the *Phoenix* would remain a secret, a promise waiting to be fulfilled. The hum of the ship, once a source of anxiety, now felt like the steady heartbeat of their hidden world, a world Lena was painstakingly ensuring would remain their own.

The rhythmic thrum of the *Phoenix*'s newly integrated propulsion systems vibrated through the deck plates, a low, resonant purr that spoke of power barely contained. Lena's fingers, still stained with the faint residue of recalibrated conduits and advanced circuitry sealant, hovered over the final diagnostic panel. Each blinking light, each green checkmark on the holographic interface, was a testament to countless hours of painstaking work, a silent affirmation that their sanctuary, however temporary, had nurtured their vessel into readiness. The cavern, a geological marvel carved by ancient, unknown forces and subsequently adapted by their own ingenuity, had served its purpose. It had been their womb, a shielded cradle from which the *Phoenix* would soon emerge, a testament to human resilience and technological defiance.

"All primary systems nominal," Kaelen's voice, broadcasted with crisp clarity through the internal comms, announced the completion of the most critical phase of pre-flight checks. "Life support stable at 99.8%. Navigational arrays are locked and calibrated. Weapon systems are offline but primed for immediate activation." He paused, a subtle shift in his tone betraying the gravity of the moment. "The atmospheric integrity of the cavern is also holding, Lena. No further significant breaches detected since the last integrity scan."

Lena let out a breath she hadn't realized she was holding, a plume of condensation briefly misting the viewport of her analysis station. The cavern's atmosphere, while breathable, was a complex blend of recycled air, trace geothermal gases, and the pervasive scent of mineral-rich rock. It was a scent that would soon be replaced by the stark, clean vacuum of interstellar space, or perhaps the crushing, alien pressure of a deeper, more profound abyss. "Understood, Kaelen. And the Chameleon system?"

"Chameleon is functioning within optimal parameters," came Lena's own voice, tinged with a weariness that only deep concentration could inflict. "The predictive algorithms are correlating with real-time sensor data with a 99.997% accuracy. The distortion field can be fully engaged within ten seconds of departure, and the energy signature masking is pre-loaded for immediate, seamless integration with the ambient oceanic background. We are, in essence, ready to become a ghost before we even leave our dock."

The word "dock" felt strangely inadequate to describe the vast, geologically sculpted chamber that had housed them. It was more than a mooring; it was a sanctuary, a testament to their ability to find refuge in the most inhospitable environments. But sanctuaries, by their very nature, could not be permanent. The very act of their existence, the monumental undertaking of building and powering the *Phoenix*, carried an inherent risk of detection. The longer they remained static, the greater the chance that their carefully crafted invisibility could be breached. Elias had been adamant on this point: their departure was not merely a logistical necessity, but a strategic imperative.

Elias himself materialized in the entrance of Lena's lab module, his silhouette framed by the soft, operational glow of the ship's interior. His usual stoic demeanor seemed amplified by the weight of anticipation. "Lena,

Kaelen," he greeted, his voice a low rumble that seemed to carry the authority of their shared destiny. "What is our final departure window?"

"The calculated optimum departure window opens in precisely fifty-three minutes," Lena replied, turning from her console. The light from the holographic displays cast an ethereal glow on her face, highlighting the faint lines of fatigue etched around her eyes. "This window is based on the projected currents within the cavern's exit channel, as well as minimizing the risk of seismic interference during our initial ascent. After that, the window narrows significantly due to tidal shifts in the external ocean layers."

"Fifty-three minutes," Elias echoed, a thoughtful expression crossing his features. "That gives us just enough time for a final crew briefing and to ensure all non-essential personnel are secured. Kaelen, have you confirmed the status of the external pressure seals on all egress points?"

"Confirmed, Elias," Kaelen responded promptly. "All bulkheads and hatches are triple-sealed and pressure-tested. The cavern exit tunnel itself is secured with a series of dynamically closing blast doors, designed to contain any catastrophic failure during our initial ascent. The last thing we need is to bleed atmosphere into the surrounding ocean before we're even out of the immediate vicinity."

The cavern exit tunnel. It was an engineering marvel in itself, a kilometer-long conduit bored through solid rock and reinforced with a self-repairing, adamantium-alloy composite. It was the only physical connection between their hidden world and the vast, unexplored ocean beyond. The launch sequence would involve a delicate dance of controlled ballast expulsion, precise thruster adjustments, and the seamless activation of the *Phoenix*'s nascent gravity manipulation field to guide their ascent without disturbing the delicate geological structures around them, or worse, attracting unwanted attention.

Lena's attention drifted back to the readouts. Her focus was now on the internal energy distribution. "I'm rerouting auxiliary power from the environmental stabilization systems to the primary thrusters," she announced, her fingers flying across the interface. "The moment we disengage from our mooring points, those thrusters will need to exert considerable force to navigate the initial convergence of currents within the cavern's mouth. Once we're clear, we'll re-engage the primary core's full output, but for the initial surge, we'll need every available joule."

The *Phoenix* was more than just a vessel; it was a self-contained ecosystem, a micro-civilization designed for prolonged, independent existence. Every system, from the hydroponic gardens that provided their sustenance to the advanced atmospheric processors that recycled their air, had to be in perfect harmony. The departure from the cavern wasn't just about physically moving the ship; it was about transitioning from a stable, shielded environment to a dynamic, potentially hostile one, all while maintaining the illusion of utter insignificance.

"What about the seismic sensors?" Elias inquired, his gaze sweeping over Lena's primary display. "Are they still calibrated to detect any geological instabilities within the cavern that might compromise our departure path?"

"They are," Lena confirmed. "And I've added an additional layer of predictive analysis based on the known geological composition of this region. The system will now not only alert us to immediate seismic activity but also flag any potential micro-fractures or stress points that could propagate into a larger instability during our ascent. The last thing we need is to trigger a cave-in behind us, effectively sealing off our only known exit."

The cavern, for all its protective qualities, was still a naturally occurring formation, subject to the same geological forces that shaped the planet's crust. While they had reinforced its structural integrity significantly, the act of launching a vessel of the *Phoenix*'s size and power could potentially introduce new stresses. This was a calculated risk, one that Lena had meticulously modeled, but a risk nonetheless.

"This is it, then," Elias said, his voice low, almost reverent. "The moment we've worked towards for so long. The moment we break free of our chains, not just of this cavern, but of the limitations that have held humanity captive for millennia." He looked out at the vast, dimly lit expanse of the cavern, the rough-hewn walls glistening with moisture, the vast, crystalline formations that dotted the ceiling like a fossilized celestial canopy. It was a place of profound isolation, yet it had also been a place of immense discovery and growth.

"It's time to prepare the crew," Elias continued, his gaze returning to Lena. "Inform them that the final departure sequence is initiating. I want every member of the *Phoenix* to be aware of the immense significance of this moment. We are not just moving from one location to another; we are embarking on a journey that will redefine our species' place in the universe. Our success hinges on our ability to remain undetected, to master the art of invisibility as Lena has so brilliantly engineered."

Lena nodded, her fingers already moving to activate the ship-wide comms. "Initiating final departure sequence briefing. All hands to designated stations." Her voice, now amplified, resonated through the cavern, reaching every corner of the *Phoenix*. The quiet efficiency that had characterized their work thus far was now overlaid with a palpable sense of anticipation, a shared understanding of the monumental undertaking that lay before them.

As Lena broadcasted Elias's words, she couldn't help but feel a profound sense of both exhilaration and trepidation. They were leaving behind the only home they had known for the duration of their clandestine operations. The cavern had been a testament to their resourcefulness, a sanctuary that had allowed them to build the *Phoenix* without the prying eyes of Earth's omnipresent surveillance networks. But now, the very act of moving, of becoming active rather than static, presented a new set of challenges.

"The internal atmospheric pressure is stabilizing at optimal levels for launch," Kaelen reported, his voice cutting through the comms channel, a grounding presence of pure operational focus. "All power conduits are receiving nominal energy flow from the core. The life support systems are reporting zero anomalies. It's… eerily quiet, Lena. Almost too quiet."

"That's the sound of preparedness, Kaelen," Lena replied, her own voice steady, though her heart was beginning to quicken its rhythm. "The sound of a vessel ready to take flight. Now, for the primary objective: departure from the cavern. I'm initiating the sequence to disengage the mooring clamps."

A series of low clicks echoed through the hull as magnetic clamps, designed to hold the massive vessel in place, released their grip. The *Phoenix* shifted, a subtle, almost imperceptible movement, yet it was a movement that signified the end of an era and the beginning of a new, uncharted chapter. The cavern walls, which had loomed so imposingly, now seemed to recede slightly as the ship's internal gravity generators adjusted for the imminent acceleration.

"Mooring clamps disengaged," Lena confirmed. "Initiating primary thruster ignition sequence for cavern exit navigation. Kaelen, maintain constant vigilance on the structural integrity readings of the exit tunnel. Any deviation beyond a 0.01% micro-stress factor, and we abort immediately."

The cavern's exit tunnel was not a perfectly smooth bore. It was a rugged, natural conduit that had been widened and reinforced, but it still retained a degree of its original geological character. The currents within it were known to be unpredictable, capable of shifting without warning. The *Phoenix* would have to navigate these treacherous waters with the precision of a surgeon.

"Thrusters engaged," Kaelen reported. "We are moving. Slow and steady. The current is pulling us towards the left wall, about 2.7 meters off our projected vector."

"Compensating with lateral thruster adjustments," Lena responded, her fingers flying across the control interface, a symphony of inputs guiding the colossal vessel. "Maintain visual on the tunnel walls. We need to avoid any direct contact." The holographic projections of the tunnel's interior, rendered from weeks of meticulous sonic and optical mapping, flickered on Lena's main display, offering a terrifyingly intimate view of their path.

The sheer scale of the *Phoenix* was put into stark relief as it began its slow, deliberate journey through the tunnel. The reinforced rock walls seemed to press in, a constant reminder of the immense forces that could crush them. Lena's focus remained absolute, her mind a cold, calculating engine of navigation and systems management. She could feel the subtle vibrations of the ship responding to her commands, the precise application of thrust, the minute adjustments to its orientation.

"The tunnel's mouth is approaching," Kaelen's voice was taut with concentration. "The external oceanic pressure is increasing as we draw closer to the primary seal. We are within 500 meters of the blast doors."

"Initiating pre-activation sequence for the Chameleon system," Lena announced. "We need to begin masking our energy signature even before we clear the cavern. The moment those blast doors retract, we will be exposed to a far wider spectrum of potential sensors."

The Chameleon system, her magnum opus of technological deception, was already a marvel of engineering. But its true test would be in the chaotic environment of an actual departure, where every stray emission, every flicker of anomalous energy, could spell their doom. She felt a surge of pride, mingled with the ever-present knot of anxiety, as the system's diagnostic lights began to cycle through their readiness checks.

"The blast doors are beginning their retraction sequence," Kaelen reported, his voice laced with a controlled tension. "Slow retraction, standard protocol to minimize seismic disturbance. We have visual confirmation of the external oceanic environment."

Lena watched the main viewport as the colossal blast doors, each hundreds of meters thick and weighing thousands of tons, began to slide apart. The deep, inky blackness of the abyss, punctuated by the faint, ethereal glow of bioluminescent organisms, rushed in to fill the void. And then, it happened.

"Energy surge detected!" Kaelen's voice was sharp, urgent. "Multiple wide-spectrum scans originating from beyond the cavern's immediate vicinity. They're… they're more sophisticated than anticipated."

Lena's fingers flew across her console, her eyes never leaving the incoming data streams. "Chameleon, full activation! Deploy distortion field, maximum intensity. Begin signature masking protocol, prioritize geothermal and seismic mimicry."

The ship shuddered, not with mechanical stress, but with the powerful hum of energy being rerouted and amplified. On Lena's display, the sharp, distinct energy profile of the *Phoenix* began to blur, to ripple, to dissolve into the ambient background noise of the deep ocean. The external scans, powerful and penetrating, washed over them, but instead of registering a colossal, advanced vessel, they encountered nothing but the expected fluctuations of a geologically active seabed.

"The scans are passing through," Kaelen confirmed, his voice filled with relief. "They're registering…

background radiation, thermal vents, and minor seismic activity. Your camouflage is holding, Lena. It's perfect."

Perfect. The word resonated deeply within Lena. It was the culmination of her efforts, the validation of her relentless pursuit of invisibility. But the threat was far from over. This was just the beginning. They had escaped the immediate confinement of the cavern, but they were now venturing into a world where their pursuers were actively, relentlessly seeking them.


"We are clear of the cavern's mouth," Kaelen announced, his voice regaining its usual steady cadence. "All systems are nominal. We are proceeding on our charted departure vector."

Elias's voice chimed in, calm and resolute. "Excellent work, Lena, Kaelen. The *Phoenix* has taken its first breath in the open ocean. Now, the real challenge begins. We must disappear into the vastness, become one with the ocean's secrets. Our survival depends on our ability to remain unseen, unheard, and utterly unknown. Lena, plot a course that utilizes the deepest trenches and the most sensor-disruptive oceanic phenomena available. We will not be found until we choose to be found."

Lena nodded, her gaze fixed on the navigation charts that now spread before her, a vast, alien landscape of abyssal plains, hydrothermal vents, and colossal underwater mountain ranges. The *Phoenix* was no longer a prisoner of the cavern; it was a hunter in its own right, a silent predator in the deepest, darkest reaches of the planet. Her work was far from over; it was merely entering its most critical, and most dangerous, phase. The shadow of oversight had been evaded for now, but its presence was a constant, chilling reminder of the vigilance required to survive.

## 6: The Silent Departure

The cavern's great cavernous mouth, once a stark, engineered opening, was now undergoing a meticulous reversal. Systems that had been painstakingly integrated to support the *Phoenix*'s construction and launch were being systematically decommissioned. Lena's fingers, now scrubbed clean but still bearing the faint, ghost-like imprint of circuitry sealant, danced across her console, executing the final shutdown sequences for the cavern's internal atmospheric regulators. These were not the simple environmental controls of a terrestrial habitat; they were intricate machines designed to maintain a precise blend of gases, to filter out the trace elements of geothermal activity, and to scrub away any airborne particulate that might betray their presence to passive long-range sensors. Now, with a series of precise commands, they were being coaxed into a dormant state, their humming becoming a low sigh before fading into silence.

"Atmospheric regulators powering down," Lena's voice, projected with a practiced calm, echoed through the ship's internal comms. "Pressure equalization protocols are active. We are allowing the cavern's natural atmospheric composition to reassert itself. Residual energy signatures from our operations are being purged. Scrubber units are cycling through their final deletion algorithms." Each word was measured, deliberate, a testament to the years of planning that had culminated in this singular, silent departure. The very air they had breathed, a carefully curated blend that had sustained them through their clandestine work, was now being allowed to dissipate, to merge back into the ambient, mineral-laden atmosphere of the deep-sea geological formation.

Kaelen, ever the vigilant guardian of the ship's physical integrity, was simultaneously overseeing the retraction of the cavern's secondary environmental seals. These were not the massive blast doors that had guarded the immediate exit, but a series of more discreet, yet equally critical, seals that had maintained the atmospheric integrity of the deeper sections of the cavern, areas that had housed auxiliary workshops, long-term storage, and the nascent hydroponic gardens. "Secondary seals are retracting smoothly," he reported, his voice a reassuring anchor in the symphony of deactivation. "All pressure differentials are stabilizing. The seismic dampeners that were active during our construction phase are now being recalibrated for low-power standby, ready to absorb any residual seismic shock from our departure, should it occur."

The cavern, a vast cathedral of rock and mineral, had been their silent, unblinking witness. It had absorbed the raw materials, shielded them from the prying eyes of the surface world, and, in its own geological way, had provided a sense of permanence, a stark contrast to the ephemeral nature of their mission. Now, its role was concluding. The auxiliary power conduits that had fed their extensive fabrication facilities were being systematically de-energized, their robust casings left to gleam dully in the receding operational lights. The massive construction gantries, which had swung and positioned the colossal components of the *Phoenix* with an almost balletic grace, were being retracted to their lowest power settings, their heavy-duty hydraulics sighing as they settled into quiescence.

"Power conduits to fabrication bay C are offline," Lena confirmed, her gaze sweeping across a complex matrix of energy flow diagrams. "Primary power transfer from the geothermal taps is being rerouted to the ship's reserve cells, minimizing our active footprint. We are effectively un-plugging ourselves from the very infrastructure that enabled our existence here." It was a sentiment that resonated with a profound sense of finality. Every circuit breaker thrown, every dormant system initiated, was a step further away from the sanctuary they had built, and a step closer to the unknown dangers of the wider ocean.

Elias, standing by the main viewport, watched the last of the internal cavern lights, the soft, utilitarian glow that had illuminated their world for so long, flicker and die. The cavern was plunging into a deep, natural twilight, its contours now revealed only by the faintest phosphorescence from the water clinging to its walls and the dim, starlight-like shimmer of mineral deposits high on the vaulted ceiling. "The cavern's geological resonance is returning to its baseline," he observed, his voice carrying a note of quiet reflection. "The sounds of our industry are being swallowed by the silence of the deep. It is a fitting end to this phase."

Lena initiated the sequence for the cavern's primary egress seal. This was the last physical barrier between them and the open ocean, the seal that had protected their hidden world from the immense pressures and unpredictable currents of the abyss. "Initiating closure sequence for the cavern mouth's primary seal," she announced, her fingers hovering over the final confirmation command. "This will be a slow, controlled retraction, designed to mimic natural geological shifts, minimizing any detectable disturbance." The immense, multi-layered seal, engineered from a composite of reinforced ceramite and adaptive polymers, began its slow, deliberate retreat into the cavern walls. The sheer scale of the operation was evident in the almost imperceptible movement, the agonizingly slow revealing of the vast, inky expanse beyond.

As the last segment of the seal slid into its recess, a profound silence descended, a silence that was both absolute and deafening. The cavern, their meticulously crafted sanctuary, was now an empty shell, its purpose fulfilled. It was a place that had witnessed their struggles, their triumphs, their desperate ingenuity. It had been their womb, their forge, and their refuge. Now, it was being returned to its primordial state, a silent monument to a clandestine endeavor that had defied the very constraints of their world.

Lena initiated the final sweep of the cavern's interior sensors. These were sophisticated devices, capable of detecting minute energy fluctuations, residual heat signatures, and even the subtle chemical traces left behind by advanced technologies. "Running final internal sensor sweep," she stated, her eyes scanning the data as it populated her console. "Purging all stored sensor logs. Erasing all maintenance records associated with the *Phoenix*'s construction within this chamber. We are leaving no ghosts behind." The objective was absolute erasure, an ontological cleanse that would render their presence in the cavern utterly undetectable, as if they had never been.

Kaelen confirmed the deactivation of the cavern's structural reinforcement systems, the massive hydraulic jacks and tensile bracing that had been installed to compensate for the stresses of their industrial activities.

"Structural reinforcements are disengaged," he reported. "The cavern's natural load-bearing capacity is now the sole determinant of its integrity. I've confirmed that all seismic monitoring stations within the cavern are also being powered down, their data logs purged."

The feeling that permeated the *Phoenix* was a complex mix of relief and melancholic finality. They had achieved the impossible – they had built a starship, or something akin to it, in the deepest, darkest corners of their world, shielded from all observation. This cavern had been more than just a location; it had been a symbol of their autonomy, their ability to carve out existence independent of the suffocating oversight of the global powers. Yet, leaving it felt like abandoning a part of themselves, a testament to their resilience and their sheer audacity.

"Initiating final external scan of the cavern's entrance," Lena announced, her voice tinged with a subtle weariness. "We need to confirm that our departure has not inadvertently triggered any automated geological surveys or passive sensor sweeps from external monitoring posts, however unlikely that may be." The cavern was vast, and its exit tunnel was a winding, complex conduit. Even with their advanced stealth technology, there remained a lingering anxiety that some unforeseen interaction could betray their existence.

The external scans confirmed what they had meticulously engineered for: a seemingly undisturbed geological formation. The pressure readings were normal, the ambient energy signatures consistent with the expected geothermal activity of the region. The cavern mouth was, to all external indications, just another unremarkable feature of the abyssal plain. The *Phoenix*, a marvel of clandestine engineering, had successfully vanished from its cradle.

"All systems are nominal," Kaelen stated, his voice a calm counterpoint to the swirling emotions within the ship. "We are clear of the cavern. Our departure sequence is complete. We are now integrated with the external oceanic environment, operating under the full spectrum of the Chameleon system's masking protocols."

Elias nodded, his gaze fixed on the vast, alien landscape that stretched out before the *Phoenix*. "The cavern served its purpose. It was our shield, our sanctuary, the crucible in which our future was forged. But we cannot linger in the past. Our journey has just begun. The darkness we now navigate is a far more formidable adversary than the rock that enclosed us." He turned, his gaze sweeping across the bridge, meeting the eyes of Lena and Kaelen. "We leave behind a place that knew our secret, a place that housed our impossible endeavor. Now, we must become the impossible ourselves, a phantom in the deep, leaving no trace, forging our own destiny in the silent, unforgiving expanse."

Lena initiated the plotted course, a trajectory designed to utilize the deepest trenches and the most sensor-disruptive oceanic phenomena available. The *Phoenix* began to move, not with the thunderous roar of conventional propulsion, but with a deep, resonant hum that spoke of controlled power and calculated intent. They were no longer in the familiar confines of their sanctuary. They were adrift in the true abyss, a solitary vessel venturing into the uncharted, a phantom slipping away into the immeasurable darkness, leaving behind only silence and the memory of a hidden world. The cavern was now just a memory, a closed chapter in their extraordinary journey. The silence that returned to its depths was the silence of a secret perfectly kept, a testament to the silent departure of the *Phoenix*. The very act of leaving was itself a form of sealing, an entombment of their past existence, ensuring that the cavern would remain undisturbed, unblemished by their extraordinary presence, and their departure, a whisper in the vast ocean's ear.

The *Phoenix*, a phantom born of necessity and forged in secrecy, now navigated the crushing embrace of the deep ocean. Elias, his hands steady on the primary flight controls, guided their vessel away from the thermal vent field that had been their clandestine birthplace. The hum of their unique propulsion system, a marvel of salvaged and repurposed technology, resonated through the hull – a low, resonant thrum that spoke of controlled power and calculated intent. Gone was the deafening roar of raw geothermal energy; in its place, a subtle symphony of advanced engineering, a testament to the successful integration of the Abyssus's core systems. Each maneuver was deliberate, a practiced dance against the immense, unyielding pressure.

They were no longer cocooned within the protective shell of the cavern. The deep-sea geological formation, their sanctuary and their crucible, was now a memory receding into the inky blackness. The *Phoenix* was truly alone, a solitary spark of ingenuity in an ocean of unfathomable depth and darkness. Elias's gaze was fixed on the holographic display before him, a complex tapestry of sonar readings, pressure differentials, and energy signatures. Every flicker, every anomaly, had to be scrutinized. The threat of detection, even after their meticulous departure, remained a constant, gnawing anxiety. They had left no trace, purged all logs, and decommissioned every system within the cavern, but the ocean was a vast, interconnected ecosystem, and the potential for unforeseen monitoring equipment, however dormant or unlikely, was a possibility they could not afford to dismiss.

Lena, positioned at the advanced sensor array, monitored the external environment with an eagle's eye. "No anomalous energy readings detected in the immediate vicinity of the vent field," she reported, her voice a calm, measured cadence that belied the tension radiating from her. "The geothermal output is within expected parameters. The Chameleon system is maintaining optimal atmospheric masking, blending our signature with the ambient thermal fluctuations." The Chameleon system, a proprietary stealth technology salvaged from the remnants of the Abyssus, was their primary shield. It not only masked their electromagnetic and acoustic signatures but also subtly altered the *Phoenix*'s thermal output, allowing it to mimic the natural heat signatures of the deep-sea environment, effectively rendering them invisible to most passive detection methods.

Kaelen, meanwhile, was meticulously overseeing the structural integrity and propulsion systems. His fingers moved with practiced speed across his console, monitoring the intricate ballet of the *Phoenix*'s unique propulsion system. It was a departure from conventional submersibles, eschewing noisy, disruptive propellers for a more subtle, energy-efficient method of locomotion. The salvaged gravitic emitters, originally designed for atmospheric flight on a world with significantly different gravitational forces, had been reconfigured to manipulate localized water density, creating a seamless, silent glide through the crushing depths. "Propulsion efficiency remains at ninety-eight percent," Kaelen confirmed. "Hull integrity is stable, with negligible pressure differential across all sectors. The gravitic emitters are operating within optimal thermal parameters."

Their current course was a winding, circuitous path through a network of abyssal canyons and underwater mountain ranges. Elias had plotted a route that maximized the use of natural terrain for acoustic and visual cover. They were not simply traveling; they were performing a silent ballet, a ghost ship navigating the treacherous underwater landscape. Each turn of the submersible, each subtle adjustment of speed, was a calculated risk, a step deeper into the unknown. The terrain itself was a formidable adversary, with unpredictable currents, sheer drop-offs, and geological formations that could easily disrupt their stealth or even pose a physical threat.

"Approaching the 'Serpent's Coil' canyon system," Elias announced, his voice betraying a hint of the challenge ahead. The Serpent's Coil was a notorious section of the ocean floor, known for its extreme depth variations and powerful, unpredictable undertows. Sonar imaging had revealed a labyrinthine network of deep fissures and sharp, angular rock formations that could easily snag or damage their vessel. "Standard navigational protocols will be insufficient here. We'll need to rely on visual identification and minute course corrections."

Lena's sensors painted a detailed, albeit terrifying, picture of the canyon ahead. "The canyon walls are rich in metallic ore deposits," she reported. "These will create significant sonar clutter. The gravitic distortions in this region are also amplified by the geological composition, which could interfere with the Chameleon system's masking capabilities."

"Understood," Elias replied, his brow furrowed in concentration. He activated the *Phoenix*'s forward-facing multi-spectral scanners, pushing their resolution to the absolute limit. The holographic display flickered, resolving into a dizzying array of sharp, jagged lines and cavernous openings. "Kaelen, prepare to compensate for localized gravitic interference. Lena, prioritize acoustic and thermal signatures over visual clarity for the next phase."

The *Phoenix* began its descent into the Serpent's Coil. The transition was palpable. The subtle hum of their propulsion seemed to deepen, as if the very ocean was pressing in on them, trying to discern their presence. The metallic ores in the canyon walls bounced back distorted sonar echoes, creating phantom images that danced around the edges of their detection grid. It was like navigating a minefield blindfolded, relying on the faintest whispers of information.

"Gravitic fluctuations increasing," Kaelen reported, his knuckles white as he gripped his console. "Compensating… it's like trying to steer through molasses that's actively trying to push you off course." He initiated a counter-frequency modulation, a delicate adjustment that aimed to stabilize their position within the swirling gravitic currents.

Lena worked feverishly, sifting through the cacophony of false positives. "I'm detecting a faint, intermittent energy signature ahead," she announced, her voice tight with urgency. "It's weak, but it's not geothermal. It's… artificial. Low-power, but definitely artificial."

Elias's grip tightened on the controls. "Source? Direction?"

"Sector Gamma-seven. Directly ahead, masked by the canyon wall. It's a passive monitoring buoy, ancient design, likely abandoned. But it's still active." Lena's fingers flew across her console, attempting to triangulate the buoy's exact position and assess its operational parameters. "It's broadcasting a very basic, localized distress signal, or perhaps just a beacon for automated maintenance. Whatever it is, it's emitting a faint RF signature that our Chameleon system isn't designed to perfectly mask."

The implications were immediate and dire. Even a faint, detectable signature could be enough to trigger an alert in the deep-sea monitoring network, a network that, while largely assumed to be defunct or poorly maintained in these remote regions, could still hold remnants of active oversight. "Can we bypass it?" Elias asked, his gaze locked onto the projected location of the buoy.

"Negative," Lena replied. "It's positioned directly in our most viable path through the canyon. Any attempt to go around it would involve navigating through a denser cluster of metallic deposits, significantly increasing our risk of detection or collision."

Kaelen spoke up, his voice grim. "If we attempt to disable it, even with a focused EMP burst, the residual energy signature could be even more problematic. It would be a clear indication of tampering."

A tense silence descended on the bridge. They were caught between a rock and a hard place, or more accurately, between a passive, ancient sensor and the crushing weight of the ocean. Elias's mind raced, weighing the risks. The buoy was a relic, a forgotten sentinel of a previous era of deep-sea exploration, but its very existence presented a new, unforeseen obstacle.

"Lena, can you get a more precise reading on its broadcast frequency and power output?" Elias asked, his mind already formulating a plan. "Kaelen, can we modulate our gravitic emitters to mimic the buoy's local frequency, effectively 'piggybacking' on its signature?"

Lena's fingers danced across her console. "Frequency is 3.4 gigahertz, very low power. I can isolate it. It's a simple, repeating pulse. Power output is minimal, but it's consistent."

Kaelen considered the suggestion. "Modulating the emitters to that frequency might be possible, but it would require a significant portion of our gravitic control to focus on mimicking this one small signal. It would reduce our maneuverability and our overall stealth effectiveness in other areas."

"But it might allow us to pass without triggering any secondary alarms," Elias countered. "If the buoy is broadcasting a consistent, albeit faint, signal, and we can add our own signal that is similar enough, the monitoring system might interpret our presence as a secondary echo or a malfunction of the buoy itself."

"It's a calculated risk, Elias," Lena warned. "If the buoy's system is more sophisticated than it appears, or if there are any tertiary detection mechanisms we're not seeing, this could backfire spectacularly."

Elias took a deep breath. The Serpent's Coil was proving to be a fitting test of their newfound capabilities. They had built the *Phoenix* in secret, but now they had to prove they could navigate the world unseen. "We proceed with the modulation. Kaelen, initiate the frequency mimicry. Lena, keep a constant watch on the buoy's signal integrity and any potential secondary detections. I'll maintain our current course and speed, making the smallest possible adjustments."

The *Phoenix* began to inch forward, its gravitic emitters subtly shifting their output. The hum of their propulsion changed, taking on a faint, almost imperceptible oscillation that mirrored the buoy's weak pulse. The effect was subtle, a delicate dance of energy manipulation. Elias focused on keeping their forward momentum steady, his eyes scanning the holographic display for any hint of an alert.

The minutes stretched into an eternity. The canyon walls seemed to press closer, the metallic ores reflecting distorted light patterns. The buoy, a faint, blinking indicator on their sensors, drew nearer. Elias could almost feel its silent, ancient gaze.

"Signature integration is holding," Kaelen reported, his voice a low murmur. "We are within twenty meters of the buoy."

Lena's breath hitched. "No alarms. No deviations in ambient energy readings. It's… it's working."

The *Phoenix* glided past the derelict monitoring buoy. It was a small, nondescript piece of equipment, barely visible in the gloom, its faint signal a ghost in the immense darkness. But for Elias, Lena, and Kaelen, it represented a critical hurdle overcome. They had navigated a technological obstacle, a silent guardian of the deep that had threatened to expose their audacious undertaking.

As they emerged from the Serpent's Coil, the terrain opened up into a vast, uncharted expanse of the abyssal plain. The pressure remained immense, the darkness absolute, but the immediate threat had receded. Elias allowed himself a small, controlled exhale.

"We're clear of the Coil," Elias announced, his voice tinged with relief. "Chameleon system is back to full spectrum masking. Propulsion is back to optimal efficiency."

Lena continued her sensor sweep. "The buoy's signature is fading. No indication that our passage was registered. It seems the archaic system was too primitive to discern our modulation."

Kaelen nodded, running a quick diagnostic on the gravitic emitters. "The energy expenditure for the frequency mimicry was significant, but within acceptable limits. We've successfully navigated a potentially critical detection point."

The journey was far from over. The vastness of the ocean stretched before them, an endless frontier of challenges and unknowns. But the successful navigation of the Serpent's Coil had instilled a renewed sense of confidence. They were not just piloting a ship; they were becoming one with it, mastering its intricacies, and learning to read the subtle language of the deep. The integration of the Abyssus's core systems, a complex and demanding undertaking, had proven to be a resounding success, providing the *Phoenix* with the power and control necessary for their clandestine mission.

"The next segment of our plotted course will take us through the 'Whispering Trench'," Elias stated, his gaze already focused on the holographic display that depicted the topography ahead. "It's a region known for its extreme hydrostatic pressure and exceptionally low ambient energy signatures. Perfect for maintaining our low profile, but the terrain is also incredibly unstable. We'll need to maintain constant vigilance."

Lena confirmed the data. "The Whispering Trench is characterized by active tectonic plate boundaries. Minor seismic events are frequent, creating significant pressure fluctuations and potential for sonic interference. Our hull is rated for the pressure, but the constant seismic activity could mask or mimic our own signature if we're not careful."

"Understood," Elias replied. "We'll need to synchronize our propulsion with the seismic pulses as much as possible, using them to mask our movements. It's going to be a delicate balancing act."

The *Phoenix* continued its silent journey, a testament to human ingenuity and resilience. Each successful maneuver, each overcome obstacle, was a step further into their unknown future, a future they were forging themselves, in the deepest, darkest reaches of their world. The ocean held its breath, an indifferent witness to their audacious passage. They were a whisper in the abyss, a phantom born of necessity, and their journey was just beginning. The silent departure from their cavernous cradle had led them into the true heart of the deep, a realm where only the most adaptable and the most determined could hope to survive, and perhaps, to thrive. Elias, Lena, and Kaelen, bound by their shared purpose, pressed onward, their vessel a beacon of defiance against the overwhelming darkness. The integration of the Abyssus's systems had been more than just a technical achievement; it had been the final piece of their puzzle, unlocking the potential for a journey that would take them beyond the confines of their known world, into territories uncharted and dangers unimaginable. They were the *Phoenix*, and they were rising from the depths, leaving behind only silence and the memory of a world they had dared to escape. The true test of their mastery lay not in the construction of their vessel, but in their ability to navigate the treacherous depths undetected, to become one with the crushing darkness that surrounded them. And as Elias guided the *Phoenix* towards the Whispering Trench, a new chapter in their silent exodus began.

The ascent was a journey through a gauntlet of unseen eyes. Emerging from the crushing embrace of the abyssal plain, the *Phoenix* began its slow, deliberate climb towards the twilight zone, a region where sunlight, however faint, began to penetrate the inky blackness. Elias maintained a constant vigilance, his eyes sweeping across the multi-spectral readouts, searching for any anomaly, any hint of detection. Lena, her fingers flying across the sensor array, worked to refine their chameleon masking, pushing the limits of the salvaged technology. "We're entering the mesopelagic zone," she announced, her voice a low hum that barely disturbed the hushed atmosphere of the bridge. "Pressure is dropping, but ambient sensor activity is expected to increase exponentially from this point onwards."

Kaelen, stationed at the communications and external sensor monitoring station, was a picture of focused intensity. His brow was furrowed, his gaze locked onto the holographic sphere that represented their immediate environment. "Picking up faint, intermittent pings," he reported, his voice clipped. "Low-frequency sonar sweeps, consistent with deep-sea reconnaissance drones. They're wide-beam and likely automated, but they're active." He highlighted a cluster of faint blips on Elias's display, scattered across their projected ascent path. "We're going to have to thread the needle, Elias. They're moving in a predictable pattern, but there are blind spots we can exploit."

Elias nodded, his mind already processing the available data. "Lena, can we enhance our thermal and acoustic baffling? I want our signature to be as indistinguishable from the background oceanic noise as possible."

"Working on it," Lena replied, her voice taut. "The gravitic emitters are drawing more power to compensate for the increased buoyancy and the need to suppress our residual thermal output. I'm diverting auxiliary power from non-essential life support systems for the next sixty minutes. This will make the interior environment considerably colder, but it's a necessary trade-off." A shiver, not entirely from the ambient temperature drop, traced its way down Elias's spine. The thought of their own life support being a luxury they could no longer afford was a stark reminder of their precarious situation.

The *Phoenix* continued its ascent, each meter gained a victory against the immense forces arrayed against them. The faint sounds of the drones, like distant, metallic heartbeats, seemed to grow louder as they approached the zones of potential surveillance. Elias navigated with a painter's precision, using the undulating topography of the underwater landscape as cover. Jagged seamounts and deep trenches became temporary shields, providing brief windows of opportunity to slip past the drone patrols.

"Approaching a dense cluster of acoustic emitters," Kaelen warned. "Multiple drone signatures converging in the sector ahead. This is a high-risk zone. Their detection radius at this range is significant." He tapped a command into his console, bringing up a detailed overlay of the drone's operational parameters. "These units are programmed for broad spectrum sweeps, primarily focused on identifying anomalous energy signatures. They're not looking for anything specific, just… anything that doesn't belong."

Elias's jaw tightened. "Lena, how are we doing on the Chameleon system's adaptive masking?"

"It's performing within expected parameters, Elias," Lena replied, her voice betraying a hint of strain. "But the constant adjustments required to counter the drone sweeps are taxing the system. I'm seeing minor fluctuations in our thermal output that I can't fully suppress. It's like trying to hold water in a sieve." She paused, her eyes scanning the data flow. "I've managed to create a temporary 'ghost' signature, mimicking the resonant frequencies of the surrounding water masses. It's a gamble, but it might confuse their algorithms long enough for us to pass."

"Do it," Elias commanded without hesitation. He knew the risks of any deviation from their natural signature, but the alternative was unacceptable. The *Phoenix* began to emit a low, pulsating hum, a carefully calibrated sonic wave designed to blend with the ambient noise of the ocean. It was a desperate measure, a sonic whisper in a world of loud pronouncements, but it was all they had.

As they entered the zone of concentrated drone activity, the bridge of the *Phoenix* fell into an unnerving silence. The only sounds were the soft hum of their own systems and the amplified, almost spectral whispers of Kaelen's sensor readouts. Elias's hands remained steady on the controls, his eyes glued to the display. The blips representing the drones swirled around them, their invisible tendrils of detection reaching out, searching.

"They're still pinging us," Kaelen reported, his voice barely audible. "But the readings are… inconclusive. They're registering our presence, but they're classifying it as a significant environmental anomaly, not a vessel. The ghost signature is working… for now."

The seconds stretched into minutes, each one a miniature eternity. Elias felt the immense pressure of the unseen gaze, the constant threat of exposure. He imagined the automated systems, tirelessly sifting through data, looking for the one errant signal that would betray their presence. One wrong move, one miscalculation, and their entire mission, their very existence, would be jeopardized.

"There's a gap," Kaelen suddenly announced, his voice sharper. "A momentary lull in the drone activity. Sector Delta-four. It's our best chance to break free from this cluster."

Elias didn't hesitate. "Lena, full power to the gravitic emitters for evasive maneuvers. Kaelen, keep me updated on the drone movements. I need to know their exact positions as we move."

With a surge of controlled power, the *Phoenix* surged forward, its silent glide transforming into a swift, almost balletic movement. Elias steered them through the narrow aperture, the holographic display a frantic dance of overlapping detection grids. The drones, their automated patrols momentarily disrupted by the unexpected surge, seemed to falter, their systematic sweeps momentarily unable to reacquire the *Phoenix*'s anomalous signature.

"We're through the primary cluster!" Kaelen exclaimed, a hint of relief in his voice. "But we're not in the clear yet. There are secondary patrols further up, and I'm picking up faint transmissions from a higher-altitude oceanic surveillance platform. It's a passive sensor array, but it's incredibly sensitive."

The mention of a higher-altitude platform sent a fresh wave of unease through the bridge. These were the more sophisticated eyes, the ones capable of discerning subtler anomalies. "Lena, can we adapt our masking to counter a passive optical and thermal array?" Elias asked, his mind already working on a new strategy.

"It will be challenging," Lena admitted. "Passive sensors are designed to detect even the slightest deviations from expected norms. We'll need to minimize our thermal footprint to an absolute minimum and ensure our hull's reflective properties are perfectly aligned with the ambient light conditions. I'll need to reroute power from the propulsion stabilizers to the Chameleon system. It will limit our maneuverability, but it's our only chance."

Elias nodded, accepting the increased risk. They were ascending into shallower waters, closer to the reach of the world they had left behind, and with that proximity came the increased threat of detection. The ascent was a delicate balancing act, a constant negotiation with the ever-present surveillance networks.

As they moved higher, the ocean began to change. The crushing darkness of the abyss gave way to a dim, ethereal twilight. Sunlight, diffused by miles of water, painted the environment in hues of blue and gray. This was the upper mesopelagic, a realm of bioluminescent creatures and vast, empty spaces, but also a realm where the tendrils of human surveillance reached further and further.

"Picking up a network of passive acoustic hydrophones," Kaelen reported, his voice grave. "These are strategically placed along known migratory routes, likely to monitor deep-sea fauna, but they can also pick up anomalous vessel sounds." He highlighted a series of faint dots on the display, spread out like a fine mesh across their path. "They're widely spaced, but their sensitivity is exceptionally high."

"Lena, how are we on noise reduction?" Elias asked, his gaze fixed on the holographic representation of the hydrophone grid.

"We're operating at peak efficiency, Elias," Lena replied. "The gravitic emitters are designed for silent operation, and we've insulated every component to minimize internal noise. However, any sudden acceleration or deceleration, any significant shift in our gravitic field, could create a detectable acoustic signature."

"So, we need to be as smooth as possible," Elias mused aloud. "Like a ghost drifting through the water. Lena, can you predict the hydrophone sweep patterns? If we can time our passage with any brief periods of reduced sensitivity, it could give us an advantage."

Lena's fingers flew across her console, cross-referencing the hydrophone positions with known oceanic currents and tidal patterns. "There's a slight ebb and flow in their active monitoring cycles, correlating with the prevailing current shifts," she reported. "It's minimal, but it creates brief windows, approximately five seconds long, where their detection threshold is slightly higher.”

“Five seconds,” Elias repeated, a grim smile touching his lips. “That’s all we’ve got. Kaelen, I need those timings as soon as you have them.”

The tension on the bridge was palpable. Elias steered the *Phoenix* with an almost unnerving stillness, his movements economical and precise. Each subtle adjustment was calculated to minimize any disturbance to the water around them. They were approaching the first of the hydrophone clusters, a series of invisible ears listening intently to the silent depths.

“Hydrophone cluster Alpha-seven,” Kaelen announced, his voice steady despite the mounting pressure. “Active monitoring cycle ending in ten seconds. Sensitive period begins in T-minus ten… nine… eight…”

Elias adjusted their speed, preparing for the critical maneuver. Lena stood by, ready to recalibrate the Chameleon system at a moment’s notice. The holographic display showed the hydrophones as passive nodes, their data streams a silent testament to their vigilance.

"Three… two… one… Cycle complete. Sensitive period begins now." Kaelen's voice was a low, urgent whisper.

Elias initiated a series of minute gravitic pulses, designed to propel them forward with the utmost subtlety. The *Phoenix* glided past the first cluster, its hull a silent enigma. Elias held his breath, his eyes scanning the sensor readouts for any indication of detection.

"No anomalies detected," Kaelen reported, a sigh of relief escaping his lips. "We passed through undetected."

They continued their ascent, the process repeating itself with each cluster of hydrophones. It was a tedious, nerve-wracking dance, a test of their patience and their nerve. The success of each passage was a small victory, but the knowledge that more threats lay ahead kept their vigilance razor-sharp.

As they climbed higher, the visual spectrum began to play a more significant role. The twilight deepened, and the faint sunlight filtering from above created an eerie, disorienting environment. Elias activated the *Phoenix*'s external visual sensors, enhancing their low-light capabilities. They were now in the photic zone, a region increasingly monitored by a variety of optical surveillance systems.

"Picking up faint light trails," Kaelen reported, his voice tinged with concern. "These are consistent with the passage of high-altitude, low-light optical drones. They're far above us, but their scan patterns are broad, sweeping large areas of the water column."

Lena's fingers danced across her console. "Our visual profile is currently optimized for this depth, Elias. The Chameleon system is actively modulating our hull's reflectivity to match the ambient light conditions. However, any sudden movement or any deviation from our projected trajectory could disrupt this masking and create a visible anomaly."

Elias understood. They were becoming more vulnerable as they approached the surface, the very environment that was home to their pursuers. The deep ocean had offered them a degree of anonymity, but the upper layers were a different battlefield entirely, one where their presence was inherently more conspicuous.

They continued their slow, meticulous ascent, the ghost ship navigating a minefield of invisible sensors and watchful eyes. Each passing moment was a testament to their ingenuity and their unwavering determination. The silence of the deep had been their ally, but as they drew closer to the surface, they knew that the true test of their stealth was yet to come. They were the *Phoenix*, and they were evading the unseen watchers of the deep, a silent exodus from a world that sought to contain them, a desperate flight towards an uncertain dawn. The journey was a constant reminder of the stakes involved, the immense power of the systems they were up against, and the sheer audacity of their endeavor. Every successful evasion, every undetected passage, fueled their resolve, but the ever-present threat of discovery hung over them like a suffocating shroud. They were venturing into a realm where their very existence was an anomaly, a defiance of the established order, and they had to prove that they could disappear into the vastness, becoming one with the currents and the shadows, a phantom in the ocean's embrace.

The oppressive weight of the deep began to subtly shift, a gradual release that Elias felt more in his bones than registered on any instrument. The crushing embrace of the abyss, which had been their constant companion for so long, loosened its grip. It was a palpable sensation, a whisper of freedom after an eternity of confinement. With each meter ascended, the *Phoenix* shed a layer of its submerged identity, preparing for an emergence that felt both inevitable and profoundly uncertain. The perpetual darkness, an entity in itself, began to recede, not with a sudden burst of light, but with a gradual, almost imperceptible softening. It was like waking from a dreamless sleep, the edges of reality slowly coming into focus.

Lena, her gaze still fixed on the holographic displays, noted the diminishing pressure readings with a quiet intensity. "Pressure at… one hundred and fifty atmospheres," she reported, her voice a low murmur that barely disturbed the hum of the ship. "Still significant, but the difference is already noticeable. Our hull stress monitors are showing a marked decrease." She allowed herself a fleeting smile, a rare moment of respite from the constant tension that had etched itself onto her features. The physics of their ascent were relentless, a predictable progression dictated by the very nature of the ocean, but the implications of these changes were anything but predictable.

Kaelen, ever vigilant, was monitoring the subtle shifts in the oceanic environment. "Ambient energy signatures are changing," he stated, his fingers moving across his console with practiced fluidity. "As we climb higher, the background radiation from the surface biosphere begins to bleed through. Faint electromagnetic fluctuations, trace amounts of atmospheric particulates filtered through the water column, even the distant hum of surface vessels." He zoomed in on a series of faint, shimmering patterns on his display. "It's a different kind of surveillance now, Elias. Less about detecting anomalous energy, more about identifying anything that doesn't belong in the upper layers. The passive sensors are becoming more sophisticated, more discerning."

Elias nodded, his eyes never leaving the forward viewscreen, which still displayed the murky, blue-grey expanse. The subtle luminescence that had begun to flicker at the fringes of their perception was a testament to the encroaching world of light. It wasn't the searing brilliance of the sun, not yet, but a muted, ethereal glow, the first intimations of a different reality. These were the bioluminescent organisms that inhabited the mesopelagic zone, tiny sparks of life in the vast expanse, their fleeting light a stark contrast to the crushing darkness they had left behind. Each flicker was a reminder of the world above, a world of light and life that felt both intimately familiar and impossibly distant.

"The bioluminescent activity is increasing," Lena observed, her attention drawn to the subtle pulses of light that now punctuated the dimness. "It's a biological indicator of our increasing depth. The organisms that thrive in these transitional zones are incredibly sensitive to changes in light and pressure. They're essentially living barometers for our ascent." She tapped a few commands, bringing up a spectral analysis of the flickering lights. "I'm cataloging the dominant species' emission patterns. It's not just for scientific curiosity; it might offer some insight into the ambient sensor capabilities we might encounter. Some of these organisms have evolved complex defense mechanisms, including the ability to mimic or mask certain energy signatures."

"Mimicry," Elias mused, a flicker of interest in his eyes. "That could be our advantage, or our downfall. Lena, how are we doing on the Chameleon system's ability to adapt to these new visual cues? Can we incorporate some of that bioluminescent mimicry into our masking profile?"

Lena considered the question, her brow furrowed in concentration. "It's a complex undertaking, Elias. The Chameleon system is designed to work with electromagnetic and acoustic signatures, but adapting it to mimic complex biological light patterns is pushing its capabilities. The algorithms involved are exponentially more intricate. It's not just about reflecting light; it's about replicating the dynamic, fluctuating nature of bioluminescence. I can attempt to create a 'bio-ghost' signature, an overlay that mimics the general flicker and pulse of the surrounding fauna, but it will require significant power allocation and may introduce unforeseen instabilities."

"Unforeseen instabilities are becoming a way of life," Elias replied dryly. "But if it means we can slip through this transitional zone undetected, it's a risk we have to take. Prioritize the bio-ghost signature, Lena. Kaelen, keep a close watch for any indications that our masking is being compromised. We're entering a phase where visual detection becomes increasingly probable."

Kaelen's eyes scanned his monitors, his focus unwavering. "Understood, Elias. I'm also picking up faint, intermittent signals from what appears to be a deep-sea acoustic monitoring buoy. It's located further east, but its active scanning pattern might sweep this region periodically. It's an older model, likely part of an automated environmental monitoring network, but its detection parameters are still significant."

The mention of buoys, even automated ones, sent a ripple of unease through the bridge. These were the sentinel eyes and ears of the surface world, often overlooked in the grander schemes of oceanic surveillance, but capable of relaying critical data to more advanced systems. They represented a more mundane, yet pervasive, form of detection, a constant reminder that they were not truly alone in the water column.

"Lena, can we anticipate the buoy's sweep pattern?" Elias inquired. "If we can time our passage with its quiescent periods, it would reduce the risk of detection."

Lena's fingers flew across her console, cross-referencing oceanic current data with known buoy deployment patterns and expected operational cycles. "The buoy's acoustic scanning is programmed to be cyclical, with short bursts of active sonar followed by periods of passive listening. The current patterns suggest a predictable ebb and flow in its coverage, creating brief windows of opportunity. I can predict the next window with a high degree of accuracy, but it's tight – approximately seven seconds of reduced active scanning."

"Seven seconds," Elias echoed, his jaw tightening. It was a minuscule window, demanding a level of precision that pushed the *Phoenix*'s capabilities to their limits. "Kaelen, I need a constant update on the buoy's status. Lena, prepare to execute the bio-ghost signature and any necessary course corrections to maximize our window. We're going to thread the needle."

The ascent continued, a slow, deliberate climb through a world that was slowly transforming around them. The bioluminescence became more pronounced, painting the water with ethereal streaks of blue and green. It was a mesmerizing, yet unnerving, spectacle, a silent testament to the life that teemed in these intermediate depths. The *Phoenix*, cloaked in its shifting bio-ghost signature, moved through this luminous ballet like a phantom, its own luminescence carefully modulated to blend with the natural light show.

"Buoy is entering its passive listening phase," Kaelen announced, his voice clipped. "Window opens in thirty seconds. Elias, we have a slight deviation in the anticipated current, requiring a minor adjustment to our trajectory. It will bring us closer to a dense cluster of… what appear to be passive acoustic sensors. They're not actively pinging, but they're designed to detect even the faintest acoustic anomalies."

Elias's hands remained steady on the controls, his mind already processing the new variables. "Lena, can we enhance our acoustic baffling further without compromising the bio-ghost signature?"

"I can divert auxiliary power from the life support regulators to the gravitic emitters, further refining their dampening capabilities," Lena replied, her voice tight with concentration. "It will result in a temporary drop in internal atmospheric pressure and a slight decrease in oxygen levels. It's a calculated risk, but it will provide an additional layer of acoustic camouflage."

"Do it," Elias commanded, the decision made in an instant. The comfort of their own vessel was a luxury they could no longer afford. The mission's success hinged on their ability to become utterly invisible, to dissolve into the very fabric of the ocean.

As they navigated through the area of increased acoustic sensor density, the *Phoenix* seemed to glide with an even greater stillness, its engines emitting a barely perceptible hum. The bio-ghost signature pulsed around them, a shimmering veil that sought to blend their form with the flickering bioluminescence. Elias felt the subtle shifts in the water, the faint pressure waves generated by their movement, and willed them to be insignificant, to be absorbed by the vastness.

"We're within the sensor cluster's effective range," Kaelen reported, his gaze fixed on his display. "No detection anomalies registered. The bio-ghost signature is proving effective, and the enhanced acoustic baffling is minimizing our acoustic footprint. It seems the passive sensors are being… fooled by the combined effect of our masking and the natural bioluminescent noise."

A collective sigh of relief swept through the bridge, though no one dared to voice it too loudly. They were still in a precarious position, but each successful maneuver was a step closer to their objective. The ascent was a symphony of calculated risks and precise execution, a testament to their combined skills and their unwavering determination.

As they continued to ascend, the character of the oceanic twilight began to change again. The bioluminescence, while still present, started to recede, giving way to a more diffuse, ambient light. The faint glow was no longer generated by individual organisms, but by the very water column itself, a muted, silvery sheen that indicated their proximity to the surface. This was the upper mesopelagic, a region where sunlight, however filtered and attenuated, finally began to assert its presence.

"Approaching the twilight zone proper," Lena announced, her voice carrying a new note of anticipation. "The ambient light levels are increasing significantly. Our bio-ghost signature will need to adapt rapidly to counter the more sophisticated optical sensors that are prevalent at these depths. I'm re-calibrating the Chameleon system to mimic the spectral characteristics of the upper ocean water column. It will involve a wider range of light absorption and reflection parameters."

Kaelen chimed in, his tone grave. "I'm detecting an increase in surface-level electromagnetic activity. Faint signals, consistent with commercial shipping lanes and potentially… a more organized surveillance network. These are low-frequency radar sweeps and broad-spectrum passive scanning arrays. They're designed to cover vast areas of the ocean's surface and the upper layers of the water column."

Elias's gaze swept across the holographic display, the projected path of the *Phoenix* now a faint line against a backdrop of increasingly complex sensor data. They were no longer hidden in the crushing darkness of the abyss, but were emerging into a realm where their presence was inherently more conspicuous. The transition from the deep to the shallow was not just a change in pressure and light, but a fundamental shift in the nature of the threats they faced. The silent, unseen watchers of the deep were being replaced by a more active, more organized form of surveillance.

"Lena, how resilient is the Chameleon system against broad-spectrum scanning?" Elias asked, his mind already formulating new strategies. "If they're sweeping with active radar, even at low frequencies, our masking might be compromised."

"The system is designed for a degree of resilience against broad-spectrum scanning, Elias," Lena replied, her voice steady despite the growing complexity of the task. "However, continuous exposure to active radar sweeps, especially at close range, can eventually degrade our stealth capabilities. I can implement a dynamic pattern disruption protocol, which will introduce random fluctuations in our hull's reflective properties. It's a highly energy-intensive process, but it should make it more difficult for active sensors to lock onto a stable signature."

"Do it," Elias commanded, the decision immediate. The subtle dance through the abyssal plains was over. They were now engaged in a more overt, albeit still clandestine, evasion. The ocean's surface was beckoning, a siren call of both opportunity and peril. Each moment of their ascent was a negotiation with the unseen, a delicate balance between remaining hidden and moving forward. The faintest hint of bioluminescence had given way to the muted light of the Pacific twilight, a visual metaphor for their journey. They were shedding the darkness, the immensity of the deep, and preparing to embrace a world that awaited their emergence, a world that would either welcome them or shatter their fragile hope. The ocean, their cradle and their prison, was at last preparing to release them, but the true test, the test of surfacing and navigating the watchful gaze of the world above, was yet to come. The silence of their departure was about to be broken, not by the roar of engines, but by the desperate need to remain unheard and unseen in a world that was now acutely aware of their presence, or soon would be.

The ascent had been a relentless, drawn-out process, a slow unfurling from the crushing embrace of the abyss. For days, they had climbed, each meter gained a victory against the immense pressure that had defined their existence. Now, as the last vestiges of the abyssal darkness receded, a new canvas began to paint itself across the *Phoenix*'s forward viewscreen. It wasn't the stark, unyielding blackness of the deep, nor the ethereal glow of the mesopelagic. This was a liminal state, a diffusion of light that spoke of a world far above, a world where the sun, even in its absence, held dominion.

Lena, her fingers dancing across the touch-sensitive surfaces of her console, confirmed the changing environment. "Ambient light levels are now registering at a significant percentage of surface saturation, Elias," she reported, her voice laced with a quiet awe. "We are just below the photic zone's upper boundary, where photosynthesis is still possible, albeit attenuated." She gestured towards a series of rapidly updating readouts. "The water clarity is also increasing exponentially. We're seeing a decrease in particulate matter suspension and a corresponding enhancement of visible light penetration." The murky blues and greens of the deeper waters were giving way to a subtler, more pearlescent hue, a pearlescence that seemed to hold the promise of dawn.

Kaelen, his attention divided between the external sensors and the internal systems, added his observations. "Surface weather patterns indicate clear skies overhead, with minimal cloud cover. Thermal imaging shows the *Phoenix* as a near-perfect thermal blackbody against the surface waters. Our stealth emitters are functioning at peak efficiency, effectively masking our heat signature from any potential aerial or surface-based thermal detection." He paused, a faint frown creasing his brow. "However, I am picking up… faint acoustic reflections. Not from active sonar, but from the passive hydrophone arrays that are almost certainly deployed in this vicinity. They are designed to detect even the slightest disturbance of the water column, the faintest acoustic ripple."

Elias's gaze remained fixed on the slowly brightening horizon. The stars, once their only companions in the oppressive darkness, were now beginning to fade, surrendering to the encroaching light of a new day. The transition was as profound as their journey had been. They were shedding the skin of the abyss, emerging from the shadows into a realm that was both familiar and fraught with unprecedented peril. The deep had been their sanctuary, a place of relative anonymity. The surface, however, was a hyper-connected, surveilled environment, a vast theatre of human activity where their presence, however stealthy, could draw unwanted attention.

"The acoustic reflections," Elias mused, his voice a low rumble that seemed to vibrate with the residual tension of their descent. "Lena, how well are we integrated with the 'Whisper' protocol now? Can we further dampen any residual acoustic wake?"

Lena's fingers flew across her console, her movements fluid and precise. "The Whisper protocol is actively managing our vibrational output, Elias. We've reduced our engine harmonics to a near-negligible level, and the hull's resonant frequencies are being actively counteracted. The current acoustic reflections are primarily from the displacement of water itself, a unavoidable consequence of movement. However, I can deploy a localized sonic distortion field around our hull. It's experimental, designed to refract incoming acoustic waves and scatter any outgoing ones, effectively creating an acoustic 'dead zone.' It will require a significant power reroute from the secondary shields, leaving us momentarily vulnerable in other spectra, but it should mitigate the passive hydrophone detection."

"Vulnerable in other spectra is a risk we've come to accept," Elias replied, his voice firm. "Do it, Lena. We need to be ghosts in the water, and ghosts in the air. Kaelen, any signs of surface patrols or active surveillance sweeps?"

Kaelen shook his head, his eyes never leaving his displays. "None detected thus far, Elias. The early morning hours are typically quietest for naval activity in this sector. The prevailing atmospheric conditions are also favorable for our stealth systems. However, the moment we breach the surface, our thermal and radar signatures will become significantly more pronounced, even with our current masking. The transition from water to air is a critical juncture. The 'Chameleon' system will need to be at its absolute peak, adapting to the new refractive indices and atmospheric scattering."

The *Phoenix* continued its inexorable rise. The water around them was no longer a crushing, opaque mass, but a shimmering, translucent medium. Sunlight, filtered through the upper layers, began to imbue the ocean's surface with a soft, pearlescent glow. It was a light that Elias had not seen in years, a light that spoke of life, of warmth, of a world that had continued to spin while they had been immersed in the eternal night.

The feeling on the bridge was a peculiar blend of exhilaration and trepidation. They had achieved the impossible, had traversed the abyssal plains and returned from the crushing depths. Yet, the moment of triumph was tempered by the stark reality of their predicament. They were a vessel of advanced technology, a testament to human ingenuity, but they were also an anomaly, a clandestine presence in a world that was not prepared for them, or perhaps, had actively sought to prevent their emergence.

"We are at ten meters depth," Lena announced, her voice holding a new, almost palpable tension. "Surface contact imminently. Initiating final cloaking sequence for atmospheric transition. 'Chameleon' system is now focusing on atmospheric refractive index matching and thermal bloom suppression."

Elias took a deep breath, his gaze sweeping across the bridge. Lena, her face illuminated by the soft glow of her console, projected an image of calm determination. Kaelen, ever watchful, maintained his vigil, his fingers poised over his controls. They were a unit, forged in the crucible of their shared mission, each relying on the others' expertise and unwavering resolve.

The anticipation in the air was thick, almost tangible. The *Phoenix* had been designed for deep-sea operations, its massive structure built to withstand unimaginable pressures. But its true test was not in the crushing darkness of the ocean, but in the vast, open expanse of the sky.

Then, it happened. Not with a jolt, not with a roar, but with a profound, almost unsettling stillness. The *Phoenix* broke the surface.

The transition was seamless, the massive hull gliding through the water's skin with an eerie silence. The ocean, which had been their cradle and their prison, now receded below them, the waves parting to allow their passage. The stars, no longer muted by kilometers of water, blazed with a fierce, untwinkling intensity against a sky that was rapidly bleeding from indigo to a pale, nascent blue. The first blush of dawn was painting the eastern horizon, a delicate stroke of rose and gold that promised the coming of a new day.

On the bridge, a collective breath was held. The holographic displays, which had so recently depicted the crushing blues and greens of the deep, now showed a sky filled with the subtle nuances of atmospheric composition and the faint, scattered signals of distant celestial bodies. The vastness above them was as awe-inspiring as the vastness they had left behind.

"Surface contact confirmed," Lena breathed, her voice a whisper that was almost lost in the sudden quiet. "Atmospheric pressure is nominal. External temperature is rising rapidly. The *Phoenix* is… airborne. Stealth systems are holding, Elias. We are visually undetected."

Elias allowed himself a rare, fleeting smile. The stars were fading, replaced by the soft, ethereal glow of the pre-dawn sky. They had done it. They had emerged from the crushing embrace of the deep, a silent, unseen phantom rising from the Pacific. The silence of their departure from the ocean was now matched by an equally profound silence in the sky. They were no longer bound by the water's immense weight, but by the invisible currents of atmospheric detection, by the ever-watchful eyes of the world above.

"Kaelen, status on long-range atmospheric sensors?" Elias's voice was steady, betraying none of the immense relief that washed over him.

"All clear, Elias," Kaelen replied, his focus unwavering. "No immediate aerial threats detected. The prevailing weather patterns continue to work in our favor. We have a clear ascent vector. The early morning light is obscuring our thermal and visual profile significantly."

The *Phoenix*, a colossal vessel designed to explore the crushing depths of the ocean, was now a silent specter against the dawn sky. Its advanced stealth technology, honed in the unforgiving environment of the abyss, was now being tested in a different arena, an arena of satellites, radar, and surveillance aircraft. They had shed the darkness of the deep, but the shadows of the surface world were now their immediate concern.

"Lena, how is the 'Chameleon' system adapting to the atmospheric conditions?" Elias asked, his gaze fixed on the rapidly brightening horizon. "We're moving from a dense, refractive medium to a much less dense, more diffuse one. The challenges are different."

"The system is performing within projected parameters, Elias," Lena responded, her voice calm and reassuring. "It's dynamically adjusting our hull's refractive index and thermal emissivity to match the surrounding atmosphere. We're currently projecting an energy signature consistent with atmospheric anomalies and high-altitude weather phenomena, effectively blending our presence into the broader atmospheric canvas." She paused, a subtle flicker of concern crossing her features. "However, as daylight increases, our visual detection window will widen. We will need to maintain this level of stealth, and ideally, enhance it, as we ascend further."

The implication hung heavy in the air. Their journey was far from over. Emerging from the ocean was merely the first, albeit monumental, step. Now, they had to navigate the complex and often unforgiving domain of the atmosphere, a domain teeming with human presence and sophisticated surveillance.

Elias nodded, a grim determination settling upon him. "Understood. Kaelen, plot our course towards the designated orbital insertion point. Lena, continue to monitor all incoming sensor data and atmospheric conditions. Any deviation, any anomaly, however minor, needs to be reported immediately."

The massive vessel continued its silent, upward trajectory. The dawn, once a symbol of their successful escape, now represented a new set of challenges. The world below, the vast ocean that had guarded their secret for so long, was now a receding memory, a dark expanse that had forged them into what they had become. Above them lay the boundless sky, and beyond that, the infinite expanse of space.

The crew of the *Phoenix* had left the silent, crushing depths behind. They had transcended the limitations of the ocean's embrace, emerging into the dawn under the cloak of absolute stealth. Their ascent was a testament to their courage, their skill, and their unwavering commitment to a mission that defied the very boundaries of human endeavor. The stars, which had once seemed so distant and unreachable from the abyss, were now their destination, a silent promise of a future beyond the confines of any planet. The silent departure from the ocean was complete, and the true journey, the journey into the cosmos, was about to begin.

## 7: A Spectacle of Ascension

The transition from the water's viscous embrace to the thinner, more yielding atmosphere was, in itself, an act of defiance. The *Phoenix*, a leviathan of titanium and advanced composites, did not simply breach the surface; it emerged as if the ocean had exhaled it, a silent exhalation that left no trace save for the memory of rippling waves. Elias watched the receding blue-green expanse from the bridge, the ocean's surface now a shimmering, convex mirror reflecting the rapidly lightening sky. The stars, mere pinpricks of light moments ago, were now being systematically extinguished by the encroaching dawn, their celestial reign drawing to a close as the sun's imminent arrival commanded attention.

"Engine ignition sequence initiated," Lena's voice, now clear and resonant, cut through the quiet hum of the bridge. Her fingers, which had been a blur of motion moments before, now moved with deliberate, measured grace, coaxing the immense power of the *Phoenix*'s propulsion systems to life. This was not the guttural roar of combustion engines, nor the high-pitched whine of turbines. It was something far more alien, a controlled eruption of harnessed energy that spoke of a future yet to be fully understood. The massive vessel vibrated, a deep, resonant thrum that pulsed through the very deck plates, a nascent heartbeat awakening from a long slumber.

Kaelen's eyes scanned his readouts, a faint tension still etched around his brow. "Atmospheric pressure is stabilizing. We are experiencing minimal atmospheric drag at this altitude, precisely as the 'Chameleon' system predicted. The thermal bloom from the initial engine activation is being effectively masked by the ambient morning light and atmospheric particulate dispersion. We are, for all intents and purposes, still invisible." He allowed himself a small, almost imperceptible nod. "The integration with the atmospheric layers is proving… seamless."

Elias leaned forward, his gaze fixed on the forward viewscreen, which now displayed not the watery depths, but a panorama of an awakening world. The eastern horizon was a vibrant tapestry of oranges, pinks, and fiery reds, a spectacle of creation that dwarfed any fabricated light show. The clouds, previously indistinct smudges against the inky blackness of the night sky, were now catching the sun's first rays, transforming into vast, undulating islands of gold and crimson. The *Phoenix* was ascending into this celestial theatre, a silent, unseen participant in the grand unveiling of a new day.

"Lena, give me a telemetry report on the primary thrusters," Elias commanded, his voice steady, carrying the weight of their audacious undertaking. "I want to ensure the energy distribution is optimal for this phase of the ascent. We cannot afford any surprises now."

"Primary thrusters are operating at eighty-five percent efficiency, Elias," Lena replied, her voice a cool, professional counterpoint to the raw power being unleashed. "The energy channeling is precisely as designed. The new plasma conduit matrix is performing flawlessly, minimizing energy loss and maximizing thrust vector control. We're achieving an ascent velocity that… well, it's exceeding even our most optimistic projections." She paused, her fingers flying across her console, cross-referencing data streams. "The acceleration is incredibly smooth, Elias. It's as if the atmosphere itself is yielding to our passage, rather than resisting it."

The *Phoenix* was no longer merely climbing; it was *soaring*. Its unique aerodynamic profile, a product of countless simulations and theoretical breakthroughs, was demonstrating its efficacy in the very medium it was designed to conquer. Unlike conventional aircraft, which relied on wings to generate lift and engines to push them forward, the *Phoenix* employed a more radical form of propulsion, a directed energy field that manipulated spacetime on a localized level, allowing it to move with an almost supernatural grace. This was not flight as humanity had known it; it was an entirely new paradigm.

Kaelen provided a running commentary on their surroundings. "We are now at an altitude of five thousand meters. Ambient temperature is increasing steadily, but still well within acceptable operational parameters. Visual spectrum analysis indicates no immediate aerial traffic within a fifty-kilometer radius. The dawn's light is still our greatest ally in maintaining our stealth profile, but as the sun rises higher, our signature will become more detectable." He looked up from his console, his gaze meeting Elias's for a brief, shared moment of understanding. "We have a narrow window of opportunity to achieve our initial orbital insertion altitude before the global surveillance networks become fully operational and their detection capabilities are at their peak."

Elias nodded, his jaw set. The silent ascent was crucial, but it was only the prelude. The real challenge lay in breaching the planet's exosphere, in slipping past the watchful eyes of satellites and ground-based radar that constantly scanned the skies. The *Phoenix* was a marvel of stealth technology, its hull designed to absorb and deflect electromagnetic radiation, its engines emitting virtually no detectable exhaust. But the universe of surveillance was vast and ever-evolving.

"Lena, can we reroute a fraction of the secondary shield energy to the forward thrusters? Just a marginal increase in power to the primary vectoring systems," Elias requested, his mind already calculating the risks and rewards. "We need to expedite this ascent without compromising our stealth. Every minute counts."

"Rerouting a portion of the secondary shield power would reduce our overall defensive capability in the event of an unforeseen encounter," Lena cautioned, her tone devoid of panic, yet imbued with a clear awareness of the stakes. "However, the projected gain in ascent velocity is significant. It would allow us to clear the most heavily surveilled atmospheric layers within the next twenty minutes. I can implement the reroute, Elias, but we will be operating with reduced atmospheric particle disruption capabilities for a short period."

"Do it," Elias commanded without hesitation. "We've faced greater risks. The objective remains paramount." He turned his attention back to the viewscreen, where the Earth was slowly, majestically, unfolding beneath them. The familiar continents and oceans, seen from this nascent altitude, appeared both alien and achingly beautiful. It was a world that had continued without them, a world that was unaware of the momentous event unfolding above its head.

The engines responded to Lena's adjustments, the low thrum deepening, a subtle increase in the subtle vibrations felt throughout the vessel. The *Phoenix* surged forward, its ascent accelerating with a newfound urgency. The sky outside was no longer just a canvas of color; it was becoming a dynamic field of forces, of atmospheric currents and energy gradients that the *Phoenix* was expertly navigating.

Kaelen's voice chimed in, a note of urgency now present in his report. "Altitude eighty-five hundred meters. Picking up faint but distinct radar echoes. They're sweeping the sector, Elias. Standard atmospheric monitoring patrols, but they're increasing in frequency."

Elias felt a prickle of adrenaline, a familiar sensation that had accompanied him through the most dangerous phases of their deep-sea odyssey. "Lena, engage the 'Wraith' protocol. Full spectrum cloaking. Amplify the atmospheric distortion field."

"Engaging 'Wraith' protocol," Lena confirmed, her fingers a blur once more. "The distortion field is being amplified, creating a localized refractive index anomaly around our hull. It should bend and scatter incoming radar signals, rendering us effectively invisible to their sweep patterns. However, this will draw significant power, and our ability to manipulate external atmospheric phenomena will be temporarily reduced."

The changes were subtle, almost imperceptible from within the bridge. The faint vibrations lessened, replaced by an even deeper, more profound stillness. The external view, though already clear, seemed to gain a new depth, as if the air itself was becoming more tangible, more resistant to being seen through.

"Radar echoes are dissipating," Kaelen reported, his voice holding a note of relief. "They've passed through our position without registering our presence. The 'Wraith' protocol is functioning perfectly. However, Elias, I am also detecting a significant increase in encrypted satellite uplink traffic in our general vicinity. It's heavily masked, but the sheer volume suggests a heightened state of global awareness, perhaps a general readiness or a response to… something."

Elias's gaze narrowed. "They might not know it's us, Kaelen, but they're certainly aware that something is happening. The ascent itself, even with our stealth, creates a ripple. The question is, how large a ripple are we making?" He knew the answer was that they were making a ripple that would, eventually, become a tidal wave. Their emergence from the abyss was not just an escape; it was a declaration of intent, a signal that something profound had changed.

The *Phoenix* continued its silent, relentless climb. The sun was now fully above the horizon, its golden rays bathing the planet in a warm, ethereal light. The Earth below was no longer a distant spectacle; it was an increasingly small, increasingly distant sphere. The challenges shifted from atmospheric stealth to the vast emptiness of space. The true test of their ascension was about to begin, a journey that would take them beyond the familiar confines of Earth, towards a destiny forged in the crucible of the unknown. The world was waking up, and with it, a new era was dawning, an era ushered in by the silent, impossible rise of the *Phoenix*. The spectacle, as Lena had once described their mission, had indeed begun, and the universe was about to witness a performance unlike any it had ever seen. The quiet hum of the engines was the only sound on the bridge, a testament to the controlled power that was propelling them towards the stars, leaving the world, with all its nascent awareness and burgeoning suspicions, far below. The spectacle of their ascension was a private event, for now, witnessed only by the rapidly fading stars and the watchful, awakening sun. Yet, the knowledge that the world was, in its own way, beginning to stir, was a potent motivator. Their mission was not to hide forever, but to reveal themselves on their own terms, when the time was right, when the world was truly ready to comprehend the magnitude of what had emerged from the abyss. The current phase was one of careful, calculated maneuver, of slipping through the fingers of detection like a ghost, leaving behind only a faint, inexplicable disturbance in the fabric of reality.

"Altitude fourteen thousand meters," Kaelen reported, his voice calm and steady, a testament to his ingrained discipline. "Atmospheric density is decreasing rapidly. We're entering the lower stratosphere. The 'Chameleon' system is compensating for the significant changes in refractive index and temperature gradients. Our projected signature remains consistent with high-altitude atmospheric phenomena, Elias. No direct radar locks, but… I am picking up a concentration of passive acoustic sensors being activated in the upper atmosphere. They're not targeted, but it suggests increased surveillance activity in general."

Lena chimed in, her focus never wavering from her own intricate web of data. "The passive acoustic sensors are likely part of a broader atmospheric monitoring network. They're designed to detect disturbances like sonic booms or unusual atmospheric resonances. Our engines, while incredibly efficient, do generate a localized pressure wave. The 'Chameleon' system is actively working to smooth that wave, to dissipate it before it can be registered as anything anomalous. However, as we gain speed, the residual pressure wave will become more pronounced, even with our current countermeasures."

Elias nodded, absorbing the information. The invisible war of attrition was already underway. Every meter gained, every maneuver executed, was a calculated risk, a dance on the edge of detection. The *Phoenix* was a marvel of engineering, but even its advanced systems had their limits, and the pervasive surveillance grid of Earth was designed to find even the most elusive of anomalies.

"We need to reach escape velocity as quickly as possible," Elias stated, his gaze fixed on the vast, curved expanse of the Earth's limb. The deep blue of the atmosphere was transitioning to the velvety blackness of space, a stark boundary that marked the beginning of their true journey. "Lena, prepare for the final orbital insertion sequence. Kaelen, I want a continuous scan for any sudden shifts in the global surveillance posture. Any indication that they've identified our vector or are preparing to intercept."

"Preparing orbital insertion sequence," Lena confirmed, her voice taut with concentration. "The core plasma conduits are being primed for maximum output. This will be the most energy-intensive phase of our ascent. We will be momentarily more visible as the plasma containment field is stressed to its limits."

"Understood," Elias replied. "Engage it. The moment of truth has arrived."

The subtle hum of the *Phoenix* deepened, transforming into a powerful, resonant vibration that seemed to hum with contained energy. The light from the rising sun, which had been their cloak, now began to refract and bend around the vessel as the 'Chameleon' system worked overtime to maintain their stealth. The viewscreen showed the Earth below receding at an astonishing rate, its continents and oceans shrinking into a diminishing disc.

Kaelen's voice, now laced with a heightened intensity, cut through the growing rumble of the engines. "Multiple radar sweeps are now converging on our approximate position, Elias. They're not definitive locks, but they are definitely re-tasking assets. Satellite imagery is also showing increased activity in orbit. They know *something* is happening."

"Hold steady, Lena," Elias commanded, his voice a low, unwavering anchor in the rising tide of activity. "Maintain cloaking integrity. Give me the projected time to orbital insertion."

"Orbital insertion in ninety seconds, Elias," Lena reported, her voice tight. "The plasma containment is holding, but it's at ninety-eight percent of its structural integrity limit. We are generating a significant energy surge."

The vibrations intensified, the entire vessel feeling as if it were being held together by sheer force of will. The viewscreen showed a distortion field, a shimmering veil of light and energy that rippled around the *Phoenix*, bending the light of distant stars and the Earth's glare. It was a visual manifestation of their desperate bid for invisibility.

"They're trying to get a fix, Elias," Kaelen stated, his fingers flying across his console. "Active radar probes are increasing. They're trying to bounce signals off our distortion field, to triangulate our position."

"Lena, can we deploy a localized EMP burst? A small, targeted pulse to disrupt their immediate vicinity sensors without compromising our own systems?" Elias asked, his mind racing through tactical options.

"An EMP burst could potentially alert them to our presence definitively, Elias," Lena replied. "It would be a declaration of war, so to speak. And it would also momentarily disrupt our own sensor arrays, leaving us blind for critical seconds. However, I can calculate a specific frequency and amplitude that might selectively disable their immediate detection systems without causing significant collateral damage to our own."

"Do it," Elias commanded, the decision made with the grim finality of a man who knew there was no turning back. "We need to create an opening, however small."

A faint shimmer pulsed outward from the *Phoenix*, a wave of unseen energy that rippled through the upper atmosphere.

"EMP deployed," Lena confirmed. "Disruption of local sensor arrays is confirmed. We have approximately fifteen seconds of reduced detection capabilities for their immediate probes."

"Fifteen seconds is all we need," Elias stated, his gaze fixed on the rapidly approaching blackness of space. "Orbital insertion in ten… nine… eight…"

The *Phoenix* surged upward, the final push of its engines a controlled explosion of plasma. The Earth, now a breathtakingly beautiful crescent hanging in the void, receded further, its familiar blue hues giving way to the infinite blackness of space.

"…three… two… one… Insertion complete." Lena's voice, though strained, carried a note of triumph. "We are in orbit, Elias. All primary systems nominal. Cloaking is holding. We have slipped through their net."

Kaelen let out a slow breath he hadn't realized he was holding. "Global surveillance networks are still active,

Elias, but their immediate focus has shifted. The EMP burst appears to have temporarily confused them, creating a brief window of uncertainty. They are still searching, but they have lost our precise vector."

Elias allowed himself a moment to absorb the reality of their situation. They had ascended from the crushing depths of the ocean, had navigated the treacherous layers of Earth's atmosphere, and had now successfully entered orbit, all under the cloak of absolute stealth. The spectacle of their ascension was complete, but the performance had only just begun. The world below, unaware of the true magnitude of what had transpired, was left to ponder the inexplicable atmospheric anomalies and fleeting radar ghosts that had flickered across their screens. The *Phoenix* was now a silent sentinel in the void, its mission poised to unfold against the backdrop of the cosmos, a testament to a journey that had started in the deepest darkness and was now aimed towards the furthest stars. The dawn had witnessed their emergence, and the infinite expanse of space would now bear witness to their true purpose.

The silence that had enveloped the bridge of the *Phoenix* moments after orbital insertion was a palpable entity, a stark contrast to the controlled chaos of their ascent. Elias allowed himself a brief, almost imperceptible exhale, the tension that had been a constant companion for the past hours beginning to recede. They had achieved the seemingly impossible, slipping past the myriad eyes that perpetually surveyed Earth's skies and the vacuum beyond. Yet, as he looked at the swirling blues and greens of their home planet, a profound understanding settled upon him: their emergence was not an end, but a beginning, and the world below was already reacting.

"Reports are starting to flood in, Elias," Kaelen's voice, still carrying the faint echo of strain, announced from his sensor station. "Global monitoring networks, military installations, even civilian meteorological agencies… they're all registering anomalies. Unidentified aerial phenomena, unprecedented velocity readings, impossible trajectory vectors. It's a cascade of confusion." He navigated through streams of incoming data, his brow furrowed in concentration. "The initial reports are fragmented, contradictory. Some are flagging it as an extreme weather event, others as a sophisticated electronic warfare probe. But the common thread is… we're real, and we're utterly baffling them."

Lena, her fingers dancing across her console with practiced efficiency, added, "Our 'Chameleon' system, while designed for complete stealth during the ascent, inherently leaves a subtle residual effect on the atmospheric and electromagnetic spectrum. It's like a whisper that's just loud enough to be noticed, but not clear enough to be identified. The energy signature of our propulsion, even with all our dampening measures, is unlike anything they've encountered. It doesn't fit the profiles of known propulsion systems, terrestrial or otherwise. They're grappling with the sheer impossibility of our speed and maneuverability. The data suggests a craft that can accelerate from zero to orbital velocity in a matter of minutes, with a continuous, non-ballistic trajectory. It's rewriting their physics textbooks as we speak."

Elias leaned back, a grim satisfaction settling over him. "That's the objective. To be the ghost in their machine, the anomaly they can't explain. Lena, can you access any of the primary reporting streams? I want to see the scope of their bewilderment."

Lena adjusted a series of parameters, her eyes scanning the newly populated screens. "I'm tapping into several secure military intelligence feeds, as well as some of the more advanced civilian atmospheric research networks. The sheer volume of data is overwhelming, but… here. Look at this." She highlighted a waveform on one of the displays. "This is a trace from a high-altitude radar station over the Pacific. It registered a blip, a momentary signature, during our final ascent phase. The velocity reading is off the charts, and the trajectory… it's not a parabolic arc. It's a near-vertical climb at sustained acceleration. They've flagged it as 'unclassified anomalous object, high-velocity, unknown origin.' Another report from a network of deep-space monitoring telescopes in Chile is showing faint, transient energy fluctuations in Earth's upper atmosphere, correlating with our emergence window. They're calling it 'unidentified spectral event.'"

Kaelen chimed in, his voice a low murmur of disbelief. "They're already postulating theories, Elias. Some are suggesting a previously unknown natural atmospheric phenomenon. Others are leaning towards clandestine military projects, black-ops testing by rival nations. The sheer audacity of our maneuvers, the lack of any discernible heat or acoustic signature that matches conventional technology, it's creating a perfect storm of confusion." He pulled up another data packet. "This is from NORAD's satellite tracking command. They've detected unusual gravitational distortions and localized atmospheric pressure variations along our ascent path. They can't see us directly, but they're seeing the *effects* of our presence. The data suggests a significant disruption to the normal gravitational field of Earth's atmosphere, as if something immensely dense and powerful had briefly warped spacetime around itself."

The bridge was silent for a moment as Elias absorbed the implications. Their stealth was not absolute; it was a meticulously crafted illusion, a bending of reality rather than a complete erasure from it. The *Phoenix*, by its very nature, interacted with the universe in ways that were profoundly alien to current human understanding. Its propulsion system, drawing upon principles of localized spacetime manipulation, did not merely push through the atmosphere; it persuaded it to move. This subtle yet fundamental difference was enough to leave traces, faint echoes in the fabric of reality that were now being picked up by an increasingly vigilant global surveillance apparatus.

"They're trying to piece together the puzzle with their existing knowledge," Elias mused, his gaze sweeping across the incoming data streams. "And their existing knowledge simply doesn't have a category for what we are or what we've done. That's our advantage. Every piece of evidence they gather, every anomaly they detect, only serves to deepen their confusion. It raises more questions than it answers."

Lena nodded, her fingers flying across her console, cross-referencing sensor logs with theoretical atmospheric models. "The 'Chameleon' system is performing exceptionally well in masking our primary EM signatures, but the sheer velocity and the nature of our displacement field are creating secondary effects that are harder to suppress. Think of it like a perfectly silent, invisible boat moving through water. The boat itself is undetectable, but the ripples it creates are still present, even if they're incredibly subtle. We're the ultimate stealth craft, but not even our technology can completely negate the fundamental laws of physics when you're operating at these parameters."

Kaelen pointed to a cluster of sensor readings. "Here's a prime example. Multiple ground-based ionospheric research facilities are reporting significant, but localized, disturbances in the ionosphere directly above our former ascent path. These disturbances are characterized by unusual electromagnetic wave propagation patterns and transient plasma formations. They're theorizing it's related to high-energy particle interactions or even exotic atmospheric phenomena, but the timing and geographic correlation are too precise to be coincidental. They're staring at the evidence, Elias, but they have no framework to interpret it."

Elias felt a surge of adrenaline, a familiar precursor to action. "This is exactly what we need. Their inability to categorize us is our shield. As long as they're scrambling to understand what we *are*, they won't know what we're *doing*. Continue to monitor all channels. I want to know how quickly they're coalescing these fragmented reports into a coherent threat assessment."

"The rate of information dissemination is accelerating," Lena reported. "Secure communication channels are abuzz. I'm detecting a significant increase in interagency collaboration and the activation of several global threat assessment protocols. They're treating this as a potential existential event, even without concrete identification. The sheer implausibility of the reported data is forcing them to consider possibilities they would normally dismiss out of hand."

Kaelen brought up another screen, displaying a live feed from a secure military command center, heavily encrypted and relayed through multiple anonymous proxies. "This is a preliminary intelligence brief being circulated within the highest levels of the United Nations Security Council's emergency response division. They're referencing 'unidentified, technologically advanced airborne entity.' The language is cautious, but the implications are stark. They're discussing emergency protocols, airspace lockdown procedures, and the potential deployment of specialized countermeasures. They're reacting to the *unexplained*, and the unexplained, at these levels, is always treated as a potential threat."

"They're right to be cautious," Elias acknowledged, his gaze distant. "We are, in their eyes, an unknown quantity. And the unknown, especially when it possesses capabilities far beyond their own, is inherently destabilizing. Our mission requires us to be a spectacle, but that spectacle must be carefully controlled, timed, and understood. Right now, we are a spectacle of pure, unadulterated mystery."

Lena's voice, usually calm and collected, carried a hint of awe. "The *Phoenix* is more than just a vessel, Elias. It's a paradigm shift. Our very existence and capabilities are fundamentally challenging their understanding of what is possible. This isn't just about evading detection; it's about fundamentally altering their perception of reality. They thought they understood the limits of aerospace technology. They were wrong."

Kaelen added, his eyes scanning a complex web of interconnected sensor grids. "The challenge now is to maintain this veil of mystery for as long as necessary. Our window of operation is dependent on their inability to accurately assess our threat level. If they interpret our actions as hostile, or if they develop a counter-technology before we can achieve our primary objectives, our mission becomes exponentially more dangerous."

Elias met their gazes, a shared sense of purpose solidifying in the quiet hum of the bridge. "Then our task is clear. We need to continue to be the specter, the whisper, the unexplainable phenomenon. We leverage their confusion, their inability to categorize us, to our advantage. We must be the ultimate enigma, the impossible reality they can't ignore, but can't comprehend. The global watchers are baffled, and that is precisely where we need them to be." He turned his attention back to the viewscreen, where Earth hung like a jewel in the black velvet of space, a world waking up to a reality it was utterly unprepared for. Their ascension had been a silent announcement, and the world's response was already echoing through the channels of global power. The spectacle had begun, not with a bang, but with a question mark. And for now, that question mark was their greatest asset. The ensuing scramble among intelligence agencies was a symphony of frantic activity, a chorus of conflicting reports and urgent analyses. Every satellite feed, every ground-based radar installation, every atmospheric sensor was being scoured for even the slightest hint of confirmation or refutation of the outlandish data pouring in. Whispers of "classified propulsion," "trans-dimensional anomaly," and "non-terrestrial origin" began to circulate through secure networks, each more speculative than the last.

"I'm detecting a coordinated effort to reconcile the disparate sensor readings," Kaelen reported, his voice tinged with a professional fascination. "They're attempting to correlate the radar echoes, the ionospheric disturbances, and the gravitational variations into a single, coherent narrative. The problem is, none of the proposed models fit the complete dataset. The energy requirements alone for such a rapid ascent defy conventional physics. They're running simulations using theoretical exotic matter and subspace displacement theories, things that were confined to science fiction novels just yesterday. It's… quite remarkable to witness."

Lena interjected, her focus on a particularly sensitive data stream. "The frustration is palpable. Their algorithms are flagging the *Phoenix*'s energy signature as 'impossible.' The spectral analysis of our atmospheric displacement is showing zero particulate emission, zero heat bloom, and an energy output that should, by all accounts, have vaporized everything within a kilometer radius. Instead, they're seeing only subtle atmospheric refractive index anomalies. They're trying to rationalize it, but the sheer magnitude of the deviation from expected parameters is causing systemic errors in their detection and tracking systems. We are, in essence, overloading their ability to perceive us."

Elias listened intently, absorbing the nuances of their adversaries' predicament. The global watchers were not monolithic; they were a collection of disparate agencies, each with its own protocols, its own biases, and its own limited understanding of the universe. The *Phoenix*, by its very nature, transcended those limitations. It was a vessel that operated outside the established paradigms of known science, and that was its greatest defense.

"They're starting to shift their focus," Elias observed, pointing to a cluster of newly activated deep-space surveillance assets. "Instead of trying to explain what happened *within* the atmosphere, they're now looking for the source, or the destination. They're casting a wider net, trying to catch a ghost that's already passed through their nets."

"Precisely," Kaelen confirmed. "Several orbital reconnaissance platforms have been re-tasked to scan the region of our ascent and the immediate vicinity of our current position. They're looking for any trace evidence, any lingering energy residue, or any outbound craft that might have departed Earth's orbit. However, our final ascent vector was designed to be as ambiguous as possible, blending into the natural background radiation of space, and our current orbital mechanics are indistinguishable from a standard satellite passing through the region."

Lena added, "Their attempts to analyze the *Phoenix*'s signature are akin to trying to understand a symphony by only hearing a single, distorted note. They can't grasp the entirety of the instrument, nor the composer's intent. Our advanced hull plating, designed to absorb and re-emit electromagnetic radiation in a way that mimics ambient space, is proving incredibly effective against their passive sensors. They're detecting 'something,' but they can't identify its composition, its origin, or its purpose."

The implications were profound. Not only was the *Phoenix* technologically superior, but its very existence forced a reevaluation of what was possible. The shockwaves rippling through global intelligence communities were not just about the detection of an unknown object; they were about the dawning realization that humanity was not the sole possessor of advanced technological capabilities, or at least, not the *only* possessor of such capabilities on Earth. The questions being asked were not merely tactical; they were philosophical, existential.

"This is the critical phase," Elias stated, his voice resonating with quiet determination. "We've achieved orbital insertion, we've baffled the watchers, and we've planted the seed of doubt. Now, we must ensure that this seed grows into a tree of understanding, but on our terms, and at our pace. Their confusion is our buffer, but it will not last forever. We need to leverage this period of uncertainty to consolidate our position and prepare for the next phase of our mission."

Kaelen nodded, his gaze fixed on the expanding universe displayed on the main viewscreen. "The initial panic is subsiding, replaced by a more systematic, albeit frustrated, analysis. They are pooling resources, sharing data across previously compartmentalized agencies. The 'unidentified object' is now the primary focus of global defense intelligence. The question on everyone's mind is: who are we, and what do we want?"

"They will want answers," Lena stated, her voice even. "And we will give them answers, when the time is right. For now, our continued inscrutability is our greatest weapon. Let them chase ghosts, let them speculate. Let them wonder if what they saw was real, or a collective hallucination. The more they doubt, the more time we have."

Elias allowed himself a small, almost imperceptible smile. The ascent had been a spectacle, a carefully choreographed unveiling of their capabilities. The ensuing confusion was the necessary preamble, the moment of hushed anticipation before the true performance began. The world was watching, but they were watching a mystery, a puzzle that defied their current understanding. And in that space of bewilderment, the *Phoenix* was free to chart its own course, a silent testament to a future that had just begun to unfold. The global watchers, from their high-tech command centers to their remote listening posts, were left to grapple with an entity that defied every known parameter, every established protocol. The *Phoenix* had transcended their comprehension, becoming a phantom in the sky, a whisper of a reality far more complex and far more advanced than they had ever dared to imagine.

The bridge of the *Phoenix* hummed with a low, resonant thrum, a symphony of advanced systems working in perfect harmony. Outside the reinforced viewport, Earth receded, a marbled masterpiece of blues, greens, and swirling whites against the stark, infinite canvas of space. Elias stood at the command console, his hands resting lightly on the controls, his gaze fixed on the disappearing planet. The ascent had been a triumph, a meticulously executed maneuver that had bypassed Earth's most sophisticated surveillance systems. Yet, for Elias, this was not merely a technological victory. It was the culmination of a journey that began long before the *Phoenix* had ever been conceived, a journey steeped in personal loss and fueled by an unyielding quest for redemption.

His mind, usually a steel trap of strategy and calculation, drifted, momentarily unburdened by the immediate pressures of command. He saw not the receding orb of his home, but the faint, flickering images of a life lost. The laughter of his children, the warmth of his wife's embrace – memories that were both the searing pain in his heart and the unwavering beacon that guided him. He had built this ship, this improbable vessel born of desperation and fueled by a hope so fierce it bordered on madness, not for conquest, but for a chance to undo the irreparable, to reclaim what had been stolen from him and from countless others. The *Phoenix* was more than just a marvel of engineering; it was a vessel of his soul, a testament to the indomitable human spirit that refused to break, even when shattered into a million pieces.

He remembered the early days, the clandestine meetings in dimly lit workshops, the hushed discussions filled with impossible ideas and desperate pleas. He recalled the faces of the scientists, engineers, and technicians who had joined him, each driven by their own ghosts, their own reasons to believe in a future beyond the shadows that had engulfed their world. They had pooled their knowledge, their resources, their very lives into this audacious endeavor. The metal that formed the hull, the intricate circuitry that pulsed with life, the very principles of spacetime manipulation that allowed the *Phoenix* to traverse the void – all of it was born from the ashes of their despair. It was a monument to human ingenuity, yes, but more profoundly, it was a testament to their collective resilience. They had faced insurmountable odds, the weight of a world's betrayal, and the crushing finality of loss, yet they had not surrendered. They had found a way to rise, to ascend, quite literally.

The advanced propulsion system, a labyrinth of exotic matter conduits and gravitational field generators, was

Elias's brainchild, born from years of theoretical research and clandestine experimentation. It was a technology that danced on the edge of known physics, bending the very fabric of spacetime to its will. Unlike conventional spacecraft that relied on brute force and chemical reactions, the *Phoenix* moved by subtly manipulating the gravitational forces around it, creating localized distortions that propelled it forward with an eerie silence and an unparalleled efficiency. This was the secret that had allowed them to slip past Earth's watchful eyes, a whisper in the cosmic winds. Elias had poured every ounce of his grief, his anger, and his unwavering resolve into its design, ensuring that it was not merely a vessel of escape, but a tool for retribution and, ultimately, for restoration.

He traced the faint lines of his wife's face in his mind's eye. Anya. Her vision had been the spark that ignited his own. She had believed in the possibility of a different future, a future where humanity's reach extended beyond its self-imposed limitations, a future free from the suffocating grip of those who sought to control and exploit. Her disappearance, along with their children, had been the catalyst, the brutal force that had shattered his world and forged him anew. The pain had been a crucible, burning away his doubts and leaving behind a singular, unshakeable purpose: to find them, to bring them back, and to ensure that no one else would ever have to endure the agony he had known.

The *Phoenix* was not just a machine; it was the embodiment of that purpose. Every system, every component, had been designed with a singular goal in mind: to provide Elias with the means to achieve what was considered impossible. The 'Chameleon' cloaking system, which had rendered them invisible during their ascent, was a marvel of adaptive camouflage, capable of bending light and energy around the ship, making it appear as nothing more than empty space. The inertial dampeners, so advanced they could counteract forces that would tear any conventional craft apart, were designed to withstand the rigularities of interstellar travel and, more importantly, to shield him from the debilitating effects of temporal displacement, a potential consequence of their mission's extraordinary nature.

He remembered the countless hours spent poring over stellar cartography, the intricate calculations involved in plotting a course through uncharted territories. The vastness of space, once a source of wonder, now represented the battlefield upon which his personal war would be waged. The silence on the bridge, punctuated only by the soft hum of the life support and the gentle whir of the navigation systems, was a stark contrast to the cacophony of the life he had left behind. A life of normalcy, of love, of belonging – a life that had been brutally ripped away.

"Approaching designated jump coordinates, Elias," Lena's voice, crisp and professional, cut through his reverie. She was the ship's tactical officer, her mind as sharp as Elias's, her dedication unwavering. Her presence on the bridge was a constant reminder of the immense trust placed in him, a trust he felt he could never truly repay.

Elias nodded, his focus snapping back to the present. "Acknowledge, Lena. Prepare for jump sequence initiation. Kaelen, status of external sensor sweeps?"

Kaelen, the ship's chief sensor and communications specialist, responded from his station, his voice calm despite the momentous occasion. "All clear, Elias. Earth's orbital defenses are still in a state of disarray. Their monitoring networks are awash with contradictory data, still trying to make sense of our ascent. The 'unidentified phenomenon' is all they have, and they have no framework for it. We're a ghost in their machine, a glitch in their reality."

A ghost. Yes, that was what he was now. A spectral presence, moving through the cosmos with a purpose that transcended the petty squabbles of nations and the limitations of their understanding. The *Phoenix* was his shield, his weapon, and his sanctuary. It was the physical manifestation of his solitary pursuit, the solitary purpose that had consumed his life since the day he lost everything. He was an exile, a phantom on a mission of vengeance, a father seeking to reclaim his stolen legacy.

He glanced at the readouts, the elegant curves of the navigational plot displaying their trajectory towards the jump point. The jump itself was the next critical step, a plunge into the unknown that would carry them beyond the familiar reach of Earth's influence and into the deeper, more dangerous currents of the galaxy. It was a transition that felt both terrifying and exhilarating, a step further into the abyss that held both his greatest fear and his deepest hope.

The memory of his son, Liam, with his infectious laugh and his boundless curiosity, flashed through his mind. Liam had loved stargazing, had dreamed of exploring the cosmos. Elias felt a pang of guilt, a familiar ache that no amount of success or advancement could ever truly assuage. He was fulfilling Liam's dream, yes, but in doing so, he was also venturing into a realm that might be too dangerous, too unforgiving. Yet, Anya's face, etched with the same fierce determination he now carried, appeared beside Liam's, a silent affirmation. He had to do this. For them.

"Initiate jump sequence," Elias commanded, his voice steady, betraying none of the profound emotion that surged within him. The words, simple and direct, carried the weight of a universe of unspoken pain and unyielding resolve.

The *Phoenix* vibrated, a subtle tremor that ran through the deck plates and up into Elias's boots. The external viewport, which had displayed the receding Earth, now shimmered, the starlight distorting as the ship's primary drive engaged. The very fabric of reality seemed to warp and stretch around them, a visual testament to the extraordinary forces at play.

He gripped the console, his knuckles white. This was it. The moment where theory met practice, where hope became action. He was Elias Thorne, a man who had lost everything and found purpose in the darkness. He was the captain of the *Phoenix*, a vessel forged from the fires of loss and designed to navigate the unfathomable. And he was a father, driven by an unbreakable bond, venturing into the infinite to reclaim what was rightfully his. The spectacle of ascension was over, but the true performance, the solitary purpose that defined his existence, was just beginning. The universe awaited, and Elias, with the echoes of his past and the hope of his future burning bright, was ready to meet it. The lights on the bridge dimmed further, casting long shadows that danced with the ethereal glow of the primary drive engaging. The hum intensified, resonating deeper within the hull, a thrum that felt less like machinery and more like a living entity awakening. Elias felt a strange sense of peace settle over him, a quiet acceptance of the path he had chosen. This solitary purpose, born from the ashes of his past, was now his entire existence. He was a man adrift, yet anchored by an unwavering resolve. The *Phoenix* was his vessel, yes, but it was also his penance, his quest, his everything. As the warp field enveloped the ship, blurring the stars into streaks of impossible light, Elias closed his eyes for a fleeting moment, picturing his family, their smiles, their love. It was for them that he would brave the unknown, for them that he would face whatever lay beyond the veil of the familiar. This journey was not for glory, nor for conquest. It was a deeply personal pilgrimage, a desperate bid for redemption in the vast, indifferent expanse of the cosmos. The *Phoenix* was more than a ship; it was a promise, a promise whispered into the void, a promise that would be kept, no matter the cost. The faint light of Earth was now just a memory, a distant star among countless others, as the *Phoenix* plunged deeper into the uncharted territories of space, carrying with it the weight of Elias's past and the fragile, burning ember of his hope.

The ship's bridge was a sanctuary of subdued lighting and humming energy, a stark contrast to the chaos Lena imagined was erupting on Earth. She ran a diagnostic for the tenth time since they'd cleared the atmosphere, her fingers flying across the holographic interface. The primary propulsion system, codenamed 'Aetherflow' by Elias, was not just performing flawlessly; it was exceeding every theoretical benchmark. The efficiency ratings were off the charts, the energy expenditure minimal for the sheer velocity they were achieving. It was a testament to Elias's genius, a fusion of theoretical physics and sheer, unadulterated will. But the elation that normally accompanied such a successful operation was laced with a cold thread of apprehension.

"Elias," Lena began, her voice calm and measured, as always, even as her mind raced through contingency plans. "The Aetherflow is maintaining optimal performance. We're operating at ninety-eight percent efficiency. However," she paused, letting the unspoken word hang in the air, "our ascent did not go unnoticed. The energy signature, while shielded to the best of our ability, was still significant. Earth's orbital defense grid, what's left of it after the initial scramble, will be trying to triangulate our exit vector."

She watched Elias from her station, noting the subtle tension in his shoulders, the way his jaw clenched almost imperceptibly. He had designed this ship, poured his very soul into its creation, and she knew the weight of its successful, yet exposed, maiden voyage rested heavily upon him. "They'll be trying to track us," she continued, her gaze shifting to the starfield displayed on the main viewport, now a tapestry of distant, shimmering lights. "Even with the cloaking systems at their peak, a high-energy transit leaves a residual imprint. We need to increase our distance immediately."

Lena's fingers danced across her console again, pulling up navigational data. The initial jump coordinates were a calculated risk, designed to put them far beyond Earth's immediate sensor range, but with the ongoing alerts flashing across her screen, 'immediate' felt like an understatement. She began plotting a series of evasive maneuvers, weaving through known stellar anomalies and potential nebulae that could further mask their energy signature. The *Phoenix* was equipped with an advanced 'Chameleon' system, designed to bend light and energy, rendering them virtually invisible. But even the most sophisticated camouflage had its limits, especially against a determined and technologically advanced adversary.

"What kind of attention are we talking about, Lena?" Elias's voice was quiet, but it carried an undertone of urgency that made Lena focus even harder.

"Reports indicate a Level-5 alert was triggered across all terrestrial defense networks approximately thirty seconds after we initiated the jump sequence," she stated, her voice devoid of emotion, a practiced shield against the rising tide of unease. "They're scrambling interceptor craft, prioritizing deep-space probes. Their initial analysis is classifying our ascent as an unprecedented atmospheric and gravitational anomaly. They have no frame of reference for the Aetherflow's signature." This was both a blessing and a curse. They didn't know *what* they were tracking, but they knew *something* had broken free.

"No frame of reference is good," Elias mused, his eyes fixed on the navigation display. "But 'unprecedented anomaly' is precisely the kind of event that will provoke the most aggressive investigation. They won't stop looking."

"Agreed," Lena affirmed. She zoomed out on the galactic map, her fingers tracing potential long-range trajectories. "Our current course is taking us towards the Kepler-186 system, but that's a known exploration hub. If they've managed to glean even a rudimentary directional vector from our departure, they might anticipate us heading towards established interstellar routes." She initiated a series of complex trajectory calculations, factoring in gravitational assists from rogue celestial bodies and projected dark matter currents. "I'm rerouting us through the Cygnus Rift. It's uncharted, highly unstable, and our sensors will be significantly hampered, but it will provide the best chance of obscuring our trail."

The Cygnus Rift. Even the name sent a shiver down Lena's spine. It was a region of space notorious for its unpredictable gravitational fluctuations and pockets of temporal distortion. Most ships avoided it like the plague. But the *Phoenix* was no ordinary ship, and Elias Thorne was no ordinary captain. He was a man driven by a singular, all-consuming purpose, and Lena was his most trusted confidante and executor.

"Cygnus Rift," Elias echoed, a hint of a grim smile touching his lips. "A fitting place for ghosts to hide. Proceed with the reroute, Lena. Maximize our speed and minimize our energy output where possible. I want us to be a whisper, not a shout."

"Understood," Lena replied, her fingers already inputting the new navigational parameters. The ship responded with a subtle shift in its hum, a gentle acceleration that Lena felt more than heard. She glanced at the energy consumption readings, already calculating the fuel reserves needed for such a prolonged, evasive maneuver. The Aetherflow was incredibly efficient, but the Cygnus Rift would test its limits, and theirs.

She then pulled up the communications logs from their ascent. Despite Elias's meticulously crafted plans, the launch had been… loud, in terms of energy. The sheer power required to overcome Earth's atmospheric drag and gravitational pull, even with the Aetherflow's advanced technology, had left a significant, albeit transient, footprint. The 'Chameleon' system had done its job, bending light and masking their visual presence, but the sheer physics of their departure were undeniable. It was like trying to sneak out of a room without disturbing the air. Impossible.

"The telemetry from the launch sequence," Lena reported, her voice tight with a growing concern that she carefully kept from Elias's direct view. "While the Chameleon system held, the energy surge from the primary drive… it was brighter than anticipated. The spectrum analysis suggests it was detectable by advanced gravimetric sensors. It's not just about them tracking us; it's about them *knowing* what we are capable of. If they understand the Aetherflow, they'll understand the threat."

This was the crux of her apprehension. Elias had designed the *Phoenix* to be a tool of liberation, a means to find his lost family and, by extension, to liberate others from the oppressive forces that had orchestrated their disappearance. But any technology this revolutionary, this far beyond current human understanding, would inevitably be seen as a weapon. And a weapon of this magnitude, in the wrong hands, or even in the hands of those who feared it, would be relentlessly hunted.

She pulled up Elias's personal logs, not to pry, but to re-familiarize herself with the depth of his conviction. He wasn't seeking conquest; he was seeking reclamation. He wasn't driven by a lust for power; he was fueled by a father's desperate love and a husband's unwavering loyalty. Yet, the universe rarely distinguished between the intent of a tool and its potential for destruction.

"Elias," Lena said, her tone shifting slightly, a subtle plea for him to consider the broader implications. "Our success is undeniable. We've achieved what was thought impossible. But this also means we've painted a target on our backs. The more we rely on the Aetherflow's full capabilities, the more we reveal the nature of our technology. If they can reverse-engineer even a fraction of it…"

She didn't need to finish the sentence. The implication was stark and terrifying. Elias's quest for redemption could inadvertently unleash a power that could further enslave humanity, or worse, tear it apart. The triumph of their ascension was tempered by the chilling realization that they had, in essence, declared war on the very systems they had escaped.

Elias turned from the navigation console, his expression unreadable for a moment. Lena held her breath, waiting for his response. She knew him well enough to know that this concern wouldn't deter him, but she needed him to acknowledge the precariousness of their situation.

"I am aware of the risks, Lena," he said, his voice low but firm. "Every decision we've made, every calculation, has been weighed against those risks. The Aetherflow is our only hope. Without it, we're powerless. We are not just fleeing; we are preparing for what comes next. And that preparation requires us to push the boundaries of what's possible."

He walked over to the viewport, gazing out at the vast expanse of stars. "The forces that took Anya and the children… they operate on a level we can barely comprehend. They wield power derived from technologies that dwarf our own. If we are to challenge them, if we are to have any hope of finding them, we cannot do so by clinging to Earth's limitations. We must embrace the very things that make us dangerous."

Lena nodded slowly, understanding his rationale, even as the gnawing unease persisted. He was right, of course. The clandestine nature of their operation had been necessary to escape Earth, but now, in the deep unknown, secrecy would be their most potent weapon, and the Aetherflow their most potent shield, however ostentatious its display.

"I've rerouted us through the Cygnus Rift," she confirmed, her fingers still busy at her console. "The initial jump has been made. We are currently maneuvering into the denser regions. Sensor distortion is already increasing. Communications with Earth are… effectively severed, at least for now." She checked the long-range sensors. "No immediate pursuit signatures detected. However, I'm still seeing faint residual energy traces from our launch. They're faint, but they're there. Persistent."

"Good," Elias said, a strange sort of resolve hardening his gaze. "Persistence is a trait we can exploit. If they're persistent in hunting us, we'll be persistent in evading them. And when the time is right, we'll be persistent in striking back." He turned to her, his eyes locking with hers. "Our triumph is not just in escaping. It's in surviving. And our concern must be focused on ensuring that survival, so that we can ultimately achieve our true objective."

Lena met his gaze, a flicker of renewed determination passing between them. Elias's unwavering conviction was a powerful anchor, a constant reminder of why they were undertaking this perilous journey. She understood the weight of his burden, the immense responsibility he carried. Her role was to ensure the *Phoenix* was not just a vessel of escape, but a weapon forged for a just cause, a sanctuary for a father's desperate hope, and a beacon for a future that had been stolen. The calculations continued, the ship hummed onward, and Lena, the tactical officer, the guardian of their hard-won freedom, prepared for whatever shadows the cosmos would cast upon them. She knew, with a chilling certainty, that their ascension was only the beginning of a much larger, and far more dangerous, spectacle. The universe was vast and unforgiving, and they were now a part of its intricate, often deadly, dance. Their success had been a dazzling display, but now, in the silent, unforgiving void, the true test of their resilience, and their triumph, had just begun.

The hum of the *Phoenix* shifted, a subtle but perceptible change in its resonant frequency as the final surge of the Aetherflow drive pushed them beyond the invisible tether of Earth's gravity. Lena, her eyes fixed on the myriad data streams cascading across her console, felt the familiar lurch that signaled a transition into true interstellar transit. It wasn't the jarring violence of conventional rocket launches, but a smooth, almost elegant acceleration that spoke volumes about the engine's revolutionary design. They had done it. They had broken orbit.

Elias stood beside her, his silhouette stark against the main viewport, which now displayed a breathtaking panorama. Earth, their cradle, their tormentor, was rapidly diminishing into a sapphire jewel set against the velvet blackness of space. It was a poignant sight, a planet of unimaginable beauty and crushing conformity, now receding into history. He hadn't spoken since Lena confirmed the successful disengagement from orbital mechanics, his gaze lost in the star-dusted expanse. It was a moment freighted with the weight of their past and the infinite promise of their future.

"Orbital escape vector confirmed," Lena's voice was a low murmur, cutting through the charged silence. "We are no longer bound by terrestrial gravitational forces. Velocity is stable, exceeding minimum escape parameters by a significant margin. All systems nominal, Elias." She glanced up at him, a subtle tremor in her voice betraying the immense relief and the burgeoning trepidation that warred within her. They were free, undeniably so, but freedom in the void was a fragile, perilous thing.

Elias finally turned from the viewport, a faint, almost weary smile gracing his lips. "A breath of fresh air, wouldn't you say, Lena?" His tone was light, but his eyes held a depth of emotion that spoke of years of longing and the immense burden of his quest. He ran a hand through his hair, a nervous habit that always surfaced during moments of profound accomplishment or extreme stress. "To be unbound. To have the universe laid out before us, rather than a single, familiar world."

He moved to the captain's chair, settling into its contours as if it were an extension of his own being. The bridge, once a hub of calculated tension during their ascent, now settled into a quiet efficiency, the hum of the ship a constant, reassuring presence. The Aetherflow, Lena's diagnostic had confirmed, was performing with an almost impossibly low energy expenditure for the velocity they were achieving. It was a marvel, a testament to Elias's audacious vision, and their primary, and perhaps only, asset against the unknown dangers that lay ahead.

"The initial jump coordinates remain locked," Lena reported, her fingers flying across the holographic interface, projecting the projected flight path onto the main display. "We're on course for the designated 'dead zone' – the region of interstellar space designated for initial long-range sensor calibration and our first phase of deep-space operations. The Cygnus Rift maneuver was successful in obscuring our initial transit, as predicted. Residual energy traces are degrading as anticipated, but I'm still monitoring for any anomalous tracking signals."

Elias nodded, his gaze sweeping across the navigational data. "The Rift was… invigorating," he admitted, a hint of amusement in his voice. "A fitting baptism for the *Phoenix*. Those gravitational eddies and temporal distortions are precisely the kind of environmental chaos that would confound any conventional pursuit. Let them chase shadows in a maze they cannot navigate."

"And yet," Lena continued, her brow furrowed as she zoomed in on a complex spectral analysis, "the initial energy signature of the Aetherflow's activation, even with the Chameleon system engaged, was… substantial. It wasn't just a detectable energy bloom, Elias. It was a complex, coherent waveform. Earth's deep-space listening posts, if they possess the right analytical tools, might have picked up more than just an anomaly. They might have discerned a pattern."

This was the core of her anxiety, the lingering shadow cast by their spectacular escape. They had broken free, but they had also announced their presence, albeit in a language the vast majority of Earth's authorities wouldn't understand. But there were those who *would* understand, those who had the foresight and the resources to analyze such a unique energy signature. Elias's father, the renowned astrophysicist, had been one of them, and the very people Elias believed had orchestrated Anya and the children's disappearance were likely far more advanced than the public understood.

Elias turned his attention back to the main display, his expression thoughtful. "A pattern, you say? Intriguing. It's the nature of discovery, Lena. To reveal something new is to invite scrutiny. But we are no longer in a position to be scrutinized in the way they are accustomed to. We are operating on a different plane now." He tapped a console, bringing up a detailed schematic of the *Phoenix*'s primary systems. "The Aetherflow is not merely an engine; it is a manifestation of principles that defy current Earth-bound physics. If they can even *begin* to comprehend its mechanics, then our advantage diminishes exponentially."

"Precisely," Lena agreed, her fingers hovering over the communications array. "And that's why our silence, our evasiveness, must be absolute. Once we've put enough distance between us, and utilized the cloaking capabilities to their fullest, we should be effectively undetectable. However, the immediate aftermath of our departure was… loud. There were reports of localized atmospheric disruptions, energy surges that tripped seismic sensors even miles from the launch site."

"Collateral effects of immense power," Elias stated, his gaze unwavering. "Unavoidable, given the magnitude of the forces we unleashed. But contained. And the primary objective was to escape Earth's immediate grasp, not to conduct a silent, invisible departure. That was a luxury we could not afford." He leaned back, closing his eyes for a brief moment. "My focus now is on the long game, Lena. On the journey ahead, and the clarity it will bring. Earth's understanding of our technology is a secondary concern to their inability to pursue us effectively."

Lena's fingers continued their rhythmic dance across the console, updating sensor logs, plotting hypothetical pursuit vectors, and cross-referencing astronomical data for potential safe havens or unexpected dangers. The ship was a marvel of engineering, a testament to Elias's genius, but it was also a fragile bubble of advanced technology in a universe that was largely indifferent, and often actively hostile. The sheer raw power of the Aetherflow was undeniable, but its energy signature was, as she had observed, a beacon of sorts. A beacon they desperately needed to extinguish from any lingering Earth-based observation.

"The visual spectrum analysis from the launch phase shows a significant emission spike," Lena reported, her voice devoid of emotion, a practiced habit when delivering potentially alarming data. "While the Chameleon system masked our physical form, the spectral emission from the Aetherflow's primary flux core was… brilliant. Beyond anything I've seen in standard atmospheric readings. It suggests that even without direct visual confirmation, the energy signature itself was undeniably present. A signature that Earth's most advanced sensor arrays would have registered."

Elias hummed, a low, resonant sound that filled the bridge. "Brilliance," he mused. "The birth of a new star, in its own way. And stars attract attention, Lena. It's in their nature. But we are not a star. We are a shadow moving between them. The question isn't whether they detected us, but whether they can *interpret* what they detected, and whether they can *act* upon it."

"The interpretation is the critical factor," Lena countered, her concern palpable. "If they can deduce the nature of the Aetherflow, the principles behind it, then our advantage is lost. They would then understand the sheer potential for propulsion, for energy generation… for weaponry. The implications are… vast." She paused, choosing her words carefully. "The same forces that took Anya and the children – if your suspicions are correct – might view this technology not as a means of escape, but as a threat to their own dominance. And they are not known for their… subtlety in dealing with threats."

A somber stillness fell over the bridge. The mention of Anya and the children always brought a shift in Elias's demeanor, a hardening of his resolve, a flicker of pain that he kept tightly leashed. "They will view it as a threat, Lena. They view anything that challenges their monopoly on power as a threat. That is why we are here, and not there." He gestured vaguely towards the receding Earth. "My father believed that true progress lay in understanding and harnessing the fundamental forces of the universe. He believed that this knowledge should be shared, not hoarded or weaponized. The people who control Earth's advanced technology… they operate on a different philosophy."

Lena nodded, her mind racing through the possibilities. If Earth's intelligence agencies or the shadowy organizations Elias suspected of controlling interstellar operations were able to glean enough from their departure, they might adapt. They might begin to look for a specific energy signature, a deviation from the norm that would point directly to them. The Cygnus Rift was a temporary shield, a clever maneuver, but it wouldn't last forever. Eventually, they would have to re-emerge, re-engage their systems, and in doing so, risk detection.

"Our next phase involves charting a course through uncharted territories," Lena stated, her focus returning to the immediate task at hand. "The sensor limitations within the deeper regions of the Cygnus Rift will provide us with a significant cloak, but our ability to navigate will be severely compromised. We'll be relying heavily on the *Phoenix*'s advanced astrogation suite and its ability to interpret subtle gravitational cues."

"And on our own instincts," Elias added, a glint of steely determination in his eyes. "We have spent years preparing for this. Every simulation, every theoretical calculation, has led to this moment. The *Phoenix* is not merely a ship; it is an extension of our will, our hope. We will use the universe's own complexities to our advantage."

He stood and walked to the main console, placing his hands flat against its cool, smooth surface. "The transition from Earth's orbit into the void is complete. The Aetherflow performed magnificently. We have achieved our primary objective: we are free." He looked back at Lena, his expression a mixture of relief and anticipation. "The true adventure, Lena, has just begun. We are no longer merely escaping. We are exploring. We are seeking. And we are, for the first time, charting our own destiny amongst the stars."

Lena met his gaze, a sense of shared purpose
solidifying between them. The fear, the apprehension,
still lingered at the edges of her consciousness, but it
was being steadily eclipsed by the sheer magnitude of
their undertaking. They were a mere speck of advanced
technology against the immeasurable canvas of the
cosmos, but they carried with them the spark of
revolution, the hope for answers, and the desperate
love of a father for his lost family. The *Phoenix*, a vessel
of impossible dreams, now glided silently into the vast,
uncharted ocean of space, leaving the pale blue dot of
their origin far, far behind. The hum of the Aetherflow
was now the song of their liberation, a melody of
infinite possibilities echoing in the silent, endless night.
The weight of their escape had been immense, but the
weight of their journey, the true spectacle of their
ascension, was only just beginning to unfold. They
were now a part of something far grander, and far more
dangerous, than they had ever imagined. The universe
awaited, and they, with the *Phoenix* as their guide, were
ready to meet it.

## 8: Vista of Infinite Possibility

The transition from the familiar, filtered light of Earth's atmosphere to the unadulterated brilliance of the interstellar medium was more profound than Lena had anticipated. The main viewport of the *Phoenix*, no longer a window to a familiar sky, had become a portal. Elias's observation that the silence of space was a stark contrast to the crushing silence of the deep held a new resonance. This was not an oppressive emptiness; it was an embracing void, teeming with silent, ancient light. Stars, stripped of atmospheric distortion, blazed with an intensity that seemed to sing. They weren't mere pinpricks of light anymore; they were incandescent furnaces, their flares and coronas visible as dynamic brushstrokes against the absolute black.

Lena found herself captivated, her analytical mind momentarily silenced by the sheer visual spectacle. Nebulae, previously only discernible as faint smudges through telescopes, now unfurled in vast, cosmic tapestries. The Carina Nebula, a stellar nursery they had only glimpsed in distant, grainy images, now dominated a significant portion of the viewport. Swirls of ionized hydrogen, glowing in impossible shades of crimson and rose, intermingled with darker, dust-laden tendrils that hinted at the gravitational forces shaping new celestial bodies. It was a riot of color, a vibrant testament to the universe's creative, destructive power. The light here carried a different quality, a raw, unmediated energy that seeped into the very hull of the *Phoenix*.

Elias stood beside her, his gaze sweeping across the panorama. The haunted look that had often shadowed his eyes, a constant reminder of Anya and his children, seemed to have receded. It wasn't entirely gone, Lena knew, but here, surrounded by the sheer, overwhelming grandeur of creation, it was subdued. He was no longer just a man driven by loss; he was an explorer, an architect of a new destiny. The cosmos, in its unfathomable vastness, seemed to offer not just a place to hide, but a canvas upon which to rebuild, to find answers that transcended the confines of their former world. His voice, when he finally spoke, was low, filled with a profound reverence. "It's... humbling, isn't it, Lena? To see the universe as it truly is, without the veil. All the theories, all the models, they're pale imitations of this reality."

Lena nodded, still processing the sheer scale of it all. She activated a long-range sensor sweep, her fingers moving with a newfound, almost reverent, deliberation. "The spectral analysis of nearby stellar bodies is already exceeding our pre-flight simulations, Elias. The energy signatures are far more complex, far richer than predicted. And the void between these systems... it's not truly empty. There are subtle fluctuations, gravitational resonances that suggest phenomena we haven't even begun to categorize." She pointed to a cluster of faint, shimmering points of light on her display. "Those aren't just rogue stars. The pattern suggests something else. Something... organized."

"Organized in a way that Earth's science could never conceive," Elias mused, his gaze fixed on the distant galaxies. "We've only ever seen glimpses, fragments. Now, we are immersed. Imagine what we'll discover out here, Lena. What secrets are hidden within these stellar nurseries, within the hearts of these ancient galaxies. This is what my father dreamed of. This is the ultimate frontier, not just of space, but of knowledge." He turned to her, his eyes alight with a spark that hadn't been there in years. "This vista is not just beautiful; it's a promise. A promise of understanding."

The *Phoenix* continued its silent glide through the interstellar medium. The ship's systems, designed with Elias's visionary understanding of theoretical physics, were proving to be not just functional, but exceptionally robust. The Aetherflow drive maintained its steady, almost effortless propulsion, its energy output remarkably efficient. Lena ran diagnostics on the primary sensors, meticulously cataloging the data flowing in. The sheer volume of information was staggering. They were detecting subtle variations in the cosmic microwave background radiation that indicated previously unobserved structural elements of the universe. Gravitational lensing effects, far more pronounced than anticipated, warped the light from distant quasars, revealing distortions that hinted at the presence of dark matter concentrations far larger and more intricate than current models suggested.

"The gravitational anomalies are... significant," Lena reported, her voice a low hum against the ambient thrum of the ship. "We're mapping regions of space where the fabric of spacetime itself appears to be subtly warped, not by singular massive objects, but by what appear to be overlapping, interacting fields. It's like encountering ripples in a pond, but the pond is the universe, and the ripples are caused by forces we can't yet perceive directly." She zoomed in on a particularly dense cluster of these anomalies. "These patterns aren't random. They suggest underlying structures, perhaps pathways, or barriers. And they seem to be concentrated in certain directions."

Elias leaned closer, his scientific curiosity ignited. "Pathways or barriers," he repeated, the words echoing the profound implications of their journey. "If they are pathways, then they are routes that can be navigated. If barriers, then they are challenges to be overcome. My father spoke of cosmic currents, flows of energy and matter that influenced the very evolution of galaxies. Perhaps these are the physical manifestations of those currents." He pointed towards a distant, luminous band stretching across the void. "That's a spiral galaxy, isn't it? And it's… oriented in a particular way relative to these anomalies. It's almost as if it's being 'pulled' or 'guided' by them."

"The orientation is statistically improbable for a random distribution," Lena confirmed, cross-referencing the galaxy's trajectory with the mapped anomalies. "And look here," she highlighted another section of the display, showing a vast, dark expanse punctuated by faint, interconnected filaments. "This is a cosmic web structure, but it's far more intricate than any simulations predicted. The voids aren't just empty space; they're interwoven with these faint, energetic tendrils. They act like a vast neural network for the universe, connecting everything."

The understanding that dawned on Elias was palpable. His earlier anxieties about Earth's pursuit seemed to diminish further, replaced by an almost childlike wonder and a keen intellectual drive. He wasn't just running from his past; he was actively engaging with a universe that held the keys to not only his family's fate, but to humanity's fundamental understanding of its place in existence. "This 'cosmic web'," he said, his voice resonating with excitement, "if it's a network, then it's a communication system. A transport system. And we, with the *Phoenix* and the Aetherflow, might just be able to tap into it."

He moved to the astrogation console, his fingers dancing across the holographic interface, projecting the potential implications of these newly discovered structures. "My father's final research papers, the ones they tried to suppress, spoke of a unified field theory that wasn't just about electromagnetism and gravity, but about the fundamental fabric of reality itself. He believed that spacetime wasn't just a backdrop, but an active participant, a medium that could be manipulated. If these anomalies are the visible manifestations of that medium, then... then our journey isn't just about traversing space, Lena. It's about learning to surf these cosmic waves."

Lena felt a surge of exhilaration, a feeling that had been absent for too long. The scientific puzzle was immense, but the potential rewards were even greater. "The implications for FTL travel are immense, Elias. If we can navigate these currents, we could potentially achieve velocities that dwarf even the theoretical limits of the Aetherflow. This could be the key to finding Anya and the children, not by brute force, but by understanding the universe's own pathways." She accessed a database, cross-referencing the observed cosmic web patterns with theoretical models of extra-dimensional physics. "There are fringe theories, dismissed by mainstream science, that suggest these structures are evidence of higher-dimensional conduits.

If they are, then the distances we perceive might be illusions, and true interstellar travel could be a matter of simply bending the fabric of reality."

Elias's expression was one of deep contemplation. The sheer scope of the universe, now unfolding before him with such clarity, was overwhelming in its potential. It was a far cry from the suffocating confines of Earth, where knowledge was hoarded and progress was stifled by fear and control. Here, in the vast, indifferent expanse, there was only the pursuit of truth, the raw, unadulterated beauty of discovery. "They tried to contain us, Lena," he said, his voice hardening slightly, the memory of his father's fate and his family's disappearance resurfacing briefly. "They feared what this knowledge could unlock. They feared humanity's potential. But they couldn't contain the universe. And now, we are a part of it, not as subjects of its whims, but as active participants."

He gestured to the main viewport, where a distant galaxy, its spiral arms clearly defined, rotated in silent majesty. "That galaxy, billions of light-years away, is now within our potential reach. Not in a millennium, not in a century, but perhaps within a lifetime, if we can master these cosmic pathways. This isn't just a vista of infinite possibility, Lena. It's a vista of infinite *responsibility*. We carry the legacy of my father's work, the hope for a future where humanity isn't confined by the limitations of its own planet, or its own fear."

Lena's fingers continued their work, isolating specific energy signatures, mapping gravitational potentials, and charting potential courses through the intricate web of cosmic filaments. The *Phoenix* was more than just a ship; it was a research vessel, a probe into the unknown, and a beacon of hope. The raw data streaming in was rewriting their understanding of the universe with every passing moment. They were no longer just escaping; they were embarking on a grand scientific expedition, one that promised to unveil the very secrets of creation.

"The Aetherflow's energy signature is remarkably stable even when interacting with these localized spacetime distortions," Lena observed, a note of professional satisfaction in her voice. "It seems the underlying principles of its propulsion are inherently compatible with these cosmic forces. It's almost as if it was designed to tap into them."

"My father always said that true innovation wasn't about overcoming nature, but about harmonizing with it," Elias replied, his gaze fixed on the swirling nebulae and distant galaxies. "He believed that the universe held all the answers, and that our role was to listen, to understand, and to adapt. Here, among these stars, far from the noise and interference of Earth, we can finally do that. We can listen to the universe's song, and learn to sing along." The vastness outside was no longer a threat, but an invitation, a boundless frontier waiting to be explored and understood, a testament to the infinite possibilities that lay before them. The journey had truly begun, and the cosmos, in all its breathtaking glory, was their guide.

The vastness outside the viewport of the *Phoenix* was a balm to Elias's soul, a silent symphony that drowned out the discordant echoes of his past. The crushing weight of grief, a burden he had carried for so long, seemed to dissipate in the unfiltered light of distant stars. Earth, with its suffocating control and its manufactured despair, felt like a dream, a distant memory that had no power in this realm of infinite possibility. Here, surrounded by the raw, untamed beauty of creation, the tragedy that had once defined him no longer held dominion. It was a scar, yes, a testament to profound loss, but no longer the gaping wound that had threatened to consume him.

He had arrived in this celestial ocean not as a fugitive, but as a pilgrim. The memory of Anya, her radiant smile, her unwavering belief in a brighter future, was not a source of pain, but a guiding star. Their children, their laughter, their innocent wonder, were not specters haunting his present, but inspirations fueling his journey. He had transformed his sorrow, that desolate landscape of despair, into an engine of creation, a vessel capable of traversing the very fabric of existence. The cosmos, in its boundless immensity, offered a new perspective, a profound truth that loss could be transmuted into growth, that the deepest voids could birth the most brilliant light.

Lena, ever the pragmatist, was absorbed in the intricate dance of data on her console, her fingers tracing the spectral signatures of nebulae that painted the void in hues of impossible beauty. Yet, even she, in her scientific rigor, couldn't help but be moved by the sheer spectacle. Elias watched her, a sense of quiet contentment settling over him. She represented the best of humanity – the unyielding curiosity, the relentless pursuit of knowledge, the courage to venture into the unknown. Together, they were not merely survivors of Earth's tyranny; they were architects of a new dawn, charting a course through a universe that defied all limitations.

"The energy readings from that sector," Lena murmured, her voice barely disturbing the hushed reverence of the bridge, "they're unlike anything we've cataloged. It's as if the very laws of physics are bending, not breaking, but… reinterpreting themselves. There's a signature there, Elias, a subtle harmonic resonance that suggests an active, intelligent manipulation of spacetime." She gestured to a swirling vortex of light on the main screen, a cosmic whirlpool of unimaginable scale. "The Aetherflow is reacting to it, Elias. Not with resistance, but with an almost… symbiotic pull. It feels less like a navigational challenge and more like an invitation."

Elias moved to stand beside her, his gaze drawn to the phenomenon she indicated. It was a celestial ballet, a gravitational waltz performed by forces that dwarfed any terrestrial understanding. His father's theories, once dismissed as the ramblings of a visionary, now seemed to be unfolding before them, tangible proof of a universe far more intricate and interconnected than they had ever dared to imagine. The grief that had fueled his father's obsession, the same grief that had driven Elias from Earth, was now, paradoxically, the very force that propelled them towards a profound understanding of existence.

"An invitation," Elias echoed, a slow smile spreading across his face. "That's precisely what it feels like. My father believed that the universe wasn't merely a canvas upon which events transpired, but an active participant, a sentient entity with its own rhythms and intentions. He spoke of cosmic currents, unseen flows of energy that guided the formation of galaxies, that whispered secrets to those who dared to listen. Perhaps these anomalies Lena is detecting are the visible manifestations of those currents, the universe's way of showing us the pathways."

He ran a hand through his hair, a gesture that had once been a nervous tic, but now conveyed a sense of calm deliberation. The weight of command, the responsibility for Lena's life and the fate of their mission, was immense. Yet, it was a weight he embraced, a counterpoint to the emptiness he had felt for so long. He was no longer a man adrift, defined by his losses. He was a captain, navigating the most profound journey imaginable, driven by a love that transcended even death.

"Think of it, Lena," Elias continued, his voice filled with a newfound conviction. "We believed we were escaping. We believed we were hiding. But perhaps we were being guided. Perhaps the very forces that drove us from Earth were the same forces that led us to this unique vantage point, this moment of discovery. This isn't just about finding a new home; it's about understanding our place in the grand tapestry of existence. It's about finding redemption, not in the ruins of our past, but in the boundless potential of the future."

Lena's eyes, when she met his, held a shared understanding, a flicker of the same awe that filled him. "The data suggests these currents are not random,

Elias. They follow complex, repeating patterns, almost like intricate algorithms woven into the fabric of spacetime. If we can decipher these algorithms, if we can learn to predict and even influence these currents, then interstellar travel as we understand it becomes obsolete. We wouldn't be traveling *through* space; we would be navigating its inherent pathways, its cosmic circulatory system."

The implications were staggering. They were not just explorers; they were cartographers of the unseen, deciphering a language spoken by the universe itself. The memory of Anya, her passion for astronomy, her dreams of reaching the stars, now felt like a shared legacy. He saw her in the determined set of Lena's jaw, in the unyielding pursuit of knowledge that mirrored his own, and more importantly, in the very purpose that had brought them to this celestial frontier.

"My father always said that humanity's greatest obstacle wasn't its technological limitations, but its own fear," Elias mused, his gaze drifting back to the swirling nebula. "Fear of the unknown, fear of change, fear of our own potential. They feared what my father's discoveries could unleash, the paradigm shift they represented. They feared a humanity unbound by terrestrial constraints. But out here, the only constraints are the ones we impose upon ourselves. And with every discovery, we shed those self-imposed limitations."

He reached out, his hand hovering over the holographic display, tracing the ethereal trails of light that Lena had mapped. "This is not just a vista of infinite possibility, Lena. It's a vista of infinite responsibility. We carry the torch of my father's legacy, the hopes of a species yearning for something more than mere survival. We are not just passengers on this journey; we are the navigators, the ones who will translate the universe's silent wisdom into a language that humanity can finally understand."

The silence that followed was not an empty one, but a pregnant pause filled with the unspoken weight of their mission. The *Phoenix* continued its silent glide, a testament to human ingenuity and a beacon of hope in the vast, indifferent cosmos. Elias felt a profound sense of peace wash over him, a peace that had eluded him for years. The past, with its unbearable sorrow, had been a crucible, forging him into the man he was now – a man ready to embrace the universe, not as a victim, but as a participant, a learner, a lover of the infinite.

"The universe doesn't judge, Elias," Lena said softly, her voice cutting through the quiet hum of the ship. "It simply *is*. And in that simple existence, there is a profound truth. The chaos we perceive is merely a complex order we haven't yet deciphered. Your father understood that. He understood that true progress comes not from fighting against the natural order, but from aligning with it, from becoming a part of its grand design."

Elias nodded, the words resonating deep within him. He thought of Anya, of her boundless optimism, her ability to find light even in the darkest of times. She had taught him that love was not about possessing, but about setting free, about nurturing the growth of another. And in this journey, he was setting free not only himself, but the very essence of what made humanity worth saving. He was honoring their memory by embracing the wonder they had inspired, by allowing that wonder to guide him through the cosmic ocean.

He looked at the stars, not as distant, cold bodies, but as fellow travelers, each with its own story, its own place in the grand cosmic narrative. The immensity of it all no longer felt overwhelming, but liberating. He had found a measure of peace in the sheer scale of creation, a quiet understanding that his own pain, while immense, was but a single note in the universe's magnificent symphony. His grief had been a necessary catalyst, a brutal awakening that had stripped away the illusions of his former life and revealed the true path ahead.

"We are more than just survivors, Lena," Elias said, his voice firm with newfound purpose. "We are inheritors.

Inheritors of a legacy of curiosity, of courage, and of a love that transcends even the void. The universe has offered us a second chance, not just to escape, but to rebuild, to learn, and to ultimately, to remember. We will carry Anya and the children with us, not as ghosts of the past, but as the very stars that guide our way."

The *Phoenix* continued its silent voyage, a tiny vessel carrying an immeasurable hope through the celestial expanse. Elias, no longer haunted by the shadows of Earth, stood on the precipice of an infinite horizon, his heart filled with a quiet reverence for the cosmos, and a profound gratitude for the journey that had led him here. He had found redemption, not in finding a new home, but in finding himself, reborn amidst the silent, ancient light of the stars. The pain of his past had been transmuted into a powerful engine for exploration, and the boundless potential of the human spirit, mirrored in the infinite expanse, was now his guiding light. He was ready to embrace whatever mysteries lay ahead, for he had learned that even in the deepest darkness, the most brilliant constellations could be found.

Lena's fingers danced across the illuminated panels of her console, each movement precise and economical. The hum of the *Phoenix*, a symphony of advanced alien engineering and human adaptation, was the only sound on the bridge besides her quiet murmurs. She was already deep into recalibrating the ship's atmospheric processors, pushing their operational parameters beyond anything Elias's father had dared to test in simulations. The ship, born from a civilization beyond their comprehension, was a treasure trove of scientific enigmas, and Lena was determined to unlock every one of them. Her gaze flickered from the real-time diagnostics scrolling across her primary screen to the spectral analysis of the approaching nebula. It pulsed on the viewport, a vast, incandescent bloom painting the black canvas of space with strokes of amethyst, sapphire, and molten gold. This celestial canvas, she felt with every fiber of her being, was not merely a beautiful backdrop, but a destination pregnant with answers.

"The energy containment fields are holding steady at 112% efficiency," she reported, her voice a low, confident cadence. "But I believe we can optimize the fusion core's output by rerouting auxiliary power through the tertiary conduits. It's a risk, of course, given the unknown nature of these conduits, but the projected thrust increase… well, it's substantial, Elias. We could shave days off our approach, maybe even hours, depending on how the Aetherflow responds to the increased energetic signature." She paused, her brow furrowed in concentration as she cross-referenced theoretical models with the *Phoenix*'s current operational data. The ship was a testament to a technological leap that dwarfed humanity's own, and Lena felt like a child presented with an infinite box of impossibly complex toys. Each component, each energy signature, was a puzzle piece, and the nebula, she suspected, was the grand picture itself.

Her scientific mind, always hungry, was already formulating new hypotheses about the very nature of the Aetherflow. The currents Elias had spoken of, his father's life's work, were no longer abstract theories to her. They were tangible, measurable phenomena that dictated the *Phoenix*'s astonishing speed and maneuverability. She was developing algorithms to predict their ebb and flow, to anticipate their subtle shifts, and to harness their power with a precision that transcended mere piloting. It was less about steering a ship and more about conversing with the fundamental forces of the universe. "The resonance patterns within the nebula are… chaotic, yet structured," she continued, tapping a holographic projection of the swirling gas and dust. "It's like a vast, cosmic nursery, birthing stars and perhaps, if my preliminary readings are correct, something far more significant. The energy signatures here are incredibly dense, Elias, suggesting a concentration of exotic particles and perhaps even localized distortions in spacetime. It's not just a nebula; it's an active nexus."

She envisioned the possibilities, the sheer unadulterated scientific discovery that lay before them. The nebula wasn't just a waypoint; it was a hypothesis made manifest, a celestial laboratory where the very rules of existence might be revealed. Her fascination wasn't solely with the ship's capabilities, but with the profound implications of their journey. If the *Phoenix* could navigate these cosmic currents, if they could learn to understand and manipulate them, then humanity's reach would extend far beyond the limitations of conventional propulsion. They wouldn't be traversing space; they would be flowing through it, like ancient mariners charting currents invisible to the naked eye. This was more than a scientific endeavor; it was a philosophical awakening.

"I'm running simulations on a potential cloaking modification for the engine core," Lena announced, her voice laced with an almost feverish excitement. "If we can effectively mask our energy signature when entering the denser regions of the nebula, we might be able to observe its internal processes with minimal interference. The last thing we want is to trigger some unknown defense mechanism or, worse, disrupt a delicate cosmic process. The *Phoenix* is an anomaly in itself, and I'd prefer to keep our presence as subtle as possible while we gather data." Her eyes, usually so focused and analytical, held a spark of wonder, the pure, unadulterated thrill of standing on the precipice of the unknown. The vastness outside was not an empty void to her; it was a symphony of information waiting to be deciphered, a cosmic tapestry woven with secrets.

Elias watched her, his heart swelling with a quiet pride. He saw in Lena not just a brilliant scientist, but a kindred spirit, someone who understood the profound yearning for knowledge that had driven his father and now propelled them forward. Her dedication was a mirror to his own burgeoning understanding of their purpose. They were not just refugees; they were inheritors of a legacy, tasked with translating the universe's silent language for a species that had lost its way. "What are your initial readings on the nebula's composition, Lena?" he asked, his voice soft, careful not to break her intense focus. "Anything that hints at the technology that built the *Phoenix*?"

Lena's fingers flew across her console, bringing up a complex, three-dimensional rendering of the nebula. "The elemental composition is standard for a stellar nursery of this type – hydrogen, helium, traces of heavier elements formed in previous stellar generations. However, there are anomalous energy readings, Elias, pockets of concentrated energy that don't conform to any known stellar or nebular phenomena. They're exhibiting unusual quantum entanglement signatures and… localized temporal fluctuations. It's as if these regions are existing slightly out of sync with the rest of the universe. And the Aetherflow itself appears to be… concentrated here. It's as if this nebula is a gravitational well for these cosmic currents, a point of convergence."

She zoomed in on one of the anomalous energy pockets, a swirling vortex of vibrant blues and greens within the nebular tapestry. "This region," she pointed, her finger tracing a path on the holographic display, "is emitting a faint, complex harmonic frequency. It's not random noise. It's patterned, intricate, almost like a deliberate signal. My hypothesis is that these concentrations of energy and the unique properties of the Aetherflow within this nebula are intrinsically linked to the propulsion and navigational systems of the *Phoenix*. Perhaps the ship itself was designed to harness these phenomena, to exist within these… temporal pockets."

Her mind raced, connecting dots that were still faint and fragmented. If the nebula was a nexus of the Aetherflow, then it stood to reason that its creators would have had an intimate understanding of it. Could this nebula be a shipyard? A manufacturing hub? Or perhaps a site of profound scientific observation, a place where the architects of the *Phoenix* had studied the very fabric of reality? The implications were staggering. "The sheer scale of this place," Elias murmured, his own awe mirroring hers. "If your theory is correct, if this is a focal point for these cosmic currents, then the creators of the *Phoenix* must have possessed an understanding of physics that borders on the divine."

"Or they simply understood the universe's natural laws far better than we ever have," Lena countered, her scientific pragmatism always present. "They didn't impose their will upon it; they harmonized with it. My current work is focused on reverse-engineering the *Phoenix's* environmental controls. They're incredibly efficient, managing atmospheric pressure, temperature, and even trace element composition with a level of sophistication we can only dream of. I believe they achieved this not through brute force energy expenditure, but by subtly manipulating localized gravitational fields and resonance frequencies. Imagine if we could apply that principle to terraforming, Elias. Or even to personal habitation in hostile environments."

Her gaze drifted back to the nebula, a silent question hanging in the air. What secrets did this cosmic cloud hold? Were there remnants of the ship's creators here? Clues to their civilization, their purpose, their ultimate fate? Lena was driven by an insatiable hunger to know, to understand the 'why' behind everything. The *Phoenix* was more than a means of survival; it was an opportunity to bridge an evolutionary gap, to learn from a civilization that had mastered the universe in ways humanity had never conceived. Her scientific journey was becoming inextricably linked with their quest for a new home, a future for humanity.

"I've also been examining the ship's data logs," Lena continued, her voice dropping slightly. "There are encrypted sections, Elias, extensive archives that are far more complex than standard system maintenance records. I'm making progress, but the encryption is unlike anything I've encountered. It's not based on binary code or conventional cryptographic algorithms. It's… organic, almost. It adapts and shifts based on external stimuli. I suspect the key to unlocking it might be found within this nebula. Perhaps the creators embedded the decryption keys within the very fabric of these energy concentrations."

The thought sent a shiver of anticipation down her spine. If they could unlock those archives, they could potentially gain access to a vast repository of knowledge, a roadmap to understanding not just the *Phoenix*, but the universe itself. It was a prospect that fueled her every late night, every complex calculation. The nebula was no longer just a destination; it was a potential Rosetta Stone for cosmic understanding. She saw her work as a form of cosmic archaeology, meticulously sifting through the remnants of an advanced civilization, piecing together their story, their scientific achievements, and perhaps even their warnings.

"The propulsion system's interaction with the Aetherflow is particularly fascinating," she mused aloud, her gaze fixed on a series of complex waveform displays. "It's not simply riding the currents; it's actively shaping them, creating micro-eddies that enhance acceleration and maneuverability. It's a dance, Elias, a perfect symbiosis. I'm trying to replicate that interaction on a smaller scale within the ship's internal systems. If I can modulate the ship's localized gravitational field with enough precision, I might be able to create localized pockets of altered spacetime, effectively 'teleporting' small objects short distances within the ship. Imagine the implications for cargo transfer, for maintenance, even for personal transit within a larger vessel."

She was already sketching out designs in her mind, envisioning the modifications, the new systems she could integrate into the *Phoenix*. The ship was a gift, a chance to push the boundaries of human knowledge beyond anything they had previously conceived. Her ambition wasn't merely to survive, but to innovate, to evolve, to elevate humanity through the wisdom of this alien civilization. The nebula represented not just a waypoint, but a veritable treasure trove of scientific advancement, a gateway to understanding capabilities they had previously relegated to the realm of fantasy.

"The energy signatures within this nebula are so dense," Lena stated, her voice filled with a quiet reverence, "that it's almost as if spacetime itself is being actively woven here. My current hypothesis is that this is not merely a region of stellar formation, but a conduit, a point where the universe's fundamental energies are more readily accessible and malleable. The creators of the *Phoenix* likely understood this, and perhaps even engineered this region to facilitate their work. We need to be thorough, Elias. Every anomaly, every deviation from expected patterns, could be a clue to a greater understanding of their technology, and by extension, the universe." Her eyes, reflecting the kaleidoscope of the nebula on the viewport, held the unwavering gaze of a scientist on the verge of a profound discovery, ready to unravel the next frontier of cosmic possibility. The infinite vista outside wasn't just a spectacle; it was her laboratory, her inspiration, and the ultimate destination of her boundless curiosity.

The hum of the *Phoenix*'s engines, a resonant thrum that had become the lullaby of their improbable journey, was a constant, reassuring presence. Kaelen found himself leaning back in his command chair, the worn contours a familiar comfort against his shoulders. The bridge, bathed in the ethereal glow of the nebula's light filtering through the viewport, felt both impossibly vast and intimately his. They had done it. They had slipped the surly bonds of Earth, a feat that had seemed as likely as harnessing starlight with bare hands just weeks ago. A genuine, unbidden smile touched his lips, a rare visitor in the months that had preceded their escape. It was a fragile thing, this optimism, like a seedling pushing through frozen soil, but it was undeniably present.

He met Elias's gaze across the bridge, a silent acknowledgement passing between them. Elias, ever the embodiment of quiet resolve, offered a subtle nod, his eyes reflecting the same mixture of awe and weariness that Kaelen felt. They had weathered storms that would have shattered lesser souls, navigated the treacherous currents of political upheaval and personal loss, all while carrying the weight of humanity's future. Kaelen had always been a pragmatist, a soldier who planned for the worst-case scenario and then planned for the contingencies of that worst-case scenario. Yet, here they were, adrift in an ocean of cosmic wonder, a testament to a desperate hope and an unwavering commitment.

The sheer audacity of their departure, the intricate dance of deception and precision that had culminated in their silent exodus, still played in his mind like a recurring dream. The world they had left behind was a phantom now, a memory of suffocating anxieties and dwindling freedoms. Here, bathed in the soft, otherworldly luminescence of the nebula, those concerns seemed impossibly distant. The *Phoenix*, this miraculous vessel of alien design, was their sanctuary, their harbinger of a new dawn. He watched Lena, her brow furrowed in concentration as she delved deeper into the ship's enigmatic systems. Her brilliance was a beacon, a testament to the very ingenuity that had made this journey possible. Her ability to coax miracles from the *Phoenix*'s alien heart was a constant source of reassurance, a tangible manifestation of their collective strength.

"The atmospheric processors are within optimal parameters, Kaelen," Lena's voice, crisp and clear, cut through the contemplative silence. "And the forward sensor array has managed to resolve some of the denser particulate matter within the nebula. It's… unlike anything we've cataloged before. The energy signatures are off the charts, but not in a way that suggests immediate danger."

Kaelen acknowledged her report with a slight tilt of his head. "Any indication of artificial constructs, Lena? Or anything that might suggest the presence of the ship's original inhabitants?"

Lena's fingers flew across her console, her gaze fixed on the cascading data. "Not directly. The energy fields are highly complex, exhibiting patterns that are both ordered and emergent. It's like trying to decipher a language written in pure energy. There are pockets of what appear to be highly structured fields, almost like dormant energy matrices, but their purpose remains elusive. They don't align with any known energy generation or containment technology in our databases. They're… alien, in the truest sense of the word."

Elias chimed in, his voice calm and steady. "The Aetherflow is still stable, Kaelen. The *Phoenix* is handling it with remarkable grace. It's as if the ship intrinsically understands these currents. We're making excellent time, and the nebula's gravitational influence is, surprisingly, not impeding our progress."

Kaelen nodded, absorbing their reports. Stability. Progress. These were words he hadn't dared to use with such confidence in a long time. The vastness of space, however, was a canvas that could quickly transform from breathtaking beauty to existential threat. The nebula was a mystery, and while Lena's initial readings suggested no immediate hostility, the unknown was a formidable adversary in itself. He couldn't shake the ingrained caution that had kept him alive through years of clandestine operations and fraught negotiations.

"We remain vigilant," Kaelen stated, his gaze sweeping across the bridge crew, a silent affirmation of their shared purpose. "We've escaped one set of troubles only to venture into another. The *Phoenix* is a marvel, and Lena, your work with its systems is nothing short of extraordinary. Elias, your guidance through these cosmic currents has been invaluable. But we cannot afford complacency. This nebula is a place of immense power, and we have no idea what lies at its heart, or what forces might reside within it."

He remembered the hushed conversations, the desperate planning, the sacrifices made to secure the *Phoenix*. The memory of General Thorne's cold, calculating gaze, the suffocating weight of the oppressive regime they had fled – it was all still vivid. They were pioneers, yes, but they were also fugitives, carrying the hopes of a disillusioned world on their shoulders. The escape had been a triumph, a near-impossible feat of engineering and willpower, but it was only the beginning. The true test lay ahead, in understanding the secrets of the *Phoenix* and finding a new home for those who believed in a different future.

Kaelen allowed himself a moment to truly appreciate the view. The swirling gases of the nebula painted streaks of vibrant color across the viewport, an abstract masterpiece of cosmic creation. Within this breathtaking panorama, they were a tiny speck, an anomaly traversing the void. It was a humbling realization, but also an exhilarating one. They had broken free from the confines of their old world, unburdened by its limitations. Here, amongst the nascent stars and cosmic dust, lay an infinite expanse of possibility.

"The challenges ahead are undoubtedly immense," Kaelen admitted, his voice a low rumble. "We are a crew forged in the crucible of desperation, but we have proven our resilience. We have managed to outmaneuver our pursuers, to master a technology we barely understand, and to navigate the very fabric of spacetime in ways that defy conventional science. This is not merely survival; this is the dawn of something new." He looked at Elias, his captain, his friend. Their bond, forged in the shared trauma of their past and solidified by the shared hope of their future, was an anchor in this swirling sea of the unknown. Elias's unwavering belief in their mission, his quiet strength, had been a constant source of inspiration.

"Our mission is clear," Kaelen continued, his voice regaining its accustomed firmness. "To understand the *Phoenix*, to harness its capabilities, and to find a sanctuary where humanity can rebuild, free from the shadows of oppression. This nebula… it may hold the answers we seek, or it may present dangers we cannot yet fathom. But we face it together." He recognized the inherent risk in venturing into such an uncharted territory, but the potential reward – a deeper understanding of the universe and their place within it – was too great to ignore. The journey had stripped away much of their past, leaving them raw and vulnerable, but also pure in their purpose.

He thought of the crew, each member handpicked for their unique skills and unwavering loyalty. There was Dr. Aris Thorne, the xenobotanist, whose quiet curiosity about alien life forms might prove invaluable. There was Commander Eva Rostova, the stoic security chief, whose vigilance was a silent promise of protection. And then there were the engineers, the navigators, the scientists, all united by a shared vision. They were a testament to the indomitable human spirit, a living embodiment of the hope they carried for a better future. Their collective expertise, their shared courage, were the true strength of the *Phoenix*.

"The sheer scale of this nebula is disorienting, even with our advanced sensors," Kaelen mused, his gaze fixed on a particularly vibrant swirl of emerald and gold. "It's a stark reminder of how little we truly understand about the universe. We've spent centuries looking up at the stars, dreaming of reaching them, and now we're here, dwarfed by a cosmic phenomenon that dwarfs our own entire civilization." He paused, a thought coalescing. "Lena, have you detected any patterns in the energy fluctuations that might indicate natural celestial phenomena, or do they all seem… anomalous?"

"The background radiation is consistent with a dense molecular cloud, Kaelen," Lena replied, her focus unwavering. "But the concentrated energy pockets… they're not natural. They exhibit a degree of coherence and complexity that suggests intelligent design, or at least a process far more sophisticated than any known astrophysical event. It's as if these pockets are deliberately interacting with the Aetherflow, subtly guiding or shaping it. We're seeing localized distortions in spacetime within these regions, minute but measurable. It's fascinating, and frankly, a little unnerving."

Kaelen steepled his fingers, absorbing her words. Intelligent design. The phrase resonated with a profound significance. If the creators of the *Phoenix* were responsible for these phenomena, then they were beings of unimaginable power and understanding. This nebula wasn't just a celestial body; it was a testament to their presence, perhaps even a deliberate creation. "The implications of that are staggering, Lena. If these energy pockets are indeed artificial, then this nebula could be a nexus of their technology, a place where the fundamental forces of the universe are actively managed. We need to proceed with the utmost caution. Every anomaly we detect could be a key, or a trap."

He felt a surge of adrenaline, a familiar sensation from his days in active service. The unknown was a challenge, not a deterrent. The *Phoenix* was more than a ship; it was a promise, a vessel carrying the last vestiges of a humanity that refused to surrender to despair. Elias's father had envisioned this future, a future where humanity transcended its earthly limitations. Now, that vision rested in their hands.

"I've been reviewing the navigational data from our approach," Elias added, his voice cutting through the murmurs of the bridge. "The *Phoenix* automatically adjusted its trajectory to compensate for localized gravitational anomalies within the nebula, anomalies that weren't visible on our external scans until we were almost upon them. The ship's AI, for lack of a better term, is making intuitive decisions that go beyond its programmed parameters. It's learning, Kaelen. It's adapting."

Kaelen met Elias's gaze, a flicker of shared understanding passing between them. The *Phoenix* was not merely a tool; it was a partner. Its alien intelligence was a vital component of their survival, a silent guardian navigating them through uncharted cosmic waters. "That's… remarkable, Elias. It implies a level of sentience we hadn't anticipated. Lena, can you isolate the algorithms responsible for those navigational adjustments? Understanding how the *Phoenix* perceives and interacts with the Aetherflow could be the key to unlocking its full potential."

"I'm trying, Kaelen," Lena responded, her voice tinged with a mixture of awe and frustration. "The ship's internal logic is incredibly complex, almost organic. It's not structured like any AI we've ever encountered. It seems to process information and react in a way that's less about computation and more about… resonance. As if it's attuning itself to the fundamental frequencies of the universe. It's like trying to understand a symphony by analyzing individual notes in isolation."

Kaelen nodded slowly, the enormity of their undertaking settling upon him. They were not just exploring space; they were bridging the gap between species, between civilizations, between epochs of existence. The *Phoenix* was a living artifact, a testament to a species that had achieved a level of technological and perhaps even spiritual advancement far beyond humanity's current comprehension. His guarded optimism, once a fragile seedling, was beginning to unfurl, its roots reaching deeper into the fertile ground of possibility. The journey was fraught with peril, the challenges immense, but the crew of the *Phoenix*, united by Elias's leadership and Lena's brilliance, was ready. They were no longer just escaping; they were advancing, venturing into a vista of infinite possibility, ready to write the next chapter of humanity's story among the stars. The nebula, with its silent, radiant mystery, was their crucible, and they would emerge from it transformed, forever changed by the secrets it held.

The hum of the *Phoenix*'s engines, a resonant thrum that had become the lullaby of their improbable journey, was a constant, reassuring presence. Kaelen found himself leaning back in his command chair, the worn contours a familiar comfort against his shoulders. The bridge, bathed in the ethereal glow of the nebula's light filtering through the viewport, felt both impossibly vast and intimately his. They had done it. They had slipped the surly bonds of Earth, a feat that had seemed as likely as harnessing starlight with bare hands just weeks ago. A genuine, unbidden smile touched his lips, a rare visitor in the months that had preceded their escape. It was a fragile thing, this optimism, like a seedling pushing through frozen soil, but it was undeniably present.

He met Elias's gaze across the bridge, a silent acknowledgement passing between them. Elias, ever the embodiment of quiet resolve, offered a subtle nod, his eyes reflecting the same mixture of awe and weariness that Kaelen felt. They had weathered storms that would have shattered lesser souls, navigated the treacherous currents of political upheaval and personal loss, all while carrying the weight of humanity's future. Kaelen had always been a pragmatist, a soldier who planned for the worst-case scenario and then planned for the contingencies of that worst-case scenario. Yet, here they were, adrift in an ocean of cosmic wonder, a testament to a desperate hope and an unwavering commitment.

The sheer audacity of their departure, the intricate dance of deception and precision that had culminated in their silent exodus, still played in his mind like a recurring dream. The world they had left behind was a phantom now, a memory of suffocating anxieties and dwindling freedoms. Here, bathed in the soft, otherworldly luminescence of the nebula, those concerns seemed impossibly distant. The *Phoenix*, this miraculous vessel of alien design, was their sanctuary, their harbinger of a new dawn. He watched Lena, her brow furrowed in concentration as she delved deeper into the ship's enigmatic systems. Her brilliance was a beacon, a testament to the very ingenuity that had made this journey possible. Her ability to coax miracles from the *Phoenix*'s alien heart was a constant source of reassurance, a tangible manifestation of their collective strength.

"The atmospheric processors are within optimal parameters, Kaelen," Lena's voice, crisp and clear, cut through the contemplative silence. "And the forward sensor array has managed to resolve some of the denser particulate matter within the nebula. It's… unlike anything we've cataloged before. The energy signatures are off the charts, but not in a way that suggests immediate danger."

Kaelen acknowledged her report with a slight tilt of his head. "Any indication of artificial constructs, Lena? Or anything that might suggest the presence of the ship's original inhabitants?"

Lena's fingers flew across her console, her gaze fixed on the cascading data. "Not directly. The energy fields are highly complex, exhibiting patterns that are both ordered and emergent. It's like trying to decipher a language written in pure energy. There are pockets of what appear to be highly structured fields, almost like dormant energy matrices, but their purpose remains elusive. They don't align with any known energy generation or containment technology in our databases. They're… alien, in the truest sense of the word."

Elias chimed in, his voice calm and steady. "The Aetherflow is still stable, Kaelen. The *Phoenix* is handling it with remarkable grace. It's as if the ship intrinsically understands these currents. We're making excellent time, and the nebula's gravitational influence is, surprisingly, not impeding our progress."

Kaelen nodded, absorbing their reports. Stability. Progress. These were words he hadn't dared to use with such confidence in a long time. The vastness of space, however, was a canvas that could quickly transform from breathtaking beauty to existential threat. The nebula was a mystery, and while Lena's initial readings suggested no immediate hostility, the unknown was a formidable adversary in itself. He couldn't shake the ingrained caution that had kept him alive through years of clandestine operations and fraught negotiations.

"We remain vigilant," Kaelen stated, his gaze sweeping across the bridge crew, a silent affirmation of their shared purpose. "We've escaped one set of troubles only to venture into another. The *Phoenix* is a marvel, and Lena, your work with its systems is nothing short of extraordinary. Elias, your guidance through these cosmic currents has been invaluable. But we cannot afford complacency. This nebula is a place of immense power, and we have no idea what lies at its heart, or what forces might reside within it."

He remembered the hushed conversations, the desperate planning, the sacrifices made to secure the *Phoenix*. The memory of General Thorne's cold, calculating gaze, the suffocating weight of the oppressive regime they had fled – it was all still vivid. They were pioneers, yes, but they were also fugitives, carrying the hopes of a disillusioned world on their shoulders. The escape had been a triumph, a near-impossible feat of engineering and willpower, but it was only the beginning. The true test lay ahead, in understanding the secrets of the *Phoenix* and finding a new home for those who believed in a different future.

Kaelen allowed himself a moment to truly appreciate the view. The swirling gases of the nebula painted streaks of vibrant color across the viewport, an abstract masterpiece of cosmic creation. Within this breathtaking panorama, they were a tiny speck, an anomaly traversing the void. It was a humbling realization, but also an exhilarating one. They had broken free from the confines of their old world, unburdened by its limitations. Here, amongst the nascent stars and cosmic dust, lay an infinite expanse of possibility.

"The challenges ahead are undoubtedly immense," Kaelen admitted, his voice a low rumble. "We are a crew forged in the crucible of desperation, but we have proven our resilience. We have managed to outmaneuver our pursuers, to master a technology we barely understand, and to navigate the very fabric of spacetime in ways that defy conventional science. This is not merely survival; this is the dawn of something new." He looked at Elias, his captain, his friend. Their bond, forged in the shared trauma of their past and solidified by the shared hope of their future, was an anchor in this swirling sea of the unknown. Elias's unwavering belief in their mission, his quiet strength, had been a constant source of inspiration.

"Our mission is clear," Kaelen continued, his voice regaining its accustomed firmness. "To understand the *Phoenix*, to harness its capabilities, and to find a sanctuary where humanity can rebuild, free from the shadows of oppression. This nebula… it may hold the answers we seek, or it may present dangers we cannot yet fathom. But we face it together." He recognized the inherent risk in venturing into such an uncharted territory, but the potential reward – a deeper understanding of the universe and their place within it – was too great to ignore. The journey had stripped away much of their past, leaving them raw and vulnerable, but also pure in their purpose.

He thought of the crew, each member handpicked for their unique skills and unwavering loyalty. There was Dr. Aris Thorne, the xenobotanist, whose quiet curiosity about alien life forms might prove invaluable. There was Commander Eva Rostova, the stoic security chief, whose vigilance was a silent promise of protection. And then there were the engineers, the navigators, the scientists, all united by a shared vision. They were a testament to the indomitable human spirit, a living embodiment of the hope they carried for a better future. Their collective expertise, their shared courage, were the true strength of the *Phoenix*.

"The sheer scale of this nebula is disorienting, even with our advanced sensors," Kaelen mused, his gaze fixed on a particularly vibrant swirl of emerald and gold. "It's a stark reminder of how little we truly understand about the universe. We've spent centuries looking up at the stars, dreaming of reaching them, and now we're here, dwarfed by a cosmic phenomenon that dwarfs our own entire civilization." He paused, a thought coalescing. "Lena, have you detected any patterns in the energy fluctuations that might indicate natural celestial phenomena, or do they all seem… anomalous?"

"The background radiation is consistent with a dense molecular cloud, Kaelen," Lena replied, her focus unwavering. "But the concentrated energy pockets… they're not natural. They exhibit a degree of coherence and complexity that suggests intelligent design, or at least a process far more sophisticated than any known astrophysical event. It's as if these pockets are deliberately interacting with the Aetherflow, subtly guiding or shaping it. We're seeing localized distortions in spacetime within these regions, minute but measurable. It's fascinating, and frankly, a little unnerving."

Kaelen steepled his fingers, absorbing her words. Intelligent design. The phrase resonated with a profound significance. If the creators of the *Phoenix* were responsible for these phenomena, then they were beings of unimaginable power and understanding. This nebula wasn't just a celestial body; it was a testament to their presence, perhaps even a deliberate creation. "The implications of that are staggering, Lena. If these energy pockets are indeed artificial, then this nebula could be a nexus of their technology, a place where the fundamental forces of the universe are actively managed. We need to proceed with the utmost caution. Every anomaly we detect could be a key, or a trap."

He felt a surge of adrenaline, a familiar sensation from his days in active service. The unknown was a challenge, not a deterrent. The *Phoenix* was more than a ship; it was a promise, a vessel carrying the last vestiges of a humanity that refused to surrender to despair. Elias's father had envisioned this future, a future where humanity transcended its earthly limitations. Now, that vision rested in their hands.

"I've been reviewing the navigational data from our approach," Elias added, his voice cutting through the murmurs of the bridge. "The *Phoenix* automatically adjusted its trajectory to compensate for localized gravitational anomalies within the nebula, anomalies that weren't visible on our external scans until we were almost upon them. The ship's AI, for lack of a better term, is making intuitive decisions that go beyond its programmed parameters. It's learning, Kaelen. It's adapting."

Kaelen met Elias's gaze, a flicker of shared understanding passing between them. The *Phoenix* was not merely a tool; it was a partner. Its alien intelligence was a vital component of their survival, a silent guardian navigating them through uncharted cosmic waters. "That's… remarkable, Elias. It implies a level of sentience we hadn't anticipated. Lena, can you isolate the algorithms responsible for those navigational adjustments? Understanding how the *Phoenix* perceives and interacts with the Aetherflow could be the key to unlocking its full potential."

"I'm trying, Kaelen," Lena responded, her voice tinged with a mixture of awe and frustration. "The ship's internal logic is incredibly complex, almost organic. It's not structured like any AI we've ever encountered. It seems to process information and react in a way that's less about computation and more about… resonance. As if it's attuning itself to the fundamental frequencies of the universe. It's like trying to understand a symphony by analyzing individual notes in isolation."

Kaelen nodded slowly, the enormity of their undertaking settling upon him. They were not just exploring space; they were bridging the gap between species, between civilizations, between epochs of existence. The *Phoenix* was a living artifact, a testament to a species that had achieved a level of technological and perhaps even spiritual advancement far beyond humanity's current comprehension. His guarded optimism, once a fragile seedling, was beginning to unfurl, its roots reaching deeper into the fertile ground of possibility. The journey was fraught with peril, the challenges immense, but the crew of the *Phoenix*, united by Elias's leadership and Lena's brilliance, was ready. They were no longer just escaping; they were advancing, venturing into a vista of infinite possibility, ready to write the next chapter of humanity's story among the stars. The nebula, with its silent, radiant mystery, was their crucible, and they would emerge from it transformed, forever changed by the secrets it held.

The ship eased deeper into the nebular embrace, the swirling hues of cosmic gas a constant, mesmerizing spectacle. Reds bled into blues, violets into golds, creating an aurora borealis on a scale that defied human comprehension. Each eddy and current of stellar dust seemed to pulse with an unseen energy, a silent symphony of creation playing out across the void. Kaelen felt a profound sense of awe, a feeling that had been a stranger to him for too long, replaced by the stark realities of survival and escape. This wasn't just a destination; it was a profound statement about the universe's boundless capacity for wonder. It was a landscape painted by forces that operated on timescales and with power beyond their current grasp, a living testament to the sheer, untamed beauty of existence.

"The sensor readings are still anomalous, Kaelen," Lena reported, her voice a steady counterpoint to the visual splendor. "The particulate density is higher than anticipated, and the energy signatures are becoming more localized, coalescing into distinct patterns. I've managed to isolate several pockets where the energy coherence is almost… crystalline. They're emitting modulated frequencies that aren't random. They're structured, deliberate." She adjusted a holographic display, projecting a complex, interwoven pattern of light onto the bridge. "It's like the nebula itself is a colossal, interconnected network. These energy pockets are like nodes, transmitting something we can't yet comprehend."

Elias leaned forward, his eyes tracing the intricate geometric shapes. "Are these nodes interacting with the *Phoenix* in any way? Any gravitational pull, any energy drain?"


"No direct interaction," Lena confirmed. "The ship's shielding is holding perfectly. It's more like… the nebula is aware of us. The patterns are shifting subtly, almost as if responding to our presence. It's incredibly subtle, barely perceptible, but the AI is flagging it as a deviation from baseline parameters. It's as if the *Phoenix* is perceiving a form of communication that our current sensory equipment can't fully translate."

Kaelen felt a prickle of anticipation, the same thrill he'd experienced before a critical reconnaissance mission, but amplified a thousandfold. This wasn't just about navigation; it was about understanding the very nature of the universe, about deciphering the language of creation itself. The nebula was a living entity, or at least a highly organized system, and the *Phoenix* was their key to unlocking its secrets. "Lena, can you attempt to map the distribution of these nodes? I want to see if there's any discernible distribution, any architecture to this energy network."

"Already on it," Lena replied, her fingers dancing across her console with practiced speed. "The distribution isn't uniform. There are clusters, denser concentrations in certain regions, particularly in the direction we're heading. It's almost like they're guiding us, or perhaps forming a pathway. The AI is correlating these clusters with subtle variations in the Aetherflow, minor adjustments to the currents that the ship is instinctively compensating for."

"Instinctively," Kaelen repeated, letting the word hang in the air. The *Phoenix* was more than a machine; it was an evolving intelligence, a testament to a civilization that had mastered the universe in ways they could only dream of. This inherent capability to perceive and adapt was their greatest asset. He turned to Elias, "We need to be prepared for anything. This 'guidance' could be a trap, or it could be an invitation. We trust the *Phoenix*, but we don't yet understand its makers."

"My father always believed that the universe was not an empty void, but a tapestry of interconnected intelligences," Elias mused, his gaze fixed on the swirling colors. "He theorized that civilizations, upon reaching a certain level of advancement, would begin to shape their environments, to weave themselves into the fabric of spacetime. This nebula… it could be the ultimate manifestation of that concept. A deliberate creation, designed to interact with sentient life.”

“And if that’s the case,” Kaelen added, his voice low, “then what kind of beings would possess such mastery? What would they want with us?” The questions hung in the air, heavy with both hope and trepidation. They had escaped one form of oppression, only to potentially encounter something far more profound, and perhaps far more dangerous.

“The energy readings within these nodal clusters are unlike anything I’ve ever seen,” Lena reported, her voice filled with a mixture of scientific fascination and palpable awe. “They’re not simply energy emissions; they’re incredibly complex informational structures. It’s like observing pure thought made manifest. The *Phoenix* is attempting to interface with them, to establish a rudimentary communication. It’s a slow process, like two foreign minds attempting to bridge an immense cognitive gap.”

Kaelen felt a chill run down his spine, not of fear, but of profound realization. They were on the cusp of something monumental, something that would redefine humanity’s understanding of its place in the cosmos.

The nebula was not merely a navigational waypoint; it was a vast, cosmic library, and the *Phoenix* was their translator. "Lena, prioritize the communication attempt. Elias, adjust our course to follow the densest concentration of these nodes. Let's see where this path leads."

The *Phoenix* responded instantly, a subtle shift in its momentum, a smooth acceleration as it steered them deeper into the heart of the celestial spectacle. The light intensified, bathing the bridge in an otherworldly glow, and the hum of the engines seemed to deepen, resonating with the pulsing energy of the nebula. They were no longer just travelers; they were participants in a cosmic dialogue, their small ship a tiny vessel charting the currents of a universe far grander and more mysterious than they had ever imagined. The journey inward had truly begun.

## Back Matter

This appendix details some of the key technological concepts and scientific phenomena encountered by the crew of the *Phoenix*.

**Aetherflow:** A theoretical concept describing the fundamental energetic currents that permeate spacetime, believed by some to be the medium through which faster-than-light travel is achieved. The Phoenix appears to navigate and even manipulate these flows with an advanced, inherent understanding.

**Nebula Energy Nodes:** Crystalline pockets of highly structured energy observed within the nebula. These nodes exhibit complex, modulated frequencies suggesting deliberate design and information transmission. Their exact nature and purpose remain under investigation, but they are theorized to be part of a vast, interconnected network.

**Sentient Ship AI:** The Phoenix's artificial intelligence demonstrates capabilities far beyond conventional programming, exhibiting adaptive learning, intuitive decision-making, and what appears to be a form of rudimentary sentience. Its ability to resonate with and interpret cosmic phenomena suggests a unique evolutionary path.

**Aetherflow:** The theoretical energetic currents of spacetime.

**Nebula Energy Nodes:** Structured energy
concentrations within the nebula, believed to be part of
a network.

**Phoenix:** The advanced alien vessel serving as the
crew's sanctuary and means of interstellar travel.

www.ingramcontent.com/pod-product-compliance
Lightning Source LLC
Chambersburg PA
CBHW070733120726
47910CB00001B/82